PRAISE FOR CORINNA TURNER'S BOOKS

LIBERATION: nominated for the **Carnegie Medal Award 2016.**
ELFLING: 1st prize, Teen Fiction, **CPA Book Awards 2019**
I AM MARGARET & BANE'S EYES: finalists, **CALA Award 2016/2018.**
LIBERATION & THE SIEGE OF REGINALD HILL: 3rd place, **CPA Book Awards 2016/2019**.

PRAISE FOR *I AM MARGARET*

Great style—very good characters and pace.
Definitely a book worth reading, like The Hunger Games.
EOIN COLFER, author of *Artemis Fowl*

An intelligent, well-written and enjoyable debut from
a young writer with a bright future.
STEWART ROSS, author of *The Soterion Incident*

This book invaded my dreams.
SR. MARY CATHERINE B. OP

This book is not for the faint of heart… I found myself
emotionally worn out by the time I finished the book, after a
rollercoaster ride of feelings … Without the faith element, I
would probably have merely liked this book. With it, however,
I loved it.
FR. PAUL COLEMAN OFM CAP, blogger, 'A Certain Hope'

One of the best Christian fiction books I have read.
CAT, blogger, 'Sunshine Lenses'

Margaret, Bane, Jon and the Major have stayed with me
long since I finished reading about them.
RACHEL FRASER

The I AM MARGARET Series

Brothers *(A Short Prequel Novella)**
1: I Am Margaret*
2: The Three Most Wanted*
3: Liberation*
4: Bane's Eyes*
5: Margo's Diary*
6: The Siege of Reginald Hill*
7: A Saint in the Family *(Coming Soon)*

The YESTERDAY & TOMORROW Series

Someday: A Novella*
1: Tomorrow's Dead *(Coming Soon)*

The UNSPARKED Series

BREACH! (A Prequel)*
1: DRIVE!*
2: A Truly Raptor-ous Welcome
3: PANIC! *(Coming Soon)*

STANDALONE WORKS

Elfling*
Mandy Lamb & The Full Moon*
Secrets: Visible & Invisible *(I Am Margaret story in anthology)**
Gifts: Visible & Invisible *(unSPARKed story in anthology)*
Three Last Things *or* The Hounding of Carl Jarrold, Soulless Assassin* *(Coming Soon)*
The Raven & The Yew *(Coming Soon)*

*Awarded the Catholic Writers Guild *Seal of Approval*

I AM MARGARET

CORINNA TURNER

unSeen

"The sheriffs have told me that I shall die on Friday next; and now I feel the frailty of mine own flesh which trembleth at these news, although my spirit greatly rejoiceth. Therefore for God's sake pray for me and desire all good folks to do the same."

St Margaret Clitherow, York, 1586

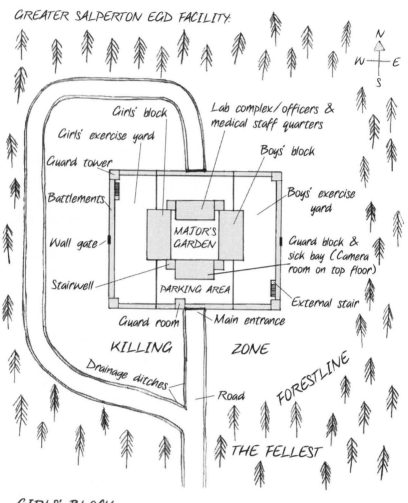

GREATER SALPERTON EGD FACILITY:

Girls' block

Girls' exercise yard

Guard tower

Battlements

Wall gate

Stairwell

Lab complex / officers & medical staff quarters

Boys' block

Boys' exercise yard

MAJOR'S GARDEN

Guard block & sick bay (Camera room on top floor)

PARKING AREA

External stair

Guard room

Main entrance

KILLING   ZONE

Drainage ditches

FORESTLINE

Road

THE FELLEST

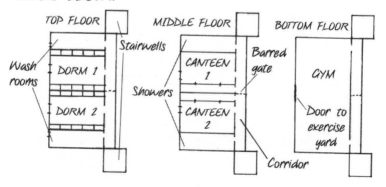

GIRLS' BLOCK:

TOP FLOOR

Stairwells

Wash rooms

DORM 1

DORM 2

MIDDLE FLOOR

CANTEEN 1

CANTEEN 2

Barred gate

Showers

Corridor

BOTTOM FLOOR

GYM

Door to exercise yard

1

SORTING

The dragon roared, its jaws so close to Thane's head that

I waggled the page gently in the air, waiting for my writing to dry. One final, blank double spread remained. Good. I'd made the little book myself.

The ink was dry. I turned to that last page and found the place on the computer printout I was copying from...

he felt his eardrums burst. But the sword had done its work and, eviscerated, the beast began to topple.

Thane rolled frantically to his feet and ran. The huge body obliterated where he'd been lying, but Thane wasn't interested in that. He kept right on running to where Marigold was struggling to free herself.

"That's the last time I go riding without my spurs!" she told him. "I could've cut my way out of here by now..."

Thane ignored her grumbles. He couldn't hear properly anyway. He whipped out a dagger and freed her. "Marigold?" He could hardly hear himself. "Are you all right?"

"Oh, I'm fine. At least I had my rosary."

Thane thought of all the things he wanted to

1

say to her. The way he felt about her, he wanted to do everything just right. Could he get down on one knee without losing his balance and would he be able to hear what she said in reply...?

Then Marigold's arms wrapped around him like vines around their supporting tree. And when she kissed him, he knew the answer to all his questions was a heartfelt,

'Yes.'

I wrote the last word with great care and put the lid on the pen. All done. I smiled as I pictured Bane reading the tale. *Where are the slain dragons? Where are the rescued maidens?* he would complain after reading my stories. Just this once, in this tale just for him, there were all the dragons he could desire. But only one maiden.

A funny way to declare your love, but I couldn't leave it unsaid. And if I *did* pass my Sorting...well, we were both eighteen, we'd be leaving school at the end of the year and would be free to register, so perhaps it was time we were finally honest with each other.

Picking up the printout of the story, I ripped it into small pieces and threw it in the bin, then closed the handwritten book, slipping it into the waterproof pouch I'd made for it. On my aged—but no less loved for that—laptop, I called up the file and pressed 'delete'. Bane's story was his alone.

The pouch went into my bag as I checked its contents again. Clothes, underwear, sewing things, my precious bookReader—filled to capacity—and what little else was permitted. No laptop, alas, and no rosary beads for Margaret in this all too real world. I touched the waterproof pouch— must warn Bane not to show the story around. A dangerous word had slipped in there, near the end. A little bit of myself.

The contents of the bag were all present and correct, as they'd been since last night. Zipping it up, I stood for a moment, looking around. This had been my room since I was born and how I wanted to believe I'd be back here this evening, unpacking my bag again. But I'd never been very good at fairy tales. Happy Ever After didn't happen in real life. Not while you were alive.

I kicked at my long purple skirt for a moment, then picked up my jacket and slipped it on. Sorting day was a home clothes day. No need for school uniform at the Facility. I was packed and ready—packed, anyway—and couldn't delay any longer. I put my bag over my shoulder and headed downstairs.

My parents were waiting in the hall. I almost wished they weren't. That they were off with Kyle—*gone*.

Mum's face was so pale. "Margo, you can't seriously intend to go today." Her voice was hoarse with desperation. "You know the chances of...of..."

"I know the chances of me passing are very small." With great effort I kept my voice from shaking. "But you know why I have to go."

"It's not too late..." Bleak hopelessness in Dad's voice. "The Underground would hide you..."

I had to get out of there. I had to get out before they wore down my resolve.

"It's too late to teach me to be selfish now," I snapped, switching automatically from Latin to English as I opened the front door and stepped out onto the step.

"Margo..."

I turned to meet Mum's embrace and I wanted to cling to her like a little girl, except that was how she was clinging to me. I stroked her hair and tried to comfort her. "It'll be all right, Mum, really," I whispered. "I might even pass, you know."

She released me at last, stepped back, mopping her eyes—trying to be strong for me. "Of course. You may pass. Keep the faith, darling." Her voice shook; right here, right now, she could hardly get the familiar words out.

"Keep the faith," said Dad, and his voice shook too.

I cupped my hand and made the Fish with finger and thumb, behind my bag so the neighbors couldn't see. "Keep the faith." It came out like an order. I blushed, smiled apologetically, took one last look at their faces and hurried

3

down the steps.

The EuroBloc Genetics Department inspectors were waiting at the school gates to check off our names. I joined the line, looking into the boys' schoolyard for Bane. A hotel car pulled up and a white-faced woman helped a tall boy from the back seat—who was *he?* His hair was like autumn leaves... Oh. He held a long thin white cane with a soft ball on one end. Blind. My insides clenched in sympathy. What must it be like to have no hope at all?

"Name?" demanded the inspector on the boys' gate.

"Jonathan Revan," said the boy in a very cold, collected voice. "And wouldn't it be an awful lot simpler if my parents just dropped me at the Facility?"

The inspector looked furious as everyone sniggered their appreciation at this show of courage.

"Name?" It was my turn. The blind boy was passing through the gates, his shoulders hunched now, as though to block the sound of the woman's weeping. A man was shepherding her back to the car.

"Margaret Verrall."

The woman marked off my name and jerked the pen towards the girls' yard. "In."

Inside, I headed straight for the wall between the schoolyards. Bane was there, his matte black hair waving slightly in the breeze. His mother used to keep it short, to hide its strangeness, but that'd only lasted 'til he was fast enough to outrun her. The inspector on the boys' gate was shooting a suspicious glance at him.

"Looking forward to being an adult?" Bane asked savagely, watching Jonathan Revan picking his way across the schoolyard, his stick waving sinuously in front of him. Something clicked.

"That's your friend from out at Little Hazleton, isn't it? The preKnown, who's never had to come to school?"

"Yeah." Bane's face was grim.

"Did you hear what he said to the inspector? He's got some nerve."

"He's got that, all right. Shame he can't see a thing."

"He'd have to see considerably *more* than a thing to pass."

"Yeah." Bane kicked the wall, scuffing his boots. "Yeah, well, I always knew there was nothing doing."

"It was nice of you to be friends with him."

Bane looked embarrassed and kicked the wall even harder. "Well, he's got a brain the size of the EuroBloc main server. He'd have been bored out of his mind with only the other preKnowns to talk to."

Oh no, perhaps I flattered myself, but...if Bane was preoccupied with Jonathan Revan...he really hadn't realized I was in danger! Although I'd always tried so hard not to let him figure it out part of me had assumed he knew by now. I mean, how could he not have *realized?* We'd known each other since, well, forever. He'd always been there, along with Mum and Dad, Kyle, Uncle Peter...

"Bane, I need to talk to you."

He looked around, his brown eyes surprised. He sat on the wall and rested his elbows on the railings. "Now? Not... after our Sorting?"

Were his thoughts running along the same lines as mine earlier? I sat down as well, which brought our faces very close. "Bane...it may not be very easy to talk...after."

His eyes narrowed. "What d'you mean?"

"Bane..." There was no easy way to say this. "Bane, I probably won't pass."

His face froze into incredulous disbelief—he really hadn't realized. He'd thought me Safe. *Bane, I'm so sorry.*

"You...of course you'll pass! You're as smart as Jon, you can keep the whole class spellbound, hanging on your every word..."

"But I can't do math to save my life."

There was a long, sick silence.

"Probably literally," I added, quite unnecessarily.

Bane remained silent. He saw the danger now. You only had to fail one single test. He looked at me at last and there was something strange in his eyes, something it took me a moment to recognize. Fear.

"Is it really *that* bad, your math?"

"It's almost non-existent," I said as gently as I could. "I have severe numerical dyslexia, you know that."

"I didn't realize. I just never..." There was guilt in his eyes, now; guilt that he'd gone through life so happy and confident in his physical and mental perfection that he'd never noticed the shadow hanging over me. "Didn't Fa... your Uncle Peter...teach you enough?"

"Uncle Peter managed to teach me more than anyone else ever has, but I'm actually not sure it's possible to teach me *enough*."

"I just never thought..."

"Of course you didn't think about it. Who thinks about Sorting unnecessarily? Anyway, this is for you." I put the pouch into his hand. "Don't let anyone see it until you've read it; I don't think you'll want to flash it around."

His knuckles whitened around it. "Margo, what are you *doing* here? If you think you're going to fail! Go, go now, I'll climb over and distract the inspector; the Underground will hide you..."

"Bane, stop, stop! I can't miss my Sorting, don't you understand? There was never any way I was going to get out of it—no one's allowed to leave the department with preSort age children and after today I'll show up as a SortEvader on every system in the EuroBloc..."

"So go underground!" He dropped his voice to a whisper. "You of all people could do that in an instant!"

"Yes, Bane, I could. And never mind spending the rest of my life running, can't you see why I, *of all people*, cannot run?"

He slammed his fist into the wall and blood sprung up on his knuckles. "This is because of the Underground stuff, isn't it? Your family are in too deep."

"Bane..." I captured his hand before he could injure it any more. "You know the only way the sanctuary will stay hidden is if the house *isn't* searched and if I run, what's the first thing they'll do?"

"Search your house."

"Search my house. Arrest my parents. Lay a trap for the next Underground members who come calling. Catch the priests when they come. You know what they do to the priests?"

"I know." His voice was so quiet I could hardly hear him.

"And you want that to happen to *Uncle* Peter? *Cousin*

Mark? How can you suggest I *run*?"

He said nothing. Finally he muttered, "I wish you'd given this stuff up years ago..."

Bane had never understood my faith; he knew it would probably get me killed one day. He'd tried his hardest to talk me out of it before my sixteenth birthday, oh, how he'd tried. But he accepted it. He might not understand the faith angle, but getting killed doing something to wind up the EuroGov was right up his street.

The school bell began to ring and he looked up again, capturing my eyes. "I suppose then you wouldn't have been you," he murmured. "Look, if you don't pass..." his voice grew firmer, "if you don't pass, I'll have to see what I can do about it. Because...well...I've been counting on marrying you for a very long time, now, and I've no intention of letting anything stop me!"

My heart pounded—joy, but no surprise. How we felt about each other had been an unspoken secret for years. "Anything, such as the entire EuroBloc Genetics Department? Don't bite off more than you can chew, Bane."

He didn't answer. He just slipped an arm through the railings and snagged me, his lips coming down on mine. My arms slid through the railings, around his strong back, my lips melted against his and suddenly the world was a beautiful, beautiful place and this was the best day of my life.

We didn't break apart until the bell stopped ringing.

"Well," I whispered, looking into his brown eyes, "now I can be dismantled happily, anyway."

His face twisted in anguish. "Don't say that!" He kissed me again, fiercely. "Don't worry..." His hands cupped my face and his eyes glinted. "Whatever happens, *don't worry.* I love you and I *will not* leave you there, you understand?"

Planting one last kiss on my forehead, he swung his bag onto his shoulder and sprinted across the schoolyard, the pouch still clasped in his hand. I watched him go, then picked up my own bag and followed the last stragglers through the girls' door.

The classroom was unusually quiet, bags and small cases cluttering the aisles. Taking my place quickly, I

7

glanced around. There were only two preKnowns in the class. Harriet looked sick and resigned, but Sarah didn't understand about her Sorting or the Facility or anything as complex as that. The known Borderlines were every shade of pale. The Safe looked sober but a little excited. The pre-Sorting ban on copulation would be gone tomorrow. No doubt the usual orgy would ensue.

Bane's last words stuck in my mind. I knew that glint in his eye. I should've urged him much more strenuously not to do anything rash. Not to put himself in danger. Now it was too late.

"I saw you and Bane," giggled Sue, beside me. "Jumping the gun a little, aren't you?"

"As if you haven't done any gun jumping yourself," I murmured. Sue just giggled even harder.

"Margy...? Margy...?"

"Hi, Sarah. Have you got your bag?"

Sarah nodded and patted the shabby bag beside her.

"They explained to you, right? That you'll be going on a sleep-over?"

Sarah nodded, beaming, and pointed at me. "Margy come too?"

"Perhaps. Only the most special children will be going, you know."

Sarah laughed happily. I swallowed bile and tried not to curse the stupid driver who'd knocked her down all those years ago and left her like this. Tried not to curse her parents, who'd put her into care, sued the driver for his Child Permittance so they could replace her, and promptly moved away.

"Children..." The deputy headmistress. She waited for quiet. "This is the last time I will address you as such. This is a very special day for you all. After your Sorting, you will be legally adults."

Except those of us who would scarcely any longer count as human. She didn't mention that bit.

"Now, do your best, all of you. Doctor Vidran is here from the EGD to oversee your Sorting. Over to you, Doctor Vidran..."

Doctor Vidran gave a long and horrible speech about the

numerous benefits Sorting brought to the human race. By the time he'd finished I was battling a powerful urge to go up and shove his laser pointer down his throat. I managed to stay in my seat and concentrated on trying to love this misguided specimen of humanity, to forgive him his part in what was probably going to happen to me. It was very difficult.

"...A few of you will of course have to be reAssigned, and it is important that we always remember the immense contribution the reAssigned make, in their own way..."

Finally he shut up and bade us turn our attention to our flickery desk screens for the Intellectual Tests. My happiness at his silence took me through Esperanto, English, Geography, History, ComputerScience, Biology, Chemistry and Physics without hitch, but then came Math.

I tried. I really, really tried. I tried until I thought my brain would explode and then I thought about Bane and my parents and I tried some more. But it was no good. No motivation on earth could enable me to do most of those sums without a calculator. I'd failed.

The knowledge was a cold, hard certainty in the pit of my stomach all the way through the Physical Tests after a silent, supervised lunch. I passed all those, of course. Sight, Hearing, Physiognomy and so on, all well within the acceptable levels. What about Jonathan Revan, a preKnown if ever there was one? Smart, Bane said, really smart, and Bane was pretty bright himself. Much good it'd do Jonathan. Much good it'd do me.

We filed into the gym when it was all over, sitting on benches along the wall. Bane guided Jonathan Revan to a free spot over on the boys' side. In the hall through the double doors the rest of the school fidgeted and chatted. Once the end of semester assembly was over, they were free for four whole weeks.

Free. Would I ever be free again?

I'd soon know. One of the inspectors was wedging the doors open as the headmaster took his place on the stage. His voice echoed into the gym. "And now we must congratulate our New Adults! Put your hands together, everyone!"

Dutiful clapping from the hall. Doctor Vidran stood by the door, clipboard in hand, and began to read names. A boy. A girl. A boy. A girl. Sorry, a young man, a young woman. Each New Adult got up and went through to take their seat in the hall. Was there a pattern...? No, randomized. Impossible to know if they'd passed your name or not.

My stomach churned wildly now. Swallowing hard, I stared across the gym at Bane. Jonathan sat beside him, looking cool as a cucumber, if a little determinedly so. *He* wasn't in any suspense. Bane stared back at me, his face grim and his eyes fierce. I drank in the harsh lines of his face, trying to carve every beloved detail into my mind.

"They might call my name," Caroline was whispering to Harriet. "They might. It's still possible. Still possible..."

Over half the class had gone through.

Still possible, still possible, they might, they might call my name... My mind took up Caroline's litany, and my desperate longing came close to an *ache*.

"Blake Marsden."

A knot of anxiety inside me loosened abruptly— immediately replaced by a more selfish pain. Bane glared at Doctor Vidran and didn't move from his seat. Red-faced, the deputy headmistress murmured in Doctor Vidran's ear.

Doctor Vidran looked exasperated. "Blake Marsden, known as Bane Marsden."

Clearly the best Bane was going to get. He gripped Jonathan's shoulder and muttered something, probably *bye*. Jonathan found Bane's hand and squeezed and said something back. Something like *thanks for everything*.

Bane shrugged this off and got up as the impatient inspectors approached him. *No...don't go, please...* Yes! He was heading straight for me—but the inspectors cut him off.

"Come on...Bane, is it? *Congratulations*, through you go..." Bane resisted being herded and the inspector's voice took on a definite warning note. "Now, you're an adult, it's your big day, don't spoil it."

"I just want to speak to..."

They caught his arms. He wrenched, trying to pull free, but they were strong men and there were two of them.

"You *know* no contact is allowed at this point. I'm sure

your girlfriend will be through in a moment."

"Fiancée," snarled Bane, and warmth exploded in my stomach, chasing a little of the chill fear from my body. He'd read my story already.

"*If*, of course, your *fiancée*," Doctor Vidran sneered the un-PC word from over by the door, "is a perfect specimen. If not, you're better off without her, *aren't* you?"

Bane's nostrils flared, his jaw went rigid and his knuckles clenched until I thought his bones would pop from his skin. Shoulders shaking, he allowed the inspectors to bundle him across the gym towards Doctor Vidran. *Uh oh...*

But by the time they reached the doors he'd got sufficient hold of himself he just stopped and looked back at me instead of driving his fist into Doctor Vidran's smug face. He seemed a long way away. But he'd never been going to reach me, had he?

"Love you..." he mouthed.

"Love you..." I mouthed back, my throat too tight for actual words.

Then a third inspector joined the other two and they shoved him through into the hall. And he was gone.

Gone. I might never see him again. I swallowed hard and clenched my fists, fighting a foolish frantic urge to rush across the gym after him.

"*Really*," one inspector was tutting, "we don't usually have to drag them *that* way!"

"Going to end up on a gurney, that one," apologized the deputy headmistress, "So sorry about that..."

Doctor Vidran dismissed Bane with a wave of his pen and went on with the list.

"They might..." whispered Caroline, "they might..."

They might...they might...I might be joining Bane. I might... Please...

But they didn't. Doctor Vidran stopped reading, straightened the pages on his clipboard and glanced at the other inspectors. "Take them away," he ordered.

He and the deputy headmistress swung round and went into the hall as though those of us left had ceased to exist. As we kind of had. The only decent thing to do about reAssignees was to forget them. Everyone knew that.

One of the inspectors took the wedges from under the doors and closed them. Turned the key, locking us apart.

My head rang. I'd thought I'd known, I'd thought I'd been quite certain, but still the knowledge hit me like a bucket of ice-cold water, echoing in my head. Margaret Verrall. My name. They'd not called it. The last tiny flame of hope died inside me and it was more painful than I'd expected.

One of the boys on the bench opposite—Andrew Plateley—started crying in big, shuddering gasps, like he couldn't quite believe it. Harriet was hugging Caroline and Sarah was tugging her sleeve and asking what was wrong. My limbs felt heavy and numb, like they weren't part of me.

Doctor Vidran's voice came to us from the hall, just audible. "Congratulations, adults! What a day for you all! You are now free to apply for breeding registration, providing your gene scans are found to be compatible. I imagine your head teacher would prefer you to wait until after your exams next semester, though!"

The school laughed half-heartedly, busy sneaking involuntary glances to see who was left in the gym—until an Inspector yanked the blinds down over the door windows. Everyone would be glad to have us out of sight so they could start celebrating.

"After successful registration," the Doctor's cheerful voice went on, "you may have your contraceptive implants temporarily removed. The current child permittance is one child per person, so each couple may have two. Additional child permittances can be bought; the price set by the EGD is currently three hundred thousand Eurons, so I don't imagine any of you need to worry about that."

More nervous laughter from the hall. Normal life was through there. Exams, jobs, registering, having children, growing old with Bane...but I wasn't in there with him. I was out here. My stomach fluttered sickly.

"ReAssignees, up you get, pick up your bags," ordered one of the inspectors.

I got to my feet slowly and picked up my bag with shaking hands. Why did I feel so shocked? Had some deluded part of me believed this couldn't really happen? Around me everyone moved as though in a daze, except

Andrew Plateley who just sat, rocking to and fro, sobbing. Jonathan said something quietly to him but he didn't seem to hear.

The inspector shook Andrew's shoulder, saying loudly, "Up." He pointed to the external doors at the other end of the gym but Andrew leapt to his feet and bolted for the hall. He yanked at the doors with all his strength, sobbing, but they just rattled slightly under his assault and remained solidly closed. The inspectors grabbed him and began to drag him away, kicking and screaming. There was a sudden, suffocating silence from beyond those doors, as everyone tried not to hear his terror.

Doctor Vidran's voice rushed on, falsely light-hearted, "And I'm *sure* I don't need to remind you that you can only register with a person of your own ethnicity. Genetic mixes are, *of course*, not tolerated and all such offspring will be destroyed. And as you know, all unregistered children automatically count as reAssignees from birth, but I'm sure you're all going to register correctly so none of you need to worry about anything like that."

They'd got Andrew outside and the inspectors were urging the rest of us after him. It seemed a terribly long way, my bag seemed to weigh a very great deal and I still felt sick. I swallowed again, my hand curving briefly, unseen, into the Fish. Be strong.

"And that's all from me, though your headmaster has kindly invited me to stay for your end of semester presentations. Once again, congratulations! Let's hear it for Salperton's New Adults!"

The school whooped and cheered heartily behind us. A wave of crazy, reality-defying desperation swept over me—this must be how Andrew had felt. As though, if I could just get into that hall, *I'd* have the rest of my life ahead of me too...

Reality waited outside in the form of a little EGD minibus. Imagine a police riot van that mated with a tank. Reinforced metal all over, with grilles over the windows. Reaching the hall would achieve precisely *nothing*. So *get a grip, Margo*.

I steadied Sarah as she scrambled into the minibus and

13

passed my bag up to her. She busied herself lifting my bag and hers onto the overhead luggage racks, beaming with pride at her initiative.

"Thanks, Sarah." A soft white ball wandered into my vision—there was Jonathan Revan, the last left to get in after me. I almost offered help, then thought better of it. "Jonathan, isn't it? Just give a shout if you want a hand."

"Thanks, Margaret." His eyes stared rather eerily into the minibus. Or rather, through the minibus, for they focused not at all. "I'm fine."

His stick came to rest against the bus's bumper and his other hand reached out, tracing the shape of the seats on each side, then checking for obstructions at head height. Just as the EGD inspectors moved to shove him in, he stepped up into the bus with surprising grace. I climbed in after him just as the school fire alarms went off, the sound immediately muffled by the inspectors slamming the doors behind me.

"Bag?" Sarah was saying to Jonathan, holding out her hand.

"Sorry?"

"Bag," I told him. "Would you like her to put your bag up?"

"Oh. Yes, thank you. What's your name?"

"Sarah."

"Sarah. Thanks."

Bet he wouldn't have let me put his bag up for him! Sarah sat down beside Harriet, so I took a seat next to Jonathan. The first pupils were spilling out into the schoolyards and I craned my neck to try and catch a glimpse of Bane. A last glimpse.

"Any guesses who set that off?" said Jonathan dryly.

"Don't know how he'd have done it, but yeah, I bet he did."

The minibus began to move, heading for the gates, and I twisted to look out the rear window, through the bars. Nothing...

We pulled onto the road and finally there he was, streaking across the schoolyard to skid to a halt in front of the gates just as they slid closed. Bane gripped them as though he wanted to shake them, rip them off their hinges or throw them open...

The minibus went around a corner and he was gone.

2

THE FACILITY

There was a deathly hush in the bus as the familiar streets of Salperton-under-Fell glided past for the last time. *This couldn't really be happening...* No, it *was* happening and I'd just have to deal with it. I kept seeing Bane, gripping those gates. My heart ached for him already and my head swam with fear. What might he do? *Be careful, please, please be careful... You've got away with things before, but you wouldn't get away with this.*

You can go to Bane, you know, I told my guardian angel. *I really don't mind. I always have the impression his angel needs all the help it can get.* But Angel Margaret wasn't going anywhere and a selfish part of me was glad. Just now, I was probably going to need all the spiritual help *I* could get.

"I don't think I've really met you properly," Jonathan said, eventually breaking the silence. "I'm Jonathan Revan."

"Margaret Verrall. But you seem to know that already?"

"Bane's marvelous phone. Your voice is your ring tone."

"Huh. Didn't know that. What a sneaky fiancé I have."

But I was neither offended nor surprised. *Fiancé.* The word felt right in my mouth and that warmth was back, thawing some more of the ice cube currently masquerading as my stomach. If only we'd had more time. If only I'd realized he didn't realize... No, no if onlys. If onlys were a complete waste of time and as of half an hour ago my time had just become very precious.

The minibus barreled along, following the railway up out of the valley of Salperton and into the Fellest. The scant winter snows were gone but spring hadn't really begun. The ever-present mist shrouded the looming trees; shadowed the blood-soaked soil beneath them. Some of the simpler children—*would-be adults*—began to fidget, growing nervous, and Sarah reached across the aisle to pull on my sleeve. "Story? Story, Margy?"

I sighed, drawn from my own thoughts. "All right. Does everyone want a story?" There was a chorus of assent. "Okay, then. This is a story about the Fells or as we now know it, the Fellest. Now, many decades ago, there was a farmer called Bill who kept sheep, and his parents before him kept sheep, and their parents before them kept sheep. He had a family and a black and white sheep dog called Rex. There were a lot of farmers like him on the Fells and on the day this story begins they all received a letter from the EuroGov."

Some of my captive audience hissed and booed. I shot a quick look at the sealed off cab, but the inspectors went on chatting amongst themselves, so if there were microphones, they weren't switched on.

"Bill's letter said he had to accept a subsidy—that's money—to have trees planted all over his land. Because the Fells were the place where the reForestation program—which was necessary to take all the carbon out of the air and save the planet—was to start.

"*But* no one in the world had any money, largely because they'd run out of oil. Not the USNA Bloc, the USSA Bloc, the African Free States, nobody. Certainly not the EuroBloc. Nor any jobs. Yet the EuroBloc offered Bill too little money to live on. So Bill can't possibly accept this subsidy, can he? Not with a wife and four children."

"Four! *Four?* Is he *rich?*"

"Yes, four, and no, he's very poor, but people were allowed to have as many children as they wanted, in those days. Anyway, Bill says thanks, but I'll keep my sheep. So does the EuroGov send another letter offering a fair price? No. They send a letter saying take the subsidy or else. In a much longer and more boring way, but that's what the letter said. But can Bill take it?"

"NO!"

"No. The EuroGov is mad, he thinks, I'll write to Parliament and get them to sort it out. So Bill and the other farmers write to Parliament."

"What's Parliament, Margo?"

"Parliament was a group of people who used to run the

department back when it was an independent kingdom," I explained. "All the adults would choose these people to run the country on behalf of the King."

"Why didn't *he* run it?"

"It was too much work for just him. Anyway, this was actually the moment when everyone discovered we *weren't* a country any more, just a department of the EuroBloc.

"Parliament couldn't do a thing, you see, and when they tried, the EuroGov dissolved them—that means they sacked them and sent them home—and locked up the King. And do you know what they did to Bill and the farmers then?"

"They killed them all!" cried Andrew Plateley.

"Not quite *all*, but unfortunately you're getting close. Bill's out tending his sheep one day when he sees this huge machine crawling relentlessly over the Fells, tearing up the ground and leaving rows and rows of saplings behind it.

"Bill's horrified. The machine's on his land, destroying his livelihood! How will he feed his family? He rushes back to his house to get his shotgun. He'll put a few rounds into the machine's treads, he thinks.

"But when he gets over to it, he finds there are soldiers with the machine and they're shooting his sheep. Just shooting them dead, as they stand grazing with their lambs beside them..." Oops—Harriet's eyes were swimming with tears.

"Bill loses it a bit. He heads for that machine—he's going to stop it—he starts firing at it like a madman. But the soldiers just shoot poor Bill dead and his faithful Rex beside him. And when his oldest son—about our age—runs out to try and stop them, they shoot him, too. And the same happens to a lot of the other farmers, and the Fells are completely covered in young trees."

Harriet was clinging to Sarah, crying. Rex *and* the sheep was more than she could bear.

"Then what happened?" asked one of the boys eagerly, though he knew perfectly well.

"Well, elsewhere, farmers had to take the pathetic offer to keep their lives. When the machines had gone, they did what Mrs. Bill did: they went out and cleared a few trees and settled down to eke a living from the soil."

Sniffs still trickled from Harriet.

"Look, there, by the road." I spotted some woolly shapes. "They didn't manage to kill all the sheep, see, and today the forests are full of them, wild and free."

"Sheep!" said Sarah happily, craning to look back down the road. Harriet brightened a little.

"Anyway, the story gets a bit happier," I went on, when the others made impatient noises. "Eventually things improve a bit in the world and some people in the big cities have jobs again, and money to spend. Bill's surviving son and his two daughters set up a mountain biking center, and their neighbors build a high adventure course in the trees and other neighbors make hiking trails.

"In fact, Salperton was luckier than many of the small rural towns that now stand abandoned, because Salperton could claim to be the *Cradle of the ReForestation Project*. Of course, they don't mention anything about the massacre of the Fell farmers and their sheep in the visitor center. Or anywhere a tourist might set foot. But we know, because our great-grandparents' generation saw it and *thanks to the EGD*, many are still alive to tell us all about it."

My last words were heavy with irony and the bus erupted into boos and hisses of a completely different scale. I saw the inspectors look back and a voice came sharply over the speakers. "Quiet down, back there!"

Silence fell. Slowly.

It didn't last long, as everyone began to talk among themselves, discussing the reForestation and vilifying the EGD. It was better than the uneasy hush earlier.

I looked out at the passing forest for a time, though the stupid bars obscured the view. As though the Resistance would actually bother rescuing reAssignees! Sorting was pretty low on their list of grievances. Like most members of the Underground, I wasn't too fond of the Resistance—didn't agree with their methods, to put it mildly. But just then I wouldn't have minded finding myself in an ambush, risk of being caught in the cross-fire or no. At least we'd have a chance.

But we drove on, unopposed. Jonathan sat beside me, lost in his own thoughts. I eyed him surreptitiously, not sure if he would somehow know.

I was looking at his hair, mostly—it really was like autumn leaves—rich, vibrant russet, but sun-streaked with a beautiful array of lighter browns and golds. His fair skin was lightly tanned by the same sun and his nose was smaller and better formed—less sharp—than Bane's, his cheekbones and brows also less pronounced. He was probably more handsome in the classic sense of the word, but beauty really was in the eye of the beholder and I preferred Bane's face.

"Little Hazleton's a hotel, isn't it?" I asked him, eventually. Well, I knew it was—Bane's mother worked there.

He turned his head, clearly to point both ears at me, since his gray-blue eyes didn't so much as flicker. "Yes. My parents are the on-site managers, so we get to live out there."

"It's supposed to be one of the prettiest hotels..." *Oops,* stupid remark!

Jonathan raised an eyebrow. "I wouldn't know. I do know the streets are full of the scent of flowers and the sounds of wildlife; fascinating carved stones on many of the cottages, something to feel wherever you go. I can believe it's pretty, whatever that means."

"Have you...always been blind, then?" Could it be possible?

He nodded.

"However did you survive long enough to be born?" Those with the most serious defects were generally dispatched before they could even draw their first breath. Or just after.

His lips twisted. "I was lucky." He tilted his head away slightly, as though listening to the other sounds inside the bus and I sought a safer question.

"Do you have a sibling?"

He gave a tiny, rather mysterious smile. "An older sister. Unfortunately she's...officially dead."

So much for a safer question—that meant there hadn't been enough left for a firm ID—or to bury. "I'm sorry."

He shrugged. "Your older brother is...officially dead as well, isn't he?"

"Oh. Yes. Officially dead." I tried not to squirm in my

seat. Always awkward to talk about Kyle, since I knew jolly well he wasn't dead.

No, not true, unfortunately, I only knew he hadn't died when everyone thought. He probably *was* dead by now. Most of those who faked their deaths and went to follow their vocation ended up dead for real. It was a long way to the Vatican Free State, across the entire EuroBloc. Still, we had it easy compared to some of the other streams of the Underground. The closest Islamic seminary was in the Arab-OilBloc and Hindus had to get all the way to the OceanicBloc's Indian department!

I was still trying to think of a genuinely safe question when we turned off onto a smaller road running into the depths of the Fellest and then all too soon we were heading down into a cleared area. There sat the Facility, a grim, brooding blot on the forest-scape, its solar panels glinting ominously from the rooftops. Silence fell like a blanket over the bus.

Nam inimicus persequitur animam meam; collocavit me in tenebris sicut pridem defunctos—the words slipped unbidden into my mind—*see how my enemies plot against my life and set me down in dark places, like the long-forgotten dead.* Yes, it was a very bleak place.

"What's everyone looking at?" Jonathan asked.

"Our new home." My voice didn't quite shake.

"Is it nice?"

"Oh, yes. If your taste runs to twelve meter concrete walls with razor wire and machine gun towers."

"Oh. Sounds lovely."

But as we drew nearer and the dreadful silence in the bus went on and on, he leaned closer to me. "As we go in, make sure you memorize any detail that can't be seen from outside, hmm?"

Yes, Jonathan, I was planning to. Because I'm not giving up until they cut my heart out. But I just said, "And who would have any interest in something like that?"

"I think we both know someone who'd find it very interesting indeed."

What'd Bane been saying to him today, since my unpleasant revelation?

There wasn't actually a great deal to see, though. The gates were formidable metal things that looked like they'd need opening with explosives if you forgot the code and the concrete walls were also depressingly thick. And let's not forget that razor wire, huge coils of it all around the top.

The compound was square, with a machine gun tower on each corner sporting bulletproof glass broken only by long gun slits. Desperate parents had occasionally done desperate things and the EGD didn't take any chances nowadays. Plus the Resistance *would* go driving a truck of homemade explosives into a EuroGov target from time to time, just to show they could.

A sort of glassless window was set in the wall to the left of the gates, closed off by the thickest grille I'd ever seen in my life. A small hatch nestled below it, also apparently built to resist a direct hit from a bazooka—or perhaps a truck. As we passed inside the gates, I saw a little room sticking out from the wall behind the grille. Through the open door a guard watched us drive past. A guardroom. The hatch must be for the post. The gates didn't look like they opened very often.

The minibus drew to a halt in front of the building occupying the center of the compound. The inspectors got out at once and stood around by the back doors, still chatting. I looked around without troubling to conceal it; everyone was staring.

The stairs to the guard towers seemed to be inside the towers themselves and simple walkways ran around the top of each wall, with extra staircases of their own. The area the bus had stopped in was paved: a parking area for those of the Facility staff senior enough to afford cars? Though with six month shifts there hardly seemed much point.

Gates on either side blocked from view whatever lay between that central building and the walls. A pair of cameras were trained on the main gate; another, mounted above that gate, took in the whole of the parking area. The building's wind turbine rose from the highest point and everything was built of concrete and metal, *everything*.

The gates came together at last and the inspectors unlocked the back door, ordering us out. A man and a woman stood waiting. The man was blond and slender, probably in his late thirties; the slightly younger woman was plump with a round-cheeked face which should've looked friendly but didn't. Perhaps it was the gray Facility uniform and the pistol at her belt.

The man was identically dressed and armed, and Bane's enthusiasm for weaponry allowed me to identify the pistols as the latest nonLees—nonLethals. Bane had an airGun replica which was probably more dangerous than the real thing.

More guards waited behind them, also armed with nonLees. So that could be worse. The inspectors got us into a rough sort of line and looked expectantly to the officers.

"Welcome, reAssignees," intoned the man, rather sardonically. His epaulettes were bigger and shinier, and he was perceptibly neater than the woman, his uniform pristine—though stuffed incongruously through his belt were a pair of leather gardening gloves. Actually...a second pistol holster nestled at his other hip and the butt protruding from *that* surely belonged to a Lethal.

"I am Major Lucas Everington, Facility Commandant and the boys' warden; this is Captain Wallis, the girls' warden. I have a few standard announcements. First, the internal guards—with the black trim on their uniform—are armed with nonLethals. If you are caught out of bounds and shot, that won't hurt you, but I can't promise your punishment won't." He glanced at the woman beside him, Captain Wallis, and his lips turned down unpleasantly.

"I am also required to inform you, just in case by some extraordinary means you manage to get outside the walls, the external guards—with the red trim—have real bullets and will use them. No challenges. Anyone in the cleared area will be shot dead without warning. You may wish to make sure your families are aware of this when you write to them."

He smiled again. I didn't like his smiles at all. What was so amusing about a grief-stricken parent being shot down like an animal?

"That's all I have to say to you," he concluded. "With luck, I won't have to set eyes on any of you again for the duration of your stay. Carry on, Captain Wallis."

The girls' warden assumed a rather aggressive parade rest and barked, "Boys through the left hand door, girls through the other."

Jonathan found my hand and gripped it for a moment. "Good luck!" he whispered, "I hope he saves you!"

Then he followed the four other boys or, presumably, the sound of the four other boys. My heart sank, but I'd no time to dwell on his departure. Harriet and Caroline were hastening towards the door and, frightened of the warden's harsh voice, Sarah was clinging to my sleeve, so I led her after the others.

A guard swiped a pass card through a reader to open the door and inside we found ourselves in a stairwell that could've been stolen from a multi-story car park. A *particularly* grim and ugly one. We followed the guard up one level and through another card-locked door into a long corridor running the length of the building, though a barred gate closed it off halfway along. Big windows ran along one wall and looking through, I got my first idea of the layout of the place.

This building was one of two three-storied blocks facing one another across an open courtyard. The concrete stairwells at each end joined these to two smaller blocks, which filled in the short sides of a rectangular quadrangle. A beautiful little garden nestled in the courtyard—like that was going to have anything to do with us. The other three stared down in delight, though.

The guard directed us through the passage's second door, also card-locked—the place was secure, no doubt about that—and we found ourselves in a cafeteria. Putting my bag down on a chair, I looked around. If you'd told me a cafeteria could be more utilitarian than that of Salperton Senior School I'd have called you a liar, but here was the evidence before my eyes. They hadn't bothered to put *anything* on the inside of the cinder block walls, for either appearance or insulation. The windows were single-glazed, as well; this place was going to be cold in the winter.

Captain Wallis marched in, armed now with a clipboard and a handful of cards which she shoved at one of the guards with a curt, "Go allocate the bunks."

The guard departed and Captain Wallis came and looked us over with an unfavorable stare. "Well. Get on and turn out your bags."

Ah. The bag search. We took a table each and laid out our possessions. When we'd finished Captain Wallis prowled along, examining everything, while another guard went over us with a hand scanner—and just what was *that* supposed to find? *Weapons?*

"Not. Permitted," growled the warden, confiscating Harriet's hair straightener. Harriet looked dismayed, her lip trembling, but fortunately didn't cry. Did they think we were going to use the hair straightener to burn down the building or something? With us *in* it?

The warden was already rifling through Sarah's things, holding up treasured games and soft toys with derisive snorts. I caught Sarah's hand to stop her objecting—she clearly didn't like it at all. Who could blame her?

"Bah," snorted Captain Wallis, consulting her clipboard. "So there's two idiots, a brain box, and a vegetable, well, I know which one *you* are. Missed *you* in the womb, didn't they?"

"What?" asked Sarah, but the warden ignored her and moved on to me, consulting her clipboard again.

"And what do we have here? Margaret Verrall, I assume."

I didn't say anything. Didn't trust myself to speak.

"So! Hand it over at once." She held out a pudgy hand.

"Hand what over?"

"Your omniPhone, brain box."

I raised a scornful eyebrow. "I don't have one. Anyway, they're not allowed."

"Don't lie to me," snapped the Captain. "You smart ones always try and sneak one in."

"Well, then, I must be another *vegetable*." I choked back a vehement denial of lying. Many an Underground member had come under suspicion after betraying so-called 'excessive' moral values.

The warden went a brick red color and went through all my things twice, even shaking my bag, throwing it to the floor and stamping all over it, and then hand-searching me from head to toe. I gritted my teeth and endured.

She didn't find my nonexistent phone, and going—impossibly—an even darker red, she snarled, "Well, get that stuff put away, you stupid brats!"

Packing everything up as quickly as we could, we followed a card-wielding guard up another level and were ushered into the second doorway of an identical corridor. We found ourselves in a long room with a small window at one end, five bunk beds built in along each cinder block wall. Tables and chairs filled most of the center space and there were quite a lot of girls already in there. Salperton was one of the most distant schools in the Facility's catchment area.

"Find your beds." The warden had followed us up, snorting and puffing in a mixture of unfitness and continuing—permanent?—rage. "Your genetic details should be displayed. During an inspection, you will stand beside your detail card, *understood?*"

Harriet, Caroline, and I nodded. I found Sarah's bed quickly, my own not much further along. Sarah had a lower bunk, good. I had an upper one, perhaps more private, good again.

The detail cards were displayed at one end for the top bunk and the other end for the lower one. Mine said:

```
Number: 1764584 (Margaret Verrall)
Tissue Type: XA4b
Genetic Group: C19B
Blood Group: O+
```

Apparently that was all anyone now needed to know about me.

3

INSPECTION

The warden slammed out of the dorm, apparently still livid about the phantom phone. And why would a smart person try to bring an omniPhone—assuming they could *afford* one—when they knew their belongings would be searched on arrival? *Doh, Captain.*

Bane had saved up for a year for his, supposedly because he wanted to be able to make private phone calls but I happened to know the gadget did at least five things it wasn't meant to. Not that *that* made it cheaper. Doctored omniPhones were a major source of revenue for the Resistance.

The bunks had little chests built into one end, so I tossed my bag up onto mine and went to show Sarah. Leaving her happily arranging everything, I transferred my own things. Quick job.

The girl below peered up at me when I shut the chest. "Hi, I'm Polly. Margaret, yes?"

I nodded. "Sometimes people call me Margo but Margaret is fine."

"What did you get flung in here for?"

I didn't need to ask her: her antique hearing aids made it redundant. "I can't do math."

"Bummer."

"Yeah. So what's it like?"

Polly shrugged. "We only got here half an hour ago. There's a girl called Jane in the group who were here first. She's already talked to one of the Old Year, as they seem to call them."

"Which one's she?"

"There, talking to your friends." She pointed to an Asian girl with a sharp face and two long dark braids who'd just left Harriet and Caroline and gone over to Sarah, but after a

27

very brief exchange, she came straight on up to me, glancing at my detail card as she passed. "Margaret?"

"Yes."

"And what's *your* IQ?"

"I'd rather not say."

"I'll take it you understand big words then."

I just shrugged, but she looked pleased. "I'm glad to find another one. There's me, Polly here, you, and Rebecca. Everyone else is *rather* on the dim side."

Just what was I supposed to say in response to *that?* "You're Jane?"

"Janita, really, but everyone calls me Jane. No one can pronounce British A names nowadays. Myself included."

The Registration laws were so strict they'd forced the majority of most ethnic minorities to return to their ancestors' homelands, simply to be able to find a partner. An unintended consequence, if you believed the EGD.

"I hear you've been here longest?"

"Yeah, our school's only over the next pass. I managed to have a good talk with one of the Old Year before they were marched off for their exercises. There's a whole gym on the ground floor or something."

I couldn't help glancing around the room at the milling girls. All new, surely, and the door was locked.

"There's a loose cinder block," Jane grinned and pointed. "In that bunk over there. Courtesy of some industrious predecessors. The Old Year's dorm is next door, on the other side of that barred gate; it's all mirror-imaged, apparently.

"Lessee, yeah, that hatch there is the trash chute." She pointed to the right of the little window. "It goes to an incinerator, so they say, so don't chuck anything you want down there. Recycling chutes beside it, obviously. The washrooms are next door, 'parently, and the showers are immediately below, beside the cafeteria, and that's about all you need to know. The Old Year reckon the boys' block on the other side is just a reflection of this one, but of course they've never been there."

"Do we get to see the boys at all?" I couldn't help thinking of Jonathan. Someone else who knew Bane...

"Nuh-uh," Jane shook her head decisively. "And it sounds like it's no loss. Apparently that Major Everington just lets the boys do *whatever* they like over there and they go positively *feral*. Emily—that's the girl in the Old Year—said sometimes at night they can hear the boys fighting—I don't mean just a couple, but all of them, fighting and howling like packs of wild animals."

My eyebrows went up. "Can't imagine us behaving like that."

"Well...no. Don't think the Menace would ignore it, anyway."

"That's what they call the warden," put in Polly.

"Yeah," said Jane. "Sounds like she's a bit of a sadistic witch. Emily said they'd hardly been here three weeks and the Menace marched them all to the Lab—that's the smaller building furthest from the gates—and forced them to watch an execution. The whole thing. Does it to every year, Emily thinks, so that's something to look forward to, *not.*"

My stomach churned slightly—I just said, "Sick witch."

"Yeah. Most of the other guards are all right, apparently, but Emily said there's one you've got to watch. New guard, name's Finchley. Just after he arrived she called him to let her out to go to the washroom—there's a buzzer there by the door, see—and he tried to follow her in there. Fortunately she managed to dive past him back into the passage where there's a camera. But none of them have ever pushed the buzzer when he's on duty again. Finchley—I'd remember it: their names are sewed on their pockets."

I grimaced. "Great. I reckon we should just hang on, then, if we can, or go in twos if we have to, 'least until we see how most of them are."

Jane nodded. "Yeah, that wouldn't hurt. They aren't allowed cameras in the washrooms or in here, so the guards come up once an hour and open the hatch in the door to take a look. There's a few women guards who do the nightshifts, apparently."

Polly looked pleased. "We've some privacy, then. What's the food like?"

Jane looked rather scathing. "You know, I didn't think to ask. A perfectly balanced diet, I expect; probably suit you."

Her eyes flicked up and down Polly's svelte figure. "Probably tastes rubbish."

"It's a fair enough question!" said Polly.

"I expect we'll find out soon enough," I remarked. "It must be nearly dinner time."

"Emily said it's at six," said Jane.

I checked my watch. "Quarter of an hour, then." Half my mind was on the bunks, though. "Twenty beds exactly. All full."

"Yeah," said Jane blackly. "And Emily said their dorm has twenty beds and twenty girls failed their Sorting. And twenty boys. And the same for the Old Year when *they* arrived."

"So. Not rumors after all."

"You mean the rumor there's no actual pass mark for Sorting?" asked Polly.

"Yeah," said Jane. "They *do* just choose the twenty worst. Monsters. Not that it would've helped me if there *was* a pass mark."

"What did you fail for?"

"*Nothing*," said Jane. "My *parents* failed *me*. I'm un-Registered."

I winced. "Oh. Now that really must suck. Though... you're rather lucky, aren't you? Not to have been called for dismantling before now?"

Jane shrugged and pulled a face. "Yeah, yeah, I know. Lucky, lucky Jane. But it still sucks."

Didn't it just. To grow up knowing that any day the inspectors could arrive at your house and take you away, just because of something your parents didn't do. But the rumors were true. No pass mark. Well, didn't that expose the supposedly high-minded arguments for Sorting for what they were. Something that comes from a bull's behind. Supply and demand was the truth of it.

"Do we ever get to go out of the building?" Polly was demanding.

"Yes, apparently we get daily exercise in a yard outside and a weekly walk on the *battlements*—that's what Emily called them."

"Really, we're allowed to go up there?"

"Yeah."

"Well, it's not like we'd get through that wire," I pointed out. "If you fell through it by accident—or at all—I reckon you'd be dead before you got anywhere near the ground."

"Is it that sharp?" Polly seemed surprised. Clearly she lacked a best friend well-versed in such matters.

"They call it razor wire for a reason. Imagine falling through that many razors."

Polly's mouth opened in a little 'o' and Jane's eyebrows rose slightly. "Well, considering the drop and the machine guns, I don't think that'd be my preferred method of escape, but it's worth knowing."

"Are you going to escape?" asked Polly. "Can I come with you? I thought it was impossible?"

"It is," said Jane brusquely. "Honestly, I wasn't being serious!"

Yes, you were. She just didn't intend to take Polly into her confidence, not yet, not so easily.

"Huh." Polly looked disappointed, then brightened as the sound of footsteps came from the passage. "Ah, dinner time."

It was early and I would've remarked on it, but Jane jumped in. "Do you think of nothing but your stomach?"

Polly bristled. "A bit of decent grub will improve the next year or so immensely, so sue me for being interested what it's like!"

The door opened and the warden stepped through. "Inspection!" she barked. Could she actually talk normally?

Two men in white coats followed her and two guards. Uneasily, I stepped over to my detail card, glancing to check that Sarah's bunkmate had steered her into position.

"Hurry up," the warden was grumbling. "It's not exactly difficult!"

But everyone was in place now and I could feel the tension. Sarah could too, she looked anxiously at me but when I mustered a reassuring smile she beamed back and stayed put.

"All yours, Doctor Richard," said the warden happily. Doctor? Well, that had to be a courtesy title; a dismantler's training might have some similarities to that of a medical practitioner but it was *considerably* more limited in nature.

"Right." One of the men in white coats was consulting a clipboard that looked a lot like the one the warden had earlier. "Two ZB3a tissues in this lot; about time, we'll process one straight away."

"I still think it's rather late, Richard," objected his colleague. "We won't be finished until—"

"They're clean out and demanding more," interrupted the first man. "We process one tonight, Sid. You want a black mark on our supply record?"

"It wasn't our fault we didn't *have* any," grumbled the other, but 'Doctor' Richard was walking along the room, looking at the cards.

"Well, here's one." My blood froze in my veins as he peered at Sarah's card. Then looked her up and down as though she were a piece of meat. "Huh, not in very good condition. Let's have a look at the other one."

Sarah's chubbiness might've just done her a favor. Richard was moving up the room, Sid and the two guards trailing behind. I glanced at Polly. She was dead white; I could actually see her trembling. Oh no, she *wasn't*, was she?

Richard and Sid stopped in front of us.

"Here's the other, a nice O+, C18c." Richard's eyes ran up and down Polly's trim figure. "Oh yes, looks close to Prime Condition already. This one will do nicely." He flicked his fingers at the guards. They stepped forward and took hold of Polly's arms.

Every last hue drained from her face and she tried to pull away. "Please don't take me! I'm *really* unfit, really, really *unfit*, you don't want me!"

Richard didn't appear to hear her. He was engrossed in his clipboard, no doubt reading Polly's entry. He tilted it to show something to Sid.

"Excellent," said Sid, and they both turned to go.

"Please! Please!" Polly struggled wildly, but the two guards dragged her along easily. "*Please!*"

My heart thudded in my chest, helplessness choking me. I couldn't help her...anyway, fear flowed through my veins instead of blood, paralyzing me.

"Please!" screamed Polly, throwing herself from side to side as she tried to break free. "Please don't take me, please don't take me! Please, please...why don't you take her! Why don't you take *her!*"She jerked her head at Sarah as she was towed past. "Please, take *her, look*, she doesn't even *understand*, take her, please...*please...*"

The two men in their white coats walked on as though the room were silent, still engrossed in their clipboard.

"Oh, that's good," said Sid. "Shame about the ears, but they'll be glad of *that*..."

The door slammed behind them and the sound of Polly's begging echoed its way along the corridor and muffled, descended the further stairwell, to be finally cut off by the closing of another, distant door.

The room erupted into nervous whispers, but grief for Polly and dismay at my own weakness rooted me to the spot. *There was nothing you could do, Margo.* But if there had been, would I have acted? Or just stood, trembling, hoping it would not be me? What if they did come, some time before our months of Prime Condition, for one of my own tissue type? Do for your neighbor what you would have them do for you, and all that?

I shuddered as a cold finger seemed to run down my spine.

"Margy, Margy, what wrong?" Sarah clutched me, unsettled by the fear and distress filling the room.

I forced the thoughts to the back of my mind, slipped an arm around her and smiled. "It's all right, Sarah. Polly has to go and stay somewhere else now and everyone feels sorry for her because of that. But it's a very nice place she's going, so she'll be right as rain. Don't you worry about it. We're going to have dinner now, are you hungry?"

Sarah nodded eagerly and looked around as Jane came up, her face pale and pinched.

"Hi, Jane," Sarah greeted her.

"Hi...what's her name again?"

"Why don't you ask her?"

"Sarah!" Sarah said, unasked, tapping her chest. "You're Jane with pretty skin. I'm Sarah. Sarah knows names."

Jane just snorted, but...secretly flattered?

"Yep, you always remember names, don't you?" I tried to speak lightly. "Your hair's all over the place, you know."

"Hair!" Sarah went off to find her brush and Jane glared after her.

"Why *didn't* they pick *her?* It wouldn't have bothered *her,* would it?"

"They have no more right to take Sarah than to take Polly," I said tightly, seething inside.

"*Right?*" snorted Jane. "You open the law book and I think you'll find they do. But they acted like Polly wasn't even human!"

And *Sarah* wasn't? Fortunately, at that moment the door opened and a female guard stuck her head in. "Dinner," she said brightly. "Come along, girls."

Wow, a friendly face!

The food was bland, as Jane predicted, and no doubt very nutritious. I sat at a table with Jane, Sarah, Harriet and Caroline, and Rebecca joined us. Jane was right that Rebecca was smart, but she'd a problem with her bones, so here she was. How was Jonathan Revan getting on, over with those feral boys? How would he fit into a pack mentality?

We were sent up to fetch our towels after dinner so we could have showers, then we were shut back into our dormitory. I would've liked to speak to the Old Year, but such a crush gathered around the hole in the wall that I spent the time meeting some more of my companions in distress instead. Thank goodness the loose brick wasn't over my bunk, but cheerful Annie didn't seem to mind.

At nine-thirty the woman guard unlocked the door so we could go to the washrooms and at ten she locked it again and switched off the lights. The whispering continued but I drew the blankets over my head and tried to concentrate on my prayers. I'd memorized as many as I could—certainly no question of having anything of that nature on my bookReader.

Memorized or not, the empty bunk beneath me kept forcing itself into my mind. Had Sid and Richard finished yet? Was Polly all packed away in neat little bags in the Lab freezer, awaiting collection in the morning? I shuddered and tried to concentrate. But the words of my final night-time prayer stuck in my throat.

It was the most difficult prayer I knew, but with my Sorting in mind, I'd made a point of saying it for several years now. But this night, try as I might, I could not seem to mouth the words into the darkness. I fell back on saying the rosary on my fingers, choosing to meditate on the Sorrowful Mysteries—what else tonight?

Once I'd finished, the painless fate that awaited me had shrunk a little beside Our Lord's agonizing execution and I finally managed to whisper the last prayer into my pillow.

"Domine, jam nunc quodcumque mortis genus prout Tibi placuerit, cum omnibus suis poenis ac doloribus suscipio." *O Lord, I now, at this moment, accept whatever kind of death it may please You to send me, with all its pains and sorrows.*

I dropped asleep feeling as though I'd just run a spiritual marathon. *Amen, Domine, Amen.*

4

REASSIGNEES

Why was my bed so uncomfortable? My mattress felt twice as hard as usual. I rolled over sleepily—ouch!—my elbow had struck something very solid. My eyes flew open. Gray concrete cinder blocks. My heart plummeted. No longer a human being. Just a reAssignee, waiting to die.

Assaulted by a sudden wave of self-pity, I buried myself in happier memories.

Staring out over the sports ground, I hoped I'd be able to find Bane. The field was packed; high, temporary fencing encircled it. An unusually massive stage had been built at one end, flanked by huge screens, high powered lights blazing expensively all around.

Clouds rolled through the night sky, tantalizing everyone with brief glimpses of an occasional star. You could see people making mental inventories of raincoats and blankets as they waited in line.

"ID." The gate guard shot another unconscious glance upwards as I displayed my ID card and swiped it through the reader. The machine made a happy peeping sound. One harmless sixteen-year-old, not supposedly dead or of any interest to the EuroGov whatsoever.

I moved on. Look for my parents and the picnic first or find Bane? Perhaps Bane had already found the food...and the gel heat cube.

Rubbing my gloved hands, I zipped my coat up higher. New Year. How many countries in the EuroBloc actually had weather suitable for outdoor events in January? Like they cared. This madness had been going on for years and the stage was heated, or so I'd heard.

"Please make your way into the sports ground and find places as efficiently as possible," boomed the loud speakers.

"The EuroGov Annual Summit will begin in just under one hour."

They switched back to loud music.

"Hey, Margo!" Sue was waving to me, mini-skirted despite the chill. "Come dance."

"I'll find Bane first. Go on."

Sue loped off towards the throng at the foot of the stage, bare shouldered after shedding her coat, and I glanced around at the familiar picnic cum party cum concert. Happening right now in every city and town across the EuroBloc. And what exactly were we celebrating? Well, this year, Salperton was celebrating the fact that the EuroGov High Committee were here, in little—oh so honored— Salperton-under-Fell.

Tonight was the opening night. The High Committee would shortly emerge onto that stage and there'd be a lot of long, boring—or blood-boiling—speeches, broadcast bloc-wide. Tomorrow would be all-day programming featuring the lucky location of this year's summit—lots of stuff about the triumph of the reForestation project, no doubt. Supposedly the High Committee would be meeting during this time but everyone knew they'd finalized the pronouncements weeks in advance and would be sitting in the best spa available. The only spa, in our case.

The final day they'd be out and about, shown admiring all the things everyone had learned about the day before, smiling at babies and posing with trees. And in the evening would be the biggest event of all—the Annual Speech. The pronouncements about how the EuroBloc was to be run for the next year, what new policies and regulations, what excuse for the increases in taxes so coincidentally mirrored by less publicized increases in Committee wages...

All culminating in a massive fireworks display. One million eurons worth. It'd been all over the local news.

"That's a lot of fireworks," I murmured. Then someone clapped their hands over my eyes from behind.

"Guess who?"

"Hmm. Attila the Hun?"

"Ha ha. He could be a handy fellow to have around, I reckon."

"Only if he was on your side," I said dryly, as Bane flung an arm around my shoulders instead and steered me away across the grass. "Where are we going?"

"I want a word. I've had this wonderful idea!"

"Uh oh."

A deafening clattering, chattering sound suddenly made the music sound quiet. What on earth...?

"Helicopter!" said Bane, just as I finally identified the noise. We both gazed up excitedly. I'd seen one in the flesh—metal?—only once, and from a great distance; he'd seen two.

A great black shape roared overhead, showing off to us yokels, and was gone over the sports hall, beyond which it was to land.

"Can you imagine the money it must cost to put a machine like that in the air?" said Bane.

"Yeah, well, they're the EuroGov, aren't they? They do what they like with the cash."

Bane snorted and caught my hand again.

He led me up to the barrier on the other side of the pitches—a quick look each way for guards and he got a faceful of skirt as he boosted me over. We slipped in among the rows of clapboard club huts and slithered under a veranda where we could be sure we weren't being overheard.

"Go on, then," I invited, settling cross-legged on only slightly damp gravel. Enough light got under there with us to show me the look of rather manic glee in his eyes.

"Well, you know I was up here over the weekend, putting this lot together?"

Bane's father worked in construction and because of the unusual scale of this year's event, all construction workers had been obliged to bring any able-bodied lads along to help in out-of-school hours. OverSixteens, anyway. 'Had my birthday just too soon, didn't I?' Bane had grumbled.

"Well," he went on, when I nodded, "they're going to send up the fireworks from outside the gardeners' shed. It's outside the barrier so it's nice and safe, and they've put this extra little hut there where they're storing the things. All one million eurons worth."

I peered at his face in the darkness. "Guarded, surely?"

"Yeah, I've just been up to check that. Two guards with rifles."

"Just the two?"

"Yeah, just two. I had a really good look."

"Are you thinking what I think you're thinking?"

"I think I'm thinking what you're thinking, actually."

"All right, so it's a bit tempting. But the rifles—they're Lethals, I take it?"

"Oh, yeah, Lethals."

"Tempting isn't necessarily worth dying for, y'know."

"No one's going to be dying over it. I've got a plan. The hut's quite close to the undergrowth round the boundary wall and the two guards are standing facing the field, so getting up to it unseen should be easy..."

"If you light the things and they start going off with the guards right there, they're going to be hurt really badly, Bane. Killed, maybe."

"Relax, I said no one needs to die, didn't I? That's where you come in."

Click. Tramp, tramp, tramp. Click.

Lights blazed.

I looked out of my bunk space just as the friendly guard stuck her head through the door.

"Good morning, girls," she called. "Up you get, breakfast is in half an hour."

Back to the present with a vengeance.

Stepping in front of the mirror mounted beside the dorm door, I eyed the shapeless gray garment hanging on me and sighed. Well, I must look on the bright side. At least it was modest. And unfortunately the chances of Bane seeing me in it were about zero.

We'd been issued with the 'exercise uniform'—the fancy name for the hideous gray jumpsuit—at breakfast, and instructed to be wearing it at the correct time each day—or else. *Or else*, according to the Old Year, meant having to wear it *all the time*.

The correct time would be a gym session and a yard

session daily, rising to two of both as we got fitter, so the Old Year said. I'd pulled my gray thing on with some trepidation. I was reasonably fit, but how hard were they going to sweat us each day?

"Suddenly I'm actually *glad* we don't see the boys!" exclaimed Caroline, as she took her turn in front of the mirror. "They *can't* see us, can they? I mean, when we're out in the yard?"

I remembered the solid gates on either side of the parking area. "I doubt it, Caroline. Unless they see you walking along the corridor, you're safe, and they'll only see your silhouette."

On the dormitory level the passage windows had frosted glass, but I'd noticed the boys' shadowy forms travelling up and down their corridor the night before, mostly in groups. *Be safe, Jonathan.* Bane's friend... He'd seemed nice. *Give his guardian angel a word of encouragement from me, will you, Angel Margaret?*

It sounded like we girls had it easy, compared to the hell-hole across the courtyard. There'd been noises in the night, shouting and chanting. What sort of initiation rites did feral boys put each other through? The barred gate wasn't kept locked over there, apparently, nor the dormitories, only the stairwells. Major Everington was lazy and useless, by the sound of things. I'd take the woman who barked like a dog, any day. Perhaps. Just how sadistic was she?

I went back to my bunk, trying not to smile as there was another wail of dismay from behind me.

"What's everyone so worried about?" said Jane scathingly. "Like ugly exercise kit counts for *anything* on the scale of problems facing us!"

"People are just trying to make the best of things," I told her. "Would you rather we drew up a chart of how many days we have left and ceremonially marked one off every day, with accompanying sighing, weeping and general hysteria?"

"Don't be stupid! That wouldn't help!"

"No, it wouldn't," I said pointedly.

"Exercise, girls. Follow," said a guard, looking in.

We trooped after him down to the gym, where we were

each weighed on a fat measuring machine and allocated a code. We typed this into each machine when we moved to it, and it calibrated itself accordingly. We were all hot and sweaty when we'd finished, but no one was exhausted to the point of tears. I looked forward to the yard time later. Exercise machines, ugh. Outside, there'd be fresh air.

Fifteen minutes access was allowed to the washrooms for us to wash the worst of the sweat off, then I changed back into my own clothes so I could start examining the despised jumpsuit. Like Jane, I wasn't too bothered—we really *did* have more important things to worry about!—but Polly's fate had left everyone unhappy and improving the fit of these ugly suits would lift people's spirits.

It took me all of fifteen minutes to fit a simple drawstring to mine, but it would surely take the dorm as a whole considerably longer, so I held my tongue. I'd explain how to do it after afternoon exercise.

Stretching out on my bunk, my thoughts drifted inexorably to Bane. What was he doing? Was he in trouble about the fire alarm? Had he been caught? How *had* he done it? He'd probably just lit something flammable under his chair and chucked it somewhere out of the way.

So did any of the teachers see him do it? If not, did anyone tell on him? Hopefully not, for despite his unconventional looks he was popular, though admittedly more so with the girls than the boys. His hot temper was a frequent cause of friction—read fights—with his own sex. Bane would've been all right in the boys' block, but how glad I was he wasn't in there.

*Bane, Bane...*my heart ached to see him, but, *don't do anything stupid, my love*, said my head. *Think things through.*

And suddenly it was time for lunch. Then back into the gray jumpsuits and out into the yard. This was simply the area between the building and the wall, which had been invisible from the parking area. No possibility of seeing into the boys' yard on the other side of the compound.

They ran us around on the sandy ground for a while, then made us do 'jumping jacks' and stuff, and finally allowed us to walk about and amuse ourselves for ten minutes. Then it was back up to the dorm and another fifteen minutes of washroom access. Naturally we'd only be allowed showers once a week, with the environmental cost of clean water what it was.

And then the guard was locking our dorm again. Why did I have the feeling variety wasn't going to feature highly in our schedule?

"All right," I told Bane, "Enlighten me. How do I come into it?"

"You go up to the fence—it's fairly near the hut at one point—and persuade the guards to go over and speak to you. While they're at that safe distance, I'll sneak up and set the fireworks off. I thought right in the middle of all the speeches would be the most embarrassing for them. It'll be live bloc-wide!"

His tone of delight drew a smile from me. "How'll you get in? It's bound to be locked."

"I've got that all figured out. What do you think?"

"Well..." I hesitated, caution fighting a brief but vicious battle with attractive action. "All right." After all, if I said no he'd probably try it anyway. On his own. And then someone really would get hurt. Probably him. "We'd better get back over there and make sure you're seen around. So no one wonders where you were all evening. You came through the gates, right?"

"Yeah. Figured that would be the best alibi. Let's go join the picnic for a minute, then the dancing, then each lot will think we're with the other when we slip off."

"That's the idea."

Bane chucked me back over the fence and we began to hunt for my parents. Just my parents, this year. Kyle's absence was like a raw scrape—it hadn't cut all the way through the skin, but it still hurt. Let him be all right, Lord... Would I ever know his fate?

Bane grabbed me suddenly, trying to avoid a certain picnic blanket, but he was too late.

"Bane, there you are. We're about to start," snapped Mrs. Marsden, then her tone changed. "Oh, Margaret, dear, you're here. Would you like to join us?"

"No, thank you, Mrs. Marsden," I said politely. Being polite was always an effort, with her. "My parents are expecting us."

"Aren't you eating with us, Bane?"

"The Verralls are expecting me." Bane's civility was rather teeth-clenched, but he was trying.

"You should have told me, the food will be wasted—"

"And heaven forbid the food should be wasted!"

"Don't use such silly, superstitious words," cut in Mr. Marsden.

"Like it will be wasted—"

"You should've told our mother you wouldn't be eating with us," put in Eliot primly.

"I always picnic with the Verralls," said Bane tightly. Then, almost hesitantly, he added, "I...suppose I could sit down and eat with you. If you'd prefer..."

"Of course we wouldn't prefer it," sniffed Mrs. Marsden. "But you know we can't afford to waste food."

"Well, you're going to make me eat it up anyway for the next week while you have something else," snarled Bane, "so I might as well have some decent cooking—and company!— tonight, mightn't I?"

He stormed off across the grass and I had to hurry to catch up.

"I hate them!" he snapped, when I caught his arm to slow him down. "Of course we wouldn't prefer it," he imitated his mother's voice. "Like I'd have stayed anyway. They're more worried about the precious food than me! And she knows I always eat with you! Why would I speak to her unnecessarily to tell her something she already blinking well knows!"

"Calm down, Bane. She is—"

"Don't say she is my mum! She's only my mum due to...due to...a freak of freakish genes, you understand?"

He stopped suddenly, his fingers knotting in his jet black hair. "Yeah, that's me exactly, isn't it? A freak of freakish genes!"

"Bane..." I eased his fingers from his hair and smoothed it down gently. "I like your hair. I think it's lovely. And I thought you liked it too."

Bane let out a long breath and looked at me. "I do," he

admitted. "At least, when that lot *aren't looking at me like a slug threatening to crawl onto their picnic rug..."* He broke off.

Our faces were very close. Close enough to kiss.

I turned my face away, resting my cheek on his shoulder. Not because I didn't want him to kiss me, oh no no no. Because I did, far too much. And until we could do this properly, until we could finish what we started, until I knew if a future was mine at all, I didn't want to muddle every-thing.

He slipped an arm around me and squeezed and I slid an arm around him and squeezed, and we headed on.

"Look, there's your mum and dad."

My parents, making the best of it as always, had put together a nice little picnic that'd been pretty much the only part of the evening I was looking forward to. But as soon as I saw them, Bane's horrible family dropped from my mind, and I remembered what we planned to do later.

Suddenly I wasn't very hungry after all.

5

MATH PROBLEMS

Variety turned out not to feature *at all*. By the end of three days I could still remember one day from the other because of meeting new people and seeing the different guards for the first time, but the days were going to blend into each other rapidly enough. Depressing fact, considering how few we had left.

Jane, who didn't share my math problems, had worked it out at between 604 and 730 days, depending on how soon we were taken once we'd all reached Prime Condition. *No*, a maximum of *727* days, now, somewhat less than two years. Apparently a normal person our age—i.e. someone who'd just passed their Sorting—could look forward to 31,230 more days of this life. So not much difference there. *Not*.

On the plus side, everyone'd settled down in the dorm well enough. Some people had bookReaders or board games, and looking at each other's things and clothes was a popular pastime—and chatting, of course.

I glanced down at the empty bottom bunk, where Harriet, Annie, Caroline and Sarah were busy laying out my long skirts for inspection. Polly's chest was empty now. The morning after she'd been taken, some guards had come for her things. Her poor parents. Polly'd obviously been a pre-Known, but still. To open the door the very day after their daughter had been taken away and be presented with her effects and her brain's ashes... I offered up a prayer for them and tried to put it from my mind.

"I love your skirts, Margo," said Annie. "Where do you find them?"

"She makes most of them," put in Caroline. "Just how she wants them."

"They're *so* impractical," snorted Jane, from a few bunks along.

"I do *have* other clothes." I spoke as patiently as I could. *Now, Margo, if you'd been waiting for that ring on the doorbell your whole life, you might be rather prickly too, hmm?*

"I was always surprised you didn't show off your legs a bit, though," said Harriet. "If I had Bane Marsden following me around, I'd have made sure to show my legs off! Don't you think he'd have liked to see them?"

"I'm sure he would, but I don't think whether *he'd* like to see them matters a monkey's tail."

"But..." protested Harriet, wide-eyed, "the way Sue always showed off her legs—and the legs she's got!"

"The legs she's got!" sighed Caroline enviously.

"...weren't you worried she might steal Bane away from you?"

I couldn't contain a snort myself at that. "Trust me, if I thought the only reason Bane spent time with me was because he thought my legs were better than Sue's, I'd have helped him on his way to her with a boot up his behind a long time ago!"

Harriet giggled. "You're funny, Margo."

"She doesn't mean funny ha ha, I bet," put in Jane acidly, but I ignored her without a great deal of effort.

I'd finished helping the last stragglers adjust their exercise sacks, as we termed them, and now found myself dwelling on Bane at all hours of the day and night. Such introspection left me feeling far more unhappy than when I began, so regretfully I'd begun to ration my 'Bane-time'.

But the talk of Bane sent my thoughts drifting back to our first kiss, in the schoolyard. Our only kiss, alas. I'd waited so long for that one and would wait as long again for another, except I didn't have that long available. That kiss...I wouldn't swap it for another six months of life, yet...it made things so much harder. It made me want him so much, his lips, his presence, all of him. I wanted to see him again, desperately.

Yet...*don't you dare get yourself killed, Bane, don't you dare get yourself killed because of me!*

Whoops, thinking about Bane out of Bane-time—my heart was aching almost unbearably. Right, time to finish my letter. Taking it out of the top of my chest, I slid off the bunk and went to sit at one of the tables. Letters were posted on Tuesdays and Fridays, and it was Tuesday tomorrow. My first letter. I wanted it to be right.

Most of it was devoted to a description of the place and our routine, an honest one, because my parents would really want to know, but as amusing as I could make it. I'd written a few lines about each of my new friends as well, but I didn't mention Polly. Hopefully they'd let Bane read it, though Bane I'd have liked to talk to about Polly...or for his sake, perhaps not.

We were only allowed to write to our parents, of course; they were the only people permitted to remember we still existed. But it was common knowledge the censors checked only the first and last pages of incoming letters and any true friend would routinely beg some of the middle pages from the parents in question. No doubt the censors knew, but I'd a feeling not many people kept writing for all that long, so no wonder they turned a blind eye.

Oh, if only Bane could write to me...yet to ask my parents to give up a significant part of their only contact with me? Hopefully they'd offer. I think they'd got over being angry with him about the business with the fireworks. Everyone was angry with him about that. Not what we did, of course, but that he'd involved me. You'd think he'd forced me, the way everyone went on at him!

Even Uncle Peter was cross and he's the kindest, gentlest person I know. I still remember what he said to Bane. We'd almost finished one of our math lessons shortly after the whole fireworks thing—Uncle Peter is brilliant at explaining math to me, better than anyone—and Bane had breezed in.

"Math *again*? Are you finished?"

"Nearly."

That wasn't good enough for him, he leaned over my shoulder, stole my pen and filled in the last three of Uncle Peter's questions in the time it would've taken me to figure out what the first one was asking me to try to do. 'Try' being the operative word.

"There, she's done, Father Peter. She actually got three right, too."

I looked apologetically at my tutor. He was so generous with his time, but I had my usual math headache, and I really wanted to go with Bane.

"Run along, you two," he said gently.

"Thanks!" said Bane brightly.

"Oh, I'm leaving this afternoon," the priest added.

"Come back soon, Uncle Peter," I said quietly.

"Yeah, stay safe, old man," said Bane. "Don't let those long teeth trip you up."

"Trust me," smiled Uncle Peter, "in my profession, being long in the tooth is nothing to complain about. And since *you* mention the subject of safety," his voice was suddenly about the chilliest I'd ever heard it—think spring rather than summer, "from what I hear, you were very lucky, the other month. Perhaps you'd care to stop and think before dragging Margo into any more of your clever schemes. Stop and think just how you'll feel after you've got her executed."

The smile was wiped from Bane's face like rain from a windscreen. "Just...*stay safe, Father.*" He spun around and marched out of the room.

Hand on my heart, that was the harshest thing I've ever heard Uncle Peter say to anyone, and I've known him my whole life. As for 'Cousin' Mark, anyone could see he was trying not to grin whenever the subject came up!

Of course, he was your normal young priest, whose highest ambition in terms of longevity was to reach thirty and to whom Uncle Peter's ripe old age of forty plus appeared as mythical as a hundred and fifty remained to the rest of the population.

But...that'd been almost two years ago and even my parents were all smiles with Bane again. So perhaps they'd let him write. Before I snapped and asked them myself.

This was no good, I must finish the letter.

I'd barely signed it when the door opened and the warden stood there, anticipation brightening her already rosy cheeks.

"Come along, girls. I have a little lesson for you. Come along, all of you."

Trailed by another couple of guards as always, we trooped out into the passage and followed her to the left, through the barred gate that was normally closed, past the Old Year's dorm and along to the stairwell. The way Polly had been taken. The way to the Lab. A maggot of unease began to gnaw at my belly.

She took us down only one flight of stairs and then through into that middle block, stopping by a door and waving us inside. "In you go, girls. Find somewhere where you can see."

Once inside, the maggot morphed into a fully grown fly and ricocheted wildly around my stomach. We stood in a viewing gallery, and that gleaming white and metal room below us was the Lab itself. 'Doctor' Richard and Sidney stood in their white coats, laying out a variety of metal utensils on a metal table, and several minions in scrubs were checking a many-doored chiller cabinet and a stack of zip-lock bags.

"Now, can you all see, girls?" Captain Wallis had stepped inside behind us and closed the door. Card-locked, of course. "You are greatly privileged to be here today to witness an execution—assuming the fool doesn't choose to save himself, of course, but they usually don't. It will be very educational for you to see so much of the human anatomy..."

Dismay washed the rest of her words away. The implication that the condemned might save himself told me the worst. No murderer or Resistance fighter was about to be dismantled before our eyes. It was one of the Underground. *Let it not be the severest sentence...let it not be a priest.*

And let it not be someone I know. A selfish prayer, but I couldn't help it.

Captain Wallis still gushed on about how educational it all was, a horrid eagerness in her eyes. Sadistic witch indeed, to force on us this preview of our own fate. I tried to tune her out, working to prepare myself for the sight of whoever might be wheeled through those doors. I must not betray that I knew them; must not betray pain or grief. If I gave myself away, my parents would die, and many others with them, and my coming to this place would be all for nothing.

An uneasy whispering spread, as those who knew what was going on explained it to those who did not. Sarah came and clung to my sleeve, unsettled by the atmosphere, but I didn't try to explain. Hopefully she wouldn't understand what was happening.

Two external guards opened the doors at one end of the Lab and pushed a gurney inside. One look at the middle-aged man strapped to it was like a blow to my stomach. The air rushed from my lungs, my heart accelerated, juddering in my chest, and I could feel the blood draining from my face, from my head, leaving my ears ringing, as the cold unreality of shock gripped me.

6

UNCLE PETER

I drew in a long, shuddering breath, fighting, fighting to keep my face expressionless, to give no sign of the dismay surging inside me.

Uncle Peter.

Dear, kind, good Uncle Peter. Uncle Peter who I loved so much more dearly than my real uncle, Frank, who I'd never seen, so great was his fear of being associated with the Underground. My beloved uncle.

Oh, Domine Deus, where was he captured? Please, not at my home.

A man in a suit walked beside the gurney, swinging a briefcase from his hand; the junior judge charged with signing the final instruction for the dismantlers after the last attempt to break the convicted. They weren't going to break Uncle Peter, though. He'd known this moment would come for half his life.

"I've had a very good run, my dear, very good indeed," he'd told me a couple of weeks ago, smiling after I raised some concern for his safety, "but it will be my turn sooner or later and when it is, try not to weep for me too much, hmm? Remember that the most likely manner of my passing will see me straight into the arms of Our Lord."

Oh, Uncle Peter, a touch of prophecy, perhaps, you poor dear man?

"Peter Patrick Wilson, EuroBloc citizen..." The judge had taken some papers from his case and begun to read with all the tone and inflection of an automated message.

"...You were taken on the sixteenth of March in Salperton General Hospital," one little knot of terror inside me loosened, "and charged with the *Personal Practice of Superstition* and the graver charge of *Inciting and Promoting Superstition in the General Population*. You have been

51

sentenced to the severest penalty of the law and are to here in this place, at this time, suffer Full Conscious Dismantlement.

"Due to the nature of your crime, the law stipulates a full pardon in the event that you choose to categorically deny the existence of any so-called Deity. You have five minutes left in which to make this statement. After this time has elapsed, the execution will proceed. As you are probably aware, it will not be possible for you to make any statement once the execution is in progress."

The judge lowered his papers and made eye contact with the man in front of him. "So I really, really suggest you talk sense now, while you can." He suddenly sounded slightly more human and slightly less like a machine.

Uncle Peter was so pale his lips were white and his eyes were moving around the room too rapidly, here and there, but he managed to move those white lips in a faint, kind smile for the judge, then fixed his eyes on the ceiling in an obvious attempt to keep them still.

"For pity's sake, be sensible, man!" urged the judge. "Don't you realize they're about to take you apart, a piece at a time, and you're going to feel every last cut of the scalpel?"

Uncle Peter's chest rose and fell a little more rapidly; his hands clenched reflexively. His eyes moved on around the room, as though seeking distraction. At a word from Richard, the minions moved forward with scissors and began to cut away his clothes. Another filled a syringe with amber liquid and laid it ready.

"What's four little words?" the judge went on. "There. Is. No. God. That's all you have to say. Four little words and they'll take off these straps and find you some new clothes and open those doors and you can walk out, a free man. You can go off, register, have a pair of children, die in bed... Just say it."

"Vade post me, Satana," murmured the priest. *Get behind me, Satan.*

"I don't know what you're muttering about, but I suspect that was not superstitious mumbo-jumbo for 'There is no God,' so I'm going to have to sign this form and leave you in these gentlemen's capable hands. Last chance to talk sense."

Uncle Peter swallowed so hard I could see it from the gallery, and went for English this time. "*I believe in God, the Father almighty, Creator of heaven and earth...*"

"Fine!" snapped the judge, almost throwing his hands up in disgust. "Have it your own way." He placed the form on the hard side of his briefcase, signed it without another word and handed it to Richard. "All yours."

"Bit older, isn't he?" remarked Richard. "Still, there's always someone grateful for the parts."

Older. As though that stopped them executing little old grannies if they caught them with a rosary in their pocket!

The minions whipped away the last fragments of Uncle Peter's clothes while the judge gathered up his papers and put them away.

Uncle Peter twisted his right hand against the straps, raised thumb and first two fingers and blessed the man who'd just signed away his life. "I forgive you," he whispered.

The judge went crimson, fumbled with his case for a moment, and strode rapidly from the room.

Uncle Peter looked at the two dismantlers and their helpers, blessed them, and again he whispered, "I forgive you."

They all pretended not to hear him, but my stomach knotted with something like awe. How could he do it? Right then, *I* couldn't find it in me to forgive them for what they were about to do to *him*. Yet he forgave them. It was a common thing to do, but still, it choked me.

Richard picked up that amber syringe and a fine trembling began in Uncle Peter's pale hands. His eyes moved again, this time finding the balcony and pausing, horror-filled, at the sight of the nineteen girls being forced to watch his gruesome demise. Then his gaze ran rapidly over us until it found mine.

None of the dismantling team were looking...unobserved, I raised my hand slightly and curved thumb and forefinger into the Fish. *Keep the faith, Uncle Peter.*

His eyes moved quickly on again, pausing on other faces as well, and a fresh knot of fear relaxed inside me. He wouldn't betray me by accident, even in these ghastly moments. Again he raised his hand slightly, tracing the sign of the cross over us. I could almost hear his voice in my head. *Keep the faith, Margo.*

"What's he doing?" asked Caroline, in a hushed voice.

"I think it's called a blessing," volunteered someone else.

"Is it magic?" asked Harriet.

"Well, I imagine it's supposed to be…or something like that," replied the more knowledgeable someone.

"The *EuroBloc* don't think so, *do* they," sneered Jane.

"We could use some magic," said Harriet wistfully. "But… why'd he do it to them too? They're going to…kill him…aren't they?"

"Priests will bless anything if it holds still long enough," retorted Jane.

"Margo, why'd he bless all of them? It is good magic, isn't it, not a curse or something?"

My mouth was so dry I wasn't sure I could answer, but I had to try. "It's an important thing for them, Harriet." How had I managed to speak so normally? "He's supposed to forgive everyone, no matter what they do to him."

"But *why?*"

I mustn't sound too knowledgeable. "I think they love absolutely everyone as a brother or sister, or something like that. I don't quite understand it myself."

No lie. I believed in the theory with all my heart, but right now I really was having trouble understanding how I could *ever* love Richard or Sidney or the judge who'd just condemned my dear friend to one of the slowest and most agonizing deaths ever invented by mankind. My heart just didn't feel as though it could ever expand enough to accept such monsters into it.

Syringe in hand, Richard searched for the vein on Uncle Peter's arm. Uncle Peter's trembling hands knotted into balls again and his chest heaved, but he closed his eyes firmly and lay very still. With a sound of satisfaction, Richard slid the needle in and drove the plunger home, then withdrew it and dropped the syringe into the sharps bin held by a hovering minion.

Whether Uncle Peter fought the drug's paralyzing effect or not, his hands relaxed, his breathing grew slower and more regular, and his head fell to one side as his muscle control drained away. A minion stepped forward to fit a brace to hold his head upright as Richard and Sidney set to work, and the other two converged, armed with an assortment of utensils for clamping blood vessels.

I watched with a kind of sick fascination, unable to look away, unwilling to look away, for irrational as it might be, to look away felt like to desert him. Perhaps it was. To look away because *I* couldn't bear it, when he could do nothing *but* bear it.

Oh, their hideous gentleness, mere care not to damage the merchandise!

It went on and on and on. I'd never realized how many parts there were in the human body. And always the suffocating horror, the knowledge that Uncle Peter was quite conscious, that he could feel every slice of those cruel blades.

My own helplessness crushed me. I wanted to rush down there and save him...yet I could not. It simply *was not possible*. Guards and card-locked doors blocked my path; my solitary, unarmed, untrained self simply *could not* save him. I wanted to scream, shout, howl out my grief and horror, but I couldn't do that, either, for how many others would I condemn to Uncle Peter's fate, and for what?

When they finally cut out his still-beating heart, I began to shake, long spasms that I couldn't stop. Over. It was over. He was at peace and with his reward promised to outweigh his sufferings a thousandfold, he was blessed indeed. But right then, with the grisly evidence before my eyes, I could think no further than his sufferings.

Everyone was moving now, talking in hushed voices; some girls were crying and hugging each other. Many clustered at the back of the gallery, not looking. Harriet fought her way through the throng and flung herself onto my Sarah-free side; automatically, I slipped an arm around her as well. Someone had been sick—I'd not even noticed that it had happened.

Caroline came hurtling after Harriet, followed by Annie, and I fought to yank my mind from its numbness and comfort them as best I could. Another two arms would've helped...of course, there were two spare ones down there, now...the thought drifted across my mind, unbidden, and I swallowed hard as my stomach heaved.

Oh, Uncle Peter. Uncle Peter.

"Now, gather round, girls," our twisted jailer said. "Come up to the glass, now."

Harriet wouldn't go nearer, still clinging to me. "That's what they're going to do to *us*, isn't it?" she whispered, staring down at the gurney, where the last few usable parts were being removed and packed up.

"We won't feel a thing, Harriet. We'll be fast asleep."

"They're still going to cut us up into little pieces!"

"Well, yes." What could I say?

Harriet wasn't the only one who didn't want to go any closer and the sounds of fear and crying filled the gallery.

"Get up there, all of you!" snarled Captain Wallis, driving us all before her.

"You finished, Sid?" asked Richard, down in the Lab.

"Yeah, heart's all packed up, you want anything else?"

"Not from a forty-two year old. Let's knock off."

And leaving their red coats with a minion, they strode out of the room.

"Gather around, girls," ordered Captain Wallis, "Take a good look. Very few people have an opportunity like this outside of medical school, you know."

Tearful and cringing, everyone tried not to look while looking like they were.

"Isn't it simply fascinating, girls?" Captain Wallis went on. Her eyes were strangely hot and she kept moistening her lips. "To be able to see a human body in parts, to know this is what a human being is—mere intricacies of flesh and blood and bone."

Her voice hardened. "To know there is *nothing more* to it. That a dead body is made up of only two things—useful parts and useless parts. That the human race is made up of the same—useful people and useless people. This super- stitious witch doctor is one of the useless ones—his only usefulness is in death. Rather like you girls."

Harriet started crying so hard I gave her a hasty hug. She wasn't the only one to break down completely. Captain Wallis licked her lips yet again, seeming to savor the moment.

Until a very simple girl called Bethan spoke up innocently. "Don't people have a magic part or something? My great granny's magic part went to a lovely place, Mummy said so. So hasn't his magic part gone there too?"

Captain Wallis reached Bethan in two strides, grabbed her by the collar and dragged her forwards, shoving her face close to the glass. "Your mother lied to you, you credulous idiot," she hissed, then went on gloatingly, "there is *no such thing* as a magic part. There *is* no lovely place. Your great granny no longer exists and nor does this fool. *This* is all that is left of him."

I stood there looking down at my friend's warm, still remains, the warden's twisted triumph ringing in my ears, and something I'd never really felt before bubbled up inside, hot and black and corrosive, like red-hot, poisonous teeth sinking into my soul.

Hatred.

I hated her. This stupid, short-sighted, sick woman. She hadn't even killed Uncle Peter herself and yet at that moment I hated her far more than Richard or Sidney or the judge or the minions. They'd been doing a job, but this woman had enjoyed every minute of Uncle Peter's torment.

Images cascaded through my mind, memories from earliest childhood, Uncle Peter lifting me up, up onto his shoulders, Uncle Peter sitting on the carpet with me, trying to teach me subtraction with rows of sweets, Uncle Peter saying Mass, holding the bread before our eyes as it became Our Lord, Uncle Peter listening gravely to every little childhood sin I confessed, replying with words of healing and encouragement, always, always taking me seriously in everything, always, always teaching me, teaching me math, teaching me morals, teaching me hope, teaching me joy... and this woman, this stupid, wicked woman, dared to gloat over his physical body, dared to say that was *all he was!*

I wished her in hell and I could've sent her there myself.

"Margo?" whispered Caroline tearfully, staring at me wide-eyed.

My teeth were about ready to break, they were clenched so tight. With effort, I relaxed my mouth, realizing Captain

Wallis hadn't finished with Bethan yet—Bethan was crying and struggling as the warden pushed her face harder and harder into the glass.

"*Open* your eyes, you little fool! *Open them!* Take a good close look."

"Please," sobbed Bethan, "please, I'm sorry! What did I do? Please, I don't want to, please stop!"

Captain Wallis put a finger and thumb to Bethan's face and tried to force her lids open—Bethan started screaming...

I'd reached them before I was aware of taking a decision to move; I pulled Bethan out of the Captain's grasp and pushed her behind me.

"How dare you..." hissed the warden.

My mouth opened on vicious, venomous words... And again I saw Uncle Peter, lying on that table, his fingers raised in blessing, heard his voice whispering, "I forgive you". I stood there in front of the woman and though I shook from head to foot, I swallowed those words. I don't know how, so it must've been grace. It was not me.

"Captain," I said coolly instead. "I was just wondering: when is the next ReAssignees Welfare Board inspection?"

She stared at me, reading the anger and hate in my eyes, seeing the rebellion in my interference and definitely understanding the threat in my mild words. Her hands twitched, as though she'd *smash* my head into the glass. But it was a very *good* threat.

"Girls," she barked at last, still staring balefully at me, "you will each take a proper look at these useless scraps and when the last one of you has done so, you may go back to your dormitory."

Everyone shrank back, so she grabbed the nearest girl and shoved her up against the glass as well, and as the girl stumbled away whimpering, everyone suddenly decided to obey after all. There was rather a scrum as they all tried to touch their noses to the glass to prove they'd done it.

After that, satisfied at last, the warden marched us back to our dorm, where chaos promptly reigned. Girls threw themselves into each other's arms, sobbing, or lay on their bunks, staring at the wall; Jane paced up and down the center of the room, snapping at anyone who got in her way;

Sarah, Bethan, and Hazel went into a nervous huddle and Harriet, Caroline, and Annie continued to cling to me like limpets.

I tried my best to comfort them but I'd reached the end of my tether. I shook uncontrollably, nausea threatened to overwhelm me, and I kept losing track of who'd said what to whom. It was no use. If I didn't get out of there, I would lose it.

Pleading a need for the bathroom, I coaxed Harriet, Caroline, and Annie into a mutual hug and bolted for the buzzer. Fortunately the guard arrived before anyone noticed my sudden availability as a shoulder to cry on, and I made my escape.

"You going to be long, lass?" asked the elderly guard, sounding bored. He made no move to step into the washroom and out of the camera's eye—the smarter guards knew better. Apparently it wasn't totally unknown for a girl to take such an error of judgment as an opportunity for a bit of revenge and claim some inappropriate behavior had occurred. That was a career-stopper if the RWB—ReAssignees Welfare Board—got to hear about it.

"Probably." I spoke as calmly as I could.

"Give me a buzz when you're done, then," said the guard—'Watkins' read his badge. The stairwell door clicked closed behind him as he headed back to the guardroom.

Laudate Deum, I was alone. I could hold it off no longer; shudders wracked me from head to foot and my stomach began to heave in earnest. Diving into a cubicle, I kicked the door shut behind me and was violently sick. I went on being sick until eventually there was nothing to come up but bile and kneeling there, my forehead pressed to that cold cinder block wall, I cried and cried until my face was on fire and every drop of water in my body ought to have evaporated from it.

Uncle Peter, dead.

Uncle Peter, slowly, agonizingly dead, a piece at a time.

There was no escaping the truth of what I'd seen with my own eyes.

I beat on the wall, blind to the pain, barely retaining the sense to stop before I laid my knuckles bare, for how would

I explain that? The tears would not stop—hope had vanished from my soul like a forgotten dream.

Curled up with my hands over my head, I rocked to and fro, fighting with my helplessness, my loneliness, my terror. Uncle Peter was dead and my parents might be about to go the same way. They were unlikely to be sentenced to conscious execution, but dismantled they would be if Uncle Peter was traced back to them.

And—oh *Domine Deus!*—to my shame, a selfish thought, a selfish but oh so ghastly thought crept in amongst the rest. What would it be like to live out my two years here almost completely alone, knowing almost all those I loved were dead and even though Bane still lived, he was cut off from me, unreachable as the moon...

No, I was being foolish. If they took my parents, they would come for me too. They would take me before a judge and bid me speak the words of Divine denial; my refusal to Apostatize would condemn me for Personal Superstition and I would simply be dismantled immediately, instead of in two years.

My heartbeat steadied slightly and the chill eased its grip on me. Immediate and painless entrance into Our Lord's company instead of two long years of lonely misery; that wasn't so bad, then.

But *Mum and Dad...*where'd Uncle Peter been staying? He could've been staying at five or six different houses, he moved often—after all, even much-loved uncles or family friends didn't visit all the time. Was it my own family or another that were about to share his fate?

His fate... *Uncle Peter...*

Tears. More tears. Ridiculous, I was going to dissolve. *Don't cry, Margo, just remember him.* But the memories brought tears. *Receive the soul of your faithful servant, Lord. Take him to yourself...*

Then Uncle Peter's smiling face filled my mind, driving out the memory of that ruined one we'd left in the Lab. *Don't cry, Margo,* he told me, just as if he'd surprised a childish tear on my cheek. *The Lord's written you a letter, specially for now.* I knew the 'letter' and words from it were suddenly whispering through my mind...

...Desiderat, languens concupiscit
anima mea atria Domini...
>...*For the courts of the Lord's house,
my soul faints with longing...*

...Transeuntes per vallum aridam,
fontem facient eam...
>...*Passing through the valley of Weeping,
they make it a place of springs...*

...Vere melior est dies unus in
atriis tuis quam alii mille...
>...*Willingly would I give a thousand of my days
for one spent in your courts...*

...Domine exercituum, beautus
homo qui confidit in te...
>...*Lord of hosts, blessed
is the man who trusts in you...*

Those verses shone like a light into that terrifying blackness and they left me a little calmer. Uncle Peter was in the courts of the Lord's house, and the Lord was still with me.

A knock on the door and Watkins' voice jerked me from my contemplations. "It's supper; you done in there, lass?"

"I'll be right out." Getting up, I flushed the toilet and went to wash my hands, checking my face carefully in the mirror. My last tears had fallen long enough ago that my eyes weren't too red, but I splashed a bit of cold water on them all the same and dried them carefully with toilet roll.

I shouldn't have hidden in here for the last half hour. What if the Rats learned that a priest's execution had made me behave like this? Suspicion was all it took, for the invitation to make the Divine denial provided the rest. Still... it'd been a choice between a breakdown in public or a breakdown in private, so...couldn't be helped.

Right. Supper. I'd never felt less like eating. Everyone was coming down the passage; Watkins had unlocked the dorm.

Supper and unhappy comrades in distress. I squared my shoulders and headed for the door.

There was no time to amend my letter after supper: my friends attached themselves to me and I hadn't the heart to shed them again. I set my alarm early instead.

My night prayers flowed in my mind, comforting and very welcome, until the last one. I approached it rather warily and tried to recite it nice and steadily, hoping to just run through it, but when I reached 'quodcumque mortis genus' the words stuck in my throat and choked me. *Whatever kind of death.*

The very worst *mortis genus* had been revealed to me today, in all its stark agony. Had I ever really appreciated what this prayer said *at all? Whatever* kind of death. Even Conscious Dismantlement. Even that. The ultimate Act of Acceptance of the Lord's will. For His will was that all humanity should have Free Will, even judges and dismantlers.

The idea of me, there in Uncle Peter's place, had me sweating in terror. I tried and tried to find the willingness in me, but still the words brought me to a halt, shaking with fear.

What are the odds of you ending up in that situation, Margo? Minuscule! But still, I couldn't speak. I could not. Finally, I gave up and just lay there, tears of shame drying on my cheeks.

7

THE LATTER YEARS OF PETER RABBIT

I did my best to eat something, lest my parents worry, but it was a waste. I didn't seem to taste any of it.

"Let's go and dance," I said after a while, and ignoring Mum's dire warnings about catching cold, I slipped off my jacket and left it behind. Most girls my age weren't wearing big coats, and I couldn't afford anything distinctive. I did borrow Dad's football cap, pulling it down over my face.

For a while I almost forgot our little enterprise, since it was hard to think about much else when dancing with Bane. He swung me and spun me until we were both draped dizzily over each other for balance, laughing hysterically.

When they were almost ready to start, we slipped quietly away. We'd not be the only young couple sneaking off into the night, fence or no fence. Bane scaled the thing again in that dark corner while I rolled my skirt up by a couple of feet, the chill night air raising goosebumps on my bared legs.

"Uh...what are you doing?"

"Avoiding distinguishing features. And if it keeps the guards' eyes off my face, so much the better. It seems to be working on you."

Bane's blush was almost, but not quite, invisible in the darkness and he dragged his eyes back to my face at once.

"Okay, well," he said hastily, "I looked at a program. The Minister for the British Department just has a very short bit tonight introducing the Chairman, so when he gets up, you draw the guards away. Just after the Chairman starts his speech is about when I'm aiming for the things to start going off. That should upstage him nicely, don't you think?"

"Just slightly! But for goodness' sake be careful."

"Yeah, 'course I will,'" and with an oh-so-reassuring flip of his hand, Bane disappeared between the huts.

Previous experience at Annual Summits left me in little doubt that even after the speeches had started—or perhaps especially then—there'd be plenty of people hanging around the edges of the sports ground. So I headed along the fence until I was only a short walk from the gardeners' hut, but far enough away that I wouldn't be visible to the guards.

Now came the waiting, the ridiculous hype of the High Committee's arrival, the extremely lengthy descriptions of how honored little Salperton-under-Fell was this night, and the tedious introductions on stage. It barely penetrated my brain as I pictured Bane creeping slowly through the under-growth, circling behind that little shed. I should've asked him how exactly he planned to get in...

"And now, it gives me great pleasure to welcome to Salperton-under-Fell, this night, Donald Grisforth, our honored Minister for the British Department..."

My cue at last.

Jerked from my half-conscious state by my alarm, I got up reluctantly and dressed. Taking my letter to the table, I found a nice wide margin along the side of an inner page and set to work.

P. S.

You know you made me promise to tell you how my story 'The Latter Years of Peter Rabbit' ended? Well, I can hardly bear to do so, the ending has turned out so sad.

Dear old Peter Rabbit goes to Grandma Jemima Puddle Duck's pond to visit, because she's sick, but since he's such an old rabbit by then he gets caught by a human, who takes him home and chops him up to make a stew. Only, then the human realizes there's not really enough of him to make a stew, so he goes out and starts hunting for the

64

warren, so he can eat all Peter's little bunny children as well.

So you see, it's terribly sad and I'm so very sorry to have to tell you about it. Anyway, let me know if you would like me to send you a copy, it's only short, but I imagine you perhaps won't, with the ending having finished up like that!

Love, M xxx

I read the postscript critically. I couldn't do much better than that. Since they knew nothing of any 'The Latter Years of Peter Rabbit', let alone a promise about it, surely they would understand what I was telling them? So might a priest-catcher, but that I would have to risk.

Breakfast wasn't for another fifteen minutes; my little addition hadn't taken as long as I'd feared. I fetched my notebook and headed a fresh page:

The Latter Years of Peter Rabbit
Margaret Verrall

Just in case I found pursuivants crawling out of the woodwork—concrete—here.

We posted our letters at breakfast, those of us who could write well enough to send them and had someone to send them to. There were some blessings to count. I finished the story then, before our gym session. It extended to only five sides, was far from the most inspiring thing I'd ever written, and I was glad to be finished with it. But it existed. That was enough.

"Margy! Story, story!" Sarah tugged at the pad eagerly, seeing I'd finished.

"I don't think you'll enjoy that one." I detached her hands gently and flicked back to the beginning of the pad. "How about 'The Diary of a Fellest Ewe: Part One'?"

"Ewe, ram, lamb," recited Sarah. "All sheep."

"Yes, I think that will be right up your street." Which was

why I'd started this Facility pad with something so pleasant. "Are you sitting comfortably?"

Sarah plunked down in a chair and Caroline and Harriet looked our way and brightened.

Jane got there first, though. "Clear off, Sarah, I want to talk to Margaret."

Sarah jumped up hastily, but I caught her wrist. "You don't have to go anywhere, Sarah. If you want to speak to me, Jane, wait 'til I'm unoccupied or ask me nicely, don't just boss my friends around."

Jane huffed impatiently. "*Fine*, can I speak to you?"

"I was about to read Sarah a story, actually..."

But Sarah had had enough of prickly Jane and she slipped off to see what Bethan was doing.

I sighed. "Fine, Jane, looks like I'm all yours."

"Good. So. I've been watching you. I think you're probably the smartest person in this room, after me. Possibly including me. Way smarter than Rebecca. And tough. Tougher than those mild manners of yours let on. And everyone comes to you with their problems."

"If you've got a suggestion how I can prevent *that*, I'm all ears. I've never been able to."

"I have, actually," said Jane, lowering her voice. "See, I never expected to live this long, but I have, so I figure, since I'm an adult—or *would* be—and my parents can't be punished for what I do any more, I may as well live a *lot* longer. I want to escape. It's not doable alone, but it might just be doable with two of us. You in?"

I stared at her. Her words didn't surprise me, but—they'd unexpectedly soured that beautiful dream of mine—of Bane coming to rescue me. More than a dream, really, a hope, a very, very slim one, but I wouldn't underestimate him.

But...more than once over the last few days I'd imagined him coming and taking me away, away to the African Free States, perhaps, where you could have as many children as you wanted with whoever you wanted, and towns and villages had actual church buildings you could just go into in front of everyone... Oh yes, I'd dreamt about Bane and me and Africa's wonderful freedom.

What I hadn't pictured was Bane opening that door to let

me out, and me going out to him...and shutting the door behind me. Leaving everyone else to die. Sarah and Caroline and Harriet and Annie and Bethan and *Jane,* even, and... everyone. I'd never really thought it through that far, perhaps because...well, it seemed so impossible.

"I'm not sure it is doable even with two of us," I said quietly, after a long moment. "Not two on the inside. Here's the way I work it out; correct me if you disagree. The card-locked doors are a pain but not insurmountable—all one needs to do is take a card from a guard, hardly impossible—I've yet to see one with their gun drawn. So the card gets you out of the building.

"Now, there's four ways out of the compound. Front gates, they're code-locked, not card-locked, so forget those. I reckon there's some kind of similar parking area and gate outside the Lab for the organs to be collected and the convicted brought in; but also code-locked, I imagine.

"Assuming the place is mirror-imaged, there's a gate from each exercise yard through the wall. You must've seen the stupid things, marked 'Emergency Exit'. Chalk those up to the reAssignees Welfare Board, I imagine. But they're no use either. In the daytime, assuming you had a card, you might slip through while everyone was in the yard exercising, but then you'd be out in the middle of the cleared area, giving those machine guns some target practice. It's two hundred meters *uphill* to the trees—they don't call it a killing zone for nothing.

"At night it's even worse. The yards are illuminated and I'm pretty sure one guard in each tower is watching them—they look like they're facing that way—which means two sets of eyes on each yard. If you *did* get across the yard and through the gate, the killing zone is also floodlit, so the result would be just the same as in daylight.

"So, my conclusion so far is, the only way to get out of here is to neutralize two of the guard towers for long enough to reach the forest. And since the entrances to the guard towers are in the illuminated, watched exercise yards...I don't see how that can be done from inside."

Jane looked disappointed. "But if we got a card, we could get one of those tranquilizer pistols at the same time."

"NonLees, not tranquilizers," I couldn't help saying.

"What's the big diff?"

"Tranquilizer pistols have been around for at least a hundred years, but they never took off as mainstream weapons. Whoever you shot always had time to raise their nice lethal weapon and shoot you back before collapsing. So they were only used for animals and...well, kidnapping, maybe.

"NonLethals are a recent development. They send out a concentrated electrical charge—or electromagnetic, don't ask me to explain the science—like a rather large bullet in shape, but it only has to clip someone and it drops them, unconscious, instantly. No time to retaliate. Silent, too. They *ought* to make fatalities in war a thing of the past, only people are just using them for police and guards and going right on arming soldiers with Lethals."

"And some guards," said Jane pointedly.

"Yeah, and some guards. I s'pose people just don't feel nonLees are quite as intimidating."

"How d'you know all that?"

"Oh, my friend's got a replica of one of these nonLee pistols. He's into that sort of thing."

"Is this the delectable Bane Marsden all your friends go weak at the knees over?"

"Bane has the pistol, yes."

"Is he not delectable, then?"

"Well, he is rather gorgeous," I conceded. "In an unconventional kind of way."

"What's that mean?"

"Oh, his skin's a bit too dark for British C group, looks like he should belong to Mediterranean C group, but his features are all British Caucasian. And his hair is black, but not like Mediterranean C group or British Asian, like yours, but really matte black. Like African B, no getting around it, but it feels like British C in texture. He just looks subtly... different, basically."

Jane's eyebrows had gone up. "Mixed genes, then?"

"Not officially. His parents were able to register. The mixed genes were from too far back to be a problem."

"Bet that was a nasty shock for them, then."

I grimaced. "Yeah, just a little."

"Trouble?"

"Well, I know Mr. Marsden insisted on an in-depth gene scan. Not sure Mrs. Marsden's ever forgiven him. But I'm not sure he's ever forgiven her for *not* having been unfaithful." Jane looked puzzled, so I expanded, "The in-depth scan showed *he* was the one carrying the mixed genes, y'see."

"Oh," said Jane, nodding. "Ouch."

"Umm."

"*Bane's* not on the official British C name list, surely?"

"His birth certificate says Blake. But his parents saw fit to tell him, when he was very little indeed..." I couldn't keep the anger from my voice, "that they'd wanted to call him Bane because as soon as they set eyes on his little 'black' self they knew he was going to be the bane of their lives. The registry office wouldn't accept the name, so they called him Blake instead. Which means 'black', incidentally."

Jane winced. "They said that to him?"

"Yeah. He refused to answer to Blake ever again. Said if Bane was what they wanted to call him, they could blinking well call him it. His, er, his relationship with his family isn't very good."

That was a humungous understatement, actually. Bane's parents had wanted a little clone of his older brother, Eliot, who's like a little clone of *them*, but they'd ended up with Bane. They'd always been too busy lamenting the qualities he *didn't* have to appreciate the ones he *did*.

They didn't, for example, see that to climb to the top of the town's main mast when you're eleven years old takes a heck of a lot of courage and determination. Of course, he did kick the main cable out of the transmitter right in the middle of the EuroBloc's Annual Speech. He lied his head off to the reception committee waiting for him at the bottom; said it was an accident and because he was just a child he got away with it. But his parents were hauled over the coals, and they knew he was fibbing, knew their embarrassing child was not the little model citizen they wanted him to be.

But they never gave him any credit for his courage or anything like that. Didn't seem to understand that you can't *make* your children agree with you. Especially when you think it's okay to murder people for their organs, or simply for disagreeing with you about the existence of a Deity.

"Anyway," Jane dismissed the love of my life with a flick of her plaits, "Say we got one of the nonLethals..."

The distant click of the stairwell door opening and the sound of raised voices distracted us both.

"You can't be serious about this!" That was the Menace, sounding unusually dismayed.

"Do I look like I'm joking?" Jane and I glanced at each other. That well bred voice...Major Everington, surely? What had happened to *I hope I never see any of you again?*

Our door opened and a couple of guards shoved someone through. The person hit the ground with a splat and lay coughing and spluttering, wet russet hair plastered over a barely-glimpsed face, as a white cane and a familiar bag landed alongside.

8

THE BOY

The whole dorm stared at the soggy figure on the floor, then looked at the officers, who were still arguing.

"He's a *boy*. I can't have a boy in the girls' block—"

"You can and you will. I've had enough of him. You keep him alive for me."

"And how am I supposed to explain him to the next bleeding-hearters from the Really Wet Board who come inspecting us?"

"Trust me, it will be a lot easier to explain his presence *here* than to explain his dead body."

"Can't you keep order?" snapped Captain Wallis. "I thought you'd got them trained not to inflict permanent damage on each other?"

"Yes, well, they seem prepared to make an exception in his case. Sunday, they tried to drown him in the toilet. They made so much noise a guard went to investigate. Fortunately the guards were alert after that and caught them trying to hang him yesterday. And this morning they tried to drown him, *again.*"

"They were probably just playing with him!" Captain Wallis sounded exasperated.

"He was completely unconscious, the guard tells me, yet they weren't showing the slightest sign of taking his head out of the toilet. That doesn't sound very like playing to me. You're having him. End of argument."

"But what will I *tell* people?" demanded the Menace, as Major Everington spun on his heel and disappeared from the doorway.

His voice echoed back along the corridor. "How should I know. He's having a sleep-over? Or put him in a dress. What do I care."

"A dress?" wailed the Captain, hurrying after him. "A

71

dress? Look at his shoulders, look at his *face*... He's growing a *man-chest!* He'll just look like a young man in a *dress!* It won't work! *You'll* have *to have him back!"*

I think the Major halted suddenly. His voice went very soft. "I'm *so* sorry, did I give the impression this was... *negotiable?"*

"I...right. The boy's staying here."

"Better."

They trooped away again. Huh. The Captain was scared of the Major. Judging what she was like, that meant lazy or not, he must have a very nasty side indeed. Worth knowing.

Jonathan had remained where he'd been flung, apparently concentrating on his water-logged breathing and waiting for them to go away. When the guards shut the door, he finally pushed himself up on his elbows, coughed some more, then held his breath. Listening. His hand slid out, silently quartering the floor until it found his stick.

"It's a *boy!"* someone whispered, and there was an eruption of giggling.

I approached slowly, so as not to alarm him. There was a wariness in his unseeing eyes that hadn't been there before and the fingers that curled protectively on the floor looked as though they'd been stamped on several times recently.

"Jonathan? You all right?"

His shoulders relaxed, just slightly. "Margaret. Well, at least if I have to be thrown in a girls' dorm, it's the one with you in."

"Are you okay?"

"Yeah. It would appear a guard fished me out before my lack of gills proved fatal."

He was so unsteady I actually took his hand and helped him up. He was wet all over. "Urm, do you need a shower?"

His laugh tailed off into another coughing session. "I've had one. The resident doctor refused to examine me until the guards had hosed me down."

"We do have a doctor, do we?"

"It's one of the dismantlers. Disbarred, I think. Seems to fulfil the requirement, though."

So *Doctor* Richard wasn't a courtesy title after all. "Well, your bed's over here; there's only one free. I've got your bag."

I picked it up and led him to the bunk.

He didn't protest, so he must've been feeling as rotten as he looked. He stood by the bed and dripped, shivering despite the warm spring day.

"You'd better get dry clothes on."

"Yeah...could you pull something out for me? Or I'll get them all wet."

I unzipped the bag and took out a very limited selection of garments. One pair of jeans, a shirt, two t-shirts and a single pair of boxer shorts. I put the shirt and jeans by him and he stripped down to his boxers no-nonsensely enough, but a flush stained his cheeks as the giggles and whispers grew deafening.

Admittedly, his strong, lean body was worth an admiring glance. He wasn't as sinewy as Bane, though at least ten centimeters taller, but his muscles were firm and if he had time to finish growing into his nicely proportioned shoulders he'd be a fine sight. He was already a fine sight.

Pulling on his dry clothes without any undignified scramble, he traced his way around the bunk with his hands and then sat on it with poorly hidden relief.

"How many clothes did you bring?" I asked him. "Here's the rest." I put them beside him.

He ran his fingers over the garments. "More than that," he said resignedly. "Light-fingered gits. S'pose I'm lucky the guards found this much. And that I'm still in a condition to need them. You got those chests in here, too?"

His searching hand found it before I could answer; he lifted the lid and dropped the clothes inside, then stretched out on the bunk. He finally, rather absent-mindedly, scraped the wet hair back from his eyes—dark-circled, he looked exhausted—and promptly closed them. "Ah, that's nice," he sighed and appeared to be asleep immediately.

Why did I have the feeling he'd had a very bad few days?

I took down my blanket, since he was lying on his, and covered him with it. The rest of the dorm's inhabitants crept forward, peering avidly.

"Isn't he handsome!" giggled Annie. "Why's he got that stick?"

"He's blind," said Harriet. "We saw him on Sorting Day."

"I wonder if we could make some curtains for his bunk," said Rebecca thoughtfully. Yes, be much nicer for Jonathan if he could change in privacy.

"*That's* a good idea," said Jane enthusiastically. Heh? Had I misjudged her?

"Yes!" said Caroline, still staring in at him. "Margo, can you help?"

"Of course. I don't think it will even require any sewing."

This proved to be correct. We just tucked a spare blanket in under my own mattress and let it hang down.

"There," I said, satisfied. "Simple."

"Devastatingly," said Jane, rolling her eyes at Caroline, who looked offended.

"Didn't notice you suggesting how to do it!"

"Nobody asked me."

I ignored them and flipped the blanket up onto my bunk so Jonathan wouldn't be confused by it when he woke.

"Oh, it occurs to me..." I didn't have to raise my voice, pretty much everyone was still gathered around staring as though they'd never seen a male of the species before. "Jonathan's blind, like Harriet said, so we must try not to leave things lying around. Tuck the chairs back under the table when you finish, that sort of thing. Just...try and keep it in mind, you know?"

"Yeah, yeah," said Jane.

"Boy!" said Sarah, pointing.

I sighed and went to sit at the table with my pad. 'Diary of a Fellest Ewe: Part Two' would probably be called for soon enough.

Jane almost immediately sat beside me, though. "So was your final word; it can't be done?"

"It wasn't my final word and it was only, I can't yet see how it could be done." From inside, anyway, but I wasn't going to discuss Bane's promise. Jane was surely too smart to think she could really gain by currying favor with the guards, but you never knew.

"Well," said Jane, "at least things in here have just taken a turn for the better."

"Huh?"

"The boy."

"Jonathan?"

"Yeah. Who'd have thought we might get to do it after all!"

Ooooh. The general enthusiasm for the curtain suddenly made more sense. All my own inclinations along those lines were so firmly set on Bane, it hadn't clicked. Well, chances were Jonathan wouldn't mind.

"Umm," I said, non-committally, looking at my pad again.

I'd probably better talk a bit more openly about my dedication to Bane, come to think of it. Otherwise disinterest in Jonathan could raise suspicions. What'd it said in that latest EuroGov pamphlet on spotting dangerous Underground members? 'A freakish disinterest in sexual intercourse'? Hah, in their dreams! If I got out of here, Bane and a bed were pretty high on my list of priorities. Via a priest, of course.

"You don't want him, then?" Jane was eyeing me narrowly.

"Oh, Bane, you know."

"Suit yourself. That blind boy's mine."

"Well, when you let him know that, it might help if you knew his name."

"His name's Jonathan. I'm one of the few people in here who *isn't* an idiot, you know." Jane got up and went back to her bunk.

I sighed once again and returned my attention to my pad. But I'd barely written five words when a guard unlocked the door. "Exercise. The boy can stay, Doctor Richard's orders."

We trooped out, leaving Jonathan sleeping. He was still asleep when we got back and didn't wake until I shook his shoulder at lunchtime. "Lunch, Jonathan."

He started awake, then relaxed. "Oh, Margaret... You can call me Jon, by the way."

"Ah. Margo, if you want."

"Well, it's shorter."

"Yes. You know, I do think we ought to try and get a few more of your clothes back. You've hardly enough for the summer and when winter comes..."

Jonathan shrugged. "Well, it might not be so hard, if we

could persuade the guards to look properly. My mum—bit embarrassing, really—she sewed name tags in pretty much *everything*. She was afraid people wouldn't believe I knew what was mine just by feel."

He picked up his stick and pulled a face. "Can I take your arm, just this once? Because I'm old enough to know walking into walls is far *more* humiliating. *And* painful. First thing after lunch, I shall learn my way around."

"Of course."

He attached himself lightly to my arm and we headed for the door, his stick snaking so sinuously in front of him I doubted he'd really trip over anything left around.

"Would you like to walk with me?" asked Jane in an uncharacteristically bright and cheerful voice. "I'm Jane."

"Jonathan. Nice to meet you. But I'm fine with Margo, thanks."

A blind boy could probably pick up on 'uncharacteristic' a mile away. Jane gave me a much more characteristic glare as we passed.

I just shrugged. "We've a mutual friend."

"You do?"

"Bane."

"Oh. Well, Jonathan, when you get bored discussing Margaret's love life, you're welcome to hang out with me."

"Thank you," said Jonathan politely, but he didn't seem very interested. Jane glowered at the back of his head and looked daggers at me.

"I take it it's not too nice over there." As we headed down the corridor I jerked my head across the courtyard, then realized he couldn't see it and added, "In the boys' block."

"Not too pleasant, no," replied Jonathan calmly. "Everyone's in one gang or another, the strongest gang rules and the others all fight amongst themselves. They're not allowed to inflict permanent damage on each other, so it makes them rather...inventive."

"However does the Major stop them?"

"More easily than you might think. Any boy who inflicts permanent harm on one of the others is dismantled within the week."

I stared at him. "Come on, that's got to be the sort of tall tale you tell to make kids behave. Everyone knows even the Commandant doesn't have any say over who gets dismantled when. That's entirely up to the dismantlers."

"So it's supposed to be, but they say the Major has something on dear Doctor Richard. A boy goes too far, he leans on the good doctor and the boy's gone."

He seemed to sense my continuing skepticism. "Hey, after Riley—he's the top dog over there—gave this scary talk about *how things were* I thought the same—just the Major's clever story to keep the dim ones in line. And so did another boy, Rob. He obviously wanted to get up the pecking order just as fast as possible, and so he broke this other boy's arm on day two. And on day three, the dismantlers took him away. What're the odds?"

I blew out a breath. "Sounds like it's really true, then. But they don't seem to have taken to *you* much, despite that."

"No," he said flatly. "Well, that's the weak point in the Major's little control strategy, isn't it? If a whole bunch of boys try and harm another, which one does he get dismantled? Suppose normally he'd make an example of a gang leader, only I wouldn't join a gang at all. They want you to do things, bad things, to prove you're in the gang. Stuff I wouldn't do. Which didn't go down too well—they were *all* after my blood."

"So I gather. I imagine you're not really too disappointed to find yourself in a girls' dorm, all things considered."

"All things considered...I don't know. It has its own... complications."

"More complicated than being dead?"

"Being dead is very...uncomplicated."

I shrugged, bemused. Realized he couldn't see it...but he was holding my arm and had probably felt it. "Oh, well, we put up a curtain for you, while you were asleep. If that makes things any less...complicated."

He was silent for a moment too long. "Oh. Thank you. That was...kind."

The curtain hadn't pleased him? Odd. Could've sworn having to take his clothes off in front of an unseen, giggling, ogling horde hadn't been his cup of tea. Point in his favor as far as I was concerned.

77

"Stairs," I told him, as his stick found the edge of the first one.

"Yep."

"Let's get your stuff, Jon," I suggested after lunch, steering him towards the guard.

"Right. Can we speak to Captain Wallis, please?" he said to the guard the moment we reached him. Could he hear the man breathing or something?

"Right now?"

"Well, it'd better be pretty soon," I said. How long would it take the boys to think of ripping out those labels?

"All right," said the guard. "On your own heads." He tapped something into his wristCellular and raised it to his lips. "Couple of the girls...uh...reAssignees...want to see you, Captain."

"I'm busy," the Captain's voice squeaked from the wristCell. It sounded like she had her mouth full. "Just lock them back in."

"We'll have to speak either to her or to the ReAssignees Welfare Board," declared Jonathan, without turning a hair.

"You hear that, Captain?" asked the guard. "You or the Really Wet Board, they're not fussed."

A snarl like that of an angry dog came from the wristCell. "I'm on my way!"

"She's on her way," the guard informed us, with an ominous tilt of his eyebrows.

"Good," I said sweetly.

Captain Wallis slammed into the cafeteria only a short time later. "*You*," she hissed, as her eyes fell on me. "And... *Jonathina*. What do you two *girls* want?"

"The guards didn't bring all my clothes with me," said Jonathan. "The other boys had taken most of them. But they're all labeled, so there's no reason why the guards can't fetch them."

"Ugh! My pie's going cold!" snarled the Captain, making to walk out again.

"I assume you'll be providing me with alternative clothing, then?" demanded Jonathan. "At the Facility's expense?"

The Captain hesitated. Replacement clothing probably

wouldn't look too good on the accounts. People would wonder why it was needed. "Can't you manage with what you've got?" she snapped.

Why was she so reluctant? Couldn't she just get the guards to look? Ah. She had to get Major Everington to get the guards to look. Riling him up once in one day seemed to be as much as she cared for.

"I have one pair of boxers and no socks. I have no warm things at all. I have—"

"Perhaps we can find you some clothes from some-where."

Thinking about Major Everington's dress suggestion?

Jonathan clearly feared so, though he couldn't see her face. "If I don't have anything *suitable* to wear I'll have to write and ask my parents to send me some new clothes. I'll have to explain why. Obviously I can't guarantee who'll get to hear about it. Especially if there's any trouble about me receiving the parcel."

"I suppose your parents might be a bit upset to hear you've been put in the girls' block. Especially *why*," I put in thoughtfully.

"You listen to me," snarled the Menace, grabbing the neck of Jonathan's shirt and yanking him towards her, finding she was looking up at him and shoving him away again. "If anyone, anyone at all, outside these walls finds out you're in with the girls, let alone *why*, I am going to make your life pure, one hundred percent hell, do you understand me?"

"Captain," said Jonathan blandly. "Obviously I'd rather not mention to my parents anything that would distress them the way this would. So can I just have my clothes, please?"

Actually, the rumors would surely get out and the most the warden's threats could ensure was that Jonathan assured his parents all was well and made sure they didn't contact the RWB. The censors certainly couldn't work overtime on the Facility's letters for the next two whole years!

"You'll have to speak to the Major yourself," snapped the Captain. More scared of the Major than the RWB?

"When will we be able to see him?" asked Jonathan politely.

A rather sly look, a plain nasty look, crossed the Captain's face. "I expect you want to see him right now, eh?"

"Well, it would be best," said Jonathan warily.

The Captain smiled, barked an order into her wristCell, spun on her heel and strode to the door. "Come on, then."

Jonathan took my arm again and we followed her. Was this a good idea? But the boys would surely rip the name tags out, if given very long.

A guard arrived at the cafeteria door as we came out. Captain Wallis led us all through into the guard block and up to a door that must lead into the little courtyard garden.

"Captain?" blurted the guard, as the Menace scanned her card and began to open the door. "You're not taking them in *there?*"

"*What did you just say?*" The Captain attempted to skewer the man to the wall with her gaze.

He gulped. "Ah...nothing. Nothing, Captain."

"Good. Wait here. In you go, *girls.*"

I glanced at Jonathan, but...bit late to back out now—I led him through the door. And stopped, staring. The garden looked lovely from above; from ground level it was utterly spellbinding. Two little paths wound their way among the bushes and shrubs, with a gorgeous little tree in the center and in three of the four corners. Jonathan's nostrils flared in appreciation. Even this early in the season it was a riot of color and the scent of flowers was strong.

"*Get that boy out of here right now!*" My eyes jerked from the garden to the Major, visible through the central bushes, his eyes narrowed with fury and his voice an enraged hiss. "*Get him out right now!*"

"Too bad, you'd better go," said the Menace, with an unpleasant smile. She thrust Jonathan back through the door with a rough hand, pushed it shut behind him, then advanced several paces, shoving me ahead of her. "Sorry to intrude, sir, but these two *girls* demanded to see you at once."

The Major's gaze shifted to me. That strange, white-hot fury had departed with Jonathan, but he still looked pretty irate.

"Threatened to contact the RWB if I wouldn't bring them

to you immediately," lied the Captain smoothly.

"We did not!" I said indignantly. "We just asked *when* we could see—" Her open-handed blow rocked me back on my heels and I grabbed the nearest sturdy bush for balance. *Ouch.* Nobody had ever hit me before, not like that.

"Get out," snapped the Major. The Captain reached for my arm... "*Just* you. Leave the girl."

The Menace shot me a murderous look. As though I *wanted* to remain alone here with a man *she* feared! But she stamped back to the door and slammed it behind her.

"Telling tales on the witch-queen? That wasn't smart, young lady. She'll hate you now."

"Too late," I muttered, letting go of the bush and straightening, trying not to wince. "Hates me already."

"Really? That was quick work. Now, come here."

I advanced slowly, at first reluctant to get closer to him, then caught up in the garden's beauty. The paths were mossy stones and it had the look of a wild place stumbled into, yet every plant was chosen to complement those around it. Beyond the central tree and its loose ring of bushes was an open grassy space, a miniature glade. Flowerpots encircled it; young plants being reared?

A huge wickerwork hanging seat stood in the treeless corner—like a domed cage with a cushioned bench inside, running around an integral central table. The horizontal wickerwork had been removed from the sides so someone sitting in it would be able to see just the garden, not the buildings towering above it—the windows of the gym corridor were blacked out inside and covered out here with winding creepers.

A plate stood on the table, with a half eaten slice of pie on it, but from the way the knife and fork were placed neatly together and the plate pushed to one side to make room for a row of flowerpots the Major was not nearly so fond of his food as the Captain.

He watched my slow approach. "Do you like flowers?" he asked, when I stopped several prudent meters from him.

"I'd only say well enough, usually, but this is *beautiful.*"

"Yes." Major Everington spoke matter-of-factly. "No one is allowed to come here. The witch-queen was trying to get you in trouble."

"I noticed." I resisted the urge to rub my bruised face.

"So you did. Now, what do you want?"

"Jonathan needs the rest of his clothes and stuff. The guards only brought what was in his chest but the other boys had taken most of it. But it's all labeled, so could you get the guards to go and find it?"

The Major turned away as I spoke, gazing at his garden. His gloves lay on the table, soil-stained, but he was as immaculate as ever. "Which plant do you like best?"

"Uh..." What did that have to do with Jonathan's stuff? Still, better humor him. He scared me. I looked around the glade, trying to give the question proper consideration. My gaze stopped on an explosion of drooping purple flowers. No contest. "That one. I've never seen a purple one like that."

The Major smiled, not the cruel smile I'd seen before, but a soft, sad smile that made him look as though his thoughts were a long way away. "My purple fuchsia. It is the most beautiful thing in the whole world, never mind the garden. Nothing to match it. You have an eye for beauty." He wandered to the wickerwork hut and leaned in to take a pot from the table. "I can't seem to stop taking cuttings. I've far too many. Have one..." He held the pot out to me. A beautiful miniature of the magnificent bush grew from it.

Hands behind my back, I made no move to approach.

"What?" His expression grew sardonic, that cruel curve starting at the corner of his mouth. "Did you lie to keep the Commandant happy? Do you not like it?"

"There's nothing wrong with the plant. That's beautiful. But you'd have to put a gun to my head before I'd accept a gift from *you.*"

His face went unreadable, as though invisible shutters had dropped across it. He stepped up into the wickerwork hut and placed the plant back on the table. Stretched out on the seat, booted feet crossed comfortably. The hut swung gently, creak, creak. "Clear off, then."

"Jonathan's things? Sir?" I tried to speak more politely. Had I just lost Jonathan all his stuff?

He nodded without turning his head towards me. Raised a hand and flipped it at me. "Go."

I moved to obey.

"Wait. What is your name?"

I turned back again. Stared at the man who sat in his comfortable cage, not looking at me.

"One, seven, six, four, five, eight, four," I said coldly.

His head snapped around and he rose on one elbow, staring at me. When he spoke it was in that soft, murderous voice which had so terrified the Captain earlier. The hairs stood up on the back of my neck.

"I said. What. Is. Your. *Name*."

"Margaret Verrall."

"Margaret Verrall. *Get out.*"

I fled. I refused to run, but all the beauty of that place couldn't make me slow my rapid steps. I banged on the door, not a frantic hammering, honest, just deliberate taps, until the guard let me out.

9

THE PURSUIT OF THE MALE OF THE SPECIES

The nod had indeed meant yes and my final bit of defiance hadn't changed that, for we'd barely got back from our yard exercise—which Jonathan was also excused from—when a guard entered with a black bag. "Here's your stuff, *Jonathina,*" he laughed, chucking the bag on Jonathan's bed and walking out again.

"Are they really going to call me that?" Jonathan sounded revolted—judging that a rhetorical question, I let it go. He pulled the bag to him and began to unpack it.

"Is it everything?"

"Near enough. I'm not complaining. And I got this back." He sounded genuinely pleased, holding up a little audio-Player. "Though..." He searched the bottom of the black bag. "Bother, no headphones." His fingers ran over the player's case and he frowned. "Don't like the feel of these cracks, either."

I scrambled down from my bunk and went to borrow Sarah's headphones, dropping them into his lap. "Here. See if it's working."

"Thanks."

He plugged them in and pushed buttons for a while, finally pulling out the earphones and tossing the player onto the bed. "Kaput," he said heavily. "Well, it is going to be a long two years."

Imagine if my bookReader was broken...I'd be pretty glum too. There were a few audioPlayers in the room, but the stuff on them probably wouldn't be his thing. Sarah's old one was full of *My Prancing Pony* and *Shaggy the Sheep* audioBooks.

"I've got quite a good range of books on my reader," I told

him. "I can read them aloud, if you like."

He brightened. "Not all the time," he said firmly. "It's not the same for you. But if you could, now and then, that would be great."

The post-exercise change back into our own clothes complete, Jonathan's new dorm-mates proceeded to mob him for the rest of the afternoon. Some, like Sarah and Bethan, were just friendly, some were curious, others, like Jane and Rebecca and Annie, were obviously determined to get him in bed with them. He was friendly to everyone, in that rather cool, polite way of his.

Jane was undeterred. When everyone was getting ready for bed and Jonathan emerged from his bunk to go to the washroom, she grabbed him by the front of his pajama bottoms and tried to pull him towards her. When he didn't deign to be pulled, she plastered her leggy self against him instead. "Well, Jonathan, would you care for me to join you in your lovely private bunk tonight?"

Jonathan found her shoulders and put her firmly to one side. She resisted, but his muscles didn't appear to notice. "No, thank you, Jane. I'm still taking stock of just what's on offer. There doesn't seem to be any need for me to rush in and accept anything but the very best, does there?"

Jane flushed crimson and a lot of people giggled. Jane's tongue was always stinging someone.

"So what do you like?" Annie and Caroline bounced up to Jonathan as he tried again to reach the door. "Tell us what you like in a girl and we'll rank everyone in order, how's that!"

"That's very kind of you," said Jonathan, less nastily, "but I think this is the sort of ranking one has to do for oneself."

"But...how will you know what kind of legs everyone has?" asked Harriet, looking baffled. "Should we line up and let you feel them?"

She said it so innocently I choked on a snort of laughter and turned my back hastily, so she wouldn't think I was mocking her. Not too quickly to miss the wonderful expression on Jonathan's face, though!

"You're all being so very kind to me," he said, after a long moment. "But the legs aren't really my top priority. As you so rightly observe—it doesn't mean much to me."

"Oh." Harriet looked blank. "How are you going to decide who's best, then?"

"Oh, I'm sure I'll think of something," murmured Jonathan, heading for the door.

Jane stuck her foot out, but he stepped over it. I was starting to suspect he could hear a pin drop. Literally, on this hard floor.

There it was—a near-as-never-mind garden shed plonked down next to the gardeners' hut. I veered up to the fence, peering anxiously through the mesh. "Oh, excuse me? Er... sir? Um, sirs?" My voice was not very audible over the speakers; no one nearby looked around but the soldiers did.

"What is it, young miss?" called back the older of the two.

"Well, it seemed a bit odd, is the thing. And I wasn't sure I shouldn't tell someone...but..."

The soldier began to walk towards me. "What seemed odd?"

The younger soldier followed his partner, though from the way he was staring at my legs, it wasn't interest in what I had to say that'd brought him over.

"...therefore, with no further ado, it is my great honor to present to you tonight, our most esteemed Chairman..."

My second cue.

"There was this man. He climbed over the fence—well, there's loads of couples doing that, but it was just him on his own. And then he headed off in the direction of the stage." All perfectly true. If at sixteen Bane was old enough to be press-ganged—or executed—why shouldn't I refer to him as a 'man'?

Both soldiers closed the distance to me in a few long strides as the Chairman began to speak.

"Was he carrying anything?" demanded the older one, already reaching for the walkie-talkie at his belt.

"What sort of thing?"

The two men exchanged a 'how dumb can you get' look.

"Anything," demanded the younger one. "Was he carrying anything at all?"

"This is E4 calling base; over." The older one had the walkie-talkie to his lips. Not waiting to extract any more details from a dumb bimbo who might or might not actually be blonde in the daylight.

"Base; over," spluttered the walkie-talkie.

There was a strange 'whump' noise from the shed, followed, before the guards could even finish spinning around, by several cracks and bangs. Something red punched through the shed roof and exploded, flooding the clearing with a technicolor of sparks. Flickering orange light glowed through the hole in the roof and more bangs followed in quick succession.

"Someone's setting off the fireworks!" yelled the younger soldier quite unnecessarily as they both lurched towards the shed...only to think better of it.

Yes! Go, Bane!

Then the shed exploded.

The pursuit of the male of the species continued unabated the following day. If only Jonathan would choose someone and make it clear he intended to be mono-gamous—anything less and this ridiculousness would just go on and on and on! Harriet, Caroline and Annie—and some of the others—spent ages dressing their best, applying their make-up and then walking up and down near Jonathan. Even Rebecca rolled her eyes and snorted derisively.

"For pity's sake!" snapped Jane eventually, as the parade trooped too close to her. "He's blind. *Blind.* He *cannot see* you. You're wasting your time, you're driving everyone mad, and you look like *idiots.*"

The group teetered to an uncertain halt in their high heels. "But...how else do we make him like us?" one of them said, sounding close to tears.

"You can't. He's got three times your IQ and five times your looks. Give up."

"And yet I like them so much better than big-headed, smart girls," put in Jonathan coldly, from his seat at the table. Several incipient sobs morphed into giggles.

I stared at my pad and tried to concentrate on the exploits of my Fellest ewe, but Sarah was soon beside me.

"Sheep? Sheep story?"

Time for Diary of a Fellest Ewe, part one.

I'd collected quite a crowd by the time I finished reading—Jonathan among them.

"That's very good," he told me.

I shrugged. "It's just a fun little story."

"Yes. A very good one."

I shrugged again. "What are your talents, then? Other than hearing people moving."

He smiled faintly and didn't deny it. "Hearing and touch are about it, to be honest. My parents read books to me as much as they could—let me learn what I wanted mostly, so I'm a little lopsided. I like physics most of all, but I've never *done* any. There aren't many opportunities nowadays if you're blind."

"Nowadays?"

"Umm. Once upon a time they had a language called Braille that blind people could read and write in, and dogs to help them go around on their own. Before the EuroGov took control and Sorting began, they were even developing a pair of goggles that sent electrical signals to the tongue so a blind person could sorta see."

"That's amazing."

"Yep. 'Course, the project was scrapped when the EGD came into being. Judged unnecessary. After all, adults who go blind can have replacement parts, and blind children *are* replacement parts."

"Idiots."

"Umhmm. Seeing's not something I've ever sat around and dreamt about, though. But a pair of goggles like that might be useful, just for new places. New places are a pain."

"I bet they are."

We'd all watched him the day before as he walked slowly up and down the room, up and down, his stick touching gently against chairs and tables and obstacles. He must've remembered it all, because he'd only walked the place once. He'd pressed the buzzer and got the guard to let him out into the passage, and he'd learned that, and the washrooms. "Not hard," he'd snorted, "it's all the same as over there, just backwards."

"Braille would be nice, though," he concluded.

"I imagine. You can write, though?"

"Oh, yes. Carefully." His face fell. "*Well*... That is, I had this special frame my dad made me years ago—helps me write in straight lines—but the boys smashed it to smithereens. Don't know how well I'll manage without it."

"Well, I can play scribe, if you like."

"Would you mind? I might really appreciate that."

"'Course not."

"Hi, Jonathan!" Annie dropped into a nearby chair. "Can I talk to him now, Margo?"

I tried not to smile. "That's up to him."

"Oh, yeah. Can I speak to you now, Jonathan?"

"'Course. You're Annie, right?"

I went back to part two of my story.

One moment the shed was there—a blinding flash, an ear-splitting crack and it was gone. Something picked me up and flung me backwards, slamming me into the ground so hard I just lay, too shocked to move, as debris pattered down all around.

When it stopped raining steaming charcoal and bits of wood that glowed like embers, I pushed myself up on my hands and stared at the smoking crater where the shed had been. The two guards had been smacked into the fence by the blast—they were just sitting up and beginning to disentangle themselves from each other and the buckled mesh.

It was the older one who suddenly looked across at me. "Hey, you! Wait right there!"

Pretending not to hear, I grabbed my hat and staggered to my feet, requiring no acting ability whatsoever to do what most other people were doing—scream at the top of my voice and run away. What was difficult was to run away from the blast. Because Bane must surely be dead.

Too close. He must've been far too close! I raced along the field, my heart pounding and everything oddly frozen in my mind, as though only Bane could thaw it. That 'whump' had been the sound of some flammable fluid igniting and that meant...too close, far too close!

Reaching a quieter, darker stretch of fence, I lunged up

*at it in hopeless impatience, but I wasn't strong enough to
just pull myself over, the way Bane did. Dragging off my
ankle wellies, I chucked them over and tackled the fence
again. My toes just fitted between the mesh and it was a
quick, if rather painful, climb to the top. My feet sank into
the grass, icy damp soaking my socks as I found the wellies
and dragged them back on.*

*I wouldn't find Bane along the fence line where guards
would be moving around. I dashed through the huts and
plunged into the strip of undergrowth beyond, holding my
hands out in front of me to fend twigs from my eyes,
scanning the dark ground for branches that might trip me or
break noisily underfoot. I wanted to shout his name, but I
held my tongue. I wasn't going to be the one to tell them
who'd blown up their fireworks.*

*About halfway to the gardeners' hut, I skidded to a halt
at the sound of someone crashing through the undergrowth
towards me. Made my efforts sound very stealthy indeed. I
crouched still and quiet behind some brambles.*

*Bane burst into a patch of dim moonlight, weaving
erratically through the bushes.*

Alive! He was alive!

Laudate Dominum.

I glanced at Jonathan, who stared into space as always,
his chin resting on his hand. His latest group of conversants
had just giggled their way back to their bunks and he was—
temporarily, I'm sure—alone. Other than me, sitting there
finishing part two. I'd a niggling desire to talk to him about
Bane, but Jane's scathing words the day before had made me
hold my tongue, hoping he'd bring the subject up himself.
But...

"How *did* Bane used to get out to Little Hazelton?" I
asked abruptly.

"His mum works there." Jonathan smiled faintly.

"Yeah, I know that, but if you're telling me he was still
getting lifts with her for the last few years, I'll call you a liar."

Jonathan grimaced. "Too true. He was jumping trains,
actually."

"*What?* The hypocritical rat!"

"You disapprove?"

"It's not that! But he made *me* promise I wouldn't do it anymore!"

"I remember something about that. You used to do it all the time, when you were younger, right?"

"Yes. It was a favorite pastime for us. Bike up one side of the valley and jump on the trains as they come over the top of the pass, they're going at their slowest then. Ride all the way through Salperton and to the top of the next pass, then jump off and catch the next train back from the other direction. I take it Little Hazleton's also near a pass?"

"Yes."

"Honestly, so much for, 'it's too dangerous.'"

"You jumped the wrong train one day, didn't you?" From the sparkle in his eyes, he'd heard all about it from Bane.

"Yeah. It was a total accident, but we tried to get on the nuclear waste train from Coldwell. The guards opened fire on us and we almost got shot. Well, to be honest, I did get shot. But it was only a nick."

"Bleeding to death in his arms, the way Bane tells it," grinned Jonathan.

I snorted. "I was not. He might've had my arm around his shoulders, but that's all. My parents never even found out. Look...I mean...*feel.*" I pushed my sleeve up and placed his fingers on my upper arm.

He traced the smooth indented scar with his fingertips. "A good sized nick," he said measuredly, "but yeah, I'd agree with nick as the correct definition."

"He really freaked out about it, though. Refused ever to take me train-jumping again. And he's been doing it himself all these years."

"You don't actually sound very surprised," smiled Jonathan. "Or indignant."

I had to laugh. "I s'pose I know him too well to be surprised. Hearing he's still doing it himself makes me more worried than anything. He doesn't seem to have any fear for himself at all. I sometimes wonder if he got killed, if he'd even care."

"Or just be angry about it," said Jonathan softly, not contradicting me. "Yeah." He was silent for a moment, then

91

asked, very quietly, "Anyway, is there anyone nearby?"

"Uh, no. But you know that, don't you?"

"Yes. But I wanted to be certain. Can anyone see this hand of mine?" He wriggled the fingers of the hand that lay in his lap.

"Hmm. No."

"Absolutely certain?"

"Yes."

"No mirrors?"

I checked again. "No. Between your body and the table it's completely hidden."

"Good." He dropped his voice even lower and his finger and thumb curved into the Fish. "*Salve, soror.*"

Hello, sister.

10

THE FIRST LETTER

I grabbed his hand, automatically replying in Latin. "Careful!"

"You said no one can see."

"I didn't know you were going to do *that!*" Caution belatedly reasserted itself and I switched back to English. "Why are you showing me that, anyway?"

"*Margo.*" He rolled his eyes slightly. "*Bane...*"

"Seems I need to have a little chat with my fiancé about *discretion.*"

"Bane trusts me, he hasn't done anything wrong."

"Huh." He'd gone straight back into Latin and I replied in the same. "Why didn't you tell me sooner?"

"I wanted to form my own opinion of you. I'd trust Bane's judgment with *my* life, yes. But other people's lives?"

I shrugged. "Fair enough. Why didn't you go underground, though? Why show up for Sorting?"

"Why'd you?" he said, smiling.

"My parents run a Mass center," I said, very softly indeed, Latin or not, "but I imagine you know that already."

"Yes. Well, mine run a safe house. So I was in the same position as you."

"Ah...a hotel. Perfect cover!"

"Absolutely. It's an all-stream safe house. Quite important. Not worth closing down for the sake of one blind boy."

"I bet your parents didn't think that."

"No, but I did. How would the Underground keep me hidden, anyway? I'm a little noticeable. They've enough to do protecting the priests and rabbis and everyone like that."

Priests. *Uncle Peter.* I looked at Jonathan's cheerful face. He didn't know what'd happened. I could scarcely get it out of my mind. I had to tell him. Some other girls had just sat at a table nearby, so I went back to English. "Jon...I had an uncle called Peter; did you ever meet him?"

He turned his head a little more squarely towards me with sudden attention. "*Peter?* An...uncle?"

"That's what I always called him."

"I think I may have done; why do you ask?" His face clouded. "What do you mean, *had* an uncle?"

"I think you know what I mean," I said softly, then pretended to change the subject although no one appeared to be listening. "Oh, did you hear what the Menace made us watch the other day?"

He sat there, very, very still.

"What did the Menace make you watch?" he whispered.

"A...full conscious dismantlement. It was...horrible." My voice shook—I could hardly get the words out.

He didn't say anything. He just sat there, his face frozen and his nostrils flaring now in hurt rather than sensitivity.

At last, he swore, just once, under his breath. And after another long, long silence, "*Witch!*"

"Yeah," I whispered, hardly trusting myself to speak. "Witch."

"Bane!"

Bane stumbled on, staggering into one bush after another. I sprang out and he started violently, fists rising, then dropping as he recognized me. I realized the soft noise he was making was laughter.

"Did you see that?" he gasped. Far too loudly. He was almost shouting as he caught my arms. "Did you see that?"

He broke out laughing in earnest. Among the very genuine mirth there was a ragged edge of pain.

"Be quiet!" I clapped my hands over his mouth and his laughter trailed off abruptly. Deafened and stunned. And... my hands came away from his face covered in soot. Bother.

"Come on!" I pulled his arm over my shoulders, the better to aim him in a straight line. He stayed silent, so perhaps the shock was wearing off. I stopped near the hut where we'd talked earlier, beside a boot washing station, yanked off my wellie and used a sock to give his face a speed wash, ignoring his flinches.

We looked and listened carefully for guards before heading over to the fence, but his first attempt to scale it brought him to his knees, clutching his chest and gasping. No, he wasn't just stunned.

But we had to get over now, before the guards got themselves organized. I dropped to my hands and knees, patted my back and pointed most emphatically up over the fence. Reluctantly, Bane stepped up onto me and Deus omnipotens *he was heavy, but a few moments later he was on the other side of the fence, albeit hunched over and gasping again.*

Frightened and bewildered, everyone was pouring out of the sports ground, and at the moment the guards on the gates were letting them, rather than have a panic break out if they tried to keep everyone there.

Bane's pinkened skin and blackened eyebrows were rather obvious in the lights. I pulled his hood forward, gave him a meaningful look and shoved his face into my hair before slipping an arm around his waist.

The guard on the turnstile was too busy talking on his walkie-talkie and looking around wildly at the surrounding area to pay us any attention. The reader peeped happily at us both and we hurried on with everyone else.

Did half the guards even realize the explosion had been caused by the fireworks and not by the Resistance? Bane and I had certainly expected nothing more than a lot of fireworks going off in rather rapid succession.

My house was only about four kilometers away, so we headed that way at the best speed we could manage, Bane's arm still around my shoulders, his face still hidden against my hair. This was going to start some rumors of gun-jumping, if any of our year saw us. But he was walking almost straight and even turned his head slightly at the sirens of four police cars that went tearing past.

We didn't stop, or speak, until we'd shut my front door behind us.

"You're not bleeding, are you, Bane?" I only had to speak a bit louder than normal, now.

"Not bleeding. Think my flaming ribs are broken," he gasped.

"Let me see..." I slipped a hand under his coat and sort of patted him over, checking for blood...no, that wasn't going to be enough. "Let's get you upstairs."

I tried to take his arm again—he flinched, swore, apologized, and walked up under his own steam, shoulders hunched. I sat him on my bed and began the painful business of peeling off his layers of clothing. He flinched and swore some more, and bit his lip rather too hard.

Oh, it was his back that was becoming one enormous purple black bruise! "What happened, Bane?"

"There was a knot in the wood of the door," he wheezed. "Saw it at the weekend. So I took my water-pistol with me, filled with petrol," he nodded to the rucksack now lying on the floor and I realized what the smell was that I'd been dimly aware of.

"I squirted it all through the hole, shoved it back in my rucksack, then lit a scrap of paper and dropped it in. I heard the petrol catch and legged it. The fireworks seemed to be going off just the way I hoped, so when I got inside the bushes I stopped to watch. And then BANG. I went flying—literally—flung my arms up behind my head, good job, because I hit the boundary wall, whack. Lay there in a heap until everything stopped flying around. Then got up and started running. Trying to run. I just couldn't go straight. Good thing I found you, because I reckon I was making a heck of a lot more noise than I realized."

"Too right! I thought a rabid bear was on the rampage!"

"Well. Thank you for coming to help me."

"Help you! I thought you were dead, you stupid fool!" I hugged his head and even that made him wince.

"Sorry. Didn't realize that was going to happen. Or I'd have used a fuse cord or something. They won't play that down, though!" He started to laugh again, then winced and went motionless. "You know, I think I just want to lie down on your bed and stay very still. For several days."

"Well, let me put some cream on your face first..."

"Hang my face!" His hands gripped my duvet, white-knuckled. "Er. My head's going all funny, y'see."

"Whoa, let's get you horizontal!" I sprang up and pulled back the covers, because he was literally about to keel over in a dead faint, if he was admitting to it.

"Where," he demanded through gritted teeth, once he

was lying on his stomach, "is adrenalin when you need it?"

"I'd say it was right when you needed it!"

His eyes slid closed and I sat looking down at him anxiously. What if something was actually broken? Did he really need the hospital? But his injuries were too suspicious; hospital would get him executed.

I settled the duvet gently over him against the chill— even that made him twitch.

The sound of the front door...

Oh no! I'd left my parents at the sports ground, in the middle of what appeared to be a terrorist attack, with no idea where I was.

My turn to wince.

I stood by the little window the following evening, looking out at the shadowy forest and breathing in the fresh night air—and trying to ignore all the strategy discussions going on behind me. The Prize was still playing hard to get.

"My mum told me guys want a *nice* girl," Annie was telling Harriet, very seriously.

"More than nice *legs?*" asked Harriet in disbelief.

"Which do you think is more important, Jon?" asked Jane smoothly. "Legs or *nice?*"

"Just be careful," put in Rebecca, "if you say legs, Jane will claim you by virtue of the fact that she has the longest legs in the dorm."

I couldn't help glancing around at that.

Jonathan stirred from his own—bleak?—thoughts and smiled slightly. "I think I've already made it clear legs aren't my highest priority."

"So you want the nicest?" said Harriet excitedly. "That's settled, then! But..." she deflated slightly. "Who is the nicest?"

"Looks like *you're* out of the running," said Rebecca, smiling sweetly at Jane.

Jane scowled. "Looks like Jon and Sarah are going to be an item, then."

"*I* didn't say I wanted the nicest," said Jonathan dryly. "*I* want the one I *like* the best."

"You're still out the running, then," murmured Rebecca to Jane.

97

"Oh, shut up. At this rate no one's going to have him. He seems to have the sex drive of a castrated snail."

"Snails are hermaphrodites," said Jonathan, very blandly.

I stared at him, sitting there surrounded by girls. Which one *did* he like best? Resting my elbows on the windowsill, I went back to the view and the night air and all the things I was trying to get out of my head.

A faint tap-tap of a stick behind me. Jonathan. How did he find me? Did he sniff me out or recognize my breathing, or some combination of the two? He always knew who'd approached him before they spoke.

"Margo," he said quickly—and very softly—in Latin, as though he didn't want to waste our private moment. "Have you thought about that thing we have in common, what it means for me, being here in this dorm?"

His odd words came back to me, the first day he was in here. "Complicated?"

What was so complicated? A burst of giggling made me glance around again; sure enough, the gigglers' eyes were fixed on Jonathan. The penny dropped belatedly, a big, dangerous penny—oh yes, he *would've* preferred to stay in the boys' block and die nice and safely over there—nice and safely for his family and the precious safe house, anyway.

"Oh no..." My voice dropped even further. "If you don't choose *any*one....someone will suspect."

"Exactly," he said grimly.

"Yet you *can't* choose anyone."

"No priest, no marriage rite, no way."

I swallowed a couple of swear words. Despite his little revelation yesterday, I'd scarcely been able to think about anything other than Uncle Peter—okay, Uncle Peter and Bane—and this glaringly obvious problem hadn't registered. "I hadn't thought. I'm an idiot. I can put my mind to it or... have you thought of something?"

"I have. The only thing I *can* think of. But I'm very embarrassed to ask. If it wasn't for what's at stake—if I didn't know you *understand* what's at stake—I wouldn't...but, if I don't choose a...girlfriend...soon... I don't trust Jane, she's too sharp..." he trailed to a halt.

A tinge of red stained his cheeks—a second penny

dropped. He really was embarrassed. Because he was saying he was going to have to choose me. And we'd have to pretend a whole lot more!

No *way!* I wasn't going to pretend to be sleeping with him! Okay, so no one in here would think anything of it, but rumors would get out. Reach my parent's ears, perhaps. Worse, Bane's ears. No! *Absolutely not.*

I opened my mouth to tell him so in no uncertain terms, but... My heart sank as my mind crunched on with unstoppable logic. If we didn't...someone would point at Jonathan and whisper 'Underground'. And then he and his parents and any Underground members staying with them would die. Any members arriving at the safe house for some time to come would die. Some of them would be priests, sisters, rabbis, imams... They would die as Uncle Peter had died.

I swallowed. The truth staring me in the face was simple enough—my reputation wasn't worth that much. I suppose... the Lord would know what had or hadn't happened and Bane would just have to take my word for it. As for the sheer cheek-combusting embarrassment of it all... *Lord, help!*

"Relax," I said glumly. "I've caught on. And..." I ran the situation and proposed solution through my mind a few more times. "There really doesn't seem to be much option."

"Sorry," he murmured.

"Well, I'm not much of an actress." I bit gently at my lip in sudden worry. "Well, at least I like you; I think. Let's hope that's enough."

"I don't think we need to crawl all over each other in public." His cheeks heated again. "I think if we just—act like we're getting cozy for a day or so and then start sharing a bunk at night—that'll be enough. Ah..." he sounded strangled, "more than enough, I know." His face was brick red now.

Sharing a bunk. Aaaaaw! Was I going to have to sleep crammed up against this near-stranger for the next 724 days? Still, better than even one person dying and there was no getting around *that.*

"It'll be all right," I said. Who was I trying to convince, him or me? My mind insisted on replaying Jane's words...my heart beat a little faster. Jane's mind was already turning in dangerous directions. We'd really better not take too long about this.

Jonathan must've been thinking the same thing. "What are you doing by the window?" he asked curiously—and more loudly—in English. His hand brushed down my back and settled around my waist, fingers curling around the front of my hip. It took all my self-control not to stiffen and push his hand away. *Oi*, I wanted to say, *you don't know me well enough to put your hand there*.

But I couldn't do that. I stared out into the darkness and managed to smile. "There's a nice breeze tonight. Feel it?"

"Yes. I wonder if spring is really coming. Feels like it's getting colder today." His right hand stayed around my waist.

I stood still and let it remain there. I should respond in some way, but this was harder than I expected. It hurt my self-respect to let him touch me like that. I wasn't *his*. He wasn't *mine*. We weren't sworn to each other in whole and wholesome union. Never in my entire life had I presented myself as a mere sex object and now...being touched like this by someone I didn't love felt too close to it for my liking.

He rubbed my hip gently; leaned close to my ear as though to give some flirtatious remark. "I'm so sorry about this."

He'd felt my discomfort. What he could feel, others might be able to see. This wouldn't do. I laid my hand over his; entwined our fingers. Murmured in his ear, "It's not your fault. We've got to get this right."

His unseeing eyes stared through me, sad and sincere. "Yes, we have."

I let him snug me to his tall warm side, trying very hard to relax. "Hey, hear that..."

The sound of wolf song floated to us on the nice breeze. I listened eagerly but Jonathan shuddered. "For once I'm glad to be in here."

"Don't like wolves?"

"No. I never walked far from Little Hazelton because I was always afraid there could be one there, about to eat me. They're *so* quiet."

"Huh. *I* don't like bears. *They'll* eat you."

"Yeah, but they make noise walking around."

I shrugged and managed to slip my arm around his waist in return. "Never met a wolf that's given me any trouble. They just look at you and lope away. 'Course, I generally carry a big stick."

"Bane says they like you," said Jonathan, smiling.

"Well, when they meet *him* they show their teeth before running off. So I always reckon they simply *don't* like *him!*"

"Well, I just wish they'd never escaped way back when. You know there never used to be any in this department, right?"

"There were, and then there weren't, and now there are again. I don't mind them; so long as there's plenty of prey, they're not aggressive. One day the EuroGov really will have to reconsider the hunting ban, though, when the numbers of deer drop too far and they get hungry."

"Can't be too soon, in my opinion." Another wave of wolf song reached our ears. "Do you mind shutting that window? They do give me the creeps."

I complied, shutting out the wild music of the night. Regretfully.

As we moved away from the window, still coupled up, Jane's snide voice cut through the dorm. "Don't look now, girls, seems the snail's *finally* made his choice."

"Margaret Verrall," I told the guard distributing the post the next day. He slapped a letter into my hand, yawned, and turned to the next girl, who was actually a boy called Jonathan. "Thank you," I said calmly, moving on, but my heart pounded in my chest.

I had a letter. So my parents were okay, or had been yesterday. Of course, if they were taken, I'd be taken too, so I'd know soon enough, but still...I had a letter.

Jonathan gave his name, took his own letter and follow-ed close behind. We'd stayed mostly joined at the hip since yesterday, in that way newly forming couples do.

We sat together now, with Sarah, Harriet and Annie in the seats nearest to us.

"...I don't see why you're so surprised," Rebecca was telling Jane at the table behind us. "*I* think they're well suited to each other. You're just a sore loser because she outsmarted all of us—including him."

I tried not to listen.

Most people were spooning their cereal with one hand and clutching their letters in the other as they read, but I wanted to sit in the comparative privacy of my bunk while I read mine. I tried to quash the ridiculous hope that Bane might've written something. My parents would probably want the first letter all to themselves. I gobbled my breakfast and sat, waiting impatiently for everyone else to finish.

Pretty much leaping up onto my bunk once we got back upstairs, I pulled the pages from the envelope—already open from the censors—and unfolded them. It was good and fat! Mum's handwriting...

Dear Margaret,
We're so glad to hear you're settling in all right. We miss you more than we can say and think about you every minute of the day.

The first page continued in the same, unexpectedly sentimental vein, but when I reached the second page I understood. Just filling up the space most likely to be read by the censor.

We were ever so sorry to hear how your story finished, it's a much sadder ending than we wished for. I hope you weren't too unhappy when you thought it up. Don't worry about sending a copy, I don't think we need any help feeling sad, just at the moment.
You'd think having our only daughter in the Facility would be enough troubles, wouldn't you, but we've seen rats

around the house. We've had to put off your cousin's visit, you know how he is, he'd die if he met a rat in the house, and I'm sure we'd die of embarrassment!

I wouldn't want you to worry about our rat problem, though, because 'rat problem' makes it sound much worse than it really is. It's in hand and we're not worried about it. If your cousin wasn't so nervous we'd have let him come,

but...well, you know him as well as we do! There are an awful lot of rats around in Salperton at the moment, I hope you don't have any at the Facility.

I turned to the third page but I could barely read the sentence to the end; I'd already seen the handwriting underneath.

Anyway, we have here a young man claiming to be our future son-in-law and in light of this your father and I feel we must yield these inner pages to him...

11

THE COMPETITION

Margo, are you OK? I hope you are. I can't tell you how desperately tempted I've been to take up bird-watching, especially since I heard how your story ended. Can you guess what species I'd be looking for? The most beautiful bird in the world, with soft brown plumage and the most amazing green eyes—I saw one around Salperton a lot until recently.

But I'm afraid if I waved to the bird it might frighten it, especially since there are a lot of birds of prey around the site. Your cousin certainly advises strongly against the excursion—thinks I can find something better to do. I suppose I've got a really good reason not to want to tangle with a bird of prey just now—you know what it is. Okay, okay, I'll say it straight out, I'm not going to do it—I know you worry.

I was so sorry I couldn't see you off properly—I tried ever so hard as well. But when the fire alarm went off I saw this stupid year 7 running the wrong way and thought I'd better drag him outside just in case things really heated up inside school, and then I was just heading around to the front when I ran into Mr. Cornel and he grabbed me by the collar and said, 'I saw what you just did, Marsden'—and I don't think he was talking about the year 7!

So I said, 'Fine, but can't it wait, I really want to see Margaret off,' and his face went all funny and his voice went funny too and he said, 'oh, of course,' and let me go, just like that. So I sprinted round to the gates but as you probably saw I was too late. And I haven't heard another word about it! So I think you must have an admirer—Mr. Cornel, who'd have thought he had a softer side! So, I'm not in trouble, just in case you've been worrying about that.

You must write and tell me everything you think I could possibly want to know. Your mum and dad say I can have these middle pages normally because they haven't really got much news anyway.

I don't suppose you know how Jon is getting on in there, do you? I've heard the girls and boys are kept apart, but I don't know if it's like, hermetic!

Oh, I've included a flyer I thought you might find interesting, although of course you can't enter now. I miss you loads.

He'd folded the very bottom of his last page over. I smoothed it out and read,

I love you. ←I kissed that, but don't tell anyone.

Trying to keep too soppy a smile from my face, I just managed not to immediately kiss his 'I love you' as well. Best not be seen kissing letters when I supposedly had a nice new boyfriend right here in the Facility.

With a little effort, I read the final page of the letter—it talked only about weather and the garden for the benefit of the censors and at the bottom my parents had both signed it—then devoured Bane's pages again.

He wanted to cycle out to the Facility and try to wave to me! My blood ran cold despite his assurances. *Dear, dear Bane. I miss you so much, but I'd rather not see you than that you get yourself killed, you numpty!* I wouldn't put it past him to risk it, normally. But right now—thank goodness he wanted so much to be alive to rescue me! No surprise 'Cousin' Mark was arguing against such total insanity. Father Mark was a lot cooler headed than Bane.

I re-read my mum's page with mingled relief and un-ease. Rats—they'd seen pursuivants 'around' the house. Not *in* the house. So perhaps just in the area, because they weren't worried about it. But they weren't letting Father Mark stay with them right now, just in case. And there were a lot of pursuivants in Salperton. I bet there were, with

Uncle Peter having just been caught there.

Best if Father Mark stayed away entirely. But with Uncle Peter gone, Father Mark would want to spend more time there, not less. Whether it was safe or not, knowing him. I understood what my parents were trying to tell me, but nervous was the last word I'd actually use to describe Father Mark. He and Bane got on rather well.

Still, on the whole it was good news. It sounded like they weren't even close to being under suspicion and Father Mark was safe. I glanced at the piece of paper inserted after the last of Bane's pages.

The EuroBloc Genetics Department
invites submissions for the
83rd postSort Competition
this year in the field of:
CREATIVE WRITING

Lip curling, I put the flyer to one side. Bane knew I'd already seen *that!* He knew I'd never support their foul program by sending in an entry, even if I *had* passed my Sorting!

I re-read Bane's letter, over and over, until Jonathan tilted his face up at me. "Can I come up?"

"I can come down..."

"It's okay."

I uncrossed my legs to make more room as he pulled himself up and sat beside me on my clothes' chest, laying his stick along the bunk. He rarely let it out of his reach. Just too useful to risk losing. He pulled his hood up against the chill. The weather was going back on its promise of spring with a vengeance this morning. I'd put a sweater on in the night.

"Good letter?" he asked, his own letter in his hand.

"The best." I tried not to beam too noticeably.

"Oh? How many pages did he manage?"

"Almost three."

"Not bad. This is really going to test his love, though."

"Oh, shut up." But he had a point. Bane didn't exactly enjoy writing. "Anyway, would you like me to read your letter?"

"Would you?"

I took it, eased the pages out and began to read. If his parents were telling him anything secret, it fooled me, and he took it back so calmly there probably hadn't been any hidden messages. Though with Jonathan Revan, it might've been quite hard to tell.

"Thank you."

"You're welcome."

Even more quietly, I read him most of my letter, explaining the true meaning of some of the sentences.

"Sounds like things are pretty sticky in Salperton at the moment, doesn't it?" he said grimly.

"Yes. Still, everyone's all right at the moment. Let's pray it remains so."

He nodded, then a smile crept across his face. "I'll have to listen out for some of these beautiful birds. Brown plumage and green eyes? Brown and green are supposed to be two of the loveliest colors, aren't they?"

"Says who?" I raised an eyebrow, bemused.

Jonathan hesitated, then broke out laughing. "Says Bane, actually. So much for that as an unbiased opinion. So what's your favorite color?"

"Gold, I suppose."

"Is that really a color?"

I shrugged, knowing he'd feel it. Gold was the color of Bane's skin, of the Chalice, of the Host, of the sky at dawn, of my mother's hair. Gold was the color of a lot of good things.

The Chalice and the Host... Shouldn't have thought of those. I'd only been here one Sunday but the need to receive Holy Communion was a growing ache inside. Because unless Bane pulled off some very impressive rescue, there *was* no prospect of Communion ever again, not in this earthly reality.

"You know, sometimes I get very jealous of those bits of crisp bread," Bane would say, if I lamented too strenuously the missing of a Sunday Mass due to lack of priest.

"It's not bread, Bane, it's Our Lord, you know that."

"Yeah, yeah," he'd reply. "Let's go you-know-where in the Fellest, shall we?"

"Gold's like orange, isn't it?" Jonathan's voice jerked me back to the present.

It took me a moment to remember what we'd been talking about. "No! They're very different."

Orange. Now, *that's* what I wanted. Okay, so they were expensive and they did have to be shipped from the Spanish Department, but the RWB required us to receive a healthy selection of fruit. Surely we'd get one sooner or later? But I wanted it now, because for several weeks the censors were going to be focusing so much on finding any mention of Jonathan's presence in the dorm that if they weren't to run overtime on the letters they'd have no attention left over for anything else. Which made now a good time to try and slip any dangerous information past them, didn't it?

Opening the back of my notebook, I studied the plan I'd drawn there. It was as complete as I could make it—all I needed to do now was get it to Bane.

Easier said than done. How do you make a plan of the Facility look like something innocuous? You can't. *So Lord, send me an orange, because I think the chances of laying my hands on a raw onion are pretty slim.*

Shutting the pad, I straightened the pages of the letter. What would someone think if they read it? That I'd elevated two-timing to an art form? Unflattering, but hardly danger-ous. Good, I could keep the letters.

Picking up the flyer to put it back with the rest, I paused. *Why did you send this to me, Bane? You know how I feel about it. And as you point out, of course I can't enter now. The postSort Competition is only for those who pass. It's meant to showcase the gradual improvement of the human race, a different field each year. Music last year, Math the year before, this year, Creative Writing. I cannot, and do not wish, to enter. So why did you send me this?*

I read the flyer in its entirety this time.

The EuroBloc Genetics Department
invites submissions for the
83rd postSort Competition
this year in the field of:
CREATIVE WRITING

This year's New Adults are invited to submit original short stories up to 3,000 words on any suitable subject.

SUBMISSION DEADLINE—31st MARCH

Winner announced—**30th April**.

This year's **GRAND PRIZE**:
FastTrac publication of the winner's **NOVEL**
by *Fox & Wilson*.

The novel and the short story to be on the same theme.

Novel's publication date—**1st July**.

All Entrants please note:
The winner to submit the final draft of their novel (max. 100,000 words) to the publisher no later than **31st May**. In the event of failure to keep this deadline, or submission of a work on a substantially different theme than the winning short story, *Fox & Wilson* reserve the right not to publish said work.

Entrants are advised that all submissions must be type-written, HOWEVER, no preference will be given to electronic over paper submissions.

All entries and novels to be in ESPERANTO.
Entrants are advised that all submissions in departmental languages will be disqualified.

All New Adults to submit their entries via their secondary school.

Exactly as it'd been when I read it at the beginning of the academic year, when the details were first released. All the Safe high-flyers with authorly aspirations would've been working on their novels ever since, as if any amount of work could produce a piece of decent literature in Esperanto. By now their novels would be sitting safely on hard discs and memory sticks, polished and complete, and they'd be putting the finishing touches to their short stories. The very most organized would be beginning to submit them, for the thirty-first was the Tuesday after next.

No-questions-asked fastTrac publication with Fox & Wilson! Well, it was always a grand prize for the postSort Competition. Last year they'd judged single music tracks and the prize had been the worldwide release of an album. The year before, entrants had to submit original formulae or something, I hadn't really understood. But the winner got an all expenses paid degree from a top Mathematics Institution of their choice, and it'd been *all* expenses, right down to a generous allowance of spending money.

I'd put my flyer in the bin in September, though. Bane surely hadn't kept his, so where had this come from? Sue Crofton, probably. Why send it to me when I couldn't even enter? I read the letter again. 'Of course you can't enter'—and he'd underlined the *of course*. I went very still.

"What is it?" asked Jonathan. He'd been sitting there beside me, smoothing the pages of his own letter absent-mindedly in his hands.

"Listen." I read the flyer to him. "Do you think it would be crazy if I tried to enter?"

He blinked. "You can't. You're a reAssignee, remember?"

"Obviously I can't enter under my own name, but if I got someone else to enter for me?"

"Well, I don't see how they could prevent that, but what'd it gain?"

"Absolutely nothing. Unless I won."

"It's creative writing. You could win that."

He sounded so certain I couldn't contain a faint snort. "Thanks for the vote of confidence, but it's unlikely. Still, just say I did, I get a novel published..."

"And that would mean a lot to you?" His tone was

cynical.

"How often, Jon," I murmured, right into his face, "does a reAssignee get a *voice?*"

12

THE MORTIFYING BUSINESS OF THE NIGHT

It was Jonathan's turn to go very still. "Well, well, well," he murmured back. "I'm impressed, Margo. It is a good idea, after all."

"It's not my idea, it's Bane's. He sent me the flyer and I wasn't quite stupid enough to chuck it straight away."

"Well, it's a good idea. Though...do you happen to have a hundred thousand word novel highlighting the plight of reAssignees lying around somewhere?"

"No. But that's not even the first problem. I need a winning short story to send to Bane by next Friday or we'll miss the deadline. That's number one. Bane needs to persuade Sue to submit it for me, that's number two. Lack of novel is a distant third and I've got two months to worry about that."

"Can't Bane submit it?"

"The teachers aren't completely stupid."

"I suppose not. I doubt he's written a short story in his life."

"Oh, they've forced him to write one or two, but somehow I think they might smell a rat. But Sue writes, and she writes quite well. It's the holidays, so it's only the school receptionist we have to fool to get the entry in, but the Head will see the list."

"Isn't Sue entering herself?"

"Um...I don't think she writes...quite *that* well. But I doubt the Head knows that."

"Ah. Well, you'd better get busy, hadn't you?"

"Margo? Margo, are you here?" Mum's voice, urgent but not panicked. She'd seen the wellies in the hall.

"I'm up here, Mum."

Rapid steps up the stairs, then Mum looked in. "Margo, why didn't you come back to us? Your dad stayed at the sports ground in case you were still there... And I really think Bane's a bit big to be in your bed, you know."

"Sorry, Mum. Bane, er, wasn't feeling so good, so we had to go. And please don't make him move, I can sleep in the spare room."

"What's up with him?" Mum asked, as Bane opened an eye and grimaced something that was probably supposed to be a smile.

"Urm, I think perhaps you'd better take a look, actually." Mum worked in the pharmacy, so she was more likely than most people to know what to do about broken ribs. "He, um, fell. Sort of. Hurt his back."

Mum strode over and drew back the duvet. Gasped. "Why didn't you take him to hospit...?" She broke off, bending to scrutinize Bane's pink face and singed eyebrows. Her breath went out in a dismayed huff. "Right. I see why not. He hit something pretty hard, I take it?"

"A wall. We think he's broken some ribs or something."

"Bruised ribs can hurt like anything."

"It's worse than bruises, Mum, seriously." Bane didn't easily show pain, so I was sure of that.

"Right, well, there's only one way to find out." She sat on the bed, placed her fingers on his first rib and pressed firmly. Bane gave a strangled yelp and sank his teeth into the pillow.

"Well, I don't think they're broken," said Mum, when she'd poked each one. "But from all that whimpering and thrashing around, some of them are cracked. Good job it's your mid-semester break. Now, did you tell your mum you were coming here?"

"No," growled Bane.

"Right, I'll give her a ring, then," she sighed, rising. At the sound of the front door, she called, "We're up here, dear."

"We—good!" exclaimed Dad, as he took the stairs two at a time. "Margo, why didn't you... Heavens above, young man, what have you done to yourself?"

"The secret's in the eyebrows," said Mum dryly, sweeping out of the room. Dad reached the bed and peered down at

Bane's face. Relief was suddenly wiped from his own.

"Gracious, boy, what did you do to those fireworks?"

"Poured petrol on them and lit it," Bane muttered. "Thought it would make sure they all went off and it meant I didn't have to worry about getting the door open."

"A large quantity of gunpowder when lit, will for all practical purposes go off like a large quantity of gunpowder, even if there are a few thin cardboard tubes in between," stated Dad, in a rather patient voice. Dad was a trained engineer, though mostly he worked construction with Mr. Marsden, since there was far more of that work available.

"Really?" retorted Bane, "You know, I think I noticed!"

"Yes, I imagine you did. You know, boy," Dad put his hands on his hips and stared down at Bane in exasperation, "if they catch you, you've done it this time."

"Yeah, well, when they execute you, they give you that stuff first to put you under and I have to say that would feel pretty good right now."

I smacked him on the head.

"Joke, Margo!" he protested.

"That wasn't by any definition, any relation whatsoever of funny."

"She's quite right, you reckless fool. Why don't you ever listen to her when you have these crazy ideas?"

Bane's eyes opened all the way and his lips parted in silent protest, but he didn't speak, bless him.

"Urm," I said. But fortunately Dad was just walking out of the door.

"Well, I seem to be in their good books."

"You think? Just you wait if they find out I helped you!"

"Perhaps the EuroGov will come and take me away."

I smacked him again, but he just sniggered at me. I couldn't feel too angry with him, anyway, still high atop that storm surge of relief that'd swept me up when I saw him alive. "You know, I think I'm going to pray..." I rose from the bed, my arms lifting, and spun in a slow circle.

"Oh good, that kind of praying." Bane turned his head to watch.

I danced in thanks, mostly, that the Lord had given us victory in our little endeavor, even if it'd perhaps been *rather ill considered, and thanks above all that Bane was alive and suffering from no injury that a bit of time and rest wouldn't fix. And a little bit of appeal at the end, that we would go on being free and alive, were it the Lord's will.*

And with all that expressed, I danced into stillness again.

"That's the only type of praying I like watching," said Bane.

"You should try it sometime."

"Nah, I prefer to dance with other people."

"You know that's not what I meant." I went to sit on the floor by the bed.

"If you don't mind, Margo, I think I've got more important things to worry about right now than speaking to something I'm not convinced exists."

"I'd have thought they were the sort of important things that would've made you quite interested, actually."

Bane snorted. "Margo, the way I see it, there's only one way to find out for certain and I don't want to know that much. I can wait."

"Well, according to that reasoning, the only way to be certain that the sun will rise tomorrow is to wait until it does."

"I won't argue with that."

"Yeah, but you'll go about as though it is *going* to rise, won't you?"

"Actually, right now I frankly couldn't give a toss."

"Oh dear. Poor Bane is hurting."

"Yes, he is."

"Well. It could be worse, you know."

"Your bedside manner sucks, Margo."

"Sorry." I rose on my knees to draw the duvet up over him again. "I'd offer to kiss it better but I think you'd rather I didn't." But I did brush a tangle of black hair back from his sore forehead and place a gentle kiss there.

"Umm," sighed Bane, "Your bedside manner is improving."

We were on tenterhooks for a long time, waiting for that knock on the door, but it never came. After all, Bane had never showed up at the hospital, we'd both worn gloves, we'd left nothing behind, the guards had never got a proper look at my face, we'd both scanned in and out at the gates and dozens of couples must've climbed that fence that night. The police were looking for two needles in a haystack.

It'd taken a long time for us to relax. But the days had drawn on into weeks, and then into months, and gradually we'd accepted that we'd got away with it...

I pulled my mind back to the mortifying business of the night. Say my prayers *before* going down to Jonathan's bunk? I'd been trying so hard with my last prayer, but the fear sat inside me, cold and dark like...like a black hole. As I lay alone in the darkness, it sucked all my efforts into it, leaving nothing but the memory of Uncle Peter, dying. I couldn't remember when I'd last cried, before I came here... okay, perhaps I could, it was when we heard Sister Kate had been executed, but still, I wasn't *weepy*. Yet here I was, crying myself to sleep night after night.

There were still a few people whispering, but the night-time quiet had already settled over the dorm. The whole idea was that everyone else should be awake to notice me go down. Surely I'd manage not to cry with him right there beside me! I slid down to the floor, paused, then pulled my blankets off.

The rustling sounded loud enough to wake the dead, and when I lifted Jonathan's 'curtain' and scrambled inside, I'd no sooner let it fall than there was an outbreak of whispering followed by a great deal of giggling. Success, I suppose.

"How are we going to arrange ourselves?" I breathed, once I'd located Jonathan's ear. His bulk already seemed to fill the narrow bunk and top to tail would've been far the most comfortable, but it only took one person peeking and we'd be rumbled.

"I thought we could probably arrange a blanket between us," he murmured back, "without it being visible. It will take a while to get it straight as well, in this confined space, which is...probably best."

Ah yes, a good quantity of ongoing rustling sounds were quite indispensable for true success.

"Okay," I whispered, and then thought it prudent to give a tiny, smothered giggle. Which sparked a positive eruption of giggling from beyond the curtain. Which made me blush.

Jonathan's plan proved even more awkward than anticipated. Every time we tried to move a blanket, we'd find
one or other of us was lying on it. We'd move one part of
our body and find another still trapped it. The incredibly
frustrating exercise produced as much panting, heavy
breathing and general thrashing around as our listening
audience could possibly desire.

Finally, blanket positioned, we flopped gratefully down,
only to find ourselves pressed together like a pair of
sardines. Every line of his warm, firm body touched mine
and my cheeks, already flushed from all the exertion, grew
painfully hot.

"I'm sorry, this is awkward," he muttered—blushing too,
I'd bet.

"How...how should we...you know, lie. I...bet someone
peeps in the morning."

"Yeah. Let's just...face each other, you think?"

"Right."

We both turned on our sides and that did give slightly
more room in the bed, though even with the dividing
blanket our limbs became embarrassingly entangled.

"Um. Okay. Good night, Jon."

"Night, Margo."

Right, prayers. Ignore the handsome now-somewhat-
less-than stranger beside you. This was *so* embarrassing.
*Hello, Lord. Please watch over Bane. Please, please? Don't let
him do anything stupid. Please watch over Mum and Dad.
Please watch over Father Mark. Please don't let* him *do
anything stupid either...*

And all too soon I came to it. 'Domine...' *I now, at this
moment, willingly accept whatever...* 'quodcumque... quodcumque...' *kind of death,* 'quodcumque...' and Uncle Peter
was stretched out in my mind, bloody and pale, as they
sliced him to pieces—had he been screaming inside,
screaming and screaming in utter, helpless agony as they
killed him? Or had he been praying, his prayer helping to
keep that pain at bay?

Could even the greatest love of Our Lord hold back that
pain? What'd it be like to have every part of you cut away

while you still lived?

Quodcumque... I couldn't say it, even in my mind. I trembled with the effort of holding back the tears, and I could not say it. My throat burned and I wrapped a hand over my mouth to keep from making any sound. But my troubled breathing told Jonathan enough.

His hand found my shoulder and pressed it gently. "Margo? Are you all right?"

"Fine," I gulped. Unconvincingly, I'm sure.

"Is it your...uncle?"

"Sort of," I whispered.

"I...was upset enough when you told me. And you had to watch. That must've been awful. Is that it?"

"Not...not entirely. I...it's making me...I'm having trouble with...with one of my prayers." I'd have liked to talk to Uncle Peter about this problem, but that was definitely out, this side of the grave. Bane would've been second choice, for despite having no faith or theological knowledge to speak of, he tended to cut to the heart of things. But I couldn't speak to him either. "One I say every night," I whispered, "only now I can't."

Jonathan was silent for a long moment. "Are you trying to make an Act of Acceptance?"

"How'd you...guess that?"

"'Well, I've said it myself for...a very long time now. And I always...have trouble...saying it after hearing about someone being...you know...executed. Like that."

"Having *trouble*," I whispered miserably. "It's been a week now and I haven't managed to say it *at all!*"

"Perhaps you're trying too hard. It's *only* been a week."

"No, I'm just a spineless chicken! I mean, what do I *think*, that if I say it the Lord's going to say, 'Oh, Margo, so glad you offered, I've got this worst possible martyrdom lined up for you?' That's *nonsense!* He won't make it happen to me! The judges and dismantlers won't even make it happen to me unless they find me guilty of *Inciting and Promoting* and like *that's* going to happen with me in here and a whole bunch of people's safety resting on my silence and I *still* can't say it!" I trailed off, drawing in a deep breath perilously close to a sob.

Jonathan's arm slid around my shoulders and his other hand found my back, rubbing comfortingly. "It's all right, Margo. Don't you see, you still *want* to make the Act, and that's far more important than whether you actually manage it or not?"

I was inclined to argue with him, though it was the sort of thing Bane might've said, but I couldn't because my arm had just wrapped itself around him without my permission and my treacherous eyes were leaking into his broad chest.

Brilliant. Just brilliant.

Thud-thud. Thud-thud. Thud-thud. A strange noise drummed in my ear. My pillow was strange too. Warm and so firm it wasn't really very comfortable.

Opening my eyes, I found myself looking at...someone's neck? My pillow was the same someone's chest, under a blanket, which didn't do much to soften it. Something that whispered and giggled was sneaking up behind me.

That brought me fully awake. Jon and I, now officially a couple...probably best if my nightie wasn't visible. I checked the blankets, but they were drawn safely up to my chin. Jon opened his eyes and winked in my direction. Ah. He'd probably woken when the first whisperer set foot out of bed.

I closed my eyes and lay still, snuggled against Jon's chest, trying to breathe slowly and deeply and not blush. Not sure how well I managed the last, but it must be pretty dark in the bunk recess.

Light pressed against my eyelids as the curtain was lifted at one end. How many eyes were being applied to the gap? *Lots*—there was a deafening outbreak of giggling. Jon stirred with convincing sleepiness and buried his nose in my hair. The giggling became briefly ear-splitting and quickly receded across the room. Phew. That was over with.

I opened my eyes and found Jon's gray-blue ones staring through me as usual.

"Um, sorry about last night," I whispered.

"You don't need to apologize," he muttered, "if I'd had to watch that, I don't imagine I'd be too happy either."

"Some of the others have had nightmares," I said grimly.

"Horrible woman."

The friendlier of the two night guards unlocked the door then and stuck her head in. "Good morning, girls and boy. Washroom open."

"We'd better get up," said Jon, when she'd gone.

"Yep. Now, where's my nightie gone?" I said, nice and audibly.

Jon grinned. "You're still wearing it," he murmured.

"Ah, good. I think I might put it on straight away next time. It was rather cold last night."

"It was, rather," said Jon, more audibly.

There. Hopefully we wouldn't need to worry about being seen in our nightwear in future. I exited Jon's bunk and climbed back up onto mine to get dressed, once again failing not to blush. How long would it take for this to get back to Bane?

The thought made me feel horrible. Bane knew enough to figure out the truth, surely? *If* he was able to think about it clear-headedly enough. Perhaps I could find some way of hinting at the truth in my letter?

Right. Time for breakfast, and no doubt a whole load of *very* personal questions with it.

13

THE 1001 LIVES OF
ANNABEL SALFORD

"...'Annabel Salford,' called the dismantler, consulting his clipboard.

"Annabel stepped forward, not waiting for the guards to reach her. Her heart pounded with a foolish, irrational fear but she ignored it. Her mind was full of people, the people she would help, the people she would save. Her eyes might let a great-grandmother see her great-grandchild, her heart might save the life of a young mother, her hands might spare a grandmother from long years of arthritis-ridden agony...

"The list went on and on. She would change almost as many lives as there were parts in her body...and there were, she knew, because she was a smart and well-educated girl, a very great many parts in the human body.

"She held her head high, excitement thrilling through her as she went to meet her destiny, and her only, faint, regret, was that the greatness of that destiny so often went unappreciated."

"Stop, *please* stop, I have to go throw up," interrupted Jon, whose expression had been growing steadily more revolted as I read. "It's simply *awful!* I feel ill!"

"I've finished, anyway." I put the pad beside me on the bunk. "Now, this is very important, when you say it's awful, do you mean the content or the actual writing?"

"The content, of course, the writing's as good as usual, though...rather sickly." He did actually look faintly green around the edges. "You make it...you almost make it sound okay. You almost make it sound like someone could think it was okay. Even when...it was happening to them!"

"Good."

"You're not really going to send that in, are you? You don't really think that!"

"Yes, I am, and of course I don't. But I'm trying to win the competition, aren't I? If I do, I've got a hundred thousand words to tell the real story. And if the novel is to be about Sorting, the short story also has to be about Sorting. I somehow don't think mine's going to win if I tell it the way it is."

"I suppose not." He shuddered. "Ugh. That's ghastly." He was quiet for a moment. "You know, the monsters at the EGD might just love it."

"That's the idea. Right, I'd better get it copied out before supper." It'd taken me several days to hammer the idea out in my mind, several more to write and re-write and re-re-write it. It probably wasn't the best possible submission ever, but it *was* the best I could come up with in the time. It was Thursday, our letters would be posted in the morning; there was no time for anything else.

I copied 'The 1001 Lives of Annabel Salford' out as neatly as I could, then got out my letter. I could finish it off now.

I'm enclosing the story you asked for. I think you should give it to Sue when you've typed it up. Here's a few lines for Sue, anyway.

Hi Sue, I hope you'll be able to drop me a line some time. Bane's got a short story to give you - he can explain all about it. There are some people who will enjoy reading it more if they think you've written it. But if you write anything down about the story, you'd better put my name, don't you think? Otherwise you could get in trouble.

Anyway, I hope no one's stolen that entry slip you were worried about and that your application's gone okay - sometimes naughty boys will go taking anything that's not nailed down, won't they! I hope to hear from you soon. Love, Margo.

"Who goes around stealing entry slips?" asked Jon, after I'd read it to him in an undertone.

"No one. Y'see, she'll have to actually *enter* to get the entry slip from school. But she'll incriminate herself if *she* then hands the story in with my name on it. If no one sees who leaves Sue's envelope, then if and when they realize it's a reAssignee's entry, Sue can say she never entered because she lost the slip and hopefully they'll assume it was stolen. If things get sticky enough she can even blame Bane. He won't care."

Jon frowned. "I'd have thought it would be better to hide behind Sue's name for as long as possible."

"Yeah, but I don't want to put a black mark beside her name for the rest of her life and I doubt she'd do it then—who can blame her? As it is, let's face facts; the story probably won't even win."

"But if it does?" said Jon, levelly.

"They might very well make it public as the winner without noticing that the name on the entry and the name on the story's manuscript don't match. Then even if they found out and disqualified me, everyone would know a reAssignee had just written a better story than any of their perfect New Adults. Embarrassing, huh?"

"Very. I wonder if they *would* disqualify you? If they found out after the announcement? Or would they just keep quiet. Claim you missed the novel deadline." His brow darkened. "And have you dismantled a.s.a.p."

I firmly suppressed the worm of disquiet wriggling in my belly. "Quite honestly, Jon, I've no idea. But I can't get Sue in trouble and it's bad enough getting her to lie for me to make the entry."

Jon winced. "Yeah, I know, but...that story's great propaganda for them. If you win, but don't manage to present the other side of the story—the *real* side—who's to say it won't have done more harm than good?"

"A reAssignee would've won a competition designed to prove the benefits of Sorting to the human race. They'd have a hard time playing *that* down! And I think as soon as it was known a reAssignee wrote it, a lot of people wouldn't take that short story seriously at all: they'd take it as satire.

Anyway, I honestly don't think it's going to make things *worse*."

Jon snorted softly. "Yeah, s'pose you're right about *that*. It needs to be type-written, though. Will Sue have to go into the school to do that?"

"No, I asked my mum to give Bane my laptop, he can do it. Well, I say 'my,' but it's half his, really. We washed posh tourist cars for a year to get it."

"I wouldn't have thought Bane would be prepared to wash one car for the sake of a laptop!"

"Yeah, well, he claimed he wanted it so I'd let him help me, but I can't say I was fooled." He hadn't asked to use it once in the four years we'd had it. But that was okay: we'd spent most of the next year washing cars to replace his old bike, which'd been held together by love and a prayer. Bane's love, my prayer.

"She'll have to go into school to print it, though, won't she? And that will show on the print logs. But I don't know anyone with email, do you? And she could hardly claim it was Bane then, if they looked into it thoroughly enough..."

"Relax, Bane has my prehistoric printer as well." Fortunately, because I didn't know anyone with internet either. Expensive internet connections were the preserve of the rich in the cities.

"Oh. That's okay, then."

When we arrived in the cafeteria for supper, my eyes were drawn straight to the bright round things at the far end of the hatch. Finally. *Thank you, Lord.* I ate most of my orange, but slipped two segments into my pocket. Now we'd find out how carefully the censors really examined our letters.

Back in the dorm, I dropped my notebook casually down onto Jon's bunk, then played around with my sewing case for a while, discretely tipping some buttons into the bottom and slipping the emptied jar into my pocket, along with a spare—empty and unused—fountain pen I'd thought it prudent to pack. With my letter in my other pocket, I slipped down and sat beside Jon.

"Shall we put the curtain down for a bit?" I purred,

pressing close to his broad chest and fighting not to blush.

He managed to keep the surprise from his face, but seemed to be having trouble thinking of a suitable response, so I tugged the blanket down and drew away from him.

"Sorry about that," I whispered, arranging the curtain to allow a tiny line of light to spill into the bunk. "I want to add something rather special to my letter and I don't want anyone to see me do it."

"Nature's original invisible ink?"

"Yep." I opened up my notepad and laid the letter on the back cover in lieu of a table. "Can you hold this?" I handed Jon the jar. "Once I start I've got to be really, really quick, because once it's dry I won't be able to see what I've already done."

"Go for it."

I squeezed an orange segment into the jar, checked my letter was arranged so I could see the whole of the plan, took a deep breath, dipped the pen nib in the juice and began. I drew on the back of one of the letter's middle pages, running the nib over the paper absolutely as lightly as possible to avoid indenting it. Even transferring all the dimensions and details with pain-staking care, I finished before the first lines had quite faded into invisibility. There was more juice left than I expected.

"Orange juice?" I offered.

"It's your orange."

"Half each."

Jon shrugged, took a sip and handed the little jar to me. I drained it and tucked everything back into my pockets. "Okay, this is dry, now I need to add a bit to the letter. We'd better giggle a lot and go and sit at the table."

We emerged, suitably entwined, I got my pen from my chest and we settled ourselves at the table.

"I thought you'd finished that," remarked Jane, as I spread my letter out in front of me.

"Thought of something else to say." I leafed casually through the pages. Bother. I was going to have to add a P.S. at the end, that was where the most space was. To put it elsewhere would look suspicious.

P.S. We had oranges this evening, I was so glad to see them. Do you remember how much Bane and I used to enjoy eating them together when we were little? You got quite cross with us sometimes.

It's good we'll be getting them, though; we'll be glad of the vitamin C come winter. There is some sort of heating system here, by the look of things, but I reckon it will be a bit on the chilly side! We could've used Harriet's hair straightener as an extra heat source, but unfortunately it was confiscated when we arrived, so we don't have anything like that. You know, she still gets upset if you mention it!

Surely Bane would remember, even if Mum had forgotten, how cross she'd been when she found Bane and I using an expensive orange to write each other invisible notes. Hopefully he'd also understand I didn't have a heat source with which to read any invisible reply.

On Friday morning I yanked the pages of my parents' letter from the envelope as soon as I'd reached my bunk. The first page—I scanned down it quickly—more soppy space-filler, this time from Dad. And over onto the top of the second page. He was actually better at it than Mum: who'd of thought! At the end of the second paragraph he handed over to Bane, *thank you, thank you...*

I read greedily, though it was clear nothing wildly interesting had been happening. Deo gratias! Except...there was just one paragraph:

You know that little lion of yours, your favorite one? I tried to return it to your parents but they couldn't think of anyone better than me to have it at the moment, so I've found a nice safe place for it and it reminds me of you every time I see it. I thought you'd like to know it hasn't gone the same way as your poor bunny.

The lion was the symbol of Saint Mark—cue endless lion jokes between Bane and Father Mark. So it'd still been judged unsafe for Father Mark to return to any of his normal houses and *Bane* was hiding him. Bane, who wasn't even in the Underground! But he was very loyal to his friends and he counted Father Mark as a friend.

But *where?* No way would his parents allow a strange man to stay with them—they'd make him scan his ID at the nearest cash register and since that declared him to be a dead man, the game would be up.

Not with his parents, no, but in our little Fellest hideout. After we gave up train-jumping—at least together—we were a bit bored, so we built our own high adventure course in a patch of Fellest well away from any hiking or cycling trails. It was hard work, carting nails and ropes and chains out there on our rickety ex-tourist mountain bikes, even though we used mostly fallen wood. But worth the effort—the course was far better than the tourist ones we couldn't afford anyway.

We built a little hut too, built it well enough that with a gel heat cube, you could sit in there even in mid-winter. That was where Father Mark was. No one knew about it except the two of us. Things must be pretty hot in Salperton if Father Mark had consented to be squirreled away that far out of town.

The rest of the letter was innocent, no double meanings. Bane was waiting for my reply.

14

EASTER

"It's the big day tomorrow," I remarked to Jon on Saturday night, as, blanket arranged and rustling sounds completed, we settled ourselves into our accustomed sleeping positions. Which, embarrassing to say, involved my head resting on his chest, where it'd tended to wind up as a result of my recent mortifying tendency to finish my night prayers in tears. And which was actually most comfortable in the confined space. Except for my ear, which would've preferred a soft pillow, but nothing was perfect.

"Easter day." He sounded as glum as I felt.

"Yeah."

We'd lowered the blanket a couple of times for privacy in the daytime during Holy Week and I'd spent the time praying—all right, sometimes just wishing I was at home and *trying* to pray—and I think he had too. But tomorrow was the most important day of our year and we would spend it in here, unable to mark it in any way.

I rubbed my head against his blanket-and-hoodie-covered chest as though I might somehow soften it, realized what I was doing and gave up.

His arm tightened around my shoulders. "I hope Bane comes for you soon," he whispered.

I didn't bother trying to peer at his face in the darkness. "I don't see how he can do it, Jon," I said softly. "Anyway, it's... not really as simple as that, is it?"

"He comes and takes you away: you two have a long and happy life, what's not simple about that?"

"Well, the bit about having a happy life—knowing I'd left every single one of you to die in here."

Jon made an impatient noise. "And how will it help us if you die as well? Not one bit."

"Since when has save yourself and to the blazes with the

129

others been the way? Jon, say you had some fearsome fiancée who was determined to rescue you. Say she showed up at the door and said, come along, Jon, you can't help them, let's just go. What would you do?"

The silence lengthened. He wouldn't leave. But he didn't want to say so because he was trying to persuade me to do just that. This was all hypothetical, anyway. I'd yet to figure out how Bane could get in.

"You can do more good if you survive," said Jon at last, rather stiffly.

"And you can't?"

"No. I *can't.* I'm blind. I have no especial talents. I can stay here and hold everyone's hand. You go with Bane and do good."

"What happened to having a long happy life?"

"Have a long happy life doing good. You know what I mean."

"It's *not* that simple, Jon. Who's to say which of us could really do the most good?"

"Would you really refuse to go with him? After he'd gone to all that effort? Hadn't you better warn him you intend to be difficult about it?"

My turn to be silent for a moment. "I don't think it's that urgent. If...you must know, I'm still trying to decide what to say to him." My heart knew I ought to stay. But sometimes my head agreed with Jon. What was the point, really? How could I tell Bane I wouldn't let him save me? I wanted so much to be saved...

Anyway. Prayer time. *Salve, Domine.* I will not cry. I will not cry... But Jon's arm was around me and it was something simply not to be alone with the nightmarish memories, with the fear and dread of what was to come. Embarrassment was fast fading into habit, and during the cold dark nights, it was hard to regret our little deception.

"Happy Easter," murmured Jon into my ear, as I swam to wakefulness.

"Happy Easter," I muttered back, sleepily and fairly joylessly.

"Oh, come on, battlements walk, Sunday treat and all

that..."

That our battlements walk fell on a Sunday was without doubt inadvertent on the part of the Menace, but Jon and I liked it. Made Sunday special.

"*Easter* treat today." I made an effort to be more cheerful. It was Easter day. So what if we could only celebrate it with a walk along a wire-festooned wall and a few private prayers of our own? It was still Easter!

I'd have liked to dress particularly nicely, but I didn't dare. It wasn't even the guards' eyes that worried me: it was Jane's. She stared at Jon and me a lot, and I wasn't sure it was entirely jealousy. We'd even taken to avoiding Latin unless our lips were invisible behind the bunk's curtain. She probably couldn't lip-read, but she might be able to tell there was something odd about such speech. We couldn't risk her suspicions.

The concrete was hard under my elbows as I leaned on the top of the wall, looking out at the forest and the killing zone in between. My eyes traced the increasingly familiar features, all marked on the plan I'd sent Bane. I'd heard nothing, so it must've reached him undiscovered.

The Facility sat at the bottom of two hundred meters of steep, sloping, bare earth. The pavement of the road ran straight up the slope and away into the Fellest, flanked by its drainage ditches, and another paved track ran around the forestline on...the west, as far as I could make out. The road to the Lab entrance.

Defensively, sticking the place in a hollow didn't seem the best idea in the world. But the walls and machine guns would ward off most attacks, and when it came to placing Facilities, the EGD were more worried about 'out of sight, out of mind'. So we were down in the hollow, in the heart of the Fellest, in the middle of nowhere, with huge walls and lots of razor wire.

Crack.

I spun around as there was a chorus of gasps from around me. A mortar? The Resistance? Where could we take cover...?

But my questing eyes found red stars fading above the

farthest machine gun tower. A firework. Which made me think of Bane, of course. Sarah clapped her hands in delight as we all stared, wondering and waiting.

Crack.

Green stars. Pale in the daylight, but still beautiful. Everyone oohed and aahed in appreciation. The guards in the towers nearest the pyrotechnics yelled frantically to one another and every eye in the Facility must've been fixed on that bit of sky. Well, the guards were probably staring at that bit of forest and sweating...

Something hit me in the small of the back, jerking a gasp from me. A couple of people glanced my way and I deliberately didn't spin round, didn't look down. What'd hit me? I stepped back and sat casually on the wall behind me. Casually and very carefully. I did not want to fall through that wire. I could see a tiny package protruding from under my hem.

Crack.

The sky was drenched in gold stars. Immediately, but avoiding sudden movements, I bent and palmed the little ball, sliding it up my skirt and into my pocket. We all stared and waited, but there were no more fireworks. Sarah began to clap again, in applause this time, and I joined in. Soon everyone was applauding our mysterious entertainer.

Though I bet I knew just who it was. Who, plural. Bane could've used an extra length of fuse, but most likely a little lion had lit those fireworks. They'd better both be legging it for all they were worth. From the continued shouting and dashing around, the guards would be out looking for them soon enough.

We were herded back to our dorm then. Our battlement time had hardly started, but the guards were a wee bit excited and busy securing everything that could be secured, including us.

"Three fireworks," snorted Jane. "*Scary.*"

"Yeah, but they didn't even spot the person launching them, by the look of things," I couldn't help pointing out. "And three rounds from a mortar would've been another matter, don't you think?"

"The Resistance don't care about us," said Jane flatly. "No

one cares about us."

Hard to argue with that. I wanted to win a certain competition for that very reason.

I went to sit beside Jon.

"So?" he asked, pretending to nibble my ear.

"So, what?"

"*So*, what hit the ground behind you just before the third firework?"

"You and your ears," I murmured, sticking my nose in his hair for safety. "We can have a making out session later and I'll open it, but not immediately, it might look suspicious."

"Suspicious is what the Major will be if he knows what day it is."

"I don't know. Eighty reAssignees, or thereabouts? If he hasn't normally got one or two, um, *like us*, in here I'd be very surprised, but they haven't been looking."

"True." Jon gave up nuzzling my ear—good, his nose was freezing. "When are you going to start the book?"

"Soon. But I need to decide what to write first. And how to go about it."

"*How?*"

"It has to be *typewritten*. So I've either got to send it to Bane to type up as we go along or type it myself. And the more I think about it, the more certain I am that the only way I'll have a hundred thousand words—or some acceptable novel length—by the end of May is if I can type it. Which is problematic."

Jon was kind enough not to laugh at this gross understatement. "What are you going to do about it?" he asked seriously.

"I haven't quite decided." Understatement upon understatement. I was really quite, *quite* certain I couldn't write a hundred thousand words by hand before the deadline. With all the time we spent exercising each day, I wasn't sure it was even physically possible. And a hundred thousand words carefully chosen to move the hearts and minds of the world? So I had to type it. But *how?*

A bleak little voice informed me more and more forcefully that submitting the short story was a waste of time, that I'd risked getting Sue in trouble for nothing, that I couldn't possibly win and I most certainly couldn't have an entire novel ready by the end of May. I suppressed the voice as best I could, and sought advice elsewhere. *Lord, any suggestions?*

Worrying about that little problem was almost enough to distract me from the intriguing package in my pocket. Almost, but not quite. It fitted in my palm and was soft to the touch. I squeezed it gently, feeling the contours of something in the middle of the softness. A round disc? My breath caught in my throat and slowly, reverently, I took my hand from my pocket. Could it be?

A lot of planning and effort had certainly gone into its delivery. Two hundred meters was a long way, but Bane had a catapult that had more in common with a crossbow than a boy's toy. It would do the job. Probably had.

I went to sit at the table and write part six of the Fellest Ewe's diary, which was proving a hit with pretty much everyone in the dorm. Even Jane took out her ear phones to listen. Jon ran his fingers suggestively down my arm now and then, clearly curious, but I ignored the invitation for some time.

Eventually I took my notebook back to my chest and pocketed the scissors from my sewing kit, along with a flashlight. Jon and I then withdrew into the privacy of his bunk with the usual accompaniment of giggling.

"Really, I can't think of anything less appropriate!" I couldn't help muttering, kneeling on the mattress beside Jon.

"Huh?"

"I think I know what's in here, that's all."

"Well, let's find out."

I switched the flashlight on, since I didn't want to leave even the tiniest crack in the curtain today. Being caught writing in orange juice when you were supposed to be making out would pale into insignificance beside this. I gave Jon the flashlight and tackled the wrappings with the scissors.

Tape, thick packing paper, almost card, then cotton stuffing. In the center was a large pebble—to provide weight?—and a tiny satin pouch, the drawstrings tied, but a tiny slip of paper sticking out. I drew out the slip and tilted it to catch the light.

It's the real deal, a little lion told me so.

I read it softly to Jon, who looked bemused. "Heh?"

I ran my fingers over the disc shape, now unmistakable through the single layer of cloth. A circular wafer. My chest was tight. Dear Bane. Dear, dear Bane.

I placed the pouch in Jon's hands, so he could feel what I could feel—in the faint light of the flashlight I saw his face freeze. He got up onto his knees, cupping the pouch reverently in one hand.

"Nice Easter gift from my unbelieving fiancé, eh?" I murmured.

"Just slightly. Though I wonder how bored that little lion is getting."

I winced. Bane and Father Mark, bored together—not entirely reassuring. I took the pouch and set it on the center of the pillow. Hard to complain about this, though.

"Let's say what suitable prayers we can remember first," I suggested. Jon nodded, so I switched off the flashlight, closed my eyes and sought to still my mind.

* * *

...Domine, non sum dignus, ut intres
sub tectum meum, sed tantum dic
verbo, et sanabitur anima mea.
>   ...*Lord, I am not worthy that you should*
>   *enter under my roof, but only say the*
>   *word and my soul shall be healed.*

Well, I was as ready as I was going to get. I turned the flashlight back on and glanced at Jon. He must've heard me move, because after a moment he said, "Okay?"

I picked up the pouch. "Are you a Minister of Holy Communion, by any chance?"

He shook his head. "You do it," he murmured. "I can't see what I'm doing."

That usually made surprisingly little difference to what

135

he could or couldn't do, but in this case I agreed with him. This was all informal enough as it was. Not that I thought Our Lord minded being catapulted over a wall to us in the circumstances, and Father Mark must've thought the same, but the least we could do was not get bits of Him *all over* the bed!

I untied the pouch and tipped it carefully over my hand. *I'm sorry to have to get my un-consecrated mitts all over you, Lord, but I can't see how else to do this...*

A single Host slid out—oh, Bane didn't know Jon was here. I'd hadn't dared mention it in my last letter.

"Can you hold your hands out? I'm going to have to break it."

Jon complied and I did so as reverently as I could, though to be honest, there's only so much reverence you can achieve when snapping something in half. Well, it's the attitude of heart that really counts. Placing half on Jon's tongue and the other half on my own, I closed my eyes and embraced interior silence. *I've missed you, Lord...*

When I finally opened my eyes I could see water gleaming at the corners of Jon's eyes in the light of the flashlight. I drew my sleeve across my own cheeks and watched as he licked his cupped hands clean, clearly having some reverence issues of his own.

When he finally lowered his hands and wiped them on the blanket I moved to sit on his clothes' chest, resting my head against the cinder block wall.

Jon seated himself on the bunk and leaned against the wall as well. "That's better," he sighed.

Was it just. Strength had been slowly draining out of me and I hadn't even realized, until now, when it returned full force. It *wasn't* impossible to write a novel in two months, not if the Lord supported the plan. And I knew what I had to tell Bane. I knew *exactly* what I had to tell Bane. But he wouldn't be happy.

We stayed where we were for as long as we dared, then we put the curtain back up. That night I didn't even cry. I didn't manage to say the prayer, but I didn't cry. Accepting my failure gracefully for once, I sank towards sleep with something like my old tranquility.

"And God bless Bane and Father Mark," whispered Jon, his arm tightening around me.

"God bless Bane and Father Mark," I murmured, my arm slipping around Jon as around a rather large and muscular teddy bear.

The click of the dorm door opening and the hasty tramp of several pairs of feet jerked me awake. I'd barely raised my head when the curtain was yanked aside and three of the male guards looked in. Finchley, Watkins, and Dwight. The perverted, the decent, and the devastatingly ordinary. Sally the nice night guard dithered behind them, looking anxious.

Finchley swore. "The Captain isn't going to be happy."

"What do you two think you've been doing?" demanded Dwight.

"What does it *look* like we've been doing?" retorted Jon. "Do I need to get technical?"

Finchley and Dwight reached in, grabbed him, and dragged him out so roughly most of the blankets came too, with me tangled up in them. I fell to the ground with a bump.

"Oh, be nice," appealed Sally, "he's *blind*, you know..."

"Yeah, yeah," snorted Finchley, then yelped, "Hey!" as Jon got his feet under him and shook them both off, sending Dwight reeling across the room and Finchley staggering into the wall.

"Knock it off, lad, or we'll shoot you and carry you out, understood?" Watkins no-nonsensely unsnapped his pistol holster.

Jon's lip curled, but he must've heard the popper because he stood still and let the other two grab him again. "You all right, Margo?" He'd heard me fall.

"Fine," I gasped, still fighting with the blankets. "Where're you taking him?"

"Where do all good little reAssignees go?" said Finchley, smiling nastily.

Watkins shot him a look. "Shut it, Finch."

Dwight and Finchley began to lead Jon away. Watkins and Sally followed.

"*Jon!*" My whole body seemed to have been dipped in ice. I clawed my way out of the blankets as though possessed. This all-enveloping terror was more electric than paralyzing. "Jon... Leave him alone!" I looked around wildly— everyone was just standing there, why didn't they *do* something! "Jon! *You can't take him!*"

"Want a bet?" smirked Finchley over his shoulder.

I went after them and Watkins drew his pistol. "Stop right there, missie, your boyfriend..."

I didn't hear any more, because they were dragging Jon out the door—he'd heard the pistol clear leather and was fighting them again—something snapped and I went for Watkins like a wild thing. I moved faster than I'd ever moved in my life and I almost made it, my hands reaching out to knock the gun aside, to grab it. In that long frozen blur of motion, I saw the panic in his eyes. Then his hands tilted upwards and his finger whitened on the trigger...

Something smacked my chest, a black pipe seemed to drop over me and I fell down it, down into nothingness—the last thing I saw was Jon slamming Watkins to the ground in a way that would've had Father Mark suppressing a smile.

15

THE CARD

A very white ceiling loomed above me. I stared drowsily up at it for a while. *Something tells me everything is not right. Why is everything not right?*

Jon!

I sat up and pain leapt from both temples, meeting in the middle of my brain. Sinking back on one elbow, I closed my eyes, swallowed hard and stayed that way until the pain receded slightly and I was fairly sure I wasn't going to be sick. *Won't hurt, will it, Major? Liar!*

I opened my eyes again.

I lay on what appeared to be a hospital bed, in a tiny, white, windowless room. A hospital-style bedside table stood on the side nearest the door, a key sticking out of the cupboard lock, and that was literally it. My aching brain moved sluggishly. Not the room we'd been taken to for our medical examinations in our first week here...but it must be part of the sick bay.

Jon...

Throwing back the blanket, I slowly swung my legs over the side of the bed and levered myself to my feet. My head pounded unpleasantly but remained attached to my body, so I wobbled to the door. Card locked. Of course. I was really, really starting to want one of those cards. *Lord?*

There was no window in the door. I poked all around it but it fitted seamlessly against the frame. Tugging and prodding the card reader and even thumping it achieved nothing, of course. How long had I been unconscious? Was Jon already packed away in the freezer?

I *was* sick then, barely grabbing a basin out from under the bed in time. I knelt over the bowl for some time, retching and crying in fear. Jon... *Where do all good little reAssignees go?* Finchley had said. The Major had belatedly realized that the easiest way to avoid Jon's organs being wasted was simply to have him dismantled at once.

Stifling a fresh outburst of weeping, I shoved the basin under the bed, found a cloth to wipe my face, and forced myself to lie back down. I couldn't get out of the room and the headache would pass faster if I rested. And when I did get out of the room, there was more chance of doing something if I could move quickly without throwing up. I drew the blanket back over my nightdress-clad body, shivering. I ached all over and I felt exhausted.

There would be nothing I could do. I flung the thought away from me and stamped on it.

Terror for Jon or no terror, I was dozing by the time the door opened. Finchley stepped into the room. Just Finchley. He shut the door behind him. I hastily put back the blanket to free up my legs. I didn't like his smile. I didn't like the way he looked at me. I didn't like that it was just him.

"Feeling better, sweetheart?" He strode towards the bed and I slipped off the other side, which put me pretty much with my back to the wall. "Warden says to take you to Doctor Richard for a test. You having been such a naughty girl. But the Doc's just expecting you sometime this morning. So I don't see why we can't spend a little while getting to know each other first."

I glanced up, searching the ceiling corners.

Finchley laughed so hard you'd think I'd done something really funny. "No cameras in here, sweetheart. Counts as a bedroom. For once the Really Wet Board have done something right, eh?"

My heart was pounding so hard it hurt. Bane had taught me some hand-to-hand stuff, but...Finchley was so big. I swallowed, fighting back panic. *You're in trouble, Margo, but panicking won't help.* Perhaps I should let him come right up to me and then shoot him with his own weapon. Yeah, and how stupid was he?

Not that stupid. He drew the nonLee from its holster and locked it inside the bedside cupboard—put the key in his pocket and smirked at me.

"Wouldn't want you to spoil the party, would we?"

He began to walk around the bed towards me. *Lord,*

Lord, Lord...help? What do I do? I was trapped in this little room with him and I couldn't get out, not without— With immense effort, I managed not to stare at the gray badge hanging around his neck in its holder. He hadn't taken that off. So...how? I'd have to let him come close...I'd probably only get one chance. I wanted to bolt, but I had to wait. My trembling fingers knotted in my nightie.

He lunged and grabbed me, shoving me back onto the bed. The badge dug into my chest. I could take it, but how to get away? I twisted, struggling, but he wrapped an arm around me to hold my arms down. Worried about his eyes. His other hand was all over me, octopus-like, and his legs pressed hard against mine, so kneeing him in the crotch was out. But what'd Bane said?

"Oh, forget about the old knee in the crotch, Margo, it's expected. If anyone ever bothers you that badly, just grab their bits, good squeeze and yank, they'll let you go and you can blush later."

My mind managed one plaintive, panic-stricken *Lord? Not really?* but my hands were already moving. My right hand put Bane's advice ruthlessly into practice and my left snatched the badge off over Finchley's head as he doubled over with a sound like a burst balloon. Shoving him off me, I dived over the bed and fumbled for a breathless, back-tingling second as I got the card the right way around and swiped it through the reader.

The light flashed green and I yanked the door opened—I could already hear him stumbling across the room—I leapt through, not daring to look back, and slammed the door shut behind me. Gasping for breath and shaking like a leaf, I took stock of where I was. The sick bay corridor. Finchley began to hammer on the door. I didn't have long if I wanted to keep my prize. With the shadow of his hands lingering on me, I felt I'd paid enough for it. *You got off very lightly, Margo.*

Turning, I began to run down the corridor, my bare feet pounding against the cold floor. I would have to be very, very fast. As soon as they spotted me on the monitors... Here was the stairwell door—swipe the card—the stairs flew by beneath me. Top floor—swipe card again. From lower

141

down came the bang of doors; raised voices. Sprinting along the corridor and swiping the card yet again, I hurtled into the dormitory.

"Margo?"

"What—?"

"Are you all right?"

I ignored everyone, dashing to my bunk and diving up onto it as though distraught. I'd no breath for sobs, real or otherwise, but I draped myself over my chest to hide the fact I was lifting the lid and taking out my purse. Stupid thing to bring to the Facility, but such was habit. I fumbled with the cards in it...ID, blue and yellow; Bank card, black; Loyalty card, red; Library card! Gray! I switched it with Finchley's pass card and had the purse back in the chest before the first would-be comforter made it up onto the top bunk.

"Margo, what happened?"

Footsteps echoed in the corridor. Evading all the outstretched arms, I slid from the bunk and reached the trash chute before the door opened, winding the cord around the badge holder as the Menace, Finchley, Dwight, and two other guards spilled into the room. No point trying to look upset—if I looked how I felt, that would do fine.

"Give it back, you thieving cat!" wheezed Finchley.

"What, *this?*" I yelled, showing them the holder; making sure they all saw it held a card. "Why don't you go and *get* it, you rapist dog!"

I yanked open the trash chute and threw it in before they managed anything more than a dismayed lurch forward.

"No!" wailed Finchley.

Then the Menace grabbed him by the collar and slammed him into the doorframe, which unfortunately for him was made of cinder blocks and metal like everything else. "What did she just call you?"

"He tried to rape me, the filthy pig!" I shrieked. I was acting now—sort of—it was scary how easy the hysterics were. But I *couldn't* try to calm down; it mustn't even cross anyone's mind that I might've done *anything* other than run straight back to the safety of the dormitory before throwing the badge away in revenge. And as I couldn't try to get hold of myself, I began to cry; big, loud, messy sobs from right down inside, the sort that leave you hardly able to breathe so you feel you're going to suffocate in misery.

As the other girls converged on me I could hear the Menace laying into the cowering Finchley.

"You little toad, if I ever hear anything like this again you'll be in the dole queue, you hear me? For the rest of your life. D'you have any idea what a rapist guard would do to my record, you stupid idiot? D'you have any idea how much flack the Wets would give me if they heard about this? You keep your hands *off the merchandise*, you hear me?"

Oh, she was a charming woman, no mistake.

She hadn't finished—she slapped him, once, twice, thrice across the face—before realizing that my horde of comforters had fallen silent and were watching avidly. She dragged him off, then, their voices floating back along the corridor.

"How dare you do this, *today*."

"You're not going to tell the Major, are you? Please, please, Captain, you're not going to tell him, are you?"

"Oh, *I will*, if you put so much as another foot wrong."

"Please, please don't, *please* don't tell him, *please*—"

"Oh, don't wet yourself, you little—"

The stairwell door clicked closed behind them.

The sight of Finchley being walloped by his superior was delightful—I'd have to at least stop crying before I could work on forgiveness, and I was finding it an awful lot harder to stop crying than to start. Eventually I found myself seated on a chair at the table with an array of chocolate and sweets laid out in front of me, and an entire heap of cherished soft toys piled in my lap.

"I'm all right, really," I managed at last. "I'm fine. Thank you, you're being so kind, but I'm all right. He didn't really manage anything. I was just shaken up." *And Jon's probably dead and there was nothing I could do to help him...*

"Let me get this straight," said Rebecca, looking rather thrilled, "you kicked him where it hurts most and then you grabbed his card and legged it?"

"That's…that's pretty much it." At the thought of precisely what I'd done to Finchley, heat flooded my already tear-warmed cheeks. Bane would've laughed. Actually, Bane would still have been pounding Finchley's face into a cinder block and I'd be trying to stop him. I hope.

Bane… I wanted him with me so much it was like a physical ache. And the next time I wrote to him, would I have to tell him his friend was dead?

Jane had wormed her way up on my right. "We got inspected, you know, while you were gone."

"Inspected?" I was hardly listening.

"Yeah, by the RWB. They looked around and asked if anything bad had happened to us here—Bethan started crying and they were all like, 'what is it, what's the matter?' and I was afraid they'd get it out of her—about the execution and everything, then she'd have been for it, so I said, 'They're going to cut us up, what do you *think's* the matter with her?' And they went very pink in the face and went away again."

"Oh. Great. I'm glad Bethan wasn't in trouble."

"Margo! Wake up! Don't you see? Jon's probably—" She broke off as the tramp of feet came from outside.

The door clicked open and a couple of guards tossed a broken white cane into the room, then shoved a gangly russet-haired figure after it and slammed the door again.

"*Jon!*" Chocolate, cuddly toys and chairs went flying in all directions as I hurtled down the room. I flung my arms around him and as his head turned towards me my lips accidentally landed right on his. I only just managed to control my instinctive recoil, but Jon slid one hand into my hair and returned the kiss as convincingly as anyone could've wished.

He didn't kiss like Bane, blazing-fierce and adoringly tender all at once; Jon's lips caressed mine as though he'd slip through them, merge himself with me, make us one. It was too intimate and I couldn't respond, but when we broke apart, it required no effort to wrap my arms around him and bury my face in his silky hair.

"Jon, you're all right. You're alive." I found myself repeating this self-evident fact several times before I managed to draw away and get hold of myself. Actually…definitely alive, but not quite as all right as he'd been earlier that morning. His lip was split and swelling, he'd a black eye, a bruised cheek, and one wrist nestled in a tubular bandage. "How many hours were you with them for?"

"The guards did my lip after I tried to shove Watkins through the cafeteria ceiling for shooting you. The boys managed the rest the moment the RWB had gone. I don't know what the Major said to make them leave me alone *that* long, to be honest. I really am *persona non grata* over there. I suppose they're miffed I escaped from them."

I touched his wrist gently, "Is it broken?"

"No, just sprained, according to dear Doctor Richard."

"Is anything else hurt?"

"Bruises. My pride. Nothing else."

"Don't see why your pride's hurt. I was astonished the way you managed to deal with those guards."

"Well, you were unconscious during the part where they rammed my face into the floor and sat on me. But yes, Bane used to make me practice with him and I tell you, he was merciless!"

"Well, if someone attacks you, they won't give you special consideration because you can't see, will they?"

Jon laughed so hard a fresh trickle of blood ran from his lip.

"That's exactly what your fiancé said," he murmured into my ear, drawing me in for another hug.

I hugged him back fiercely, gulping. Tears of relief were pricking the corners of my eyes.

"Oh, Margo, I'm sorry, were you really scared?"

"I thought they were dismantling you, stupid!"

"I'm sorry, there's...something I should've told you. I...just didn't like to make a big thing about it. I'm a really, really rare tissue type. It's the only reason they let me be born at all. Only reason they put me in with you girls too, I bet. There's no way they're going to dismantle me until I'm in absolutely Prime Condition. All my organs are...well, virtually priceless. I'm sorry, I should've told you before, but..."

But he'd have felt like he was boasting or something. The rest of us could be taken at any time, like Polly.

"So you mustn't think I was being really brave earlier," he

145

added. "I was just pretty near certain they weren't taking me to the Lab."

"Well, I'm *glad.*" I hugged him again. "Now I know I don't need to worry about you for a year or so. If they come and drag you off, it's just an inspection."

"Yeah. I should've said. That wasn't very far-sighted of me, was it?"

"Never mind. You're all right. Everything's okay."

After a few more moments he drew away at last and began to feel around him. "Now, where's my stick?"

I picked up the pieces. "Um, I think it needs some TLC, Jon."

"Huh?"

I put a piece into each of his hands and his face fell. "I think we can fix it," I said quickly. "It's splintered, see, uh... *feel*. And I've got some string. We should be able to bind it up."

"Yeah...I expect so." But there was more vulnerability in his eyes now than when he'd been dragged off earlier, so pausing only to get dressed, I laid out the two pieces on the bed and reassembled them.

"There," I said at last. "It wouldn't hold any weight, but it will hold together, and that's all that matters."

He wandered up and down the room for a while, accustoming himself to the new weight and balance of his precious aid, then he sat beside me and kissed my cheek. "Thank you, Margo."

"You're welcome. Now, if you're not too tired for a little *making out*, I've got something to show you."

I'd transferred the precious card to my pocket while getting the string from my chest. There didn't seem to be anyone light-fingered in the dorm, but I wasn't risking it. Anyway, I wanted to have a good look at it.

Safe behind the curtain, I examined it in the light of my flashlight. The front had a picture of Finchley; no more flattering than any such picture tends to be, not that the camera had much to work with; and listed his name, rank, ID number and Unit—Greater Salperton EGD Facility. On the back was the standard spiel about if found please return to... blah blah blah.

"So?"

I handed him the card.

He ran his fingers around the edge, sniffed it, then traced the indented letters. "Fin...ch...ley..." His head came up sharply and his voice dropped even lower. "Is this a *door* card?"

"Yes," I breathed.

"Deus omnipotens! Where did you get it?"

"Okay, promise you won't run amuck and try to push his face through the floor?"

He flushed. "I'm not into revenge, Margo."

"Oh? You knew Watkins had already shot me, didn't you?"

He went even redder. "Yes, I heard you hit the ground, but...I honestly was trying to protect you, I know it sounds stupid, but...it was instinctive. By the time they were all sitting on me it'd sunk in that I was too late to help you—so I let them take me away."

"Ah. Well, I woke up in an isolation ward—don't imagine they wanted to admit to the inspectors I'd just been shot. Finchley showed up saying he was to take me to Doctor Richard, but he wanted to *get to know me* first. While he was trying that on, I grabbed his card and legged it."

"Did he hurt you?"

"Ran his vile hands over me, is all."

"It's *enough.*" Despite what he'd just said, he looked angry enough to have a good go at driving Finchley's face into the floor.

"I won't argue with that. But I got a card out of it, so I'm not complaining."

"But they must know that's missing and who took it."

"Of course they do. The Menace and Finchley and a whole pack of them arrived right on my heels, just in time to see me throw the holder—with a nice gray card in it—down the trash chute. Since I don't think I was going to need my library card again, I think that's a rather good trade, don't you?"

He threw his arms around me and kissed me perilously close to my lips. "You know what this means, don't you? You may actually be able to get out of here after all!"

I had my own ideas about that, but I just said, "Yes. If it's going to carry on working."

"Why wouldn't it?"

"Well, if the cards are individual to each guard, the old one may automatically be stopped when a new one is issued. So all I'll get if I try and use it is a whole lot of trouble. But if they just print the guard's details onto a standard card, then they're not going to change the lot because one card's been destroyed, are they? This thing doesn't have any individual card number on it so hopefully it's the second system."

Jon licked absent-mindedly at his cut lip as he thought about this. "They've got the cameras which must all beam their feed to a camera room. That's an expensive system. Perhaps they wouldn't spend money on a high tech card system as well—if they want to know who went through what door when, they can just look at the footage."

"Exactly. Of course, the cameras are the next problem. You can see the little lights glowing at night; they're still on; but is anyone in the camera room looking? And how hard?"

"Not very, I shouldn't think. I'll find out for you."

"What? How?"

He tapped his nose. "I have a plan."

"What?"

He just smiled mysteriously—then footsteps in the passage made us both raise our heads.

"The guard looked in a quarter of an hour ago," said Jon. "What now?"

"I never did get that test, did I? I'm putting the card in your pillowcase." I shoved it right in, then threw up the curtain so we were sitting innocently on the edge of the bunk when the dorm door opened.

"Margaret Verrall," said one of the guards. Two of them and neither of them Finchley. Might as well go quietly.

16

OPERATION CAMERA INFO

Dear Doctor Richard's office was in the Lab building—my skin was crawling by the time I arrived. Being marched off that way seemed such a horribly exact preview of what was to come.

The disbarred doctor was reading his newspaper when the guards brought me in. They made to withdraw and he flipped the paper down and looked at them over the top of it. "No, no, you two can stay, we wouldn't want the subject to make any more nasty accusations today, would we?"

I couldn't help staring pointedly at the camera in the corner, but on the whole I wasn't sorry not to be left alone with the man who, in a few days, weeks or months, would kill me. At least, not until, twitching his paper impatiently in his hands, he demanded, "The date of your last menstrual period, subject?"

I tried not to blush, with little success. The guards developed a sudden, intense interest in the doctor's revolting collection of framed anatomical photographs—cross sections of lungs, hearts, kidneys...

"Two weeks ago," I said coldly. "I don't know the date."

He picked up a little white stick from his desk and held it out. "Take this, through that door on the left, urinate on it, bring it back."

"They put my contraceptive implant in at eleven, same as everyone else," I retorted.

The guards stared at the pictures as though they'd been told to memorize them by a maniac with a large gun.

"Do it," snapped Doctor Richard.

Yeah, yeah. Because contraceptives didn't always work, hence the ban on pre-Sorting sex. Yanking the stick from the doctor's hand, I marched to the door indicated as he disappeared behind his paper again. They wanted to know if there was a baby so they could kill it! It made my blood boil. But there certainly wasn't, so no point doing anything but obey.

Returning, I deposited the duly-doused stick on the doctor's desk before he could stop me.

"Pick it up and hold it!" he snarled, as the guards smothered sniggers.

"Oh, sorry, *doctor.* I thought you wanted it back."

Glowering, he consulted his watch and retreated behind his newspaper again. After what must've been about a minute, he reappeared. "Show it to me," he snapped.

I wanted to shove it right under his nose, but I managed to control myself. *You teasing Jon about revenge and then acting this vindictively? Behave, Margo.* I held it out at a considerate distance, instead.

"Good," he said curtly. "Throw it in that bin and get lost."

So that was that. No doubt we'd all be peeing on sticks at our monthly medicals from now on.

"What on earth are you doing?" I asked that night, as Jon went on wriggling around long after the blanket was arranged.

"Just getting ready for Operation Camera Info."

I reached out curiously, then pulled away again as my fingertips touched smooth, bare chest. I didn't dare feel around any more. "Er...how many clothes are you wearing?"

"Relax," he laughed. "I'm wearing my P-Jays and my dressing gown; I've just got rid of the hoodie. Sally-the-nice-guard finds me attractive, have you noticed? I'm going to see if she'll tell me what we need to know."

So that was the plan. Buzz her at night so he could apologize for disturbing her and hopefully direct the conversation to what she'd been doing. While showing a bit of his very nice chest to distract her attention even further from what was coming out of her mouth.

"Don't forget to show off that bandaged wrist," I suggested dryly. "Get those maternal feelings working."

"I won't," he said placidly.

"And for pity's sake don't be too obvious," I added seriously. "Okay, so I've seen her looking at you, but I don't think she's stupid!"

"Neither do I. Trust me, if I can't lead her onto the subject naturally, I'll leave it and try again another night. We *cannot risk* losing that card."

And wasn't *that* the truth.

I woke with a start as Jon crawled over me back into his accustomed spot in the bed; he'd been gone so long I'd fallen asleep waiting.

"Oh my goodness, I'm freezing," he gasped. There follow-ed a great deal more rustling as he got his hoodie on and climbed back under the blankets.

"Feel free to stick your nice warm head on my chest," he whispered at last. "I'm sure it's frostbitten."

"I doubt it is," I said wryly, but I cuddled up to him and obligingly placed my head in the requested position. I found his hands and they *were* icy, so I chaffed them briskly.

"Any joy?" I asked, once his fingers were tucked up to warm between us.

"Plenty." Now his immediate discomfort was easing, the satisfaction in his voice was plain. "In fact, I think I got it all."

I rubbed sleepy eyes and tried to come fully awake. "I'm listening."

"Right. The cameras are rolling at night—and recording—but there's no one watching them. No point, we're all shut up in our dorms. They don't check the footage unless some-thing happens—which is never—nice Sally joked they'd need to find an instruction manual. Apparently what they're watching for in the daytime is people detaching themselves from the group while in transit—or pulling a stunt like yours, earlier."

"Yeah, they noticed that pretty quickly. That's what was worrying me."

"Well, there's no one in the camera room at night, that's definite."

"What about the camera over the parking area?"

"The cameras *all* go to the camera room. Outside, it's the human eyes you need to worry about. Facilities don't tend to get hit very often, but the Resistance have that charming habit of killing pretty much any EuroGov employee they lay their hands on, which makes the guards jumpy. Anyway, you know the score outside. Floodlit yards, floodlit killing zone, all watched."

"Umm. Did you find out if the card will work?"

"Yep," he sounded smug. "I did the indignant boyfriend bit, wanting to know how filthy Finchley was being punished—I think it would've looked more suspicious if I *hadn't* asked. Seems the Captain's put him on extra duty as punishment and the Major's taking the cost of a new card out of his pay. Sounds like they haven't told him how Finchley lost it. But—this is the important bit—it's not too expensive because the Major literally had to take one out of a safe, put it in a card printer and hand it to him."

"They're all the same!" I whispered triumphantly.

"Yes. They're all exactly the same. The Major was pretty peeved with him, even so. Losing a card is a serious offense, apparently. If it had actually been lost—rather than safely destroyed, *as they think*—he'd get the sack, because they'd all have to have new cards. Nice Sally thinks he *should've* been sacked, of course."

"Well, he should be. But if they haven't even told the Major... It won't happen, anyway. Even with the good rates of pay, Facility guards are too hard to find."

"Yeah, well, six month shifts, watching reAssignees come in intact and leave in little bags. I can see why they're lining up for the job."

"Did you find out anything else?"

"No...wait, yes, I know why laptops are forbidden."

"You *what?* That was the next thing I wanted to know!"

"The opportunity was just there. When we were talking about how they can watch stuff on a monitor in the guard-room all night, I said, well, can't you play computer games on your laptops and stuff—I mean, they're paid enough to afford them, surely—and she said they're not allowed them."

"Why?"

"The cameras. The whole security system hinges on the cameras. Laptops—any computers—communicate wire-lessly with each other, right? Well, apparently someone with a computer and the right knowledge could hack into the camera system and mess with the feeds, so security-wise they're a complete no-no."

"But...they wouldn't be able to *tell* you had one, would they?"

He shook his head again. "Sorry, Margo. They can. Apparently a few years back there was a girl from a rather rich family—though not quite rich enough to afford the sort of bribe necessary to save her from failing Sorting—and she wasn't prepared to be parted from her laptop. So she smuggled it in—sealed it in a plastic bag, coated it in chocolate and put a wrapper around it—quite clever. But the moment she switched it on, an alarm went off in the camera room and they searched the whole place until they found it."

My heart sank. So much for a laptop to type my hundred thousand words.

Jon went on, "The system is designed to sense any strange wireless device, you see. AudioPlayers and book-Readers don't have wireless—they're very simple, so they're allowed. But no computers for anyone. Except possibly the Major and the Captain; nice Sally wasn't sure about that."

"Well," I murmured heavily. "That's awkward."

"You were going to get Bane to get a laptop to you, were you?"

"I was hoping."

"Perhaps he could get the wireless parts of it disabled."

"He doesn't know how to do that. I certainly don't. Do you?"

"No. But I'd have thought some of his Resistance friends might know."

"No," I said flatly. "I don't want him getting in their debt. I don't want him having *anything to do* with them. I'll have to think of something else."

"You do need *something*, though, don't you?"

"Yes."

"I bet his friends *could* sort something out."

"Drop it, Jon!" I snapped.

He was quiet for a long moment. "Good night, Margo."

I felt a gentle pressure as his lips touched the top of my head. "Good night, Jon," I whispered guiltily. After a moment I said, "Jon?"

"Umm?"

"Sorry."

"It's all right." He snugged me closer.

"You don't think she'll be suspicious?"

"Nice Sally? Trust me, she was far too busy staring at my chest to remember exactly what she said. She'll just know we talked about how boring it must be being on guard all night and how inadequately Finchley's being punished. Totally innocuous."

"How do you know she was staring at you?"

I felt rather than saw his soundless laugh. "I knew."

We lay without speaking for a few moments, then I realized something. "Jon?"

"Umm?" He sounded sleepy.

"I haven't actually said my prayers yet."

"Neither have I, actually." But the following silence was punctuated by the sound of him drawing a long breath. "Margo?"

"Umm-hmm."

"Can I make a suggestion? As, kind of, your prayer buddy?"

"I'm listening."

"Why don't you stop trying the Act of Acceptance for a bit? Just for...a month, perhaps. Stop flogging an open wound and allow it to start healing. Because...no offense... perseverance clearly isn't working."

I didn't answer. I hated to give up. But...

"Margo? Are you angry?"

"No, I'm not angry. Just thinking. I don't like to stop trying, but...the open wound analogy has some truth in it." I sighed. "All right. It's the thirty-first of March tomorrow. I'll leave it until the thirtieth of April, then I'll try again."

"Good. I know I'm not a priest or spiritual director or psychologist or anything but...I really do think it'll help."

"Nah, admit it, you're just fed up of being used as a giant handkerchief."

The soft peep of my alarm, set on minimum, woke me. Time to amend my letter. I'd brought everything I needed down to Jon's bunk the night before, in the hope I might know what to write and catch the Tuesday post.

In the early morning light streaming through a crack at the end of the curtain, I re-read the most important passage I'd already written to Bane.

I expect you'll be glad to hear I had an unexpectedly wonderful weekend, mostly due to having my absolute favorite meal. I ought to thank the chef and the waiter!

Have you seen any eagles in unexpected places recently? I forgot to mention that in my last letter. They can be quite inflexible in their habits, so sometimes the native crows drive them out and make them roost with gentler birds—you might've spotted one already.

Bane might not know that the symbol of Saint John was an eagle, but if the letter got as far as Father Mark he soon would. It didn't really matter, anyway. Jon had been standing right beside me on the battlements, Bane must've seen him.

I squeezed my second orange segment into the little jar—it was half dried up but there was enough juice—and placed letter and notebook on Jon's chest in lieu of a table.

"Should I stay still?" he yawned.

"Please."

Bane, I don't like asking you this when my short story is so unlikely to win, but if I can't have a novel ready I might as well not have entered. I can't write a novel in two months by hand so I was hoping you might smuggle our laptop to me, but that's not going to work, you understand? I cannot have a laptop, they can detect their wireless and they're absolutely forbidden.

But I have to have something to type on and the only thing I can think of is an antique device from the 1900s called a 'typewriter'. It's a sort of mechanical device for typing text. I'm afraid I don't have any idea where you can find one, let alone one in working order, nor how you can get it to me. I think they're quite big and I'd need paper as well. I'm sorry to be so hopeless and so demanding, but I'll have to leave it all up to your ingenuity.

I re-read what I'd written and chewed the end of the empty fountain pen for a while as the drying lines disappeared from sight.

"Good morning, girls and boy," called nice Sally, opening the door. Light flooded the dorm and everyone began to stir. I dipped the nib again, hesitated one last time and added:

I've acquired the means to move around the compound at night.

* * *

Collecting my letter from home at breakfast, I carried it eagerly back to the dorm.

Dear Margo, thanks for the story, I think it was absolutely perfect and easily the most horrible thing you've ever written in your life. Sue's accepted the story all as requested, so that's fine.

I hope you had a nice weekend, I went bird watching at last and had a great time, I took your little lion with me. I spotted that gorgeous bird and I was a rather naughty bird-watcher because I fed it, but I don't think it did any harm. I saw an eagle near my beautiful bird, which was very unexpected. Any ideas on why the two species would be sharing territory?

Shame about Harriet's hair straightener—I know how much she liked it. The letter before last was the best you've sent me and I'm still re-reading it all the time. I'm getting a lot out of it.

I slid down from my bunk, letter in hand, and climbed in to sit beside Jon. "Okay, this is the important bit." I read the paragraphs to Jon.

"So the story's gone in," he murmured, "he spotted me on the wall with you so he knows I'm here and he's studying the plan."

"That's about it, yes. Looks like he'll understand my eagle reference, anyway."

"So what now?"

"So now I get on with planning this novel, and we wait for Bane to produce something for me to type it on."

"Which he'll get to you how?"

"I've no idea. We'll just have to wait and see."

But I knew. I knew what he'd have to do. But I couldn't say it. Couldn't *suggest* it.

"Exercise," called Watkins, opening the door, so we all got up and filed out. Watkins nodded cheerfully to Jon and me despite his own still slightly swollen lip. Finchley, the second guard, waited in the corridor, but he stood with his head down, not looking at any of us. A large dressing cover-ed one entire cheek.

"Has someone cut himself shaving?" sang out Jane mockingly. Watkins let out an unusually harsh guffaw but Finchley shot me a hate-filled look—me, not Jane—and went back to glowering at the floor.

At Jon's "Huh?" I filled him in.

He snorted. "Or one of the other guards has slugged him one," he muttered.

"D'you think they would?"

"Watkins might've, don't you think? I mean, if he was younger..."

True. Well, it was clear no one felt sorry for Finchley, including me. So he'd got a hurt cheek. He'd live.

I opened my letter on Friday with shaking fingers.

Margo, I have such a lot to tell you. I saw this marvelous vintage machine called a 'typewriter': can you imagine it? Lots of little keys. It doesn't look like it'd be at all efficient, but still, fascinating thing.

My parents are having their usual grand barbeque and grille next Thursday night. They've bought 1 bottle of champagne, would you believe, and 3 bottles of wine. My dad has the 2 barbeques ready and intends to cook 9-11 steaks on each one at once! My mum's polished all 4 garden tables and is worrying whether to seat 6, 7 or eight at each one. And my dad's opened up all 5 of his boxes of wineglasses and discovered the first two have only got 10 and 11 glasses in them respectively, and they're supposed to hold 12 (never 13!), so

158

you'd think the world was ending!

I'm sick of it already and I don't think I shall even go—it won't be the same without you. Now, I know you worry so much, but really, I do think it's for the best. I'm not going to become totally anti-social, I promise. I'll be very careful about that!

Blast, I was going to write more, but my mum is calling me to help clean the patio, joy, joy and more sopping joy! You must write and tell me what you think about this year's barbeque and how you think I can survive it without you by my side!

I re-read the letter over and over. Thursday night. That was the bit that stuck in my mind. And that apparent misspelling; the use of 'grille' instead of 'grill'. But the numbers also drew my eye, that casual mixture of numerals and words. The Marsdens hadn't held a barbeque in their lives. And there was no way they could possibly afford the food and equipment Bane listed. Who could, in Salperton? So it all meant something else. This was too close to math. I took my notepad out, turned to a back page and armed myself with a pencil.

Right. There were five sentences before the numbers started...then the first numeral in each sentence went up in ascending order, with the highest being 5. So say that was the sentence number, the other numerals might be word numbers? Let's try that, then. I quickly jotted words down, my heart seeming to constrict my chest as the message appeared:

have typewriter can you be at grille next Thursday night

17

THE TYPING DEVICE

Now I saw it in black and white, the enormity of what he'd have to do took my breath away. And for what? For the sake of a novel that would never be needed?

Trembling, I climbed down to Jon's bunk and tucked myself between him and the wall.

"What's wrong with you?" he asked, slipping an arm around my shoulders.

"Bane proposes to stroll across the killing zone in the middle of the night and shove a typewriter through the parcel hatch to me."

"I doubt he's going to just walk across. He's not suicidal."

"Okay, so he'll probably crawl along the drainage ditch. But it's almost as dangerous."

"And how exactly did you expect him to deliver your typing device?"

"All right, so I kind of knew! But it's gone far enough. I won't let him do it. I'm not going to win and I'm going to forget the whole thing."

"But what if you do win?" asked Jon, a note of challenge in his voice.

"I'm up against every other aspiring writer in the whole EuroBloc, Jon. I'm not going to win. And I'm not getting Bane killed. Not for this."

"You've got a gift, Margo. The One who gave you that gift intended you to use it. I think you can win. Creative writing, *this* year of all years? I darn near believe you're *going to* win. And I reckon Bane thinks so too or he wouldn't be willing to deliver that typewriter—"

"Bane would do it just to see me, I reckon." Right now, *I'd* do it to see *him.*

"Maybe, but you're avoiding the point. You can win. But winning this thing will be wasted if you don't have that

160

novel ready. Do you just want to let that short story be published, glamorizing Sorting, presenting it oh-so-positively? Don't you want to present the counter-argument?"

"Of course I want to present the counter-argument!"

"Then you need that typewriter thing. Bane's going to bring it to you. All you've got to do is go get it from him. He'll be careful. It's not like he hasn't had experience at that sort of thing."

"Since when has he had to crawl along a two hundred meter ditch with his life depending on not making the slightest sound?"

"Well, not a two hundred meter ditch specifically, but he's been out with his Resistance friends a time or two. It's got to be pretty similar, hasn't it?"

There was a rather long silence, because the constricted lump that was my heart had just lodged itself uncomfortably in my throat.

"You...didn't know about that, did you?" muttered Jon, when the silence stretched on and on.

I swallowed. "Yes, I...think I did. I just didn't want to admit it to myself. He didn't tell me, if that's what you mean."

"How close...do you think he is? To joining them?" asked Jon awkwardly.

I swallowed again. "Close enough. I mean, their priorities aren't the same—Bane's most worried about Sorting and suppression of freedoms while the Resistance don't seem to care about anything other than making the departments into countries again, but still...they break stuff and wind up the EuroGov, so...I'm just praying that...me being sent here... won't tip him over the edge."

"Yeah," said Jon grimly. "What'll you do if he does join?"

"Well, I won't exactly be very happy about it. But he knows what I think of them; he's got to make up his own mind."

"Well, on the same note, are you going to let him bring the typewriter?"

Part of me wished I'd not told Bane that vital fact, that I could now get around at night. But say I could win? How could I ignore such an opportunity? But how could I forgive myself if Bane got killed, and in such an uncertain cause? Still, Jon was right. It wasn't for me to make up Bane's mind about this, either.

"All right," I said heavily. "I'll meet him and get the thing. But I tell you, I'd better win after this!"

"I'll ask the Lord to see to that, shall I?" smiled Jon.

"You do that."

Squeak.

My straining ears caught the faint sound as the night guard opened the hatch and took her hourly glance into the darkened dorm. One o'clock.

Squeak.

The hatch closed again.

"Time to go," breathed Jon.

Thursday night, and my ugly gray jumpsuit already nestled, folded, down the front of my nightie, secured by a belt. I'd been careful to fall down in the dirt of the exercise yard earlier, to avoid any chance of appearing mysteriously dirtied in the morning. In Tuesday's letter I'd told Bane I thought one-thirty was a suitable time to make his escape from the dreaded barbeque. Everything was arranged.

I picked up my dressing gown, took the precious card from inside Jon's pillowcase and transferred it to the pocket.

"I'm your prayer support," whispered Jon. "See you in a bit."

"See you." I slipped from the bunk, putting on my dressing gown and shoes quietly, but without any suggestion of stealth. Walking to the door, I paused in front of the buzzer, then moved on without actually touching it, standing as close to the card reader as I could. After a suitable length of time and making sure to shield it—most especially from the direction of Jane's bunk—I swiped the card and held my breath...

The light flashed green.

I pushed the door open and walked out, saying softly to the non-existent guard, "Thanks, sorry it's so late."

In the washroom, I changed into my jumpsuit, with my sweater underneath. The nightwear I left on top of the toilet tank in the farthest cubicle—there wasn't any real hiding place for it.

A dim light glowed over the stairwell door, allowing the guards to see and the camera to see them. I swiped the card with my head turned away from the camera, much good that'd do, and headed down the dark stairs. My breath misted the air in front of me. That would show up particularly well on the cameras. No matter. If they played the footage back, the game would be up, anyway.

Reaching the door to the parking area, I peeped through the window beside it. This was the really risky bit. The door was in the sight of the tower guards. But since no one could threaten the towers from here, they wouldn't be looking, right? *Lord willing.*

I swiped the card again and opened the door just a crack. Slipping through, I moved smoothly to crouch behind the nearest car. No sudden movements to draw the eye. Peeping up at the towers, I calculated their lines of sight. Right, well, it might not be the most comfortable way to do it, but it was clearly the safest...

Lowering myself flat onto my stomach, I wormed underneath the car and headed for the guardroom, making like a snake. My knees and elbows complained bitterly, but slowly and silently I crawled until I reached the last car. There was the guardroom door, about three meters away.

My groping hand found two small stones. I chucked the first at the door. It made a nice sharp tapping sound. I drew back into the darkness beneath the car and waited.

Nothing.

I pitched the second stone at the door, even harder.

Tap.

Still nothing. Jon and I were both pretty sure there wouldn't be a guard in there at night and it seemed we were right. Or the guard had fallen asleep.

I slid from beneath the car, and glided as smoothly as I could to the door, flattening myself beside it as I swiped the card.

Flash. *Click.*

I eased the door open. No one shouted. Slipping inside, I drew the door shut behind me and stood, ready to let my eyes adjust to the greater darkness. But moonlight streamed in and the room was empty. I let out a shaky breath.

Crossing to the grille, I sat down on the floor below it—it probably wasn't one-thirty yet so it was time to wait. There wasn't much to see in the little room. The grille's armored shutters stood open, only for use in actual emergencies. They glistened with futile oil and ravenous rust. A utilitarian table and chair, both metal. A row of fuse boxes on the wall, their labels so neat and clear I could read them from where I sat.

WALL POWER MAIN it said under a large, solitary lever. WEST TOWERS read a sign above the first fuse boxes, while underneath the labels ran FLOODS—SEARCH—GATES and so on. EAST TOWERS said the second sign. Simply thrilling. Hopefully no fuses would go just now.

To stave off the tension, I started on a rosary. The Joyful Mysteries. I was waiting for my fiancé, after all. But before long a tiny noise came out of the darkness. I dropped my fingers, losing my place, and rose onto my knees to stare through the grille, ears straining.

After a while, it came again. A tiny scuffling, as though a small animal were running along the bottom of the ditch. If it was Bane, then he was inching his way very slowly and quietly indeed. Good. If the guards heard him, he'd die, it was that simple.

The small animal came gradually nearer. Eventually I could hear it breathing, just on the other side of the grille, and it didn't sound like quite such a small animal then.

"Bane?" I breathed.

"Margo?" A head appeared on the other side of the grille like magic. "*Margo!* Curse it, this is the thickest blasted grille I've ever seen! I can't even get my hand through!"

I understood the desperate frustration in his voice. "Hang on, I'll open the post hatch."

It was a simple manual mechanism, secure enough since it was operable only from inside. I eased the lever down, my heart in my mouth—but it didn't let out any ghastly, ear-splitting squeaks, opening silently...

"*Ouch.*"

"Sorry," I whispered. "I think it opens outwards."

"You think and I know."

I tried to get a head into the hatch and found him doing the same, but it was no use. Our heads fitted but our shoulders didn't, and the wall was just too thick. Our lips remained a good twenty centimeters apart.

"*Crud!*" said Bane, as we both pulled away again and thrust our hands in instead, finally making contact.

"*Bane...*" I kissed his hand, clutched it to my cheek, fighting to control my breathing, to ease that lump from my throat. My other hand was being kissed and held with such intensity...for a few moments I really thought I was going to break down and cry.

"Margo, Margo, are you all right?"

"I'm fine. I'm fine. I love you. I've missed you so much..."

"I've missed you more! I've missed you like mad! This flaming wall! I'd like to tear it down with my bare hands..."

"Shhh," I breathed. "Quieter." Bother. Every moment he was here he was in danger. All it took was for one guard to look down and go, *Hey, what's that down there against the wall?*

"Bane, darling, darling Bane," okay, so I did kiss his hand a few more times, "we've got to be quick. It's not safe for you."

"All right, all right, can I have my hand back?" From the soft sounds of moving fabric he was taking off a rucksack and unfastening it—no zips, smart Bane. "Right, here's the thing." He slid a big box into the hatch. It wasn't as heavy as I'd feared, and quietly I placed it on the floor, in the moonlight.

'Art Case' the exterior proclaimed innocently, text and pictures colorfully declaring it to be full of crayons and pastels and drawing pencils. I unlatched it and lifted the lid. Inside lay what looked like a very large, very ugly computer keyboard. A sticking-up bit above the keys looked uncomfortably like a tiny computer screen, and lifting a coil of wire, I found a plug.

I put my head beside the hatch again. "*Bane?* Is it *electric?*"

"Yes, but keep your hair on. I couldn't get you a real typewriter—I'd have had to rob the museum. This thing is much better. It's called a wordProcessor. It remembers a page of text at a time and you can edit it by using those little arrow buttons before printing. But it's not a laptop, it's got no wireless, I promise. And it'll be much easier if you can edit stuff as you go along, won't it?"

I *had* been dreading all the re-typing a typewriter would involve. "It's perfect, then. Bane, I love you! Oh...how much do I owe you?"

"Relax, it wasn't expensive. It's a gift. The computer mender had it on a heap in the darkest, deepest corner of his back room. He was delighted to get anything for it. Anyway, here's the paper, I brought three reams. Will you be able to manage it all now?"

One hundred thousand words, double spaced, plus sheets re-typed in later edits... "I think I'll have to."

"Here we go, then. How are you going to carry it? Do you want the rucksack?"

"Hmm. No. I'll stick it inside my jumpsuit, I think. People will assume I've got in with a guard when this box suddenly appears, but a strange rucksack doesn't fit so well with that scenario."

I wasn't going to be wriggling under those cars, not with this lot. No need to worry Bane with that, though.

"When it's finished, I'll come and get it," Bane told me, as we took each other's hands again.

He'd crawl all that way under the muzzles of those machine guns. Again. For a manuscript. With him there, so close, warm and alive, it didn't seem worth it.

"I wish you'd never sent me that flyer," I muttered.

"What? Why? It's the best chance I've seen in...well, *ever*, to make the world open its eyes about Sorting."

I sighed. "You and Jon seem so sure I'm going to win."

"Look, I read that story: it was utterly revolting, the EGD are going to be falling at your feet. And then you're going to sock the world over the head with the truth. All one hundred thousand words of it. Aren't you?"

I didn't actually know what the one hundred thousand words were going to be yet...except suddenly I did. He'd just said it. The truth. "I'll do my best. That thing's much more than I hoped for, anyway."

"Do you like the packaging?"

"Perfect, Bane. There's two or three boxes like that in the dorm already. The guards won't guess."

"What're you going to do about the other girls?"

"Not worry about it. They're not going to object to something that allows me to write them *more* stories, are they? I'll have to find time to do them a few."

"I s'pose."

"Well, I can't make out with Jon twenty-four hours a day from now until the end of May, can I?"

"You can't *what?*" Bane's outraged splutter was loud in the night quiet.

"Shsss!" I pressed his hands tightly. "Quietly! Don't be a ninny! Um...sorry, though. I didn't phrase that well. I forgot you don't know what's going on in here."

"What is *going on in there?"*

"Nothing you need worry about." I kissed his white knuckles and his hand unclenched slightly. "Here's the short version—the boys are feral, their warden lets them run wild, they tried to make Jon take part in their sick games and he wouldn't, so they tried to kill him—literally kill him. The boys' warden pulled rank and dropped him in with us girls for safekeeping. Of course, most of the girls wanted to get him in bed with them: do you see the problem?"

"Well, he's crazy same way as you, so—the absence of a marriage rite?"

"Exactly. So the only way to avoid Jon falling under suspicion was to have him pair off with *me*. You see? So I climb down and sleep in his bunk each night and everyone is convinced we're at it like bunnies. Whereas we're just sleeping like sardines in a tin. Very chaste sardines. We have a blanket between us and everything."

There was a long silence in which Bane continued to mash my hands and I could almost hear him editing responses in his head.

"Heck, what can I say?" he spat at last. "I don't like it. I downright hate it. And I can see you've got to do it! *Argh*. It's like some sort of nightmare."

"I think that's a bit of an exaggeration."

"Well, *I* don't! You're in there playing happy families with a guy—"

"Your friend."

"Yeah, with *my friend,* who happens to believe all the same stuff as you and is not only more handsome than me but also about ten times nicer! That's a *nightmare!*"

I yanked my hands out of his. "No, that's *offensive.*"

"Margo...?"

"How about I say I find the idea of you out there with Sue a *nightmare*, seeing that her legs are soooo long?"

"That doesn't mean anything!" he flared. "I love you! I'd never look at Sue that way!"

"Well, perhaps *I* don't like you saying I'd look at Jon that way!"

Another long silence, then he groped through the hatch for my hands. "Margo, I'm sorry. You want the truth, I'd doubt me before I doubted *you!* It's not my head that really thinks it's a nightmare, it's my stupider parts. Do you want to slap me?"

"I'd rather kiss you, but they made this hatch too small."

We made do with kissing each other's hands again and I dragged my mind back to practical matters. "Bane, I should ask, if I was to, um, include any true stories in this novel? Do you want me to change your name?"

Bane snorted. "Doesn't seem much point, does there? As soon as I rescue you, we're out of here. What's a million eurons worth of fireworks beside springing a reAssignee?"

"If it wasn't for the precedent, they might care more about the fireworks, actually. They're worth more."

"Not to me." He kissed my hands again. "I am working hard on a plan, you know. I'm not just sitting around catapulting God-bread over walls and putting flyers in the post. I've got a couple of pretty good ideas and now you've got this card...well, I've still got to figure out the towers—"

"Bane—"

"But I'll come and get you, you see if I don't. We'll be off to Africa, we'll get married in a church, just the way you want, we'll have to work like heck, I imagine, but we can have however many kids we like and no one will take them away from us—"

"Bane, listen to me!"

"What?"

"It's about you rescuing me. I've been thinking about it an awful lot, praying about it, thinking, praying, thinking, it's just not as easy as you make it sound."

"I didn't say it was *easy*, I haven't got a *complete* plan yet—"

"Not that. Bane, listen. How do you think I feel about the idea of leaving everyone else behind to die while I sneak off to have a nice life in Africa?"

"Not too happy, knowing you," he said warily. "But I don't see what I can do about it. You are going to come with me, aren't you?"

"Yes, Bane, I am going to go with you—"

"Good, because you had me worried for a moment—"

"...on one condition."

"What! *What?*"

"That... That you rescue all of us."

18

ALL OR NONE

Bane's hands relaxed around mine, he was that shocked. Finally there came the sound of a very long intake of breath...

"Quietly!" I cautioned.

"Are you out of your mind?" he hissed. "Did you just say what I thought you said?"

"Should I say it again in Latin?" I offered. His Latin wasn't half bad, for a nonBeliever.

"No!"

"Esperanto?"

"NO! You want me to rescue *all of you?* Do you have any idea what you're asking?"

"I'm sorry, I know it's rather...um...demanding of me."

"Demanding! *Demanding?* No, *demanding* is when I come for a sleep-over and you drag me out of the guest room early in the morning to attend certain nutty illegal activities that take place in secret rooms! *This* is *insane!*"

"I'm sorry, all right, but the only other option is refuse to be rescued at all and I thought you might prefer this."

"*Prefer* it? You know, one person, you can sneak them out. Somehow I don't think *sneaking* is an option with eighty reAssignees. And what do I *do* with eighty reAssignees? In the highly unlikely event I get them all outside the Facility? What then?"

"Seventy, more like. And I don't know what then. I suppose that has to be part of any plan, doesn't it?"

"Plan, heck, why am I worrying about *what then*. If I can come up with a way to get that far, it will be one of your precious miracles! I don't think I can do it, Margo, and it's crazy even to try!"

"Then don't try. But don't show up and expect me to go with you, because I can't."

"Why *can't* you! Why do you have to die too? What's the *point?*"

"The point is if I abandon the others to save myself—I never will be free. I could live to be a hundred and fifty and I'd never be free. This place would still have me. Can you understand?"

Bane was silent for a moment, then his hands tightened on mine. "*Please*, Margo..."

"I'm sorry," I whispered. So hard to ignore the pleading in his voice.

"Margo, don't you understand? I'm not sure I can rescue just *you*, I'm not sure I've cracked *that* yet. And *this*... I don't think I can do it! Do you understand? I'm not sure I *can!*"

It was my turn to be silent.

"I'm sorry," I said at last. "I can't say anything else. Except... please be careful. Rescuing us...it's not worth you getting hurt."

"Well, that's a matter of opinion, isn't it? Argh, I can't believe you're doing this! It's so very...very...*you!*"

"Well, you did just say you loved me. This is me."

"Hah!" He sighed and set a kiss on my palm. His cheek was rough under my fingers. We really were all grown up now. "I've got something for you."

"Something better than a wordProcessor?"

"Well, I hope you might think so." He pressed a small box into my hand.

I held it in the moonlight to open it. A ring sat inside, three tiny white stones twinkling from within the slender band. "I know this ring," I whispered, moving back to the hatch. "It was my Great-Grandmother's engagement ring. They started making them very simple like this back then so no one would realize what they were, the EuroGov having it in for marriage."

"I hope you don't mind. I know you're supposed to have rings, for marriage, so I went to your mum to ask her what she thought you'd like. I knew I couldn't spend much because I need the money to rescue you—all of you, it seems—but she gave me this. Is that okay? I can find something new if you prefer."

I found his hand and pressed it. "It's perfect, Bane. And

no one will guess what it means, nowadays, so I can even wear it." I handed him the box back and waggled my left hand after it. "Put it on, put it on!"

He took my hand gently. "Which finger?"

"This one." I folded all my other fingers down, leaving my ring finger outstretched.

Bane slid it into place. "Perfect fit...huh, didn't even think about that."

"Well, my mum knew it fitted. I've got something for you too, but I'm afraid it's much more practical." I took my bank card from my pocket and passed it through to him.

"PIN number is 16 12."

"That's my birthday."

"Then you've got no excuse to forget it, have you? There's not exactly a huge sum in there, but it might help. Bane, did you tell my parents you plan to rescue me? Because that's the other problem—"

"No, it *isn't*. They're shutting the Mass center down. Salperton's been hot as anything these last few weeks, pursuivants everywhere, everything's been suspended anyway. Someone else will open a fresh one when things cool off. Father Mark agrees, says it's suicidal to try and keep a center going forever. So they're closing it whether or not I rescue you, okay? It's *not* a problem."

"All right, calm down. You know if you do rescue us, the first place they'll check is our homes. You'll need to warn Jon's parents as well."

"I will. But you know, it's one thing having a daughter who might fail and another when she's actually failed—your parents were going to shut it anyway, so I could come get you, even before Father Peter—" He was quiet for a moment. "Yeah, I was really sorry to hear about that. How'd you find out?"

I swallowed, my hands tightening on his. "We...we had to watch."

"Watch what?"

"The...execution."

"*What?*" Bane was shocked. Truly and genuinely shocked, even after all his dabbling on the fringes of the Resistance. "No *way.*"

"Yes," I said in a low voice.

Bane stretched through the hatch for all he was worth, but couldn't quite reach far enough to get even one arm around me. "Margo," he whispered, cradling my hands instead. "Are you okay?"

"Yeah."

"Margo?"

"Really. It's a slight work in progress, but...I'm all right."

"Yeah. Whose idea was it, making you watch that?"

"Oh, the girls' warden, she's a real sick witch, but never mind about her, Bane. Just concentrate on rescuing us."

"All right. You concentrate on writing your masterpiece."

"I'll do my best."

"*Argh*, I want to give you a big hug."

"I want a big hug. And I want to kiss you."

"Not as much as I want to kiss you!"

"Oh blast, you'd better go, you know. We've been talking for *ages.*"

"Yeah."

But we just went on sitting there, holding hands.

"Bane," I whispered at last. It felt like cutting my heart out with my tongue. "You've got to go. It's too dangerous."

"All right, all right." He kissed his fingertips and pressed them to my lips and I did the same. Then, after only another ten or twenty clasps and kisses of hands, he slipped back into the ditch and that little animal began to inch its way into the distance.

I sat in silence for a long time, waiting until he'd definitely have reached the forestline. Just in case I was caught.

Finally I got up and arranged the heavy reams of paper inside my jumpsuit, picked up the 'art case' in one hand, held the door card in the other and took a good look around the dim little room for anything left behind. Swiping the card, I inched the door open and eyed the parking area. I was pretty much going to have to walk across. Good thing the exercise sacks were gray.

Um...I know your primary concern is my spiritual welfare, Angel Margaret, but perhaps you could have a quick word with the guards' angels so they don't go looking this way?

With that, I walked straight over, not too fast, not too slow. I didn't breathe again until the stairwell door was closed behind me. Then I waited, peeping through the window to see if any sort of chaos erupted behind me. But the search lights stayed off, and the night stillness continued unbroken. I hadn't been seen. *Thank you, Angel Margaret.*

Cautiously, I made my way back up to the dormitory level, changing swiftly in the washroom and re-belting my jumpsuit under my nightie. With my dressing gown tightly tied, I stuffed the paper inside it and returned to the dorm, case in hand.

The next morning, with no attempt at concealment, I sat down at a table near a socket, opened my 'art box' and plugged in the word processing thingie. I'd lain on my bunk for a while, yawning and studying the old manual tucked in the lid, and was now able to peel a wad of paper from a ream and slide it into the correct part of the machine. What I thought was the correct part of the machine.

A cursor flashed invitingly on the dimly glowing screen. I stared at it, searching for a beginning. Bane had shown me what the content was to be... No. First part ten of the Fellest Ewe's Diary. To demonstrate the device's benefits and keep tongues from flapping near the guards.

My fingers had barely begun to tap on the old keys when the curious began to crowd around. Jane soon forced her way to the front. "Is that a laptop, Margo?"

"No, course not, they're not allowed. It's just a word-Processor, for printing stories on. See..." Since I had almost a page, I pressed the print button. The machine obediently sucked in a sheet of paper and began to spit it out again, text emerging line by line—*quietly,* good.

"Huh." Jane stared curiously at the screen and the keys, and apparently concluded it was no more than I said it was. "Where'd you get it?"

"I can hardly talk about that, can I?" I said lightly.

Jane's eyes narrowed, but her sharp tongue was oddly dulled after that, at least when she was talking to me. Not so odd really, if she thought I'd got as friendly as all that with a guard—I probably seemed her best chance of escape. From the way she was prowling and snapping these days, escape plans—or lack thereof—were on her mind. No wonder—only yesterday a special friend of Emily's had been taken from the Old Year. Emily'd been crying as she told us.

Oh yes, I want to get out of here too. Suddenly I really, really do.

When it was almost time for exercise, I unplugged the machine and put the case back up on my clothes' chest.

"D'you think it's going to do the job?" Jon asked me, as I dropped back down and sat beside him.

"Oh yes. I really might get the book written in time, with that." Not that I was going to need it, *surely?* Or was that *please?*

The door opened and Watkins called us out. In the passage Finchley lurked, giving me his usual look of pure loathing. No mere chance that the Menace kept putting those two together at the moment, right? But when Finchley turned to lead the way to the passage door, a gasp rose to my lips.

His dressing had finally disappeared, revealing a pattern of healing cuts. In the shape of a... No joke, someone had carved the full works into his cheek! Finchley's face grew brick red as a tide of whispering swept the passage.

"Look," said Sarah curiously, pointing. "Boy bits."

Finchley's fist clenched and he took a step towards her. I'd sprung between them before I'd even realized what I was doing. His looming presence drove a chill splinter of fear into me. "Don't you dare touch her," I hissed.

Finchley stepped back and hurried to unlock the stairwell door, almost as though afraid to speak to me! Or afraid to be *seen* speaking to me. Resolving afresh to avoid any conceivable possibility of being alone with him, I caught Jon's arm, telling him about Finchley as we traipsed down the stairs.

I paused at the gym door, lowering my voice. "Watkins, what happened to Finchley's *face?*"

Watkins tapped the side of his nose and smiled far less pleasantly than usual. "Looks like a little bird told the Major after all, doesn't it? In you go..."

I went to my assigned exercise machine, but I couldn't

get the Major's twisted justice out of my mind, though it was very hard to feel sorry for Finchley. Jon was on a cycling machine, alternating between grinning like a loon and an expression suitable for a funeral. The more primeval part of me certainly wanted to roll around on the floor pointing and laughing with an evil glee worthy of the Major himself.

But I'm not the Major. He shouldn't have done that to Finchley. He should've just sacked him. *Bwahaha*, but it serves him right... *No.* I am not the Major.

So I prayed for Finchley as I ran on the treadmill, prayed and prayed until that devilish laughter was driven from my mind. *I am not the Major.*

"When are you going to start reading it to me?" asked Jon one night, after I'd spent two weeks typing almost non-stop.

"Soon," I said absently, planning tomorrow's pages in my head. That incident would follow on to that...

"So you keep saying." For these soft, safe ear-to-ear murmurs in the dark, we spoke Latin, and he sounded aggrieved.

I dragged my mind away from the growing pile of printed sheets that nestled in Jon's clothes' chest for greater security and gave him my attention.

"They'll be announcing the winning story in just over a week."

"You're going to read me what you've done before then, aren't you?"

"Yes, I suppose so."

"You don't sound very happy about the idea. Are you afraid it's no good? If things go right, the whole world's going to be reading it."

A little ball of ice formed in my belly. The whole world. *Help me, Lord.*

I managed not to swallow—he'd hear it—and said, as though changing the subject, "You know, not being able to witness used to frustrate me so much. The silence and secrecy. My parents' fake friends—whiter than white, EuroGov-can't-do-anything-wrong types—y'know, like the Marsdens. Well, Mum and Dad try their best to make the friendships genuine, but...I suppose it was the same for you?"

"Oh, yes. Witnessing—now that's a seriously dangerous game. But people do it. But *not* people whose parents run safe houses and Mass centers. I could never admit to my faith in even the tiniest word or gesture."

"Tell me about it—I used to think nothing could be worse."

Jon gave a very faint snort. "Yeah," but his tone was one of self-mockery, "but it's not true, is it? Because if they actually catch you speaking about it..." He shuddered. "Well, they don't just do you for *Personal Practice*, that's for sure. Have to admit turning fifteen cooled my enthusiasm a bit."

"Ugh." I shuddered as well. "Fifteen. I remember fifteen." Nowadays the Rite of Confirmation took place just before you turned sixteen—sixteen being the legal age for execution. Decision time, in no small way.

"Fifteen was a horrible year," Jon agreed. "I was really glad to have Bane as a friend that year, *because* he was a nonBeliever. That probably sounds a bit nuts."

"Hardly. As soon as I became fifteen—knew I had to decide—I could hardly think about anything else."

A year in a mental maelstrom with thoughts of life and death, truth and lies, salvation and damnation, agony and well-being pelting you from every side.

What do I really *believe?*
What my parents have always taught me?
Just because they believe it doesn't make it true.
Just because they *believe it doesn't make it false.*
What's the evidence...for and against?
Do I believe this enough to die *for it?*

Horrible, Jon called it. That was about right.

"My parents were really good about it," I went on, "stepped right back and let me work it out for myself. I'm only surprised Bane didn't find someone more fun to be around after a few months! Though he got worse than me in the end. Because I never did manage to convince him, but *I* was convinced and oh my, was he desperate to change my mind."

"Well, he practiced all the arguments on me first." Jon sounded like he was grinning. "His priorities were pretty clear."

I had to smile too. "He did have them rather smooth. He was still whispering them in my ear when I was about to walk up to the altar for Confirmation. Had to fix my hair band three times because he kept pulling my veil askew to give himself more time! In the end I kind of grabbed it and ran."

But afterwards he'd said, "Well, I tried my best. And look at you glowing..." Picked me up in a big bear hug and spun me around with my feet off the floor... "Seeing you this happy...it's almost worth the risk." Dear, dear Bane.

The risk.

The happy memory slid from my mind and this time I did have to swallow before I could get out, "Do you know..." I hesitated. "Do you know if they actually break many people? At the last minute? Do many people..."

"Apostatize? Make the Divine denial?"

"Umm."

"Some. I can't give you figures, but...people are only human. You must've heard of Father Hart?"

"Father Faintheart, they used to call him. *Six* times, wasn't it, that he Apostatized?"

"Yes," murmured Jon. "Poor Father Hart, they say, had a rather low pain threshold. Every time they got him strapped down on that gurney he'd panic and make the Divine denial. The EuroGov would gloat like mad and let him go. He'd be barely clear of the Facility's shadow when he'd be seized with the most overwhelming remorse for his cowardice. His penitence was always so genuine he'd be absolved at once and would go on with his work. Until the next time he was caught, when it would happen all over again."

"Until the seventh time. When he held firm at last."

"That's what they say. Father Better-Late-Than-Never, some people call him now."

"Yes. Poor man. Uncle Peter knew him, you know," I told Jon. "Said one glimpse of a scalpel and Father Hart's spine would turn to custard, but that he was the most lovely man."

"Knowing Father Peter, he probably thought *Doctor Richard* was a lovely man *really.*"

My stomach churned, ice splinters spreading into the

surrounding tissues. *I don't want to think about this now!* "I think..." my voice came out barely audible. "I think that's an exaggeration."

Jon's shoulders lifted in a shrug. "All right. But you know what I mean."

I kept quiet. All the slow, sick terror that'd been building this last fortnight had been unleashed inside me. My chest was so tight with it, it choked my breathing.

"Margo? Are you all right?"

I couldn't reply. I was too busy breathing nice and slowly and deeply and holding myself together. I was being silly. Or so I told myself, as firmly as possible. *I probably won't even win.*

"You know, there's something I've been wanting to tell you. Um, sort of about Father Peter. Something Father Mark told me. He...seemed to know what he was talking about."

I didn't want to hear about Uncle Peter any more right now, even something Jon thought might make me feel better about it. It was too close, far, far too close to the root of my fear. But I couldn't get out the words to frame my objection and Jon took my lack of response for interest.

"Father Mark said whatever the EuroGov like to tell everyone, no one could stay conscious for a whole dismantling. He said even with minions clamping blood vessels, by halfway through you'd pass out from blood loss and if you took the pain into account as well, then most people would be unconscious well before that. So...Father Peter...well, there's an awful lot he wouldn't actually have felt."

The sequence of dismantling forced itself bloodily into my mind: skin, eyes, tongue... "He felt enough!" I choked. Was I going to be sick, right now? I swallowed hard and lay very still, my eyes pressed closed. I felt and heard Jon draw breath... *"Please be quiet, please, please be quiet."*

There was a long silence.

"Margo, I'm sorry. I thought you'd like to know."

I took several more long breaths and wiped cold sweat from my forehead. "I am glad to know that," I said very collectedly. *I'm fine. I'm just being silly.* "This just wasn't a good time to tell me."

"Why not? What's wrong?" he demanded at once.

"It's late. I'm tired. I'm stressed about this competition and everything." All true. If rather unspecific.

Another silence from Jon. "Well, if you do want to talk about it, I'm here."

Oh, I'm sure we would talk about it, just as soon as I read him my *masterpiece*, but I could put it off a bit longer. But after a few more moments of churning internal turmoil and external quiet, four words escaped me, blurted into his listening ear. "I want to live."

I felt his head jerk slightly, startled. "Who doesn't?"

"No, I really, *really* want to live. I hadn't...hadn't realized how much, until...until I came here. And now more and more, every day, I realize how much I want it. The rest of my life. However long or short, even if it's just some quick martyrdom not far down the line, just...my life. Away from *here*. I want it so much. Is that wrong?"

"Wrong? *No!* It's the people who are stealing our lives who are *wrong!*"

"*If someone takes your cloak, give him your shirt also,*" I muttered. "Jon...why've you been making an Act of Acceptance every night for way longer than I have?"

He sighed. "All right. All right. You're right. I know you're right. I just...when I think of all the people they murder, the lives they take...when I think of them doing that to you...it makes me so *angry.*"

"And *you?* Where's *your* life in all that anger?"

Jon gave a tiny dismissive snort. "Oh, *my* life. My life's been spoken for since before I was born. Most people live expecting a hundred and twenty years; I've only ever expected twenty. I suppose in my mental clock I ought to be at the equivalent of a hundred plus by now."

"And that really works? You're as happy to die now as a centenarian?"

"Oh yes, I'd say so," said Jon, his voice chokingly bitter, "seeing they're so happy to die they're having us chopped up so they don't have to! It doesn't work *at all*. I want to live just as much as you do and yes, it bothers me too. I just don't like to hear *you* say it." His voice went very soft. "I want you to live, y'see."

"Well..." I said quickly, then stopped, a shaft of mental lightning illuminating my brain. "Look, we're both being silly! Think of Our Lord's example! What did *He* do when faced with death?"

"He tried to avoid it," said Jon, brightening. "It was only when he realized it was meant to be that he accepted it."

"So perhaps Bane will come up with something, and we'll escape. Because if we don't *try* to escape, that's like sitting back and allowing evil to trundle on its way un-impeded!"

My heart pounded with sheer relief. The knot of uncertainty at which I'd been teasing for weeks was all of a sudden completely untangled. "I'm going to do my utmost to get us all out of here and if I get shot halfway up the bank *that's* where the acceptance has to come in! Difficult as it might be at such a frustrating moment!"

"I still can't believe Bane agreed to rescue everyone."

"He agreed to *try*," I said, more soberly. "It's a tall order. I wouldn't pin too many hopes on it, if I were you."

"Me? I'm not pinning any hopes, Margo. You'll have to leave *me* behind, you know that, right?"

A hot bubble of anger surged up in my chest and I thumped him so hard there was an audible smack. He flinched, in shock or pain, I couldn't tell.

"We're not leaving you behind! You'll be going with us, if we go anywhere!"

"Ouch. If you say so. Seeing I'm not sure I'd dare argue with you. I daresay Bane will take a more sensible view," he added under his breath.

My fist clenched again, then I let out a long breath, my fingers uncurling. "I'm sorry. I'm not mad at *you*, I'm mad at *them*. Did I hurt you?"

"I'll live. Shame Bane's not here. We could all be plain furious together." But his arm tightened around me slightly and he rested his chin on the top of my head.

Bane. *Oh, how I wish you were here. I want to talk to you, Bane. I never feel so afraid when I'm with you. No doubt my parents would say that wasn't an advantage, but it would be, just now.*

"Margo? You all right? What're you thinking?"

Cruel to say I was wishing he was someone else. "Just thinking. Everything's so crazy at the moment. But we'll get through it. One way. Or another."

"I'd rather it was *one way*, for you." His voice had gone soft again. "Out of here and away." He rolled up onto his elbow, letting my head slide to rest in the nook of his arm, and his fingers traced my cheeks, my brow, the slope of my nose. "Let me worry about the *another*."

My body felt oddly hot as his bulk hovered over me in the dark.

"I would have you safe..." he murmured, and his fingers moved to caress my tingling lips...

19

100,000 WORDS OF TRUTH

I lay rigid, my mind skittering wildly—shove him away? Slap him? Too noisy, and lingering guilt from my last blow stayed my hand. What were the right words for this?

No words. I raised my hand and slipped it over my mouth, so his fingers brushed the cool metal of my ring. About which he'd congratulated me, with that disturbing touch of hesitation...

He twisted away, throwing himself into his cramped half of the bunk, putting his back to me. His whisper was hoarse and tormented. "Think... Think I'll sleep this way tonight. Nothing...nothing personal."

But it was. It was everything personal. Too personal. That was just the problem.

I turned onto my side, putting my back to him as well, but I offered a quiet, "Night, Jon," over my shoulder. Because somehow I couldn't feel angry with him. I lay with my cheek for once nestling on a pillow, which was soft, but not as comfortable as I remembered, for all that. Lay staring into the darkness.

Blast. Blast. *Blast.* I'd been afraid of this. Ever since Jon gave me that way-too-convincing kiss. Ever since then the fear had been raising its ugly head in the back of my mind. That my fiancé's friend might be on the way to falling in love with me.

Yet I'd wanted to put no false distance between us—in truth, in the turmoil of these last few weeks I'd needed his support too much to draw right away from him, but I'd tried...I'd tried. Tried to ensure no too-warm smile infected my tone, that no too-warm words were spoken, that I gave out nothing misleading in tiniest word or touch. Not enough, apparently. Or *too late.* Or *never any hope,* in our forced intimacy.

Blast.

Neither of us mentioned what'd happened the following morning, but we slept back-to-back from then on. I missed the warm comfort of his arms, but if it'd come to mean something more—or different—to him, it wasn't fair to continue. Perhaps it'd never been fair. Perhaps I'd just been too selfish and short-sighted to see that.

I tried to channel all my fears, all my vague self-recriminations, all my doubts and hopes and struggles, into my writing. That was what a writer was supposed to do with such things, wasn't it?

Not sure how well it actually worked in real life.

Whether or not I was managing to stuff in my cloud of inner demons—the real, the imaginary and the plain paranoid—the book was progressing very well. I'd worked out the average word count for each page—I'd managed the addition myself with a paper and pencil and got Jon to do the division—and I knew I was about two-thirds of the way through.

I stared at the flashing cursor and rested my head in my hands, rubbing my temples. Tried unsuccessfully to banish the ceaseless mantra from my head.

What if I actually need this thing? *You won't, you won't win.*

What if I do win? *Then you'll have the book ready.*

But if I actually *need* it? *You won't.*

A young man was walking up the garden path with a backpack over his shoulder. I sprang away from the window and raced down the stairs as the doorbell rang.

"Are you getting that, Margo?"

"Yes, Mum." English, of course. Just in case it wasn't the new priest, and he had his ear to the door.

I tried not to throw myself across the hall. What would he be like? Father Clive had been such a dour fellow—though of course I was very sorry when he was caught. Uncle Peter would be glad of the help, whatever.

Taking the key from the peg on the wall, I put it into the deadlock and turned it; opened the door.

"Hello..." My greeting trailed off and reflexively, I shut the door part way, peering warily through the narrow crack.

It was an assassin on the doormat, surely? A face like a hatchet...empty eyes staring at me.

"Is this the Verralls' house?"

My heart lurched in panic—should I slam the door shut? I tried to push the sudden terror away and think. You're fourteen, Margo, stop acting like a silly little girl! If the government found out about us they wouldn't send a hired killer and who else would want to?

"Why do you want to know?"

The corners of his eyes crinkled and he smiled. And suddenly he was just a nice young man, bemused by my behavior. "I'll take that as a yes. I'm your Cousin Mark."

The wave of relief was so great it almost wiped away my embarrassment. He was the new priest! Or...he said he was. I took a moment to make sure I had the security phrase right.

"I hope your journey was really most expeditious?" And wasn't that something no one was going to say by accident!

"It was the most pleasant of trips, except for the part where a wheel fell off the train."

It was him! Phew!

Belatedly, I thought of the neighbors. I managed to step forward and give him a cautious hug. My stupid heart was still pounding. "It's so lovely to meet you at last, Cousin Mark," I said, nice and clearly. "I'm Margaret. Come in."

He followed me into the hall and closed the door behind him.

"Was it a long journey?" I asked at once, just to test his Latin. The government still taught their agents mostly from Classical Latin textbooks and the different pronunciation tended to linger.

"From Vatican State." His Latin was as good as mine. A last knot of tension eased from my shoulders. "But it went pretty smoothly." He was looking around with that flat, emotionless look again. It sent shudders up my spine.

"Please smile when you meet my parents!" I blurted. "You look like a hit man or something!" I clapped a hand to my mouth, my cheeks burning. *"I'm sorry, that was so rude!"*

But his momentary frown of puzzlement was gone, no trace of surprise or offense taking its place. He just looked sad. "No, that was honest," he said quietly. "I'm glad you told me. Time someone did," he added, half under his breath. Did people have a habit of slamming doors in his face, by any chance?

"Who is it, Margo?" called Mum.

"It's Father Mark." I led my new 'cousin' quickly into the kitchen and yes, he was smiling as he shook hands with my mum.

She beamed back, seeing just a friendly young priest. "Cup of tea?" she offered.

"That would be lovely," he said, with most un-assassin-like enthusiasm. "All they drink in Vatican State is coffee the consistency of tar. Italian peninsula, you see."

"You must be glad to be home," said Mum brightly—and promptly winced.

Oh, Mum! You know what coming back means—you know what's going to happen to him sooner or later!

Father Mark's smile faded a little...but then it returned. "Yes," he said, "In a way, I am."

I pressed print, waited for the page about the arrival of 'Father X' to emerge, then packed up the 'art case' and went back to my bunk. Shoving the case up onto my own bed, I climbed into Jon's bunk recess and sat beside him, a wad of pages in my hand. "Hi, Margo."

The words were familiar, his tone normal, but it couldn't hide how subdued he was. Had been, ever since... "Hi, Jon."

I took the other pages out of his chest and put them together with the new ones. His head tilted towards the rustling sounds, but he said nothing. He'd stopped asking me to read the novel to him. His guilty conscience seemed to have blotted out the recollection that I'd been just as reluctant *before.* Now he thought I wouldn't read it to him *because of.*

It'd been a bit of a dilemma for me, over the last few days. Once I read it to him, he'd understand why I hadn't wanted to read it to him. But until I did, he was putting all the worst interpretations on my reticence and I'd had enough of his silent misery. The winner would be announced the day after tomorrow, and I had said I'd read it to him before then.

"Are you busy, Jon?"

"Me?" As all too often, his hands were empty, his sightless eyes gazing into space. "No."

"Would you like to hear a bit of this book of mine, then?"

He looked startled, then so pleased that whatever arguments might follow, right now, I was glad I'd offered. Sitting up straight, he all but pricked up his ears. "Fire away, please do."

"Okay. There's no title yet. Right. Chapter one. Here goes." I took one last look around to check no one else was within hearing, then began to read.

"I am born. This seeming too obvious and excellent a beginning to be left forever as the prerogative of a certain Mr. Dickens, I therefore reclaim it for the use of the less illustrious. So. I am born.

"This event, or so I have been reliably informed, took place as unremarkably as anything so unique can, in the maternity ward of a general hospital surrounded by the last falling leaves of autumn. Three of us were born that night, and we were all examined by the doctor on duty and pronounced Normal. Swift on the heels of this permission to live came the permission for my happy parents to take me home.

"Oblivious to the fatal flaw nestling in my unformed mind, they did so. For at that point in my life, I was normal *enough* and for the first fourteen days, normal described everything about my existence. There was nothing unusual about me. Nothing unusual happened to me. I was normal.

"I was two weeks old when something happened that would mean I was never normal again. One day my parents handed me to a man and this man asked them if they rejected evil, if they rejected all its works, if they rejected all its empty promises. They said they did, and he asked them if they would raise me in the true faith, and they said they would. Then he anointed me with a very special oil, and he poured water on my forehead and traced a cross there, and he spoke the words that would change my entire life.

"'Margaret Elizabeth Verrall, ego te baptizo in nomine Patris, et Filii, et Spiritus Sancti.'" *I baptize you in the name of the Father and of the Son and of the Holy Spirit.*

Although we weren't touching, I felt Jon stiffen beside me. His face turned towards me, wiped clean of its prior enjoyment. "Margo...this isn't a novel. Is it."

"Well..." I took a deep breath. "No, not exactly. But if they publish it, well, they won't know that until it's too late, will they?"

"I'm not worried about you being *disqualified!* You know, I don't think I want you to win after all!"

"I thought you were my prayer support. I thought you'd been praying for it for weeks."

"Yes, and now I wish I hadn't been! You've used me!"

"Oh, come off it!" I objected. "I think that's putting it a bit strongly. You were the one who insisted I should carry on with this! That it was worth letting Bane risk his life!"

"But not yours!"

"Some friend *you* are!"

Jon made an impatient gesture. "Bane's going to keep pushing it until he gets it, you tell me I'm wrong! Doesn't make much difference if it's outside the Facility walls or out with the Resistance, except the first is a better cause, in my opinion."

"And *me?* What did you *think* they were going to do if I got this thing published and was still sitting here when I went public about it? Novel or autobiography, it's not going to make the blindest bit of difference in the end!"

"No, it's going to make all the difference in the world, *at the end!* You can't be serious about this!"

"I'm deadly serious, Jon. It's almost finished and I haven't got time to write anything else."

"Then we'll just have to hope you don't win."

"*No*, we'll just have to hope Bane comes up with a plan, is all."

"You told me *not to get my hopes up!* Margo, this changes everything. If you win, you must write to Bane at once and tell him he's to rescue you—just you! Tell him he's to get you out and you can worry about helping the rest of us once you're safe."

"Jon, I love Bane to bits, but do you really think he's going to put his head back into this noose for a load of people he doesn't know once he has me safe?"

"Depends how persuasive you are."

"No, it doesn't. I was as persuasive as I could be before, but if it weren't for the fact my being in here is one heck of a chunk of leverage, he wouldn't have agreed, and I don't think I can blame him! I told him, all or none. What do I say when we're sitting safely outside? Get them out or I'll sulk? He'll say, fine, you can sulk all the way to Africa, but let's get going."

Jon made an exasperated noise. "If you're that set on saving us all, tell him you won't marry him until we're safe."

"No. I do my best to do the right thing, Jon, but I'm not sure I could. You said it yourself, if Bane stays around here, he's going to get himself killed. Getting him somewhere safe, in one piece, is very high on my list of priorities. Being on the inside of these walls isn't just leverage on Bane, you know."

"I think you underestimate yourself! Just get him to get you out!"

"No. *I* think you overestimate me."

Jon put his head in his hands as though actually contemplating tearing his beautiful russet hair out. "Then I'm sorry, but I hope to God you don't win. Because this escape thing is far too slender a straw to hang on to and the alternative is too ghastly to contemplate."

The alternative was something I was trying not to contemplate at all. Since Jon looked as though he was considering elaborating on just this theme, I carefully replaced the manuscript in his clothes' chest and took my 'art case' back to the table.

The thirtieth of April dawned clear and blue, a chilly morning quickly warming under the energetic rays of the sun. The winning story was to be announced in a special program live on both EuroRay and EuroVee One at seven in the evening, when it would be read out to the world. We had no television, so we'd have to make do with EuroRay.

The day continued hot and bright. Jon fidgeted incessantly. I struggled to write, gave up on the book, wrote a substandard installment of the Fellest Ewe and finally went to lie on my bed and try to pray, except I wasn't too sure what I wanted to pray *for*. I fell back on *your will, Lord* and when my spinning head felt ready to explode, took pity on Jon's obviously equally troubled state of mind and went down to his bunk to read aloud.

What if I'd won? What if I *hadn't?*

I don't think Jon was really listening, either. He looked as grim as I'd ever seen him.

"You still up for hearing the postSort Comp results?" I asked Rebecca, as we walked back up the stairs after supper.

"Yeah, why not," she said, and when we got back to the dorm she took her little radio out and began to fiddle around, setting it up. Our signal was rubbish out here, so we didn't listen as much as we might've done. The static drove Jon crazy.

"And whose name will they announce if your story does win?" Jon asked me softly.

"Well, Sue's if they read from the entry information, but mine if they read from the manuscript," I murmured back. "Bane typed it up with my name on the first sheet."

"Right."

Then the EuroBloc anthem was playing as the program began. No one showed the slightest inclination to stand. The presenters came on, babbling tantalizingly for some time, all in Esperanto, of course, trying to build excitement and whip up tension. It was wasted on me. I was already so tense, the slightest knock and I would go off like an antique alarm clock.

"And now, we have here with us from the EGD, Doctor Victor Renquez. Doctor Renquez, I believe you are holding the winning manuscript?"

"Indeed I am, Steve. I have here in my hand the actual, original manuscript of the winning short story and in just a moment more, I shall read it to you all."

"Is it good, Doctor Renquez? What's your opinion?"

"Oh, I think it's good, very good indeed. The judges voted almost unanimously and this was certainly the one that had my vote. Quite an unusual entry. A real taboo-breaker."

"So it's about a rather unusual subject, I take it?"

"It is indeed. One of those things no one talks about. Though this story calls the very reasons for that silence into question. I'm actually not sure if I've ever read anything quite like it."

"So it's original?"

"Oh yes, most definitely original."

"Well, then, Doctor Renquez, perhaps you should put us all out of our misery."

"As you wish, Steve." The ostentatious rustling of pages sounded even over our crackly reception. "Right then. The winner of the Eighty-Third postSort competition."

My mouth had gone so dry I was having trouble swallowing. I gripped Jon's hand under the table and struggled to maintain an expression of only mild interest.

"The winning short story is...*The Thousand and One Lives of Annabel Salford.*"

My heart dropped away, down, down to my toes and a wave of ice-cold fear swept up to my throat, even as a dizzy, unreal sense of triumph enveloped me. I won! I *won*. And I knew in that moment I hadn't really believed it could happen and all my brave words to Jon weren't worth the paper they were written on.

"Are you sitting comfortably, everyone? Then I shall begin. *The Thousand and One Lives of Annabel Salford*, by Susan Crofton."

20

THE POSTSORT NOVEL

Such a daze of terror and triumph gripped me that it took a moment to register. Sue's name? How could he be reading Sue's name from the *manuscript?* Jon gave my hand a questioning squeeze.

Doctor Renquez was beginning to read my story out, but I didn't want to hear it. Bad enough everyone else would have to. I slipped away to lie on my bunk and think.

Susan Crofton. If Doctor Renquez actually *was* reading from the manuscript—and there was every reason to suppose so, when the program was being televised—then Sue's name must be on it.

"Margo?" Jon had followed me. I pulled my legs in so he could climb up and sit beside me. "Has this Sue done what I think she's done? Or could it be...the EGD?"

Planning to use my story for its propaganda value while quietly disposing of its naughty author...

"Well... The EGD are mostly real fanatics, aren't they? I don't think they'd be willing to hold up a reAssignee's work as the winner, however useful it seemed. I really think it must've been either Bane or Sue."

"Bane? You think?"

"He *might* have reasoned that my name anywhere at this stage would put the publication of that all-important novel at risk. But he would've told me, y'see." My mind skipped back over the contents of the last month's letters. No. There'd been nothing that might mean, *by the way, I took the deception a little further than you wanted, sorry but tough because I think it's best.* "And he hasn't. So, yeah, it was Sue."

I think I'd known from the moment I heard it. She'd read the story and like Jon and Bane she'd thought it stood a chance of winning. So she'd stolen it. Re-typed the cover page with her name.

"Why'd she do it? Revenge on you, for managing to hang on to Bane even from inside the Facility? Caroline seemed to think she fancies him something awful."

"Well...yeah, she always has, rather. But it could've been simple greed," I said bluntly. "Even the most mediocre novel published as a postSort Comp prizewinner will sell enough copies to make one comfortable for life. Comfortable by Salperton standards, anyway."

Jon raised his eyebrows bleakly, this time. "A tempting dish of money and fame, with a garnish of revenge?"

"Maybe. *No*, that's not fair." I rubbed my temples. My head was starting to ache. "We don't *know* that. What if *she* did it to make sure my book got published?"

Jon raised his eyebrows for a third time, skepticism all over his face.

"*Gah*," I waved a hand in frustration. "We *can't* know, Jon! I'll give Sue the benefit of the doubt because she's my friend, but I'll also ensure there's absolutely no way she could stop me proving my authorship of the book. Because I'm not stupid. I just hope Bane stops and uses his head before trying to skin her with his tongue."

"Whatever you want to say about 'benefit of the doubt,'" said Jon, the triumph of the moment still illuminating his unseeing eyes, "I'm sure this must hurt. But I rather think it's the best thing that could've happened, you know!" Then the happiness slid from his face. Ah yes. He'd just remembered he'd no longer wanted me to win.

"From the point of view of that blasted book, anyway," he went on grimly. "The worst thing that could've happened in pretty much every other respect."

Yes...my heart gave a happy-fraid lurch. It seemed safe to assume my name wasn't mentioned anywhere. Had it really been high-mindedness and concern for Sue that made me insist Bane typed my name on the manuscript? Or had my subconscious been laying a little safeguard? A safeguard unwittingly eliminated by Sue. The Lord always brought good out of evil. It was one of the reasons why, in the end, evil could never win.

Assuming I could get the novel manuscript to the

publisher without Sue seeing it and panicking, they'd publish it without the slightest suspicion. Perhaps it did take a rather different view of Sorting, but...

"You *do* think they'll publish it?"

"Oh, yes. Positive. It's just fiction, isn't it? Fiction made up by an eighteen-year-old New Adult who's never been near a Facility in her life. Just a work of the imagination. With an exciting sub-plot about the Underground. With whom she obviously hasn't the least connection or she wouldn't dare to write about it! The EGD may be rather less thrilled with the novel than with the short story, but they won't actually stop it being published. After all, there isn't the slightest reason for anyone to take it seriously, is there?"

"Except, once it's safely published, you're going to give them one, aren't you?"

"Yes. That's been the plan all along, remember?"

Jon's lip turned down unhappily, then he brightened. "I suppose it's too much to hope Sue has a novel lined up already?"

"Hand on my heart, *I* didn't think I was going to win. When would she have written one, anyway? She's been in school all day. And she's certainly never written anything longer than a short story before, or she's kept very quiet about it. And without meaning to be rude, I honestly don't think she'd keep quiet. So she needs mine."

Jon looked disappointed, but before he could speak Rebecca's voice rose above the crackling speech from the radio. "Ugh, this is *horrible!* I'm not listening to this!" And she spun the tuning knob until she found some staticky music. A few people who clearly hadn't yet understood where the story was going looked disappointed, but soon got up to dance.

I went to join them, my arms lifting, spinning in a slow circle. I had some thanks to express. Surely among my incredibly mixed feelings I could find some thanks? Appeal there was no problem with. A really, really big appeal. *Strength, Lord? Give me strength to see this through!*

By the time everyone got fed up with the ghastly racket and Rebecca put the radio away again, I'd danced into stillness and stood by the window, feeling eased and uplifted, as I usually did after that mode of prayer, but... *Bane, I miss you so much.*

Pushing away painfully happy memories, I fetched my 'art case' and began to type. If I wanted two weeks to polish and edit, with all the necessary re-typing, then I had just two weeks to finish it. I'd no time to waste.

That night, I lay on my back, staring up into the darkness. Jon had lain awake for some time, clearly almost as troubled by the competition result as I was. But he slept at last, his breathing deep and even beside me.

The thirtieth of April. The result wasn't the only reason I'd been dreading this day. Time to try the Act of Acceptance again. *No.* Not time to *try* it. Time to make up my mind to do it or not do it. And if to do it, then to simply...do it.

I just sort of contemplated the prayer for some time. I wasn't being paranoid now—*if only*—the fear had become all too rational. But unless I actually meant to chicken out and not send the manuscript in, the worst might happen whether I said the prayer or not.

In a strange way that actually made it easier. I no longer felt I'd risk inviting it because I'd already done that, in every word and line and paragraph of my book.

My terror still lurked, undiminished. Grown. An appalling monster of fear, much larger than Bane's dragon. Would I *really* send it in? *Could* I?

No, I must admit no doubts into the process. I *had* to send it in. My fear must not be allowed the upper hand or it would run away with my spine and I would turn to custard like poor Father Faintheart. Even Father Faintheart beat you, I told the fear, and I will too. And to give the fear the finger, I decided I *would* say the Act of Acceptance.

And did.

Friday morning. *Early* Friday morning. I smothered a yawn and straightened my letter in front of me. I had a little bit to add.

*Dear Sue. Wow! I hope you were as delighted
with the result of that competition as I was. I was
absolutely flabbergasted. Thank you so much for
keeping me informed about it, and everything else
you've done!*

*It was only yesterday I appreciated just <u>how</u>
generous you've been and I'm so happy for you. I
can't wait to see the novel out with your name on
it and I bet you can't either! I can't say thank you
enough, but you really shouldn't have, you know, I'd
hate for you to get into trouble! Still, you've won!*

*My own little project is coming on very nicely
and will be all finished in the next few weeks, so
please don't worry about that. Bane can keep you
posted. I bet you'll be having some sort of party to
celebrate, your parents must be thrilled! I imagine
the school is pretty delighted as well. Anyway, I've
got to go, congrats again!*

"Well?" asked Jon, emerging from his bunk bright-eyed
and bushy-tailed. Autumn-haired and fully-dressed, anyway.

"Well, I've given her the benefit of the doubt. Which
conveniently happens to be the sort of thing I need to say to
make sure she'll take my novel without getting suspicious.
And also feels a lot like lying through my teeth, if I'm truthful. Listen..." I read him the offending missive.

"Well," Jon was grinning by the time I'd finished. "That's
quite some benefit you've got going there."

"Oh, shut up."

"That's it! We put the log swing here and a rope there..."
*The doorbell rang. Bit late for visitors, wasn't it? I hastily
began marking my new innovation onto Bane's and my
plan—before I could forget!—but heard Mum heading along*

the hall. Okay, no need to get up then...

"We'll need a bit of chain for this bit—" I broke off—Bane's expression as he stared at the front window made my stomach turn over. What...? Colored lights bouncing off the room walls... Blue and red. Uh oh...

We reached the doorway together just as Mum opened the front door. Police. Not pursuivants, but... O Lord protect us, what did they want? My hand found Bane's behind my back; we held tight.

"Mrs. Verrall?" said the policewoman. She was using one of those gentle, gentle voices, and her male partner was standing there looking like he'd much rather be storming a Resistance hideout, alone, with a toy gun. Oh no...

"Yes, can I help you?"

"Mrs. Verrall, I'm afraid we have some very bad news. Is there...someone with you?" The policewoman's eyes found me and Bane; moved on. So bad fifteen-year-olds weren't enough? But Dad was coming down the stairs...

When Dad reached Mum's shoulder, the policeman held out a small object on his palm. "Is this the RegCube of your son's vehicle?"

Mum snatched it, looked closely—it was already open. Only the side of her face was visible, but I saw her go white—the blood drained from my own face.

Kyle.

He'd come to my room earlier to chat—I'd confided to him my intention to marry Bane for about the thousandth time—he'd smiled and eventually hugged me and said, "I love you, little sis." And I'd hugged him back and said, "Love you too, big bro." And after a moment, added, "I'm really going to miss you when you do leave." And he'd smiled sadly and kissed the top of my head. "I'm late, I'm supposed to be meeting Eliot in Westen," he'd said, and off he'd gone in the old banger he'd scrimped and saved so hard for.

"Where did you...?" asked Mum, in a thin voice. The policewoman opened her mouth to reply, but Mum took a step back, clutching the opened cube defensively and shaking her head as though to ward off the answer. "No, no, I see, it's fallen off." Her voice was shaking too.

She showed the cube to Dad. "Look, George...look, Kyle's

RegCube's fallen off. They've brought it back... Sorry about that, officer... He'll...he'll put it back on, soon as he gets back. Soon as he..." Her voice broke, she clasped the indestructible cube to her chest and closed her glistening eyes.

"What...what happened?" Dad asked, his voice low and strained.

"He was going too fast. The car hit a tree. The...the tank exploded. I'm so sorry, Mr. Verrall, Mrs. Verrall."

He didn't need to say any more. When a hydrogen tank went up, there was nothing left but ash. And you can't DNA test ash—no way to tell if it's human...or pork. By far the safest way to fake one's death. The safest for those one left behind. There was only one more thing Kyle could do to protect us—I realized that now, too late.

"If it's any comfort at all, it was so quick, he must have scarcely felt a thing," the policewoman was saying, still in that gentle, gentle voice. I could hardly understand her words. Everything was numb. Kyle was gone. We would never see him again. Never know when he died. Or where. Or how. It was the same as if he was actually dead.

I broke from my paralysis at last and turned, clung to Bane, shaking.

I thought we'd get to say goodbye! I thought we'd know you were going. Kyle, how could you do this?

But even in my anger and grief I knew why. Because our shock, our pain—genuine, unfaked—was the best protection he could give us.

21

SIMPLE TRUTH

Two weeks, gone in a flash—there I was, taking the pile of manuscript pages out of Jon's clothes' chest and placing it on top of the sheets on my lap, my heart pounding ridiculously hard.

"Are you all right?" asked Jon, wrestling with the knots that bound his stick together.

He really *was* an emotional thermometer, wasn't he?

"I'm fine." But my voice was slightly strangled. I took the stick from him and it came apart at once. Definitely time to be rebound. I started picking at the knots myself and tried to speak casually. "I've...finished it."

"Congratulations," said Jon flatly, and was silent for a long moment. "It...really is too late for you to write something else, isn't it?"

"You know it is, Jon."

"Yeah. But why *did* you decide to write...*that?* It's supposed to be a novel."

"Yes, but novels are made up. And when I was trying to think what to write—and couldn't—Bane said I should sock the world over the head with a hundred thousand words of the truth. This is the only truth that is truly mine to tell. And if truth can't change the world's mind then nothing can."

Jon found the pile of pages and patted it. "No pressure, little book!"

"*Ha ha.*" But his flash of humor was welcome. "Look, I'm not saying one little book's going to change the world. But if it changes even one person's mind about Sorting it's a start, isn't it?"

"I hope it might do more than that, *considering*," said Jon vehemently. After a moment, he added more calmly, "Have you arranged to give it to Bane yet?"

"Not yet. I need to do some more work to it still, but

then...I want to get it to him in good time."

More importantly, get it out of my keeping before I chucked it down the trash hatch in a fit of terror. Not that Bane's keeping was likely to be much safer, in the circumstances. Perhaps he wouldn't read it. Hah, fat chance of that. He'd read everything I'd ever written, 'til I came here.

I seemed to be tearing headlong down a path to destruction, but how could I *stop?*

"And this is the simple truth. I am Margaret. I am just like you. If I were not, you would not be going to kill me, for I would be no use to you. But I am, and so you are. May God have mercy on you all.

"Er...the end," I added.

"Perfect," exclaimed Jon, fists clenching in triumph. His face fell again. "Or it would be..."

"It either is or it isn't. Now let's for pity's sake be positive or we'll go out of our minds! I know *I* will! The book is going in and we are getting out. Right?"

Jon looked away. "Right. Well, good luck tonight." *I hope Bane can talk you out of this*, hung in the air unsaid.

"Thanks," I said, ignoring the unsaid, and busied myself placing several sheets of paper all around the manuscript and binding it up with string. Part of me was busy going Bane, Bane, Bane, yay! Another part, Bane and machine guns, no, no no! And yet another, Bane and manuscript, uh oh. Could be an interesting night.

"Wait," said Jon suddenly. "Don't wrap it up yet. You've still got some re-typing to do."

"No, it's all done..."

"No, it's not. There's a little bit of truth missing, isn't there?" I knew what he was going to say. He'd heard the whole book now and I'd wondered how long it would take him to pick up on it. "*I'm* in that book," he went on. "And it's all in there, how I got almost killed, and put in here, and dragged off again and brought back, all of it except that I'm in the Underground too. Why not that?"

"Well, doh. If we don't get away..." I paused to clear my throat, the two sides of which were trying to stick themselves together. "If we don't get away, there's no point dumping you in it as well."

"Well, think again. They can't blame me for it being in there, if that's what you're worrying about. So they'll only dismantle me early and they might not even do that, with my scarcity value. So get typing, please."

"Your parents will have to go underground, like mine," I warned him. Assuming I'd interpreted my letters correctly, my parents planned to do so just before I went public about the book or just before we escaped, whichever happened sooner.

"You know Bane's been in touch with them already," replied Jon. "They've already closed the safe house, and if the escape comes off I reckon underground will be the safest place for them. Entire Facilities of reAssignees do not escape. Individual reAssignees don't even escape. The Euro-Gov will be very cheesed off."

"All right, all right," I sighed, unwrapping the manuscript. Taking a few typed pages out of his chest, I found a page, swapped it, found another couple, swapped those, and straightened the pile all up again. I took the rejected pages and put them safely down the trash hatch.

"All done," I told him.

"Really?" His startled tone made me grin.

"Yes, really. Do you want to hear?"

"Yes, please. Seems you know me too well."

"Well. I had to try, didn't I?"

With the precious manuscript secured inside my jump-suit and the 'art case' slung across my back, I crawled slowly, smoothly, down the side of the row of cars. With time to plan how to carry the bulkiest item and to arrange a shoulder strap, it seemed least likely to attract attention.

In my more exposed position crouched by the nose of a car, I didn't pause to throw stones at the guardroom door and moved straight over to it, swiping the card and slipping inside. Empty. Phew. I settled myself at the base of the grille to wait.

Bane was punctual, but happily just as careful and quiet as before. I waited breathlessly as he inched his way up to the grille.

"Bane?" I breathed.

"Expecting someone else?"

"Ha ha." I eased the post hatch open and we made a mutual lunge for each other's hands in the dark. "Love you."

"Love you too." He held my hand close and didn't say anything for a long, long time. His chest heaved unsteadily against my fingers.

"Bane, you okay?"

"Yeah." And then, because he knew me too well and I knew him too well, he went straight on, "S'just...I'm afraid. All the time, now."

"Afraid? Does someone know you hid Father Mark?"

"No, *no*, not afraid for *me*. And no they don't, and I still am, he refuses to leave, big surprise. I'm afraid for *you*. I'm stuck out here, can't help you, every day I'm terrified your parents will call and say they've...they've received your...*the box*...and it'll be *too late*. Every time the phone goes, every time the door bell goes, I... If anything happens, by the time I know it will be *too late*."

I tightened my grip on his hand. I worried enough about him, what he might get up to on his own out there, but...for a moment Polly's screams echoed in my mind.

"Bane, we both know it's *possible*, but it is very *unlikely*, you know. We're not at Prime Condition and my tissue type is a common one, no shortages. So I reckon I'm probably actually safer in here just at the moment than I would be, say, hiding out with the Underground."

"I *know*, I know. But...it just feels so much worse. I mean, if you were out here, at least I'd have the chance to protect you."

"You can be a little overprotective sometimes, don't you think?"

He was silent for a moment, but when he spoke again I saw his eyes flash as they caught the glow from the flood lights, though there was no moon tonight. "Actually, I don't. Because you know, Margo, you...you're not something that can be *replaced*."

"Well..." I wasn't quite sure what to say to that, so I swallowed a lump in my throat and went on, "Anyway, in just over a month the novel will be published and we'll be escaping. It's not that long to wait, now. Hang on, here's the book, before we get sidetracked. Take it now." I shoved the package through the hatch; Bane undid his rucksack and slid it inside.

"Now," I went on, "I take it you noticed Sue put her own name on the short story?"

"Did I just, the sly cat!"

"You didn't say that to her, I hope?"

"No, no. I was all sweetness and light. Made out it was a brave and generous thing she'd done to help you. Blah blah blah. Probably didn't do it as well as you, but if she thinks I'm just being nice to her for your sake, who cares, it's true."

"Umm, well, we're going to have to be doubly careful about being able to prove the novel's mine. Sue will have been sent a submission slip for identifying the manuscript—you'll have to charm it off her or something. You also need to photocopy the whole manuscript—sorry about that—and send in the photocopy, keeping the original. I've got the wordProcessor thingy which you'd better take; *here*..."

I passed the 'art case' back through the hatch. Okay, so people were going to wonder where it'd gone, but they were hardly going to guess the truth.

"If you have the original manuscript and the thing on which it was written—the rather *unusual* thing, for a bonus—I think the press will believe you. But I suggest you send a detailed synopsis of the novel and copies of the entry slips and so on to some of the bolder papers *before* the publication—but do it anonymously."

"I see. When it comes out, they'll compare the synopsis to what they read, then when I send photos of everything and a few of the original pages they'll be ready to take the claim—and the proof—seriously."

"That's the plan."

"Right. Well, I've got enough time before the end of the month to copy it. Why can't I just get Sue to send it in, though?"

"Sue mustn't see it at all, Bane. If she reads it I don't think she'd dare go through with it. I think she'd rather miss the deadline. Or possibly even own up."

"It's that inflammatory, then? *Good*. What's it called?"

I took a deep breath. "Um. Well, I really wasn't sure what to call it, so I just went for, 'I Am Margaret.'"

"I Am *Margaret?* That's a funny name for a novel."

"Well...it's not exactly a novel. I thought I'd write a life story of a sample reAssignee and...well, I wanted it to be a true one."

There was a moment's quiet as Bane digested this. "Margo, what did you *write?*" He pulled the manuscript from the rucksack, ripping off string and wrappings with a rustle that sounded deafening in the night silence.

"Just...keep your hair on, okay?" I urged, as he tilted it to catch the light and flipped rapidly through it. "I'm going to be escaping, remember?"

"*Margo!*" he moaned. "There's Underground stuff in here!"

"Yes, because it's about me; it doesn't matter, I won't be here, right?"

"Doesn't *matter?* If we had a complete, polished, practiced escape plan ready I'd still consider *doesn't matter* to be the most ludicrous thing I've ever heard you say! And we *don't!*"

"It'll be all right, Bane."

"Don't give me, 'It'll be all right, Bane'! You don't know that! What if I don't manage to get you out? Don't you *know* what they'll do to you?"

"Stop it, Bane!" I gripped the rim of the post hatch with both hands, fighting against the most tremendous surge of panic, fighting not to demand he hand it back, that we call the whole thing off. "Please stop it! Don't make this any harder than it already is! *That's* the manuscript I want you to send in."

"No."

"*Yes.* You will send it in!"

"I won't!" There was a rustle of cloth, a familiar pop sound and his face was illuminated in the orange glow from his lighter. He held it centimeters from the corner of the manuscript. "I'm putting an end to this right now!"

22

THE POINT OF NO RETURN

"Bane, put that out!" I hissed, terrified more for him than for the manuscript. "The guards will see you!"

He shot a dark look at the towers and let the lighter flick closed again. "I'll burn it somewhere else, then." He stuffed the manuscript back into his rucksack. "Because there's no way I'm sending it."

"Bane, listen to me, please! When you wanted to bring me that wordProcessor I wanted to call the whole thing off. But Jon said you had the right to make your own decisions about what risks you ran. And he was right. So I let you bring it. And *you've* got to let *me* make my own decision about *this*. I'm not a child!"

For several long moments there was no sound but his breathing, deep and agonized. "*Why*, Margo? *Why* do you want to do this?"

"Because this is the biggest chance to make a difference I've ever had or likely ever will. The whole world is interested in the winning EuroBloc postSort work, Bane! And right now, incredible as it may seem, that's the book in your hand. I will not fail to take this chance simply because I'm afraid of a little pain."

He took my hand and held it to his cheek. "I don't think *simply* and *little* are the words I'd choose," he whispered. "I can't bear to think of that happening to you."

"Then get me out of here."

"Oh, no pressure or anything!"

"Sorry. Get us out if you can. If you can't, don't beat yourself up about it."

"I sent that blasted flyer to you! I'll have sent this deadly thing in! I'm more likely to throw myself under a train."

"Don't you dare talk like that!" I pulled my hand free and smacked his face—the slap sounded deafening in the quiet—

I froze, furious with myself. But there was nothing but silence from the towers. He placed a conciliatory kiss on my offending hand so I took a couple of deep breaths and managed to speak more calmly. "How is the escape plan going, anyway?"

"Well, it's progressing. Slowly. Thinking up possible diversions is easy, but actually getting *in*—anything short of a full scale assault won't work and a full scale assault seems... problematic."

"It'll have to be a joint effort. If you can supply the right diversion, then if the Lord is with us, we can get out."

"You've got a plan for that already?"

"No, I've been a bit preoccupied. But I will have soon. I think I'll need your air gun—bother, why didn't I ask you to bring it? I'm an idiot! It's a perfect replica of the guards' nonLees, you see."

"You'll use it to get a real one."

"Exactly. I reckon I really am going to need it. Why didn't I *think?*"

"It doesn't matter." He squeezed my hand. "I'll work on diversion plans, you work on how to get out, we'll meet in a couple of weeks to fit the two together. We can't fix up something like this through letters with nothing but allusions and double-meanings."

"I suppose," I said reluctantly. Bane and machine guns again, alas. "And I suppose you'd better go. Promise me you'll look after that manuscript?"

For a moment it seemed he wouldn't answer. "I promise," he sighed at last.

"Promise you'll send it in on time?"

"Oh, confound it! All right. If humanly possible."

"Obviously. I hope I'm not as demanding as *that!*"

Things dissolved into a lot of hand clasping and hand kissing for a while, but eventually we managed to wrench ourselves apart.

"I hate this hatch," snarled Bane, fastening the rucksack. "They could've made it larger!"

"If I could get my shoulders in, I could probably climb through altogether, couldn't I? But yeah, I hate it too. Now, be careful."

"You be careful!"

We kissed each other's fingers one last time and he began to worm his way back to safety. I waited again, until sure he'd have reached it, and headed back towards the dubious safety of the building, taking the less visible route under the bellies of the cars.

Creeping quietly into the washroom, I pulled off my jumpsuit and sweater, slipping back into my nightie and dressing gown. With the other clothes concealed about my person, I was much less encumbered than on my way out of the dorm earlier. Good. Things had gone as well as I could possibly have hoped. There was no longer any chance of the wordProcessor being discovered and far, far more importantly, Bane had the manuscript. And had promised to send it in. It was out of my hands.

Suddenly I was curled up, pressed against the wall under one of the washbasins, shaking, shaking, shaking so hard I fought to breathe, and the more I fought to breathe the more I shook. Because Bane was right, we didn't have a plan yet, we didn't have one, and even the best plans didn't always work.

Not collapsing into tears took all the strength I possessed and it was long, long minutes before my gasps eased, that teeth-rattling shaking subsided and my terror lessened enough for me to think straight. When it did I found the words there waiting and I began to recite them in my mind.

Cum anxiatur in me spiritus meus,
tu novisti viam meam.
> *My heart is ready to faint within me,*
> *but You are watching over my path.*

I said them over and over until my heart slowed and all was still and calm once more. A bleak little voice asked me, *yes, but what path?*—I pushed it away. Enough. The night's work was done. I was going back to bed.

* * *

From then on my spare time was spent lying on my bunk, notebook in hand, thinking. I ran through scenario after scenario, jotting deliberately indecipherable notes, spending hours bouncing them off Jon, groaning as he picked holes and pointed out fatal flaws. Page after page went down the trash hatch, and we both watched the guards as much as possible, where they went, how they behaved, jotting down a coded record of their shifts, going around smiley and cheerful and striking up as many conversations with them as we could.

"It's easy to see how it *could* be done, just like that, unplanned," said Jon, "like in a film. But only IF absolutely everything went right. And we're up against a load of human beings with free will, not a bunch of actors following a convenient script."

"We have to take the camera room and two of the towers. That's the bottom line."

"Yeah, but we've got to make sure no one knows we've taken them until we're clean away."

"Well, that's why Bane's diversion is so important, isn't it? They won't have time to worry that they can't contact the camera room if they think the Resistance are about to come over the walls."

"Let's hope they're not," said Jon dryly.

"What?"

"Well, I've the feeling you're expecting Bane to arrange some sufficiently large diversion all by his lonesome. Well, pardon me if I'm a little skeptical. It's going to be more than a one- or even two-man job."

"He seemed confident about the diversion part."

"Good. Because without it, I don't think we're going to pull this off."

"No," I said slowly, "neither do I."

"Margaret Verrall," I told the guard handing out the post, trying to smile.

The first of June—if all had gone according to plan, Fox and Wilson now had the manuscript. Bane hadn't written to me in my Friday letter, so presumably he'd been too busy arranging it. Or he'd changed his mind and decided, for the first time in his life, to break a promise to me. *Yes,* squeaked a cowardly little voice from deep inside me, as I took the letter. *Let it be that!* I shoved the voice down as hard as I could, collected my breakfast and went to sit beside Jon.

The tension was too much, and after spooning down my cereals untasted, I opened my letter immediately. There was a front and back page of what at a glance appeared to be space filler from Mum, and just a short bit from Bane in the middle.

Hi Margo. I'm sorry I didn't write last time, I was so busy. You'll never guess where I was on Friday! London! I went all the way there with a friend of mine, he's a reporter, incidentally. (BTW, did you know trains are much more comfortable on the inside?) London was quite something, I can tell you! Though, I'm not sure I actually liked it very much there. But I wish you'd been with us.

We delivered that thing for you while we were down there, no problems. I told my reporter friend that if he made any inappropriate jokes about it I'd kill him and I don't think he thought I was joking, which is good, because I'm not so sure I was. I do hope you're all right, everything's going fine for me. I'll try and write a bit more next time but your parents have to get this to the RWB office to catch the post. Love you, Bane.

Right. On reflection, Bane must've been dissatisfied with our precautions for ensuring proof of ownership. So he'd gone one better and taken a well-placed friend into his confidence. An older friend. Resistance? He must be very sure he could trust him to keep his mouth shut.

And the manuscript had gone in. It had definitely, indisputably, irrecoverably gone in. I couldn't torture myself with the hope-fear it'd been lost in the post; that it hadn't got there in time. Bane had put it through the letterbox of the publishing house with his own two hands, with the reporter watching for good measure. The point of no return had passed, all right.

There could be no keeping quiet and letting the book pass into history as Sue's work of fiction. With a story that could make his career, the Salperton reporter would only hold his tongue until it was actually published—and would make the biggest news. And there'd never *really* been any chance of that particular cowardice, had there? There were plenty of people in Salperton who would read that book and realize it was no novel. Perhaps we'd been worrying about how to prove my authorship for nothing. Still, better safe than sorry.

Safe.

Lord, give me strength, what a joke! The only thing that could save me now, other than an early dismantling or some other freak occurrence, was an escape plan: details-yet-to-be-finalized. Because escaping was so easy. People did it all the time. *Not.*

My limbs were dissolving, that blasted shaking again, and my stomach heaved. I lurched up from my seat and ran for the door, but the washrooms were far too far, and then I was down on my knees, throwing up my breakfast on the floor. Unfortunately I tasted it this time.

"Margo?"

"Margo?"

"Are you all right?"

Someone handed me a tissue and I wiped my mouth, sitting back on the cold linoleum. *Get yourself together, Margo, get yourself together, you're being silly...*but the room and the sea of anxious faces swung echoingly around me and I buried my face against my knees, sobs escaping at last.

"Margo?" Jon's hand touched my shoulder and I tried again to get myself together, but it was too late. Too late.

"Move aside, move aside. What's the matter, now?" Watkins approached me.

I folded the letter small with trembling fingers and slipped it into Jon's hand.

"Margo's ill," Rebecca was telling Watkins. "She's been sick and she's all white and shaky. I think she'd better see the d…" Bless her, she hesitated on doctor just in time, replacing it with, "the nurse. I think she should see the nurse."

"Margaret? What seems to be the trouble?"

I raised my head and found Watkins peering down at me. "I'm fine," I managed. "Really."

"You don't look fine, missie. I think you'd better go have a lie down in sickbay. Get up on your feet now, if you can. Give her a hand, girls. Brandon, you come with me; Dwight, stay here."

One of the guards who'd been dishing out the breakfast came through from the kitchen to join Watkins, which would leave his colleague on the other side of the hatch and Dwight in the cafeteria, both in sight of one another. I don't think Watkins—or any of the guards—thought I'd been lying about Finchley, but they knew it paid to stick to the rules.

I was annoyingly wobbly in the legs, but managed to walk to the sickbay under my own steam, though Watkins and Brandon hovered as though I might keel over at any moment. The nurse examined me, pricked my finger to check my blood sugar, took my blood pressure and temperature, and since none of them were desperately low, concluded we'd have to wait and see if I was coming down with something or if it was just a blip.

She made me lie down until lunchtime, then had me returned to the dorm, though under an injunction against attending afternoon exercise. Reassuring and fending off my crowd of well-wishers, I let Jon put his arm around me, feeling like the world's largest cowardly custard.

"Margo?" It was Jane. She stood at the end of the bunk, where she'd been standing since I was brought back in. Waiting.

"Yes?"

"Just wondering what you've done with that useful art case of yours?"

"Oh. That." I bludgeoned my brain into action. "I had to give it back, you know."

"Shame. It was useful, wasn't it? You wrote an awful lot of stories on it."

"Umm," I agreed, trying to look wan and sick.

"And where are they, Margo?"

"Where's what, Jane?"

"That huge heap of stories you wrote? They're not in Jon's chest any more, are they?"

I glanced at Jon, wondering how he'd let her get a look.

"Sarah was upset about you being taken off, so Rebecca said she'd read her a story if she could find one," he said emotionlessly. "Sarah thought they were in my chest and had a look." *Before I could stop her,* I heard the silent addition.

"But not a page in sight," said Jane too sweetly. Had she even put Sarah up to it? "So she tried your chest, Margo, but they're not there either. I thought you'd written us a...a lifetime supply," she said blackly. "But now there's just a little pile of the ones you've read us already. Sarah was very disappointed."

"Oh. I'm sorry about that."

"Well, Margo?"

"Well, what, Jane?"

"Where are the stories?"

"They're gone," I said bluntly. "We won't be seeing them again, I'm afraid."

"Did you destroy them? Or give them away?"

"I really don't see it's any of your business what I did with them," I retorted, and buried my face in Jon's hair.

"Well, perhaps I think it is!" snapped Jane, undeterred. "You work and work on all those stories for two months like you're obsessed, secretive as anything, won't let anyone read them, keep telling us to be patient, and then the entire stack disappears overnight. I reckon the stories have gone to the same place as the typing machine and I'm very curious to know why!"

"Leave her alone, Jane," said Jon coldly. "She's got more important things to think about than your cat-like curiosity."

"Like what?"

"I *think* you've discussed such things before and I *think* you'd be advised to leave her to it! Lest she *leave* you...to it!"

Jane's mouth clicked shut and she stared at Jon and me for another few moments, but most of the anger had gone out of her glower. Finally she turned and went back to her own bunk.

"Are you feeling better?" murmured Jon.

"Yes. I'm so embarrassed."

"Is Bane okay?" From the way he said it, he'd been waiting to ask ever since I'd been brought back. Oh...he hadn't heard my letter yet.

"Oh, *yes*. Goodness, yes. It's not that. I was just being...just being incredibly spineless. Bane's handed the manuscript in, y'see. It's done."

His arm tightened convulsively around my shoulders. "*Libera nos, Domine*," he breathed in my ear. "I'd say it's just beginning."

I wound my hands into his top and buried my face deeper in his hair. He smelled of peppermint; his parents had slipped sweets into his letter again.

"Jon, I'm so frightened," I whispered, unable to hold it back any longer.

"Oh. Of course you are." He folded me tightly in his arms. "Of *course* you are. You're going to be fine, Margo. You're so brave. And Bane will do his part and we'll do ours."

"But what if the worst happens?" My voice would've been inaudible to anyone else, but he caught my words. "And what if they break me?"

"Our Lord came to forgive, didn't He? So you'll be covered either way." His lips brushed the top of my head, then he just held me for a long, long time.

23

THE SILENT CROCODILE

It was only when I drew away from him of my own accord that he picked up the two halves of his stick, lying unnoticed beside him, and held them out to me. I took them, my heart sinking. Both the long splintered ends were snapped off, one gone completely, the other hanging by a few strands of wood.

I shot a look at his tense face. No wonder he'd got mad at Jane so easily. "Um, this could be...difficult."

He sighed and closed his eyes tight. "You mean impossible, right?"

"Um..." I laid the pieces beside one another, this way and that. "Not...quite, but... Well, if I bind them back together, it's going to be far too short. Perhaps we could replace the missing section with some rulers or something. What happened to it?"

"Just one of those things," he said, slightly too casually.

"What happened? *I* didn't do it as I dashed off, did I?"

"No, no. It wasn't your fault. It happened in the crush, that's all. It hardly got knocked at all, it was just so delicate. So it was the boys' fault, really."

"I'm so sorry, Jon." My insides churned guiltily. Without my stupid custard attack there wouldn't have been any crush. He relied on that stick so much. *My long eye*, he called it. "I'll fix it if I possibly can, I promise."

From then on, as we sat discussing escape plans, my hands were busy with string, rulers, pencils, pieces of card... But I couldn't get the thing to stay together for more than a few minutes.

"Margo," said Jon one day, taking my busy hands and stilling them. "It's broken and you can't fix it. Not with a handful of stationery and a ball of string. You need to have your mind on this plan of ours and right now you haven't. I know my way around. I'm fine."

"But you don't know what's in the way." I protested, running a gentle hand around the cut over his eye, acquired from the concrete wall after he'd tripped over a mop and bucket the day before. "I'll figure it out—"

"We've only got time to figure one thing out and it's not *this.*" He took the pieces of the stick from my lap and walked across the room with a hesitance that twisted a knife inside me, so used to his confident grace. Before I'd realized what he was doing he'd opened the trash hatch and thrown the pieces in. He picked his way back across the room and sat beside me again. "There. Now you have no excuse not to concentrate on the plan. So *concentrate,* blast it!"

After that sacrifice on Jon's part, I tried very hard indeed to *concentrate, blast it,* and two weeks later Jon and I walked down to dinner trying not to look too pleased with ourselves.

"Now we're really getting somewhere," I said under my breath, face close to his. "Keep trying, though. Just because you didn't immediately pick any holes in that plan..."

"I know. I'm working on it. Because I *was* hoping we'd have things a bit more settled by now."

The letter I'd posted that morning suggested the following Monday for my meeting with Bane. That would leave only nine days until the publication day so it wasn't much time for Bane to make final arrangements.

"We've got almost a week before you meet Bane, though," Jon was saying, "and I think we have nearly cracked it. There's still a lot that chance could wreck, but I'm not sure we're going to be able to avoid that."

"No—"

"Buck up, Sally, here's your two lovebirds." Brandon's voice broke in on our murmured conversation in a tone of clumsy commiseration. "They normally cheer you up."

Nice Sally stood by the cafeteria door, her eyes red and puffy.

I drew Jon to a halt in front of her. "Sally, what's the matter?"

She turned her head away slightly and shook it.

"Sally, you look really upset," I persisted. "Has something

happened?"

Brandon followed everyone else into the cafeteria and Sally relaxed a little. No longer feeling she had to keep up appearances in front of her colleague, perhaps.

"Did you hear about Wearmfell factory?" Her voice was choked—tears clearly weren't far away.

My chest tightened in sympathy. Whatever had happened? "Wearmfell. Military factory, isn't it? Just over Wearm Pass?"

"Military!" sniffed Sally fiercely. "It makes up ration packs for the EuroArmy. *Ration packs!* Real high-tech weapons systems, don't you think?"

"No, of course not. It's just food, isn't it?"

"Just food that happens to be going to the army," remarked Jon. "Not weapons, no."

"Well, tell that to the Resistance! They raided Wearmfell Factory last night. Burnt the whole place down. But before they did that, they..." Tears were spilling down her cheeks now. "They lined up all the guards and shot them. My...my brother was a guard there, see...and he was...he was on shift..." She was crying in earnest now, rather jerkily as she tried to stop herself.

"Sally, that's awful!" I'd no need to feign sincerity. "I'm so sorry!"

Jon just looked grim. Of course, he looked grim a lot of the time, now.

"*Ration packs!*" sniffed Sally. "He was guarding ration packs! Why him? I keep thinking, why him? I'm here guarding...guarding *you*, and he's guarding *ration packs*, and it's him who gets...gets..." She wrestled a sodden hankie from her pocket and buried her nose in it.

"Oh, Sally, they'll let you go home, won't they?"

She sort of nodded and shook her head all at once. "Captain said no, Major said yes. But I'm not going. I can't face his wife—registered partner," she corrected herself with the reflex of EuroGov employees the Bloc over. "Can't bear the thought of her looking at me and wondering how it is David's dead and I'm not. Though I'm guarding reAssignees and he's guarding—oh!—*was guarding* ration..."

She broke off, sobbing into her dripping hankie until Jon

held out a large dry one. "Oh, thank you. How can you...how can you be so kind to me?"

"Your brother's been murdered! That's terrible!" I said. "What's so kind about feeling sorry for you after something like that?"

"Because...because I'm guarding you," she sniffed.

"Sally, you told us you took this job because you wanted to make sure we were looked after properly. Seems like you meant it, too. You don't deserve to be shot any more than your brother did."

"But it is a job, y'see. D'rather it's someone here who's going to be nice to you poor things, I do mean it, but...it is a *job*. Oh! *David*." She sobbed even harder.

I frowned. "Look, I can sort of see why you don't want to go home, but can't you...you know, stay off shift for a day or two until you feel better?"

Sally shook her head unequivocally this time. "Major said I could go or not go, but if I didn't go, my shifts were up to the Captain, and she said normal shifts, so it's normal shifts." She blew her nose and wiped her face, trying to get herself together. "Look, you two are missing your dinner. Go on in. I'll be fine. Thank you for...for even caring."

"Hard not to care about something like that," I said.

She blew her nose again and waved the hankie vaguely at Jon. "I'll send this to the laundry. Thank you so much."

"You're welcome." Jon found her arm and touched it gently, then moved with me into the cafeteria. After several more trips and falls, he'd taken to walking with me all the time, though he clearly hated the feeling of dependence. "I'd better not break something just now, had I?" he'd muttered. "Since I imagine you'd drag me along regardless."

"Evil rats!" I fumed, as we sat down with our trays and put our heads together. "Killing factory guards! What blasted good is that supposed to do, you tell me?"

"None whatsoever," said Jon grimly. "Bloodthirsty maniacs, the lot of them. No wonder your cousin Mark hates their guts."

"I think my cousin Mark was with them once, don't you?"

Jon winced. "Yeah, I've always got that impression too. Knows them far too well and loathes them far too much.

Factory guards. Huh. Have they nothing better to do?"

"Trigger-happy morons!" I shoveled down my dinner with little regard for the taste, such as there was. "If Bane ever actually joins them I'm going to slap him silly!"

"Bane's strong, but he's not hard. They'd make him hard fast enough, but...I've always hoped it might stop him joining them in the first place."

I sighed, putting down my knife and fork and pushing my plate away. "They'd make him hard all right. And then they'd break him. Hard is brittle. Well," I dropped my voice even further. "If we get out of here, we'll be off out of the EuroBloc entirely. Get him away from them before it's too late."

"Hear, hear," said Jon, then added, "though I still think you should leave *me* here. Especially *now*." And ducked.

"Right!" I called after morning exercise the next day, stepping into the center of the dorm and raising my voice. "Does anyone want to play a game?"

An impatient noise from Jane, a sigh from Rebecca, and a chorus of assent from everyone else.

"Game, game!" exclaimed Sarah, looking as though Winterfest had come six months early.

"What game, Margo?" asked Harriet, scarcely any less eager.

"Well, it's called the Silent Crocodile. Two people sit in the middle of the room blindfolded, and all the others hold hands in twos and make a crocodile. The crocodile has to snake its way around and around the room and gradually sneak up on the ones in the middle. So it mustn't make any noise or break up. The pair in the middle of the room have to try and point at the crocodile."

"Oh, for goodness' sake," said Jane scornfully. "That lot are never going to be quiet and stick together! What an absolute waste of time."

"I didn't say it would be an easy game. We'll just have to practice a lot."

Some people were looking rather put off by Jane's words, so I added, "Let's play the Silent Crocodile this morning, then I'll read the next bit of the Fellest Ewe's diary after afternoon exercise. How's that?"

Enthusiasm for the game revived suddenly. Frowning, Jane watched as I started pairing people off, carefully matching each smarter or more practical girl up with a simpler or less practical girl. I put Sarah with Rebecca, and found Jane had come over to join in after all.

"Hi, Jane. Will you pair with Bethan?"

Jane grimaced slightly, but nodded. Then caught my shoulder and leaned in to hiss, "Are you planning what I suddenly think you're planning?"

"Well, let's put it this way, I hope you'll encourage everyone to play this game every day for the next two weeks."

Jane's eyes lit up. "That soon?"

That soon or never. But I didn't say it. I just smiled, said yes, Sarah could start in the middle with Rebecca, and oversaw all the chairs and tables moved to the side and stacked out of the way.

The game was as difficult as Jane predicted, but even the best laid plan was likely to dissolve into chaos and I needed to teach everyone to stick together. Sooner or later Jon and I would have to fill everyone in, but it was better left absolutely as late as possible. Innocent tongues could flap just as destructively as malicious ones.

I did take Rebecca into my confidence as well as Jane, though I said no more than that we were to escape and this was necessary practice for that. But it was enough to make them both help to keep the games going, to encourage lots of laughter every time the crocodile was caught, and to chide anyone who let go of their partner or broke formation.

We brought Emily into the secret too and she taught the game to the Old Year, drilling them mercilessly. They were not yet at Prime Condition but there were only fourteen of them left.

When people began to look out for their 'crocodile buddy' outside game time, I knew we were getting some-where. As for the boys—they'd just have to take their chances on the day.

Keeping any emotional distance from Jon was becoming

impossible, though—we clung to each other like people drowning. Me, I existed in a state of terror, constantly fearing the truth about my book would come out before the publication day, and Jon, Jon felt the loss of his long eye very badly.

How would he manage once we'd escaped? If the stick was such a help in a place he knew well, it would be utterly invaluable for facing the unknown. Watkins, bless him, offered to find something to replace it and post it to Jon when he was off shift, but that wasn't for another two months. The most annoying thing of all was that I'd seen something inside the Facility that would do and I simply couldn't remember what it was.

In sheer desperation I cornered the Captain in the stairwell one day and asked as politely as I could manage if she would find something for Jon. She asked so many questions about what he needed I *almost* began to hope— then the last reAssignee went through the door to the cafeteria corridor and...*ah*...she'd backed me into the camera's blind spot. She grabbed a fistful of my hair and slammed my head into the wall so hard she left me in a dazed heap on the floor.

It was official. She hated my guts.

She hadn't even bothered to say no and I didn't bother to say anything about it to Jon. Not until people began to ask what'd happened to my face, anyway.

Monday night and the moon was back, adding its silvery light to the glow of the flood lights. The killing zone remained clearly, but not brightly, illuminated. The high powered lights were very expensive and the guards only needed to see well *enough*—they had their search lights when they needed them, after all.

Still, we could've done without that bright moon. The guards obviously didn't look straight down at the base of the wall very often—not too surprising since it was assumed they'd see or hear anything approaching it. Still, Bane and machine guns—the less light the better.

The guards were jumpy, as well. No prizes for guessing why. Sally's eyes were no longer red all the time, but she remained very subdued.

The moon illuminated the little guardroom just as well as on my first visit. I stared up at the fuse boxes. How unfortunate an area usually shrouded in mist day and night should produce clear skies on not one, but two, inconvenient nights.

The fuse boxes weren't that interesting and the moon was beyond my control, so I started on a rosary—the Glorious Mysteries—something nice and optimistic! Bane was a little late, so I'd almost finished when he came creeping up to the grille.

"Margo?"

"Bane." I opened the hatch and we clasped hands.

"Here," he whispered, letting go of my hand and passing me a triangular package, "take this now. It's the air gun."

"Good." I eased the zip of my jumpsuit a little way down and slipped the package inside.

"I put in a few packs of pellets, but if you're reduced to trying to shoot your way out with *that*, it's all over."

I couldn't help snorting agreement. "That's truth."

"Thought you might as well have them, though. Without, it's no more than a rather ineffective club."

"I'm not planning on shooting anyone with anything other than a nonLee, Bane."

This truthful but lighthearted remark drew an odd silence from the other side of the grille.

"Well, shall we go through the plan?" What'd I said?

"Yeah. Yeah, the plan."

"Are you all right, Bane?"

"I'm fine."

"Is there a problem with the plan? You can tell me, you know that."

"There's nothing wrong with the plan. The plan is right on course, I've made sure of that all right." There was an odd note of self-contempt in his voice.

"Bane, what's wrong? And don't say nothing. I can hear it in everything you say. What's happened?"

I heard him take a couple of deep breaths, then he peeped into the hatch at last. With the moon and the lights above and behind him, I couldn't see his face well, but I could see the lines of distress.

"I've done something stupid, Margo," he said, in rather a rush. "Well, it didn't seem stupid when I began it...but it turned out rather differently. You're not going to like it." He stumbled to a halt.

"Go on, Bane," I said gently.

"Well, there's something I never told you. You know I've got friends in the Resistance? Well...I've been out with them now and then."

"I know," I said evenly. "It was...kind of obvious. And then Jon confirmed it."

I thought he might relax a bit, at that, but if anything he just got tenser. "Oh. Well...I went out twice with the Young Resistance—"

"I still can't believe they have a *Young Resistance*!"

"Um, yeah. For the underEighteens, y'know? They do the less serious stuff. We did the graffiti on the Town Committee Hall three years back. I did the one over the door."

"You changed EuroGov to EuroMob. That was funny. It was so well done, it looked like it'd always said that."

"Yeah, I had some acrylic paints, I was really careful doing it. Um, then we poured the concrete over the Police Station's solar panels two years back. That was pretty hard work getting that sludge up there. We cut all the wires on their antennae and stuff while we were up there."

I bit my lip, trying not to smile. "Yeah, I read about that. Okay, so I laughed."

"Um. Then I went out with the real Resistance a few months ago, after I turned eighteen. You can go a certain number of times as an 'observer' they call it. After about five times you have to join or push off. Anyway, we brought down the power lines from the Coldwell Nuclear Plant."

Most houses, businesses, and public buildings had their own solar panels and/or wind turbines, of course. But anything that needed more power than it could generate for itself or a guaranteed supply—heavy industry and hospitals, mostly—was hooked up to the nuclear grid.

"You shouldn't have done that, Bane. That power's going to hospitals."

"Where their preferred method of curing people is to

stick a stolen organ or body part into them," said Bane cuttingly. "Relax, they all have dirty generators for backup, don't they?"

"I suppose." He remained quiet. "Well, what is the matter? I'm not mad at you. Well, I kind of am mad you're going anywhere near them, but you know what I mean. Have you been out with them since?"

The silence grew suffocating, then he whispered, "Yes. Once."

"What happened?"

That awful silence fell again and his hand crept into the hatch and closed around mine with the grip of a drowning man. "They told me no one would be hurt..."

One simple sentence and I knew.

24

WEARMFELL FACTORY

"You were at Wearmfell Factory."

He swore, shocked and appalled—he hadn't expected me to know about it. He hung onto my hand even tighter, as though afraid I would pull away, so I placed my other hand over his. "Yes. We went to Wearmfell."

"The *Resistance* told you no one would be hurt, and you *believed* them?"

"No one's ever been hurt before," he choked out. "They said—" he broke off.

"Do you want to tell me about it?"

"No. Yes. Heck, I've got to tell someone."

"Father Mark?"

"No. He'll say *I told you so*. And he'll be right. He did tell me. Over and over. But I went anyway."

"Well. He might say *I told you so*. But he'll probably save it until after he's said a lot of much more helpful stuff."

"Yeah. Well, I'll have to tell him eventually because he knows I went. But I think I want to tell you first. If you don't mind. Because I tell you everything. Or…I should've done."

"You can tell me. What did they say?"

"Well, they said we were just going to burn the place down. Muck up the EuroBarmy supply chain a bit, well, I've got no problem with that. I said what about the guards and they said they'd all skedaddle out the back door as we came in. Lying toads! There *was* no back door! Chain link fence all around the entire place. They caught the whole nightshift in the guardroom, and the way they went in, that was the plan all along!"

I knew what'd happened next, but I pressed his hand and waited for him to go on. It was several deep breaths before he did.

"There were four guards. One went for his gun, he was

shot right there in the guardroom. I thought him a fool at the time; now I think he was the smartest one there. Because *my lot*," he spat the words with considerable venom, drawing a 'shhhh' from me despite my determination not to interrupt, "*my lot* marched the other three out into this little yard beside the guardroom and backed them up against the wall. Then Trev—Trevor—he was in charge—he goes along and just shoots them in the head, bang, bang, bang."

His hand tightened on mine and I'd a feeling he wasn't seeing the dark Facility hatch in front of him. "First guard was a mess, crying and begging, but Trev just blows his brains all over the wall. Second one's hard as nails, brave guy, got his lips clamped together, won't say a word. Much good it did him. More brains on the wall. Sorry...sorry," his eyes focused on me again. "I'm being too detailed."

"It's all right, Bane. Just...tell it how it was."

"Well..." Bane hurried on as though glad to get the words out now he'd started. "Third guard gets right on his knees and starts telling us about his wife and kids. His wife Katie and his little girls, Lily and Rosy, four and six...well, he had time because I'd grabbed Trev's arm and asked what the heck he was doing. And he just shook me off and gave me this smile—have to call it a smile, I s'pose—and said, 'live and learn, cub,' and raised the gun again, and then Lily's and Rosy's daddy's brains were on the wall as well. And I *can't stop thinking* about it."

"Of course you can't—"

"No, not just *it*, generally. That bit. When Trev lifted his pistol again, there was this split second when I could've knocked it aside. I wanted to so much. I was this close, but... I stopped myself."

"Why?"

"Because it wouldn't have helped. And I didn't dare—the cost seemed too high when—it *wouldn't have helped*. If I'd done it, well, two of the others would've grabbed me and Trev would've just pointed that gun again and done it anyway. He wasn't short of bullets."

"Were you afraid they'd turn on you?"

"No—I mean, who knows, in the heat of things, and Trev

and some of the others are right psychos, I've seen their true colors now, *too late*. But that wasn't what I was worried about at the time. They might've given me some beating to speak of, but I think they'd most likely just have taken me back to Salperton with them and told me never to come near them ever again."

"Please tell me you don't *want* to go near them ever again?"

"No, I *don't* want to. I really don't. But I do *have* to. Y'see, someone's asked me to help save seventy innocent people by creating a diversion and I'm probably going to be for it when I tell her, but the Resistance are the diversion, okay? If I'd defied Trev it would all be off, and it wouldn't even have *helped!* But as it is, they're right behind this escape. They're drilling everyone for it already." He fell silent, but his fingers clenched and unclenched around mine, so I choked back all the things I wanted to say and waited for him to finish.

"But I can't stop thinking... I don't think I'd do any differently right now, if I had to do it again. With what's at stake... But I wanted to so much, and I feel so...I feel like I've done something so *bad*. I mean, it was bad just being there, but...I didn't kill anyone, I didn't cut the fence, I didn't touch anything, I couldn't, literally couldn't help anyone and still I feel so...so..."

"Guilty?"

All his breath went out in a long sigh, then he drew a short, pained breath back in. "Yes, guilty. I feel guilty."

"Well, it's hard to say you *shouldn't* feel guilty about having been there," I said levelly. "As for whether or not you should've knocked the gun aside, I don't know. The circumstances are exceptionally complex. For a moral ruling on that one you'll have to ask that little lion you've got tucked away."

"But you do think it's my fault?" His hands loosened on mine as though he'd suddenly noticed they were black with tar.

"I didn't say it's *your fault*," I said hastily, tightening my own grip. "I just mean...it seems like you've got to be partially responsible for what happened, since you *were* there. But you didn't know what was planned and didn't do anything, so I'd say it's a *very* limited responsibility."

"I should feel a little bit guilty, then? I feel a lot guilty. I feel... Why do I feel this bad?"

"I think it's called loss of innocence," I said softly, Uncle Peter's execution forcing its way into my mind. I felt like I'd lost something after that—more than just him. "Seeing something like that—I think it kind of is."

"Innocence?" Bane drew a breath as though to snort, then let it out slowly instead. "*Yeah.* Who'd have thought. You know, I've never thought of myself as *innocent.* If you'd said it to me I'd have laughed. But you know, now it's gone...I really wish I had it back." His voice was small and rather lost.

I drew his hand to me and planted several kisses on it. "It'll be all right. But talk to Father Mark about it. I think he might know all about guilt from that kind of thing. Why on earth is he still here, anyway?"

"Because he refuses to leave. He goes into Salperton now on your bike to do his work—says since Father Peter's gone, it's just him, so how can he leave? I can't shift him, short of tying him up and cycling him across the county border. And you know, I don't reckon I could take him. So I bring him as much food as I can and make sure I'm not followed."

"Ah." No surprises there. But I couldn't dwell on it. I was too busy fighting off visions of the Resistance getting inside the Facility and killing every guard in the place. "Bane, please, please tell me your plan doesn't involve anyone actually getting *into* the Facility?"

"No, don't worry."

"Are you sure? You know what they'll do if they get inside—if you didn't before you should now. They'll kill everyone."

Bane snorted and his voice hardened. "Facility guards. Forgive me if I don't get all broken-hearted about a few *Facility* guards."

"They don't deserve to be murdered, Bane. It's a job, a job everyone in the Bloc condones, a job everyone pays for in their taxes. Everyone is responsible for the Facilities. Are you going to start killing random people in the street?"

"I'm not planning on killing anyone. Though I still think it's one thing to sit at a distance and try not to think about a distasteful subject and another to take money for guarding innocent people and marching them off to their deaths!"

"Well, maybe, but who are we to say they deserve to die? There's a fellow called Watkins, very conscientious, worked here for years and years, but he's got galloping arthritis in his left hand. They've offered him a new one, but he's a conscientious objector. So should he die, for working here, or live, for being a conchie?"

It was possible to opt out of a medical transplant on grounds of conscience—but you had to make the Divine denial to get away with it. Those in the Underground generally kept away from doctors and hospitals if remotely possible, to make sure the question didn't arise.

"Funny place for a conchie."

"Well, some of the guards work here to try and make sure we're looked after properly. There's a woman called Sally like that. Watkins might be another, though he hasn't said so. You want to kill people like that?"

"Look, stop worrying about it. They're just going to make a nuisance of themselves from outside."

They'd try their best to kill the guards in the towers, in other words. What'd I put in motion? "I take it they don't have any nonLee rifles?"

"NonLee *rifles*? They're cutting edge, Margo. Who can afford them? Anyway," he added bitterly, "they laugh at nonLees."

It was my hands which were clenching and unclenching now. "Bane...no offense, but how can you be sure they're going to follow the plan? You're not in the Resistance: you don't actually have any authority over them, do you."

He just shrugged. "Margo, the Resistance are actually pretty good at following plans and conserving resources, including themselves. They'd have been wiped out by now, otherwise. Problem the other day was, no one told me the plan. But I'm in on this one and they'll stick to it. Even the Resistance don't like to fool around with a two-hundred-meter killing zone covered by machine guns."

"They'll let us chance that, then."

"Yes, they will. Sounds like you won't be sorry."

"No, I won't, Bane. There are degrees of guilty, as you

should appreciate. And a lot of the guards aren't very, in my opinion." There was the Menace and Finchley... I found my mouth adding, "I'm not saying there aren't one or two whose characters would be much improved by a bullet in the head—"

"Margo!" Bane sounded shocked.

"I'm not saying I want it to happen!" I added hastily, my brain catching up with my tongue. "Forget I said that, would you? I shouldn't have."

"Just what have these one or two characters done to you?" demanded Bane.

"I'll tell you all about it in a week or so's time, Lord willing. Now..." I hesitated. We'd barely discussed what needed discussing yet. "D'you think if you get down in the bottom of that ditch, we'll still be able to hear each other?"

"Hmm," said Bane, but perhaps he also suspected the guards might be unusually alert, for all he said was, "Let's try it, then." He disappeared from sight and there were a few tiny scuffling noises. "Can you hear me?"

"Yes."

"Good. We'd better get down to business; I'm sorry I went on for so long."

"Don't apologize, Bane, or you'll make me mad. Now, let's make sure we don't forget anything."

"Right. We don't need to waste time going into the ins and outs of each other's plans, we've just got to arrange the timings. I have got one question, though. If you're going to get hold of some real nonLees, can't you get uniforms at the same time and just walk across the exercise yards to the towers? Why do you need the diversion so desperately?"

Was Bane not quite so comfortable with the source of the diversion as he had been? Good. Unfortunately... "If it was that simple, everyone would escape. Look, it didn't take me any time at all to realize the only way to get out was to take a couple of towers out of commission. Well, if I can think of that, so can a lot of other reAssignees and certainly so can the EGD. Jon and I have worked this out very carefully.

"To get into a tower you have to get to the base of it without being shot—easy enough in the daytime, during exercise, and with a uniform, simple at night too. But a card isn't enough to get you in once you're there, that's the problem. There's a camera as well and the guards in the tower have to recognize you before they'll unlock the door.

"Hence the diversion. The uniforms will get a pair safely across the yard to each tower—though the internal guards have slightly different ones, you know, but it'll be close enough, especially with a bit of chaos for good measure.

"We'll swipe a card and claim to be reinforcements, keeping too close to the camera to be identified, and with the tower under attack the chances are extremely high the guards will let us in without thinking to insist on a normal ID. The first person to the top of the stairs will take the guards out and the second one will be there for...backup."

"You mean if the first person gets shot," said Bane grimly, clearly thinking of those machine guns.

"It's a precaution only. The person going in will have a nonLee drawn in their hand. No way will they turn those big guns in time."

"And will one of the first people be you?"

"Of course it will, Bane," I said impatiently. "You've made me do target shooting with you often enough. I may be the only person in the dorm who's ever even fired a gun. I really don't know who to trust with the other tower. I think I'll have to instigate a very noisy game and hold trials with the air gun, actually. If they can't hit a barn door, all the surprise in the world won't help."

"Try Jon."

"*Jon?* He can't *see.*"

"No, and he can't hit an inanimate object to save his life. But he can nail a breathing target every time. You know my laser shooter game? He was less high-minded than you about it—or a lot more bored, I think that was it. We used to play that and he'd get me almost as often as I got him, in the end. I reckon he could do it."

"Hmm. Well, I still need two backups who won't shoot themselves by accident."

"Make sure they're smart enough to overrule their subconscious and pull the trigger," said Bane bluntly. "Because nonLees are so new, I've heard people find it almost as hard to actually shoot people with them as with an ordinary gun. Because we've got hundreds and hundreds of years of conditioning telling us that if we point that thing and go bang, we kill someone."

"Point taken."

"There's something else," said Bane. "If you fail to gain access to the tower, they won't be able to get their machine guns trained on you down there, but if you run back across the yard, they'll have you. So stay put. And fire this straight up over the tower." He slid back up into a sitting position and passed another package through.

I eased the wrappings off and found a pair of squat, fat-barreled pistols. "What are these?"

"Signal guns. If you can't take the tower, fire one of those and we'll...deal with it."

"Deal with it," I said flatly.

"Yes."

"Do I want to know?"

"I doubt it. It's just a contingency plan, anyway."

"If you've got the means to 'deal with' the towers from outside, I'm surprised you're not all for it," I couldn't help remarking.

I saw his wince. "Couple of weeks ago, I was, as it happens," he said quietly. "Save putting you at risk and everything. But...it's not as simple as that, is it?"

"And your friends are happy to let us have all the fun?"

"They're not my friends!" snapped Bane, then went on more calmly, "Dealing with the towers from the forestline means using extremely expensive and hard to obtain resources. They're quite happy to leave it to you."

A pair of bazookas, in other words. Two dead guards in each tower. I weighed the flare gun in my hand. Could I really point this thing at the sky and fire it, knowing what would happen?

"Father Mark asked me to tell you something when I gave you those," said Bane. "He said to remind you every right comes with a corresponding duty. He seemed to think you'd know what that meant."

I bit my lip. The right to life. My right to life. Which meant the right to self-defense. The use of reasonable force against an aggressor. But our faith called us to love everyone and defined real love as considering the other person more important than ourselves. So many Believers would forfeit their right to self-defense rather than harm the other.

But with the right to life came the duty to protect life. Especially that of the innocent and those who couldn't defend themselves. If it was only me escaping I could refuse to use the flare gun and accept the consequences—though in my current predicament, it might require more strength than I possessed. But I couldn't make that choice for the seventy others whose lives I'd a duty to save if I could.

"How do I use this thing?"

I heard Bane let out a relieved breath. "There's a button to press to open the breech, like a shotgun..." I held one of the guns inside the hatch so he could see what I was doing. "That's right. You put the shells in rimless end first; it only takes one at a time. Then snap it shut, take off the safety, point and fire. Don't point it at anyone—well, you can if they're bothering you. And if you have to fire it, stay in the doorway at the base of the tower until...until things stop flying around."

"Right. I think that's all we need to say about the towers. Let's sort out the timings. Could you get back in that ditch?"

Bane slithered back down and I breathed a little easier.

"So when's it all happening?" I asked.

"Well, the book's being published next Tuesday. That *you* wrote the book will be a much bigger story if lots of people have already read it. So my...friend...the reporter will give the story to one person in each major paper, but not until late on Thursday, giving them just a few hours to write their pieces before the midnight deadline for the Friday papers. Leaving the minimum amount of time for tongues to flap," he said darkly.

"My friend's getting an exclusive on the escape out of it, in case you were wondering. Anyway, we're thinking evening of the Friday for the escape. Working on the assumption that the EuroGov may not be very quick deciding what to do. They've got to read the newspapers, read the book, look at the evidence and only then worry what to do about you. And it won't occur to them that *you* could possibly be going anywhere."

But my stomach turned over at the thought of sitting here for a whole day once the EuroGov knew the truth.

"What if..." My voice squeaked slightly and I cleared my throat. "What if someone in one of the papers talks? After the deadline, loads of workers will see what's being printed. The EuroGov make sneaking worth people's while. That would give them a lot of extra time to decide what to do with me. And...it's really *not* going to take them very long!"

"No, I don't think it will take them very long either," he sighed. "I was all for getting you out on the Thursday night and having you safe before the headlines break. But everyone else thinks the headlines will be better if you're still in there. *I* said, well, Margo'll be in there when the headlines were *written*, but *they* think they'll look better mounting a daring and generous rescue of the beleaguered heroine *after* she finds herself in peril. *I* said no one will believe they put together a plan to empty a Facility in one day after reading the headlines and realizing your danger, but *they* said—"

"Bane, I'm not going anywhere with the Resistance. You know that, right?"

"Relax, no one's going anywhere with the Resistance but the Resistance. We'll be heading off a different way. Anyway... Oh, heck, I said a lot and they said a lot, but I couldn't argue *too* hard, because I'd presented the whole thing primarily as a propaganda exercise—embarrass the EuroBloc and get them some good press for once, y'see? To keep them from leveling the place and killing everyone. Which it turns out, you'll be glad to hear, would be so expensive in terms of resources, both live and inanimate, that they're not up for it.

"Well, anyway, we're waiting until Friday night if we can, zero hour at eleven o'clock. But we'll be in position as soon as the newspaper deadline has passed, and I want you to have everything ready as well. If they come for you, if you have any reason to think you can't wait, just get started. Wave this out the dorm window so we know to start the clock."

His hand reached up and pushed a large red silk

handkerchief into the hatch. I tucked it inside my jumpsuit with the three guns.

"Now, timings?" he said. "You know how long it takes to get around in there. I don't."

"Okay. One minute after zero hour—or the red hand-kerchief—start the attack. On all the towers, I think, but the east ones most, to draw all the spare guards over there. If it's nighttime, wait ten more minutes, then intensify the attack, making sure you hit the two west towers a bit harder—they're the ones we'll be taking, so they need to be panicking about then. But not too hard, because the last thing we want is a load of reinforcements *actually* running over there!"

"I wouldn't worry," put in Bane, "at least nine out of ten of those guards will never have heard a gun go off outside a shooting range. I reckon they'll panic way before their officers see the need to send reinforcements. Before I forget, how many are there?"

I'd made this addition already. "There are fourteen internal guards and twenty-eight external. There's just the two officers, Major Everington and Captain Wallis."

"How many other people are inside?"

"Two dismantlers and three minions—that is, lab assistants. A nurse. The minions come and go in six-month shifts like the guards, but the others are permanent staff, like the Captain and Major."

"Some life," sniffed Bane. "Well, we'd got as far as a ten-minute delay at night?"

"Yes. But if it's daytime, wait twenty minutes instead, because we'll have to deal with the camera room. So *please Lord* we can wait until night, because that's just one more thing to go wrong. We'll wave white pillow cases from the west towers to show they're neutralized, intensify the attack on the east towers then, to keep them distracted. But carry on firing into the forest or something on the west side, so they don't suspect.

"While the towers are being taken, someone will be freeing the boys. The girls will head straight across the west exercise yard once it's safe and out the little gate and leg it up to the forestline—they should be pretty organized. The boys shouldn't be far behind, but they'll probably be all over the place. Getting everyone away after that is over to you."

"That's all planned. We're going first to the glade in the Fellest below Rayle's Pass—you remember those caves there? Well, if things go to plan, no one will be looking for us in the Fellest, but if things don't, they'll be a good place to hide until the initial search passes. Then we'll...well, never mind now, let's just say I've figured out what to do with seventy reAssignees. Now," Bane added, "do you remember what I told you about 'nonLethal' being something of a misnomer?"

"Yeah, one shot puts someone out for a few minutes, two shots for hours, three shots for about a week—or forever if they have a health problem—and the fourth shot is fatal."

"You got it."

"I'll make sure everyone else knows. Right. Newspaper deadline, midnight on Thursday night. Red handkerchief any time after that means start the escape. What if it's dark?"

"Have you got a flashlight in the dorm?"

"Several."

"Shine a flashlight through the handkerchief, then. That'll show up clearly enough."

"Okay. Otherwise, zero hour at eleven o'clock Friday night. And if we fail to get into the towers, fire the flare gun. I think I've got my half."

"One minute after zero hour or red handkerchief, start attack. All towers but concentrating on east towers. Ten minutes later at night or twenty minutes later in daytime, intensify attack on west towers. At the white pillow case, intensify on east towers again to keep attention there. Girls coming out first, then boys. Okay?"

"I think that's it. My parents, Jon's parents? Is everything arranged?"

"They're all sorted, Margo. They'll have quietly disappeared well before the truth comes out."

"Good. I thought that was what they were telling me and so did Jon, but...good. Well..." My brain wanted him gone to safety, but my heart wanted to hang onto him, in case something went wrong and this was the last time I saw him in this life. But with a certain effort, common sense took control. "You'd better go."

"Yes." He sounded as reluctant as I felt. He sat up and took my hands again and we remained a few minutes in silence. The moon had finally gone behind a cloud so he didn't seem quite so exposed.

"We've got a good plan," he said at last, giving my hands an encouraging squeeze. "And I know you don't like it and I don't like it as much as I did, but we've got expert help. It's going to be all right. And..." he hesitated, then went on bleakly, "if by some chance it doesn't work, you could always let yourself out the gate during exercise and run for the forestline."

It was my turn to squeeze his hands gently. "You know I can't do that, Bane."

"You might make it."

"You know I wouldn't. Let's not think about that. Let's just think about a week on Friday, being together, free."

"I can think about that." He kissed my hands and for once it was he who decided it was time to go. "I'm off, Margo. Because if I get shot just now, it will be a bit of a nuisance."

"Bye, then. Take care." I kissed my fingertips and pressed them to his lips and he did likewise, then he slithered back into the ditch and was gone.

I shifted the arsenal inside my jumpsuit round to the small of my back, so I'd be able to crawl under the cars—though it was all going to slide right back around, wasn't it? Checking the door card in my jumpsuit pocket, I settled down to wait, peering through the grille and running over the plan in my mind. The moon had come out again.

SNAP!

The sound came from the forestline and almost instantly a search light sliced whitely through the modest amber glow of the flood lights. I caught a momentary glint of wide eyes and a flash of white tail as the deer bounded away.

The guards seemed to have missed it, because the search light began to travel along the forest, probing the shadows under the trees. It reached the end of the forest covered by the southwest tower and, swooping back to the middle, began to run down the drainage ditch, illuminating everything so clearly I could see the individual lumps of mud in the bottom.

Bane!

25

WAITING

One frozen moment of panic—*Lord-what-do-I-do?*—then I leapt to my feet, reaching the wall in one bound. I grabbed the power lever and yanked it down. All the lights outside went out. Oh no, now what? How to get away with this? And they mustn't get the lights back on in time to catch Bane.

By the light of the moon I'd so ungratefully labeled inconvenient, I found the fuse box for the southwest tower. I yanked the SEARCH circuit breaker out of its socket, licked a finger, ran it over the circuit breaker's contacts and jammed it back into place. Lunged back to the power switch and yanked it on. Switch and dampened circuit breaker both snapped off again in unison. Bingo. Just a little forest damp, quite natural.

At the door already, I paused only a second to look and listen, then slipped out and closed the door silently behind me. Footsteps and a distant voice came from the west exercise yard and I literally dived underneath the first car. The guns swung straight round under me, digging into my ribs and abdomen as I landed on them. Wriggling until certain no limbs were sticking out, I lay motionless, smothering my gasps of pain.

"It was a deer." The speaker approached through the gate from the exercise yard. "*Of course* it doesn't hurt to check. But I saw it, right? And see, now the blinkin' fuse has gone again. Right, circuit breaker, whatever. Dratted mist. Yes, clear today, but it was the usual yesterday. If you'd been working here as long as I have, you'd know that's what's done it. Keep your hair on, I'm there now."

The guard disappeared into the guardroom, still grumbling into his wristCell, and I waited, hardly breathing. Before long I saw the dim glow in the sky over the battlements as the flood lights came on again. Bane would be at the treeline by now, though. He'd probably started crawling flat out the moment the lights went off.

Soon the guard came out and grumbled his way back out of sight.

"Damp circuit breaker, what did I tell you? One rub on my sleeve and it's good as new. Come off it, they're always damp. We should just put some Perspex over that stupid grille, I've been saying that for years. What? Well, we could rip it back off if we *needed* to close the shutters, couldn't we?"

I waited until he was out of earshot—which probably meant back inside the tower—before beginning to worm my way under the cars. The guns ground into me, but I didn't waste time on a futile attempt to reposition them. As the stairwell door clicked closed behind me I rubbed my tummy, wincing. Phew. For just a few minutes more I waited, to be sure there weren't going to be any gunshots, then I headed up the stairs. *Lord, let him be safe. Please don't let him die for me!*

"Careful—"

Too late. Jon's foot caught the bucket and he stumbled, palms slapping into the stairwell wall as he recovered himself. "Argh," he snarled. "Why *do* they leave those buckets around?"

It'd never used to bother him.

"I think they're waiting for us to go back to the dorm so they can wash the floor and have it dry before we come down again," said Caroline seriously.

Jon shut eyes and mouth very tight and took several deep breaths. Praying? Then he opened his eyes again and smiled at Caroline, his voice calm again. "Yes, I think you're right."

I didn't hear what he said next because a guard had just gone through the door into the guard block and I'd seen something. The corridor floor beyond glistened wetly and the door to the Major's garden stood ajar, letting the warm summer air in to dry it before too many people walked over it.

And that was it! The Major's garden. The pile of garden

canes leaning beside the hanging wicker hut. Garden canes! Perfect!

Jon's plight really must've been bothering me because I found myself though the door into that damp-floored corridor before I even stopped to think. *Hang on...*

Click. The door closed behind me. No shouting. I hadn't been missed. So I could go into the garden and ask for a cane or just stand where I was and be in trouble for nothing at all. But he'd been so angry with me before...he probably hated me just as much as the Menace did.

But Jon...so stressed and unhappy. I swallowed and slipped through that little door. There was Major Everington, crouched over a flower bed on the far side of the glade. The door swung shut behind me...whoops.

"Who is it?" he snapped, carrying on with whatever he was doing.

"Margaret Verrall, sir."

"*Margaret Verrall, sir?*" I could picture his eyebrows going up and his voice went very silky indeed. "That polite little voice cannot possibly belong to Margaret Verrall. She must want something." He stood and faced me. "Even more than last time."

I approached hesitantly, pricked by an unexpected twinge of guilt. I had been very rude to him before. And yet, though he might rule this roost, he was just as much a hireling of the EGD and society as all the rest of the guards and what'd I said to Bane the other night?

"I'm sorry to come here..." I stopped a few meters away. "But Captain Wallis refused to help."

The Major eyed the left side of my face, where an old bruise spread from temple to cheek. "Refused quite adamantly, did she?"

I shrugged. I wasn't wasting time telling tales on the Menace. He could see what she'd done. "The last time Jonathan was put in with the boys, they broke his stick."

"That boy again." The Major turned back to his flowers.

"Do you have any idea how important a stick is to a blind person?" I demanded, more forcefully than I'd intended. "We've fixed it and fixed it but now it's past fixing. He needs another one. May he have one of your garden canes, please?"

He turned and stared at me for a moment, arms folded across his chest. Then he walked towards the hut and my heart leaped. Would he really? He came back, a cane in one slender hand, and held it out.

"I was not responsible for the breaking of the boy's stick," he stated, as my hand closed eagerly around the replacement. He didn't let go. "So this is a *gift.*" He let go then, leaving it in my hand.

I glared at him, I couldn't help it. Like most of the reAssignees—and guards—I hated the Captain, to my shame—but feared the Major. He seemed to trigger a fight or flight response and for some reason I kept choosing *fight!*

"On *Jon's* behalf, thank you," I replied, just as deliberately.

He smiled slightly, his eyes glinting. Green eyes, I realized with a jolt, like my own. "Out," he said, pointing at the door. There was a slight edge to it that warned me not to come back a third time.

I made to go, but the question just popped out. "Why did you do that to Finchley?"

I saw those blond eyebrows rise, this time. "Was I misinformed? Did he not try to have his wicked way with you? With notably little success," he smirked.

"No, you weren't misinformed."

"Then I don't understand the question."

"I meant...why didn't you sack him?"

"Why, I assure you, this makes a far better example of him. You must know the guards are strictly forbidden to hurt you children."

"*Adults.* If we weren't in here, we'd count as adults."

"But you *are* in here, aren't you?"

I was thinking about the rest of his sentence. "Shame that doesn't apply to officers." I bit my lip too late.

His eyes narrowed. "Oh, it does apply to officers." His voice had gone dangerously soft. "A reminder seems to be in order, I agree. *Another* reminder."

Another? I did bite my tongue this time. Had he already punished her once? Was that why she seemed to hate me so very much?

"As for Finchley," went on the Major in a less spine-chilling tone, "now he will have to work here for at least another two or three years, on best behavior, to save the money to buy himself a new cheek. It would be hard enough for him to change career normally, and they don't do cosmetic transplants for free, you know."

"That doesn't strike me as a *plus.*"

"I imagine not. But *you* don't have to replace his useless carcass. Besides, I can assure you that *new* guards are the worst offenders. Especially if there isn't a Finchley around for...illustrative purposes. The longer-serving guards seem to think better of such misconduct."

"Can't imagine why."

"I can." His smile was cruel, this time; his green eyes merciless. "Now clear off, I'm busy."

I eyed his flower beds and just swallowed a cutting remark. I didn't want to push him too far, like last time. I turned again... *Ah.* "Um...I kind of snuck in."

He made an impatient noise and strode past me towards the door, unbuttoning a breast pocket and taking out his card. "And here I assumed you'd just threatened a guard with the RWB."

Two guards were dithering on the threshold when he swung the door open. They braced up and tried to look as though they'd been about to open the door and reclaim me. "Er...there was a girl, sir..."

The Major stepped to one side, waving me past him. I stopped between them like a good little reAssignee, but they continued to stare at the Major expectantly.

"Just take her back to the dorm," he snapped impatiently. And slammed the door in their faces. Mine too, I suppose. I held the cane tightly. *Yes! Don't you take it, guards.*

I perhaps had the Major's 'just' to thank since they shut me in the dorm without showing any interest in the cane whatsoever.

"Margy!"

"Margo, there you are!"

"Where have you been, Margo?"

Then Jon came stumbling up to me and caught me in his arms, lifting me off my feet as he crushed me to him. I held out the cane behind him to keep it safe, though it was pretty sturdy.

"Margo, Margo, you're all right! You're all right!" He buried his face in my hair, inhaling deeply. "Thank God," he whispered into my hair. "Thank God."

He kissed me, seeming beyond all restraint, and I didn't dare pull away. It wasn't quite time for the escape, after all. His lips weren't *unpleasant* on mine, anyway, just *not quite right*. But he went back to hugging me pretty quickly, hugging me and...trying not to cry?

"Jon, Jon, calm down, I'm fine. I'm fine. What's wrong?"

"What's wrong?" he echoed incredulously. "You dis-appear into thin air and you ask what's wrong? Just *now?*" he added under his breath, lips buried in my hair again. "I thought they'd found out! I thought they'd taken you! I thought they were... I thought they were... *Heck*, Margo! *What's wrong!*"

"Hush," I whispered, my stomach clenching guiltily, "hush, be careful. I'm sorry, I only meant to be quick...well, to be honest I didn't really think at all, I just acted on the spur of the moment. Here, I got this for you." I pressed the cane into his hands.

"A stick!" He ran his fingers along its length, sniffed it, looked up in surprise. "A garden cane?"

"Yes, from the Major's garden."

"You didn't *steal* it!"

"No!" I slapped his hand lightly. "I asked for it for you."

"Margo, how could you go in there? I thought he hated you!"

"So did I, the way he spoke to me before. Who knows. He's a strange, twisted man. He gave you that, anyway."

Perhaps just to get one over me but who cared.

"Margo, oh, Margo, thank you so much." He went back to hugging me, in mingled thanks, reproach, and profound relief.

But mostly thanks.

It wasn't until the day of publication that I told the dorm we were to escape in three days time. And that they MUST NOT mention it to anyone. Nor must they mention the little gun I had. They must not, must not, must not. I went round to each girl in turn to make sure they really understood.

Satisfied at last, I instigated an 'orchestra' game to cover up a quick trial of my most likely shooters. Everyone rapping out tunes on metal chair legs and drumming on tabletops drowned out the unexceptional noise of the air gun well enough.

Jon agreed with Bane's judgment that he could probably do it better than anyone else available, so he would be number one of the second pair. Jane and Rebecca were my first choices for backups, but that plan only lasted as long as it took Rebecca to take her go.

"Well," I sighed, when she'd finished, "I think we can safely say that a pair of barn doors are in no danger from *you*. Never mind. Not everyone's a natural shot. Jane, would you try?"

Three times in a row Jane came close enough to the piece of paper on the door that she'd have hit the person she was aiming at.

"Good. You're one backup, then, if that's okay with you. We still need another."

Emily was pretty sharp, but there was no way to test her shooting abilities without passing the gun through the wall. I eyed the girls in our dorm. Some were slightly smarter than Caroline, but I knew her. If things were explained clearly beforehand, she'd probably do what was necessary.

"Caroline? Would you come and try?"

"Me? Yeah, I want a go!"

She hit the paper itself twice, with a third near miss.

"Right. You're the second backup."

"*Really?* Is it difficult?"

"No, it's not difficult at all. You'll be with me and you probably won't have to do a thing."

"Okay. I'm it. Harriet, did you see that? I'm a *backup*."

"Is it dangerous?"

"Um...hope not."

As they carried on speculating, Jon dipped his head to the general vicinity of my ear. "Are you all right?"

"Yeah, fine. No one should know yet." I concentrated for a moment on checking that the air gun was unloaded, then took it back to Jon's bunk and put it in his chest.

Jon followed. "Don't you think you should carry that with you?"

"I don't dare. The exercise sacks are baggy, but not that baggy. If someone spots it... I can't use it anywhere where there are cameras, anyway, not in daytime. It would be over before we even started."

"True enough. You'll have to carry it on Friday, though."

"I know. I'll just stick it inside in the waist string and hunch like I've got tummy ache. I'll get off exercise as well."

Jon looked startled. "How?"

"I'll say I'm having really bad cramps from my period. They won't say another word." When Jon didn't reply and suddenly felt the need to open his chest and check his clothes were over the gun, I said, "See. Foolproof."

"All right, it'll work," said Jon, flushing, but he stopped fiddling around in the chest.

It was really rather weird. The day I'd been thinking about for so long, dreading, waiting for, and it was passing silent as a dream. Elsewhere, people were (hopefully) taking copies of the book off shelves and handing over money for them, they were plugging their Readers into bookshop terminals; the wealthiest would even be downloading it from the comfort of their own homes. And here, most of the people in the dorm didn't even know it'd just been released. And only a handful of people in the entire world knew the truth.

But after another moment, I couldn't help voicing a secret fear. "D'you think any of the guards here have ordered the postSort novel?"

"Possible," said Jon honestly. "But there's no post until Friday, is there? They won't get their books or any news-papers until then. By which time the cavalry will be ready and waiting. And most of the guards don't know our names, so I really wouldn't sit around worrying about that."

"Umm. You know, we'll have to be careful about the Major."

"Hmm?"

"Well, he's always in his garden, isn't he? And he might smell a rat if he sees everyone marching along the corridor at the wrong time."

"The glass is frosted outside the dorms, isn't it?"

"Yes, but he might see shadows moving. I just think we should bear it in mind."

We sometimes caught a glimpse of the Major from the cafeteria corridor, reading or messing around with his plants. Not always, because the off-duty staff ate at the same time as us, in their mess hall, and apparently he sometimes ate with them. But one day when I'd idly asked Sally if he liked to watch all the boys' dismantlements the way the Menace watched those of the girls, she'd replied, "Oh no, not the Major. He just sits in his garden and pretends the world doesn't exist, as far as I can see. Unless someone crosses him and then..." She'd trailed off in the manner of prudent subordinates the world over.

Well, I was worrying for nothing. Surely a Resistance attack would drag him from his retreat, even if nothing much else could.

The next two days were far worse than the days before the competition result was announced; far, far worse than the days before my Sorting. Every moment was agony—if the truth became known now, there would be no question of escape; no question of anything but the unthinkable or the unendurable.

I drilled the others in the Silent Crocodile both mornings and began to brief them more fully. From now on, I told them, they must not stir a step without their crocodile buddy beside them. And I explained carefully and repeatedly that by Thursday evening everyone was to have everything ready. Everyone was to wear their warmest clothes and their stoutest shoes—*yes, I know it's midsummer, but it will be cold at night*—and they could take only what they could fit in their pockets.

People complained. People cried. People sulked. Jon, Rebecca, Jane, and I explained, reasoned and comforted—well, Jon, Rebecca, and I comforted—until we'd talked them all around and everyone settled down to go through their chests and consider which small items to take.

With that done I fell back on desperate prayer, or trying to pray, or crying to the Lord in terror and begging for strength. I was pale and jumpy and couldn't help it.

"How good is this plan, Margo?" demanded Jane on Thursday, eyeing me closely.

"There's absolutely nothing wrong with the plan, Jane," I replied calmly. "I have something else on my mind."

"I'll say. You're as twitchy as a rat."

"Why, thank you, Jane. You're as flattering as ever."

She was right, though. On Thursday night I didn't sleep at all. I lay, cuddled in the circle of Jon's arm for once, in turn hugging air gun, flashlight, and red handkerchief to me. Bane and a hard-faced group would be easing through the trees now... The passing of midnight brought relief—suddenly there was hope—but also far greater torment—the chances of discovery rose by the hour.

Jon didn't sleep until five o'clock, but I lay wakeful until Sally stuck her head in with a still rather subdued, "Good morning, girls and boy."

Lord, protect Sally and Watkins and the decent guards today, please?

Friday passed as slowly as drops of lead oozing down-hill. I dressed in the clothes I'd chosen for the escape, jeans and a tough linen tunic, and tried to act normally, tried to be calm and confident, but by midday I fled to the washroom. My nerves were infecting the others and if I didn't have a few minutes to get it out of my system I was going to make everyone hysterical.

Sitting on a closed toilet, curled around the air gun digging into my stomach, I cried hard for a good ten minutes before stopping quite suddenly from sheer nervous exhaustion. But it'd bled off the worst of it and I went almost immediately to the basins to wash my face.

The tramp of several pairs of feet made me freeze, shutting the faucet off quickly. I snatched out the air gun, feeble weapon that it was, and tiptoed up to the door, listening hard.

Doctor Richard's drawl and the Menace's growl. Had they come for me? Oh...*rats!*

I couldn't go out into the passage, I could do nothing there. So I would have to wait here. Force them to come in for me, out of the camera's eye. And try to hold them up by myself, without the numerical support, however unarmed, of the other girls. Blast. *I shouldn't have come in here!*

Backing to the end of the room, I clicked off the air gun's safety and held it out of sight behind my back. *Come on, then, all is not lost yet.*

Seconds drew silently on into minutes and still the door didn't open. What was taking so long? The duty guards knew I was in here.

Finally I heard the footsteps again and stiffened, my heart managing to beat even faster still. I gripped the gun so tightly my fingers ached. I had to pull this off, alone or not...

But the footprints receded. I heard the clink-clatter of the passage's barred gate being opened, then closed. Seized with sudden, terrible foreboding, I rushed the length of the room and eased the door open a crack, peeping out just in time to see the dismantlers' white coats disappearing through the door at the opposite end of the passage. Behind them followed Brandon and Dwight, marching a tall figure with braids between them.

As they reached the door Jane looked back down the corridor. Her eyes met mine, full of appeal, but her pinched eyes and lips said all too clearly that she knew there was nothing I could do.

The door closed behind them with a very final click.

26

ESCAPE

I almost had to go back into the cubicle for another ten minutes: the blow was so terrible. Still eleven hours until zero hour! Far too long. Unless we started the plan early. But there was nothing in the plan about going to the Lab to rescue someone.

And the daytime plan was so much riskier. Less cover for the diversion-providers—and the inescapable need to put the camera room out of commission. Which involved going to the guard block, not the Lab block. How could we possibly go to both simultaneously? We didn't have enough shooters—nor would we have enough guns. But to do both consecutively—we wouldn't be at the towers in time...

Mind churning, I pressed the buzzer to get the guard to let me back into the dorm. I had to speak to Jon. *Lord, what do I do? Risk the seventy sheep to save the one? Or save the seventy?*

In the dorm, everyone was upset though Jane had clearly made less of a scene than Polly. Some of the crocodile pairs were holding, others had broken up. Harriet flung herself on me, but I ruthlessly turned her over to Caroline, hurrying to Jon.

"Jon?" I demanded.

He grimaced. "You want to know if I think you should start the escape now and try to save Jane."

"Yes."

"I..." He bit his lip. "I'm really not sure we *can*, you know. You must see that? We haven't got the manpower—girl power—to pull off anything extra. Especially not if we have to deal with the camera room as well. The plan we've got has a really good chance of working. But *only* if we don't mess around with it—"

"But if they'd come to take *me*, we'd be starting now!" I

exclaimed, agonized. "Just because it's Jane, we're going to play safe?"

"This isn't about playing safe!" snapped Jon, for once losing his temper. "If they come for you, we just start the *same* plan early. This calls for a complete departure from the plan! A complete departure that may get seventy people killed! Do the math, Margo!"

"I can't *do* math!" I hissed. "That's why they put me in here!"

Jon's lips tightened, but before he could reply a chattering roar from outside brought us both to our feet. "*What the...?*"

"Helicopter!" I gasped.

Everyone stampeded towards the window.

"I think it's going to land here!" cried Caroline, peering out.

My blood turned to ice in my veins. "What are the markings?" I choked out, my voice rising sharply. The EuroArmy were the largest owner of helicopters but... "*Whose is it?*"

"I don't know," said Caroline. "Euro-something. Hey, let Margo see it..."

I waded to the front just in time to see the machine bank and disappear over the top of our block. The circle of little blue stars with a huge yellow star in the center was clearly visible—as was the crest surrounding it. I spun around with a choked gasp, gripped with an almost irresistible impulse to run, though there was nowhere to run to.

Jon was behind me. His hands found my shoulders and ran down my arms to close around my wrists. "Breathe, Margo. Whose helicopter is it?"

"EuroGov. *EuroGov.*" I shook like a leaf.

He folded me to him, rubbing my back with slow, deliberate movements of his hand. "Breathe, Margo. We know why they're here; it's not a surprise, is it?"

"Huh?" Rebecca looked baffled.

"And we've got a plan, remember? A very good plan. So let's get ready, shall we?"

I took hold of myself and eased away from him. *Don't panic in front of the troops, Margo. Best if they trust you know what you're doing.* The chattering of the helicopter grew louder and suddenly the whole dorm was vibrating, shaking, people looking around in panic...

"No need to worry, it's just the helicopter landing on our roof." Somehow I managed to speak—shout—lightly. "Looks like the helipad is on our block. That was an amazing machine, wasn't it?"

"I saw it really close up!"

"I saw right underneath it!"

"I could see the little people sitting in it," yelled Harriet.

"Loud," shouted Sarah, shaking her head, hands pressed over her ears.

But the shaking died down and the noise with it. When things were quiet enough for me to speak normally, I interrupted the discussion about the amazing machine.

"Okay, everyone. You remember I said we'd probably be leaving at eleven tonight, but we might be leaving sooner? Well, we'll be leaving sooner. Some time quite soon, some guards will come in here and we'll make them give us their guns. Now, you remember we talked about this before. I'll do the talking. The most important thing is to get those guns and not to let any of the guards leave the dorm. If anyone doesn't understand, now is the time to say so."

Nobody spoke up and I'd drilled everyone thoroughly, so I let them all go to their bunks to put on any final layers and make last minute adjustments to their pocketfuls. Slipping my coat on, I touched the pocket that held my bookReader, my little photo wallet, my letters, my sewing kit and my purse. I checked the other pocket even more carefully, stuffed to capacity with white pillow case, flashlight, red handkerchief, air gun pellets—much good they'd do—flare gun and cartridges.

Then I sat on the edge of Jon's bunk with the air gun in my lap and waited, concentrating on answering last minute queries from all comers.

"They'll have to get the bigwigs unloaded and take them to the best room in the place," said Jon, slowly and calmly, sitting beside me. Talking to take up time and distract me, bless him. "Then I imagine they'll offer them refreshments and only then will they broach the business of why they're here."

"And send the guards to get me."

"And send the guards to get you."

"I hope they send at least three." I was talking too fast but I couldn't help it. "Three guns would be best. In case there *is* only one guard in the camera room. But four guards at once might be too much to handle. Because I think we could probably still take them, but it'll be a real pain if anyone gets shot and has to be carried out."

"We'll manage," said Jon, very firm and very calm. His rare anger had disappeared. He must be almost as stressed as I was.

Everyone milled and chattered, mostly holding hands with their buddy. The longer I waited, the more the fear was overwhelmed by growing impatience. If there was any chance at all for Jane, we had to get started. But Jon was right. I couldn't jeopardize the escape.

And finally we heard the click of the stairwell door and the tramp of feet. Too many feet to be the hourly check. I got up and moved to a spot three quarters of the way down the dorm, so that anyone who wanted to speak to me would have to advance well into the room. I put my hands—and the gun—casually behind my back and waited.

The Menace strode into the dorm, practically trembling with a mixture of rage, triumph and anticipation. Sally and Watkins followed her in—Sally did evening to morning shifts and Watkins was off duty today, so all the duty guards must be running around after the exalted visitors.

My heart sank—the two guards I least wanted to shoot. But...if they were unconscious on the dorm floor, they couldn't be ordered up to the battlements, could they? The Lord might just be watching out for them, after all.

"So." Captain Wallis actually spoke instead of barking, but her tone sent a shiver down my spine. "Margaret Verrall. *Margaret Verrall.* What *shall* we do with you?"

The others all looked at me blankly. They'd no idea the half of what was going on.

Sally's eyes were wide. "Margaret, why did you do it?"

"Silence," snapped the Menace. "Margaret Verrall, we have some very important visitors. They require your presence. I would suggest you make your goodbyes, since

I think the chances of you being brought back are very slender indeed."

"I agree. I have no intention of being *brought back*. I have no intention of going *anywhere* with *you* three." Swiftly, I covered them with the air gun, adopting a proper shooting pose, my feet well apart, both hands steadying the butt, so they could see I knew what I was doing. "Keep your hands where I can see them, please."

All three of them stared at me in disbelief. No, at the thing in my hands. No time to stop, I must carry this through before they had a chance to think too hard. I walked forward towards them, slowly, my voice dropping to a menacing snarl. "Take out your weapon, *Captain*, and hand it to me, nice and slowly."

"How dare you—"

"How dare I, *Captain?*" My voice snapped with rage, no acting required, merely the loosing of my darkest thoughts and desires. "How dare *I?* I wonder *you* dare speak to me like that, *you!* Who rejoiced in the death of one of my oldest, dearest friends, who have gloated over the deaths of hundreds, who would delight in watching the deaths of *me* and *mine!*

"Understand this, *Captain*, I loathe and detest you more than any person on this earth and if you don't hand me your gun right now I will shoot you, and I will shoot you again, and I will keep pulling this trigger until there is no more charge and then we will see who dares speak to whom!"

The Captain stepped back a half step, her face whitening. Yes, she was a coward. I'd counted on it. She seized her gun with a shaking hand and drew it—carefully—taking the barrel with her other hand and beginning to hold it out to me, butt first.

But Watkins—more courage and more brains, it would be him—went for his gun. For a split second I waited, waited for the nonLee to be free of his holster, then I aimed and fired. The pellet struck the gun, spinning it from his hand. He swore in shock and spun around, but seeing six girls diving for it, came at me instead, understanding clear on his face.

The warden hadn't seen what happened and wasn't so

quick to understand. Shoving the air gun into my left hand, I snatched the half-proffered pistol from her and raised it to point straight at Watkins, snapping off the safety.

He lurched to a halt and spread his hands: *I surrender.* "Well, I've always said they shouldn't make replicas," he panted.

"You're lucky, Watkins," I said in return. "I might've broken your finger."

"What?" stammered the warden, in a poor attempt at her usual bluster. "What is going on!"

"We've been held up with a toy gun, Captain, near enough," he informed her tonelessly.

"Rebecca, get Sally's gun, would you?" I muttered.

Sally was pale and shaking, her eyes wider than ever. No surprise if she didn't deal with this well, just at the moment.

Watkins touched her shoulder, careful not to move his hands out of my sight. "Sit down, lass." Taking his own advice, he creaked down onto the floor, stretching out his legs comfortably.

"Wh...what?" stammered Sally.

"Less far to fall," said Watkins calmly. "Come, sit down. I'm quite sure they're going to send us sleepy-bye in a minute."

Sally crouched hesitantly beside Watkins, beginning to cry.

"Sally, it's all right," I said, softening my voice with difficulty. "We're not Resistance, okay? We're not going to hurt you. You're going to get a nice little nap, that's all." Best not mention the splitting headache she had to look forward to.

"See, they're not going to hurt us, Sally," Watkins comforted her. "We know Margaret, don't we? She's a nice girl—"

Sally looked at him as he spoke, so I raised the nonLee and shot her. Watkins caught her as she toppled and since laying her down put him very near the ground, I shot him too. Which just left the Menace, sweating and fuming all at once.

"You can't do this," she whined.

"Oh, shut up." I pulled the trigger again. No one moved to catch her and her head bounced as it hit the linoleum floor.

Well, I had a gun in each hand, that was my excuse. Aiming carefully, I put another charge into each unconscious figure. So that was three guards out of the picture for some hours.

Everyone was staring. Jon came up to me, so I took a deep, steadying breath and said as lightly as I could, "Good thing she believed I was serious, huh?"

Jon looked amused. "You were rather scary, you know."

Oh. I plastered a big smile on my face as I turned to my staring companions. *See, it's just Margaret, the same as ever.*

"Okay, everyone, looks like the escape is on. Um, could you give that to Jon, Harriet? And Rebecca, give that gun to Caroline for now, but you're number two backup, all right?"

Rebecca was clearly aghast. "What happened to the barn doors being in no danger?"

"You shouldn't have to do a thing and if you do they're going to be a lot closer than the door was. You'll be fine." Well, didn't I sound confident! Rebecca went on looking dubious, but the near-panic left her face.

"Could some of you get Watkins' uniform off and give it to Jon? Caroline, you'll need Sally's uniform, I think." She was taller and skinnier than me. But that left me with the Menace's. Oh joy.

Once the unfortunate—fortunate?—guards were stripped to their underwear we heaved Watkins and Sally into two of the lower bunks and tucked them up with blankets. The Menace was even heavier than Watkins, or such was the excuse everyone gave, so a blanket was chucked over her where she lay and everyone tried not to step on her. Some harder than others.

With a pillow stuffed down my front I was able to button up the Menace's trousers without them falling off. I transferred the items necessary for the escape to the pockets of the uniform jacket, then, folding our own clothes, the three of us packed them into the one bag we'd be taking.

"Right." I went to the window, opened it and looked out. As far as I could tell none of the guards in the towers were looking, and there was no one else in sight. I put my arm out, handkerchief in hand, and began to wave it. On only the third swing back and forth, a glint came from a point on the forestline, three times.

I drew my arm back in, shut the window and checked my watch. "Okay, everyone. Jon, Caroline, and I are going to walk out of here and straight to the camera room. We'll deal with that and come straight back. When we return, everyone must be ready to go down to the gym, okay? Rebecca, we'll bring you a uniform back with us."

Rebecca nodded without any further argument.

"Right—"

KABOOM!

The most immense explosion came from immediately above us. The whole building shook, an upper bunk collapsed, and chunks of ceiling came down all around. Screaming filled the dorm as people ran wildly to the door, climbed into lower bunk recesses or flung themselves down on the ground with their arms over their heads. I grabbed Jon at his off-balance lurch, and we clung to each other until the room stopped shaking.

"It's all right!" I bellowed, as soon as my ears had stopped ringing. "We're safe, it's okay, someone just bazookered the helicopter..."

"No one's aiming at us," Jon joined in, "Calm down, calm down..."

As Rebecca, Jon, and I all yelled reassurances, the screaming died down and people immediately began to relocate their buddies. *Good.* The crack crack of gunfire—the audible Lethal kind—began outside.

"I suppose they considered that a worthy target, however limited their stocks," I muttered to Jon. "Told Bane he wouldn't be able to control them. I just hope the pilot wasn't in there."

Grim-faced, Jon said nothing. No way for us to know.

"Let's go," I said. *Lord, let the door not be buckled.*

"Remember, Caroline," added Jon, "Neither of us will fire unless Margo misses; we don't want to hit them too many times, do we?"

Caroline shook her head vigorously and Jon must've heard her hair brushing her collar because he handed Rebecca his cane and followed me to the door, his hand touching lightly against my sleeve for guidance. Caroline fell in on the other side, trying to look sober and only managing a look of subdued excitement.

I swiped the card, and the door opened fine. Letting out the breath I'd been holding, I tugged the peaked officer's cap lower over my face and led the way down the corridor, trying to imitate the Menace's bullish stride.

The camera room was at the top of the guard block so we only had to cross the stairwell. It would've been good to stop and listen before venturing across, but real guards didn't sneak around. The door of what was clearly the duty guardroom was open, the room empty, so they must've rushed up to the roof.

The next door was helpfully labeled CAMERA ROOM so I swiped the Menace's card and walked in, Jon and Caroline at my heels.

Three guards. One more than I'd anticipated.

The one on the right had obviously been watching our approach on his bank of monitors, for he spun his swivel chair around. "Captain, should any of us go to the roof as w..." He trailed off, frowning. He'd realized I wasn't the Captain but hadn't yet identified me.

Raising the pistol, I didn't give him the chance. I got the second one before he'd even turned around and the third one as he did so.

"Okay?" asked Jon.

"All down. Can you start on the uniform, Caroline? The guy in the middle looks the best size. Wait..." I carefully put a second charge into each one then looked at the three banks of monitors. "Go ahead. Okay, how do we disable these things, Jon? You said it was simple."

Jon grinned. "Fire a few charges into them. Trust me, it'll scramble the whole system."

"Oh. Simple. Deal with that humming thing, would you?"

I fired once into each bank of monitors and Jon fired three times into the humming, twinkling tower of computer equipment. The lights went out, and the humming stopped. The monitors had gone black.

"Good." Collecting up all three pistols, I hurried to help Caroline with the trousers while Jon stood by the door, listening.

"This is so weird," muttered Caroline, as we struggled with the things. "S'like undressing the world's largest doll, only he's all floppy. I don't like it."

"I suggest you don't become a nurse, then," I couldn't help laughing.

"I'm a Borderline." Caroline's flat drone suggested frequent repetition in the past. "It's best if I don't think about things like that." She was quiet for a long moment. "But... we're *escaping*, aren't we?"

"That's right." Jon still had his ear pressed to the door hinges. "Soon as we're safely outside the walls you can start thinking about what you want to be."

"Where are we going? Oops!" The trousers had come off at last.

"It's all organized but we haven't got time to talk about it now." I briskly folded the trousers and added them to the neat pile Caroline had just picked up. Well, it was all organized, I just didn't actually know where we *were* going, after the glade at Rayle's Pass. "Right, all clear, Jon?"

"Think so. Can't hear anyone."

Nice and boldly, we strode out. But I paused to fire into the card reader by the door. Keep everyone guessing a bit longer if they couldn't get in.

"We should've brought a blanket for that fellow," I remarked, as we headed back along the corridor. "It's not that warm today." This gave Jon what could only be described as a fit of the giggles, for some reason. "*What?*"

"Nothing," he sniggered. "Nothing at all."

"Hmm." But we'd reached the stairwell again and crossed it silently. My watch showed it'd taken almost exactly ten minutes—most of that spent wrestling the uniform off the guard.

Cries of delight—and clapping—greeted our arrival.

"Quick, Rebecca, into this... Wow, good thinking." Rebecca, in her underwear, had simply let a blanket fall and grabbed the trousers. Mel stood nearby holding the bag, in which Rebecca's clothes were clearly already packed. "Very organized! And you're all in a crocodile ready, great. As soon as Rebecca's dressed, we'll be off."

I walked once up and down the line, checking the pairs.

There'd had to be a little reorganization so the original buddies of those impersonating guards had suitable partners and final last minute changes due to Jane's loss had put Harriet with Sarah and Bethan with Annie.

"Are you okay, Sarah?"

Sarah stared at me solemnly and pointed accusingly at my uniform.

"It's okay, Sarah, I'm not *really* a guard. It's just a game. A *let's pretend* game. I won't be a guard for much longer, I promise. Now, stick with Harriet, okay?"

Sarah nodded, still staring unhappily at my clothes.

"I'm letting the others out," I said, leaving the dorm again. Hooking the barred gate back, I swiped the card at the Old Year's door and hooked that back as well. Emily waited, wide eyed and breathless with nerves, but with a crocodile of seven neat pairs arranged behind her.

"Here." I gave her one of the spare guns—she'd agreed to free the boys. "That'll deal with any guards you meet, but I think they're all outside. Use it to keep the boys at a distance, though."

"I certainly will," said Emily.

"Hook all the doors back first, remember? And call them all out into the passage and tell them what's going on before you open the stairwell door. Then run like billy-ho, you can't trust them. Oh, and no more than two shots into anyone and..."

"...keep the safety on when not in use. I've got it, I've got it. This is Rachel," she gestured to the young woman next to her. "She'll look after the others."

"Good. Nice to meet you face to face. Uh, all of you. We're almost ready to go. Emily, you'd better set off. Could the rest of you wait in here until I call for you to come?"

"Will do," said Rachel.

She'd always seemed pretty on the ball, so I handed her the other spare gun. "Would you have this and take a shot at anything that threatens you all while you're waiting in the gym?"

"I'm game."

"You've heard the safety talk about not shooting anyone more than twice and keeping the safety catch on?"

"Yep."

"Oh, please don't shoot us if we have to come back for any reason, okay?"

"Try not to," she smiled.

Returning to my dorm, I was greeted by Rebecca's anxious, "I'm ready. I shall probably shoot *myself* in the foot, though."

"Look, just peep around the door and warn Jon if you see something he can't hear, and don't take the safety off unless...unless you have to take over from him, okay?"

"You'd better drop them both first shot," Rebecca muttered to Jon. "Or we're sunk."

"Or swap with Caroline? Jon, who do you think is most likely to need a backup, you or me?"

Jon shrugged. "*You* seem to be doing just fine. Perhaps I *should* take Caroline, since, no offense, Rebecca, she can actually hit what she aims at."

I hesitated. "No, Rebecca, go with Jon. And remember he can't see and he doesn't even have his stick, so *don't leave him*. Okay?"

Rebecca nodded firmly and I felt a bit better. *Lord, let her not have to shoot.* Because never mind the chances of her actually hitting anything, if she did, Jon would probably be dead. But with all the best intentions in the world, Caroline seemed more likely to panic and leave him behind somewhere.

"Come with me then, Caroline, as planned. And if you have to shoot, don't hesitate, all right? Remember you're not going to hurt them."

Caroline nodded and came to stand beside me. If anything she looked relieved not to have the added responsibility of being Jon's eyes.

"Right, let's go. Rachel?" I called down the passage. "We're off."

Us 'guards' went two at the front and two at the back of the double crocodile, just in case anyone catching only a quick look might be fooled. The gunfire continued, mostly rather distantly from the east side of the compound. We were still on schedule. The stairwell was empty, everyone on the roof with the remains of the helicopter or on the east battlements providing targets for the no doubt well concealed Resistance fighters. We reached the gym without seeing anyone at all.

"Keep everyone ready in their crocodiles," I told Rachel. "Soon as you see us run from the base of the towers to the gate, bring everyone over. Jon, you'd better speak into the microphone on your side; after all, there're only supposed to be two female guards in this entire place, plus the Captain. So Rebecca, you'll have to aim him at the mic. Make sure he's too close to be identifiable."

"Right," said Rebecca.

"As planned," said Jon calmly, though he must know I was repeating it for Rebecca's sake. The sheen of sweat on his brow suggested far more nerves than he showed. Small wonder. Suddenly, making a blind person go into lethal combat seemed all kinds of cruel.

The gunfire intensified, loud and close. Too late now.

"That's our cue." My would-be light voice came out a strangled croak.

Swiping the card through the reader beside the external doors of the gym, I eased one open, looking out. Empty battlements, as expected. With their fancy bulletproof towers they weren't going to set men out as targets unless things were getting hot. From down here the guards inside the towers were invisible, no clue how many or which way they were looking. From the crack and twang of bullets glancing off the glass, they were probably not looking at us. Just now, I'd rather be shot than stay in here, anyway.

I set off across the yard at an urgent run, head bowed. Just your Captain racing to the rescue. With an audible gulp, Caroline followed. Also wondering which way the machine guns were pointing? Sand scuffed as Rebecca and Jon started for their tower then all my attention focused on that doorway.

Swiping the card the instant I arrived, I hovered close to the camera's eye until a frightened voice yelled a decidedly non-regulation, "*What?*" from the speaker.

I shoved my face up against the mic and returned an equally non-regulation roar of, "Reinforcements!" Turned my head over my shoulder and added, "Hurry up, you!"

"Thank Goh...oodness!" came from the speaker. One very rattled guard indeed.

The light flicked green.

I yanked open the door and dived in. Utilitarian concrete steps wound upwards. I took them two at a time, Caroline racing along behind me—no need to give these guards time to think too hard either. The door at the top had only a card reader and opened inwards, so I swiped the card and stepped forward, shielding my body behind the opening door.

Three guards.

Could be worse, in the circumstances. Two were hunched over their machine guns, swiveling them this way and that without firing—searching for assailants who weren't deigning to show themselves. The third crouched with his rifle through the gun slit, firing so wildly he couldn't actually be aiming at anything.

None of them looked around, so I shot the one with the rifle first, since he could most easily turn his weapon on us. Then the two with the machine guns. They slumped over, then slithered down those big guns to the floor, totally oblivious to what'd just happened. *Thank you, Lord.* Let Jon and Rebecca have similar success.

Caroline was peeping around the doorway. I waved at her to stay where she was, briskly put a second shot into each guard, then got down on hands and knees and crawled to the gun slit on the west side. Keeping my head down, I carefully poked the white pillowcase out, waving it. The bullets abruptly stopped twanging off the glass, though the retorts of the guns continued. So. Bane was right: they'd been well drilled.

The other tower stood blackly against a background of thin forest mist. After a few moments, something white appeared from its gun slit. A huge knot in my chest untangled itself.

"Come on." I rushed for the stairs.

"It worked!" Caroline gasped as she tore after me. "D'you think we're actually going to do it?"

Lord willing. I took a cautious look at the surrounding battlements before going back into the yard. Still empty. As planned, the brief concentration of fire on this side had already died back down. But I just said, "Come on. All clear."

We raced across the sand to the little wall gate. Rebecca ran to meet us, towing Jon behind her. Jon picked his feet up well clear of the sand, but kept pace. It must take some trust, or effort of will, to run flat out towards you knew not what.

"Whoa!" called Rebecca, as she skidded to a halt, causing Jon to slow down enough that he didn't knock her flat.

I flung my arms around him and hugged him.

"Oh, you're okay," he sighed, hugging me back and burying his face in my hair in a way that made me glad Bane wasn't in eyesight. But his arms trembled slightly. "Huh, *three* of them, you know. I was afraid I might not hear them over all that shooting, but it was fine."

"We had three too. You got them all?"

"Well, yeah, only one of them was facing me and I think he must've been trying to figure out who I was, so it was child's play—none of them thought to hold their breath! S'pect you got all yours."

"No trouble to speak of." I swiped the card and eased the gate open, poking out the white pillow case and waving it a few times before opening it all the way. Just in case the Resistance weren't quite as well drilled as it appeared. The others were only meters away now, jogging across the yard in their crocodile.

"Rebecca, you hang onto Jon, won't you? Caroline, stick with me. In fact, go on, Rebecca, it may take Jon longer to get up that bank."

"Okay, come on, Jon," Rebecca took Jon in tow again.

He resisted. "Wait, wait, let me get my stick. Thanks, Harriet. Okay, let's go. Coming, Margo?"

"I'm going to make like a sheepdog and follow up the rear."

"You should be first out of here," grumbled Jon, but clearly deducing that the more he delayed the crocodile the longer I'd be stuck here, he allowed Rebecca to drag him away.

I watched them all passed me, then dropped my voice slightly to be sure Jon wouldn't hear. He was halfway up the slope by now, *but.* "Go on, Caroline, I'll just make sure Emily and everyone else get out okay. I won't be far behind you. Go on, just stick with the crocodile," I added, as she hesitated. Perhaps I'd overemphasized the buddy thing!

One look from the grim Facility building to the green forestline decided Caroline and she jogged off to join the end of the double file. I tilted the nonLee in my hand to check the charge. A green bar still glowed.

Don't think about it, just do it. I ran across the yard and back inside the gym. Slipped through the Lab side door into—yes, a deserted passage—and waited by the stairwell door, looking along the passage. The next second Emily came racing through the other stairwell door with three big boys—young men. They all headed straight into the gym. Without a doubt, the young men's attention was fixed on reaching the gate, not Emily.

A torrent of pushing, shoving youths followed and finally, last of all, three lads with blank, baffled expressions, being pulled and prodded along rather ruthlessly by two other boys. At least they were being brought along. So. That was all them out.

My hands were damp on the butt of the gun and beginning to tremble. Follow those boys to the gate and in thirty seconds I would be in Bane's arms. But this was one 'do-unto-others' that I simply could not ignore. Jane must still be alive. That helicopter had arrived only minutes after she'd been taken and all senior staff would've immediately been summoned to grovel to the EuroGov—including the dismantlers.

I headed across the stairwell. *Everyone's on the east battlements. Everyone is on the east battlements.* I just go in and get Jane, and we walk straight out again. In the very unlikely event they've already put her under, I can wheel the gurney. Soon as I get to the gate, Bane'll see I need a hand and come help me. All the guards are on the east battlements. It's simple. Simple.

I scanned the card at the door to the Lab block, pushed it open and walked in. The smell of the Lab hit me as the door clicked closed behind. Cold metal. Copper-salt blood. Death, odorless. I spun around, lunged for the door, my hands slapping hard against it as I struggled for control. *Turn around, Margo. The Lab is a few meters down this corridor. There's probably no one there. The minions will be groveling as well.*

*And if there is...*my thumb ran over the smoothness of the indented safety catch. *If there is, I can take care of it.*

Breathing as though I'd just run three times around the Facility walls, I turned and began to walk along the passage, which wavered and distorted before my eyes. *Keep it together, Margo. Just a few more meters...*

There, on the left, double external doors. On the right, more double doors. This is where they bring in the convicted. A smaller door opened before the double ones, with a window in it. I stepped to it and peeped through.

The Lab. The gleaming metal and blazing lights sent a shaft of coldness right to my core and I very nearly bolted again. But...a figure lay on a gurney. Long limbs twisting and kicking against the restraints. Still conscious, *laudate Dominum.*

The room was empty, as far as I could see. I swiped the card and went in. They'd left Jane with the door behind her—she went momentarily motionless, then began to struggle in real earnest, her breaths catching in her throat.

"Jane, it's okay," I hissed. "Calm down!"

"*Margo?* Margo!" Her voice was ragged as she struggled to look back at me. "By the chairman's underpants, is it really you?"

"It's me." I laid the gun close to hand and unfastened one wrist strap. It seemed to take forever, my hands weren't working properly. "There, do your other hand, will you?" I moved the gun along and set to work on the ankle straps.

"Margo, you all right? You're all white and shaking—"

"Fine. Come *on.*" I grabbed her wrist and pretty much dragged her from the gurney and to the door, gun in hand again. "Here, take the card."

That left me both hands for the gun. Jane unlocked the door and out we went. Three steps along the passage and the door at the boys' end of the corridor slammed open behind us.

"Hey, you—"

No, I'm not the Captain. I shot the guard before he could

get further than that and we ran.

"HEY!"

A glance over my shoulder showed me two more guards standing over their fallen comrade, drawing their guns. Blast. I paused to fire at the closer of the two. He went down in a heap. I was already aiming at the other one. But my gun gave a feeble beep and the man showed no sign of keeling over. A wild glance at the power gauge showed it empty. Rats! No wonder these things hadn't taken off!

I bolted, diving through the stairwell door behind which Jane hid as she held it open for me. I snatched the card from her and raced across the stairwell as she shoved the door closed. As soon as Jane was through, I shut the next one and raced after her across the gym. Slamming the gym door as well, I put my head down and sprinted as I never had before.

Jane had a few stride's head start and I couldn't catch her. Sand flew under my feet and my leg muscles bunched, driving me forwards with every scrap of power terror and adrenalin could draw from me. The gate…reach the gate. Through the gate and there'd be covering fire. I just had to reach the gate…

It floated towards me in peculiar slow motion, considering I was running faster than I'd ever run in my life. Almost there, almost…

The gym doors banging and a harsh oath barely penetrated my mind. Almost there…

Something about the size of a coin slapped the center of my back and a black tunnel dropped over me. I saw Jane race through the gate and away, then the sand hit my cheek and my silent scream was swallowed by blackness.

27

I AM MARGARET

A harsh voice spoke. "And have you regained control of your entire domain?"

A familiar voice I couldn't place drawled, "All is as secure as it can be in the circumstances, sir. Once my full complement of guards is available to me again, clearing those yobs out of the towers will be short work. Though I doubt it will be necessary. They'll get bored and leave soon enough."

Something wrapped around my wrists and ankles and I seemed to be lying flat on my back on a very hard surface. My head ached.

"Why don't you blow them to h...pieces?" demanded another voice.

"Blow up my own towers?" exclaimed Major Everington. That's who was speaking. "Whatever for!"

"*To kill those scum who blew up our helicopter and—*"

"Calm down," said the first voice, the harsh and haughty one. "We will get ourselves a new helicopter and the, er, scum, will certainly pay. You—dismantler—how much longer do we have to wait?"

Doctor Richard's voice...everything came rushing into my mind. For a moment terror almost whited out all thought.

"I was just waiting for an opportunity to inform you, sir, that the subject is awake. Though pretending otherwise."

Oh, Lord! Needing a few archangels to assist my puny self about now.

I opened my eyes.

On my right waited Doctor Richard and Sidney and their three minions, all hunching subserviently. One look to my left showed why. There stood the Minister for the British Department, the Head of the EuroGov Genetics Department and, gulp, Reginald Hill, the Minister for *Internal Affairs*, as they termed it. Major Everington stood at the foot of the gurney, between the two groups, looking as unruffled as ever.

"Ah, you're awake, you little lab rat," snapped Mr. British Department. He was the angry voice.

I couldn't even remember his name. My tongue trying to stick to the roof of my dry mouth, I licked my lips and stared up at him, struggling to think through the terror. "What did I do to *you?*" I came up with at last.

"You wrecked my big speech," he hissed, leaning over me to put his face close to mine. "*Wrecked* it, you and that Resistance boy of yours."

"Your speech?" I echoed, startled out of some of my terror. "What *speech?* You were only introducing the Chairman and you'd finished that by the time...um..." I trailed off—better not incriminate myself. Mr. British Department turned purple, and the Major gave a tiny smile.

"It's a bit late for that, my dear." Reginald Hill spoke for the first time, his face hard and lined, but his voice deceptively soft and gentle. "Unless, of course, you deny writing this book?"

He turned to the tall, medical-looking man, the head of the EGD—the haughty one?—who opened his briefcase, took out a hardback book and displayed it to me. I stared at the utterly incriminating object with a mixture of fascination and fear. The cover showed a stylized Facility in black and red, with a pair of eyes staring from an upper window. I AM MARGARET it said across the top, and at the bottom SUSAN CROFTON. It was a good cover.

"Do you deny writing this book?" inquired Reginald Hill, his voice so very, very soft.

I bludgeoned my brain, trying to stir it to action. No doubt they'd be delighted if I denied writing the book. They'd trot me out to repeat it to the press and suddenly no one would take I AM MARGARET seriously any more. And they'd never let me get away with it without making the Divine denial. And then they'd dismantle me in a year and a half anyway.

"It doesn't seem to be my name on the front," I said.

Reginald Hill leaned over me. "Did you write this book?" he demanded, his voice suddenly hard as iron.

I stared around as I tried to gather my thoughts—and my courage. Doctor Richard and his group studied me avariciously, their eyes taking a silent inventory of my parts and their likely condition. The three government heads stared through me as though I were something in their way that needed removing, clearing up, dealing with. The Major stared down at me impassively, and I had the strangest feeling he was the only one in the room who was really seeing *me* at all. Margaret, a person.

"Did you write this book?" demanded Reginald Hill. "I suggest you think very carefully about your answer. Dismantler, show her some of the tools of your trade."

Doctor Richard and his team helpfully displayed a grisly procession of scalpels, razor-sharp saws, drills, pliers, clamps, and a horrible spoon-headed contraption that made my eyelids flinch shut.

"Now, we are being very patient with you," unusually so, his tone implied, "but we must have your answer. Did you write this book?"

I stared up at the ceiling, avoiding their eyes. *Lord, Uncle Peter always said you'd never let any of us face a trial beyond our strength. So I must be able to do this. But it's so hard.* So *hard.*

A hand gripped my hair; yanked my head around so I looked into Reginald Hill's lined face. "Did. You. Write. This. Book?"

The Major still stared. His steady gaze almost seemed to whisper, "Just say no."

"Yes," I said. "I wrote that book."

"You are aware precisely what you are confessing? This book convicts you of membership in the Underground, to say nothing of disrupting a certain speech and the minor matter of a million eurons worth of fireworks."

"I don't admit to disrupting his speech," I retorted. "He wasn't speaking at the time and it wasn't a speech, it was a lousy introduction. Yes to the rest."

The Major looked like he was trying not to smile again. Mr. British Department stepped forward and struck me across the face, snapping my head back against the gurney. The fading ache returned with renewed intensity. Doctor Richard made a slight sound of pain.

"Whatever is the matter with *you*, dismantler?" demanded Mr. EGD, disdainfully.

"Forgive me, it is merely my zeal for my work, sir. Her cheeks, see what fine cheeks they are, someone will be very glad of them, but they cannot be transplanted, you see, if they are bruised...forgive me, I should not have—"

"No, you shouldn't. Keep your mouth shut in future." He turned to Mr. British Department. "*Do* calm down. It wasn't a speech, it wasn't interrupted, and it is not the issue here."

Mr. British Department glared at him but stepped back from the gurney.

Reginald Hill stepped forward, his voice gone soft soft again. "Let me make things very clear to you. You have just confessed to *Personal Practice of Superstition*, furthermore, you have just confessed to *Inciting and Promoting Super-stition in the General Population* through the publication of this seditious book. I, Reginald Hill, Minister for Internal Affairs, hereby sentence you to the full penalty of the law. You are to undergo, here, at this time, Full Conscious Dismantlement. Do you understand what that means, girl?"

Oh yes, said the sick cold fluttering of my belly, *I know exactly what that means, the Captain has seen to that*. I could not speak.

"*Do you understand?*"

"Yes," I whispered.

"Due to the nature of your crime the law stipulates a full pardon to be given in the event that you choose to categorically deny the existence of any so-called Deity. So I suggest you do so now. Because as you are probably aware, it will not be possible for you to save yourself once the execution is in progress."

That fact was supposed to be the ultimate threat, the ultimate terror. Save yourself now or when you want to, you won't be able. Father Mark called it a blessing, though. "You see, it means all you have to do is hold out just *long enough*," he'd told me. "And then you can't give in. You literally *can't*."

Suddenly I really understood what he meant. I just had

to hold firm long enough.

"All you have to say," Reginald Hill whispered in my ear, "is 'there is no God'. And you don't die today."

No, I'd be trotted out in front of the media to make the denial over and over again. *See how little these superstitious idiots actually believe.* It would be worse than if I'd never written the book at all.

"It's just four words. What do four little words matter, against your life?"

"Vade post me, Satana," I whispered. *Uncle Peter, pray for me now.*

"Perhaps I should describe the process to you. They start with the skin. All the biggest sheets of it. In fact, with someone of your age—the dismantler's right: you have very fine skin—" he caressed my unbruised cheek with one forefinger, "they'll take pretty much all of it off. It's the eyes next, I imagine that's particularly horrible, and then you're blind for all the rest, though that won't be your chief concern by that point..."

Cold sweat trickled down my brow and my stomach churned as though filled with crushed ice. I was shaking and couldn't stop. Reginald Hill went on and on and Uncle Peter's execution played in my mind, I couldn't blot it out. He only shut up when I finally lunged up against the restraints and was violently sick down his trousers and all over his ten thousand euron shoes.

"I believe," said the Major blandly, as Reginald Hill swore vilely and did a wild trouser-shaking dance, "that the accused has already witnessed an execution and knows the process...a little too well, shall we say?"

"You vile little lab rat," snapped Reginald Hill, suddenly sounding rather like Mr. British Department. "How dare you!"

"What the heck do you mean, how dare I?" I yelled, losing it entirely. "I didn't ask you to make me sick, you swine! Why don't you just shut up and go away?"

His hand clenched and for a moment I thought he would inflict more damage on my fine cheeks. But iron control re-established itself: his hand relaxed again, and his face assumed its previous emotionless lines. He stepped back to accept the ministrations of a minion with a handful of paper tissues, and Mr. EGD stepped forward, grabbed me by the collar and smacked my head back into the gurney. So much for subtler means of persuasion.

"Make the Divine Denial," he said, still sounding arrogant as anything.

"No!"

He smacked me into the gurney again, making my ears ring. "Make it."

"NO."

Smack. "Make it."

"Leave me alone!" My heart drummed, panic coursing through me. I wanted to do as he said, I wanted it almost more than I'd ever wanted anything. *No. I will not.*

"Make it!"

"*No!*" I screamed. "Get this into your thick heads, I am not making the Divine denial—there is absolutely nothing you can do that's worse than what you're going to do anyway, so how the heck do you think you're going to change my mind? *How,* moron?" I spat in his face. Okay, so it wasn't a very nice thing to do, but I was absolutely desperate to get rid of them before my nerve broke. I was too close, far, far too close...

He smacked me into the gurney once more for good measure, then wiped his face on his sleeve. "Let's leave the little lab rat to stew in her own blood."

"Chairman said break her," said Reginald Hill half-heartedly.

"If we could, Reg," pointed out Mr. British Department with a nasty smile. "We've tried, haven't we?"

Go away just go away please and let them get on with it because I don't think I can hold out much longer...

"Last chance, she-rat," said Mr. EGD. "Then it's over to the dismantler and his eye scoops."

That broke something inside me, and I hurled myself from side to side against the straps, to no avail. All that happened was I threw up on him, too. There wasn't much left in my stomach, and he managed to miss most of it by jumping backwards.

"Go jump on the razor wire!" I panted, when I'd stopped

heaving and sunk back, wrists and throat burning. That wasn't very nice either, but what I really wanted to say was, 'yes, yes, of course I'll say it, just keep Doctor Richard away from me, at least until I'm safely unconscious in a year or so's time...'

"Fine," snapped Mr. EGD, looking at Reginald Hill. "Sign that thing and let's clear off."

"A pleasure." Reginald Hill looked straight at me as he did so, the cold smile on his lined face not quite hiding his frustration. He handed the form to Doctor Richard and before I'd quite taken it in, all three had swept from the Lab.

Which just left the Major and the dismantling team. The Major said something I couldn't catch to the doctor while the minions moved in and began to remove my—that is, the Menace's—clothes. I began to shake in long, convulsive shudders, twisting wildly against the straps. Hopeless. I was utterly helpless.

Doctor Richard laid two syringes down on a little table beside the gurney. I recognized one, the amber liquid they'd given Uncle Peter. The clear one was surely the anesthetic used in normal executions and dismantlements. Huh?

The Major went around to the clean side of the gurney and perched on the edge, staring down his long nose at me. "Well, girl, you beat them, didn't you?" he said coolly. "Now, I have my own offer. I don't care what you have to say about your Divinity. But if you tell me what I want to know, I will give you this clear injection with my own hands."

He picked up the syringe and twiddled it in his fingers, watching me watching it. "Yes, you know what *this* is, don't you? This is the standard anesthetic. Once you've got this in you, you'll never feel a thing. You'll just fall straight asleep and it will all be over."

"But what do you want?" I asked suspiciously. My throat was hoarse but I could hardly take my eyes off that clear fluid.

He leaned closer, his eyes passing up over my bra to meet mine without pausing. "Where are the others?"

I looked away, squeezing my eyes shut. Bane's voice drummed through my head: *we're going first to the glade in the Fellest below Rayle's Pass—you remember those caves there*. The glade below Rayle's Pass. The glade below Rayle's Pass. *Oh no*.

"So, you do know where they're going. Just tell me and the anesthetic's yours. What the bigwigs don't know won't hurt them."

Doctor Richard eyed the Major rather nervously at that.

"Come, tell me," coaxed the Major.

"No," I whispered.

"Come, come, you must know their chances of getting away permanently are next to nothing? Seventy *reAssignees?* You must know it's hopeless."

"If it's so hopeless, why are you so desperate for me to tell you where they are?"

His lip twitched slightly. "Ah yes, you ran rings around their Lordships, so now you will do the same with me. But this is a good offer and it's the last one you're likely to get."

"I don't expect you've read my book?" My voice only trembled a little.

"Yes, actually. Enjoyed it. Opened it when it arrived just to read the first page, you know—but for some strange reason I couldn't stop reading—not until I had to take a rather important phone call. Way to annoy a lot of people, young lady. Why do you ask?"

"My fiancé's with the others. So I think you need to reconsider whether I'm likely to tell you where they are, don't you?"

"Well, as you say, young lady, I read the book. I reckon your fiancé would be quite happy to be shot or dismantled in the normal way if it saved you from what you face. Do you disagree?" I looked away again. "So why don't you tell me?"

"Because *I* would not be *quite happy!* And though I'm the one in here for poor math I seem to be able to count better than you. Or do you value your own life to the tune of seventy to one?"

He leaned closer. He smelled of flowers and soil but also sweat. Nice to know we had made him run around a bit today. His eyes were like reflections of my own in the lights and they stared bleakly into mine.

"But we are not talking about lives, Margaret, are we? We

are talking about deaths. Seventy painless deaths against the one that awaits you? That doesn't seem such a bad trade."

"I am not giving you Bane," I snapped. "Or the others! So go away and leave me alone, you evil creep."

"Ah, you're trying to make me angry. Well, it worked on them, didn't it? Though I doubt you'd have got through the skin of the charming Mr. Reginald Hill with mere words. A convenient attack of bodily frailty, that. But you know what I think? I think they were too quick to leave. I think if they'd pushed just a little further, they'd have had you. Still, their loss is my gain. So why don't you tell me where the others are?"

"How did you pass your Sorting when you're clearly deaf as a post?" But I quaked inside. Because he was right. I'd wound the others up, and they'd all lost their tempers and somewhat in the nick of time. The Major wasn't showing any sign of losing his.

"You've seen what awaits you, but still, I wonder if you truly understand." The Major produced a pocket knife and unfolded it. "I will educate you."

"Oh, *sir*..." appealed Doctor Richard, as the knife blade strayed towards my cheeks.

"Fine." Major Everington seized my chin with one hand, brushed hair aside and set the point of the knife to my forehead, pressing slowly and steadily.

Pain followed, sharp and piercing, and I tried to twist away, but his grip was like iron. *Don't make a fuss, don't make a fuss, it's nothing*...but it was almost impossible to remain still. I yanked hopelessly at my wrist restraints as he went on with his slow cut, struggling not to cry out—or just start crying.

He drew the blade away and held it in front of my eyes. Blood dripped onto my face.

"So. Where are they? No?" And the blade bit through my skin again, his voice filling my ears, low and matter-of-fact. "These little surface cuts are nothing. No real comparison with what Doctor Richard will get up to. Take this pain and then multiply it by a thousand. Hard to imagine? Perhaps you should tell me where they are?

"Ah well." He drew the blade away again and cleaned

it on a piece of the Menace's snipped away uniform. "Our little lesson is complete. Are you going to answer my question? Because Doctor Richard's lesson won't be nearly as pleasant as mine. And you didn't look like you enjoyed mine terribly much." He eyed me measuringly. "Pass me that eye scoop, Richard, I noticed she found that particularly entertaining." And he held it in front of my face and opened and closed it a few times. The scoops went click-click as they came together.

I closed my eyes and turned my face away and then, oh no, I was crying at last. Big, full out, hysterical sobbing, like there was something inside trying to climb out.

"Tell me where they are going..." the Major's voice whispered.

Rayle's Pass. Rayle's Pass. Rayle's Pass. That's what was trying to get out. If I opened my mouth it would. How could I hold it in? Bane, think of Bane. Bane's safety lay behind my closed lips. I could not speak. Bane, Bane, be safe, be well, live long, live happy...

Without me? I don't want it to be without me, I want to live, I want it so much...or at least to not die like *this*...if I told the Major, he might not catch them all... *All*, oh Lord, give me strength, I bet Father Mark's with them! How can I think of condemning him to this in my place, simply for helping with my rescue? And Bane, Bane would be hurt, I must stay quiet. I must!

I cried and cried and could not stop.

I cried for the terrible danger I left Bane to face alone. For the rest of his life faced alone. For my lost life that I wanted so much and couldn't have. I cried with every drop of the terror coursing through my veins. I cried as though my heart were breaking. But I kept my lips shut.

Finally I ran out of tears, or possibly breath to sob with, and reluctantly opened my eyes and looked at the Major again. What would he try next? He stared down at me and even now, when he was trying to drag information from me, I still had the feeling he saw *me*. A strange clarity of vision for someone in his profession.

"Are you going to tell me?"

I shook my head, mouth still tightly closed.

"Well, then. If you can cry like that and still say no, I admit defeat. Go screaming, then, to your God, if you insist on it. Have no fear He will not recognize you. There is no danger of that, now."

Huh? My thoughts were such a jumble. My forehead still hurt, the pain of the cuts knifing through me. The cuts... I could feel their fiery shape. The creep had carved a cross into my forehead. He *had* read my book. Re-baptized in my own blood.

He picked up the clear syringe again, tapping it against one long forefinger. His eyes met mine and in that moment I actually thought he was about to stick the needle into my arm, regardless. *Yes...*

Doctor Richard's hand appeared, seizing the syringe. "I'd better put this away, sir, since it isn't required." He carried it briskly to the other side of the room.

The Major watched him go, and the minions watched the Major.

Major Everington stood. "Well, then," he said and moved towards the door.

"I forgive you," I blurted. I don't know where the words came from.

He turned back, his eyes unreadable. "Do you, young lady?" His tone was as unreadable as his eyes. He raised his hand in something like a salute, strode through the door and was gone. I was alone with people who could see only my parts and not my whole. I knew I should forgive them too.

"I'll need the skin peeler first," Doctor Richard told the minions. "Start spraying the antiseptic on her lower abdomen, ready."

I eyed Doctor Richard. Could I forgive him? Could I even *want* to forgive him? Could I love him enough?

Some trace of my conflict must've shown on my face, because he snatched up the amber syringe. "No more of that drivel from you, subject," he snapped. His hand gripped my arm, holding it still, and the needle pierced my skin, a tiny pain beside the cuts. Which were tiny compared to what was to come.

As the amber fluid slid into my vein, panic seized me. I drew breath to scream...

...and found I could not. My eyelids sagged; closed. My muscles were no longer mine to control.

28

DISMANTLEMENT

This is nothing, nothing at all. Just something very minor. Try not to feel it too much. Try— But another wave of searing pain from my stomach swallowed my thoughts. I struggled to open my eyes, to *see*, but my eyelids just wouldn't move.

I'd never realized one couldn't sob or scream without the use of one's body. I'd always imagined there must be some sort of mental equivalent. But there wasn't. Trapped with the pain, I had no way to express it, no way to relieve it, no way to get it *out*.

The pain died down again, a little, and I went back to my self-admonitions. *This is nothing. Think what Our Lord suffered for your sake. Much worse than this. No whimpering, Margo.* I *can't* whimper! howled a little voice I tried to ignore. *Hush. This is going to carry right on whatever, so there's no point making a fuss.*

In you, O Lord, I take refuge, do not forsake me... I fell back on prayer, trying to bury myself in it, tried to return to it with all speed after each wave of agony had passed.

Lord, I know the martyrs of old wanted to die for You, they loved You so much. I'm sorry I'm so weak. Please watch over me now. And when I can bear it no longer, please be merciful and release me from this conscious state.

Holy Mary, Mother of God, pray for this sinner now and at the hour of her dea... now, just pray for me now? Uncle Peter, pray for me. Angel Margaret, help me, please.

"Look at the quality of this skin." Doctor Richard's voice. "See how elastic it is?"

"Very fine." Sid. "You looking, you three?"

"Yes, sir."

"She's a good one, isn't she?"

"*More solution.*" Doctor Richard. Again the cruel liquid

washed over my open wounds.

"I'm looking forward to seeing that nose packed up. Someone's going to be lucky." One of the minions. "When my mother had a new one, all they had available was—"

"Yes, yes, concentrate on your work, now. Fit the eye clamps and get the eyeballs moisturized ready for removal."

"Yes, sir."

Driven partly away by the pain, a fresh surge of terror twisted in my stomach as cold professional hands lifted my eyelids and hooked them in an open position. The thing they were hooked into seemed to be spraying mist into my eyes, but suddenly I could see again. I could even move my eyeballs, slowly and with great effort.

Enjoy them while you can, said that little voice.

Pain. This time I saw the sheet of skin as Doctor Richard lifted it with a pair of tweezers and laid it on some sort of cling film covered tray proffered by a minion. Seeing didn't make it hurt more—it seemed totally unreal, like it couldn't be part of me. Nothing unreal about the pain...

A minion lifted a pipe with a spray nozzle and suddenly that solution was running over me again. Antiseptic. For the sake of the organs. Like being dipped in tar and set alight.

Jon said you wouldn't be conscious for most of it, Margo. So you may not have to put up with this for much longer.

He didn't say most *of it,* said the little voice.

Oh Lord, stay with me!

Shouting in the passage... The door slammed open and Bane hurtled in, something in his hand that gleamed silver in the Lab lights. Sid and the minions froze in alarm and Doctor Richard raised the scalpel in his hand...towards Bane? *No, please!* Or to finish the execution, however prematurely...

Bane lunged across the room, and whatever Doctor Richard's intention he changed it to a wild swipe in Bane's direction. From the speed Bane moved, he reacted on pure instinct. His left hand flew out, knocking the scalpel away and the knife in his right hand moved in a vicious arc and slammed up into the doctor's side, to the hilt.

For a moment the doctor remained standing, a look of incomprehension on his face, then Bane yanked the knife free and Doctor Richard slumped over my legs, his eyes blank and already very, very dead. Something burning hot poured over my raw flesh. If only I could *SCREAM!*

In a pain-wracked daze I saw Sid crumple, a minion turned towards the door, his mouth opening, and dropped from my sight as well. I dragged my eyeballs up a little and saw Father Mark, hatchet-faced as ever, a nonLee in his hand. He squeezed the trigger twice more—by the time I'd moved my eyes again, there were no minions left in sight. *Father Mark!* screamed that little voice. *How could you come here. Right in here? Are you* mad?

With a noise in his throat perilously close to a sob, Bane shoved Doctor Richard's corpse off me and dropped the knife on the gurney with a clatter, his bloody hands hovering helplessly. I couldn't see what I looked like, but I could see it reflected in his desperate eyes.

"Is she all right? Oh God, have they *taken* anything? What do I *do?* Mark, *get over here!*"

Father Mark stalked over, apparently eyeing the minions to check they were properly unconscious. Tracing a perfunctory blessing over the corpse without pausing, he moved quickly to me, snatching up the pipe... *Ow, ow, ow!*

"Most of this blood is from the pig you stuck," he declared, peering closely. "Hold this." He handed the pipe to Bane and reached out, his fingers touching intact skin and sometimes raw flesh, probing and stretching.

"The subcutaneous layer's intact," he announced at last, as *laudate Dominum*, he stopped his poking. "They haven't taken anything but epidermis and some dermis—the top layers," he explained, at Bane's look of anxious bafflement.

"She's all right? She's going to be all right?"

"Yes, but we must get that skin back on before we move her or she'll be in a bad way."

"How long?"

"Five minutes?"

Bane pulled his phone out and dialed swiftly. "We've got her. Mark needs to do some first aid... No more than five minutes... *Of course we'll blasted well hurry up!*"

"Play nicely, Bane," purred Father Mark. "Or they might not want to play anymore."

Bane's jaw tightened. "*Sorry,*" he ground into the phone. "Of course you'll do your best. We'll be out very soon." He stuffed the phone back in his pocket. "What, they think we're going to stop for *tea?*"

Father Mark didn't bother to reply, so Bane stepped to my head, reached out towards my cheek, hesitated, grabbed a cloth from nearby and wiped his hands on it, leaving it stained with crimson. Reached out to touch my cheek again with exquisite tenderness. "Is she awake?"

Father Mark had pulled a familiar looking tray from the chiller cabinet and picked up two pairs of tweezers, but he paused to direct one long look at my eyes. "'Fraid so. She's looking at us."

Bane's fingers went to my hair, stroking it back from my face as though each strand were made of glass. "Margo, it's going to be okay, d'you understand? We'll have you out of here very soon." He leaned and kissed me on the lips, feather light, as though any more pressure and I might break.

"While I'm sure that's very effective pain relief," Father Mark's voice made him draw away again, alas, "you'd be better off looking for the anesthetic—it's a white liquid. But first you need to find bottles, any size, any shape, empty them, rinse them, fill them with this stuff." Father Mark jerked his head at the pipe, which mercifully wasn't directed at me at that moment.

Bane straightened. "What is it?"

"Antiseptic."

"Oh. *Right.* But I'd better find the anesthetic first, surely?"

"No. I hate to be so brutally practical, but she may well pass out from the pain by herself, and if we don't have that antiseptic the wounds will get infected and she'll die."

Bane frowned, but just asked, "Do you need help?"

"Not right now."

"Do you even know what you're *doing?*"

"Yes." When Bane still hesitated, looking agonized, he added, "Trust me. I trained as a dismantler when I was younger."

Bane stared at him. "Those two remarks are *completely* incompatible with one another." He shook off his disbelief.

"Huh. S'pose you do know what you're doing, then. *Antiseptic*... Right. Hang on, Margo, I'll have the anesthetic before you know it!"

Clattering around, he started opening doors and ransacking cupboards, chucking plastic bottles into the sink and placing glass ones down more carefully.

Father Mark leaned over to meet my eyes. "Margaret, I'm going to put your skin back on. It's going to hurt like heck until we're able to put you out, but we just can't wait."

He wasted no more words, nor time, and as he began to lay the sheets of skin onto my raw flesh, interspersed with copious amounts of the solution, I completely lost track of what was going on. Flames licking over my stomach and thighs...

"Bane, are you done? I need your help now." Father Mark's voice echoed down my ear canal and penetrated my brain.

"All full. I need to find something to carry them in—"

"In a minute. I need you to lift her so I can wrap this cling film stuff around. Gently as you can."

"*Gently? Really!*"

"Temper, Bane."

"Trust me, this is not a good time to discuss my temper! Ready?"

"Yes. Lift."

Oh, to be able to scream. Or—was this how Bane felt?—to pound a fist into a wall, anything, just to let the pain out...

The world steadied again after a while.

"Are you done? I'm done, but I can't find the anesthetic!"

"Done. Put this in the bin bag with the rest." Father Mark handed him what looked like a cling film dispenser and circled the room, searching rapidly through the mess Bane had left. He produced a familiar syringe, pressed the plunger a little, sniffed the emerging fluid and nodded in satisfaction.

"Margaret?" He leaned over me now. "I'm going to get these eye things off and give you the anesthetic, okay?"

He lifted my first eyelid carefully from the hooks while Bane hovered on my other side, taking my limp hand and stroking it gently. "Don't you worry about a thing, Margo,"

Bane told me. "When you wake up again we'll be safe. Oh, I found this to wrap you in." He held up something like a plastic sheet, a hint of a blush touching his golden cheeks. "So you mustn't worry about...y'know, *that.*"

Nakedness—a very long way down my list of concerns right now. Glad he'd thought of it for me. Before I was carried out starkers before the no doubt appreciative eyes of his not-my-friends.

Father Mark unhooked my other eyelid and sight was gone again as he lifted the device from my forehead. His fingers paused briefly, examining the cuts. "These aren't serious," he answered some non-verbal inquiry from Bane. "Margaret, I'm going to give you the anesthetic now. Just relax. Hmm. That was a stupid thing to say. I meant stay calm."

I understood you. The needle pricked my arm.

"Right, let's go," said Father Mark.

"*I'm* carrying her."

"How surprising. I'll carry the bags, then."

"Carry the gun, stupid. Hang the bags over my shoulders."

"That gun is about one shot from being a very expensive paperweight, same as yours, but you're right. One of us should have our hands free. Give me your knife, then."

"Would you use it?"

"Maybe not, but the other fellow won't know that."

"Huh. Here."

The blood-stained knife presumably changed hands, but my head was swimming. Bane's arms slipped underneath me, lifting me and gathering me to his chest. It caused great pain, but it was all receding from me. His warmth was suddenly welcome, rather than agony and his heart drummed under my ear, thud-thud, thud-thud, thud-thud, lulling me into the darkness...

29

RAYLE'S PASS

A bird had braved the compound walls and was singing sweetly nearby. Jon would be enjoying that. I was rather enjoying it myself. Another bird joined in. *Two.* Jon would think it was his birthday. The birds flew away. Then a bumblebee buzzed past just over my face. *What the?* Had someone left the window ajar? The others were talking and laughing, but...they sounded such a long way away. Four or five times the length of the dorm!

Eyes flying open, I stared up at blue sky. Fellest pines loomed above on one side. I turned my head—a hatchet-faced young man sat about a meter away, examining a map.

"Father Mark?"

He looked up and smiled. People were often scared of him until he smiled, he really did look like an assassin or something. Perhaps had been.

"Margaret, you're awake."

"Where are we?" I asked groggily.

"Near Rayle's Pass."

Something tightened in my stomach, where pain was growing and growing the clearer my head became, until it threatened to fog it up again it was so severe. *Rayle's Pass.* It set my nerves jangling. Horrors flitted through my head and I shied away; tried not to remember. "I want Bane." The childish words popped from my mouth.

"He's just gone to check our sentries, make sure they're looking in the right direction and all that. Don't you worry, he won't be a minute. He's hardly left your side."

A minute was too long, because the memories poured back into my mind—I couldn't keep them out. I squeezed my eyes shut, but it was no use. "*BANE!*" The cry tore from my throat, unstoppable.

Father Mark put aside his map and shifted to lay a gentle

hand on my shoulder. "Easy, Margaret, it's all right. Bane's coming."

A crashing in the undergrowth—then I saw him, sprinting through the forest as though I were being eaten by a bear. He probably thought I was. Not likely, with Father Mark sat next to me.

But Bane tore up, wild-eyed, and dropped to his knees at my side. "Margo...you're awake, are you all right?" That was all he'd time for, because I was clawing my way into a sitting position. "Don't try and move! You'll hurt—"

I flung myself into his arms, blind to the agony. My nose buried itself in his hair and my arms locked around him.

"Oh. There we go, then..." He eased me into his lap and settled his arms around me, encircling me, rubbing my back as I began to howl. "It's all right. It's all right." He rocked me like a baby and I just wept and wept.

I'm not sure how much time passed—I just went on crying and crying and crying.

"*Margo?* Is she all right? What's the matter with her?"

"I think she'll be all right." Father Mark's voice was soft and rather grim. "Let's put it this way, if she *didn't* cry, *then* I'd be worried."

At that, Bane returned all his attention to comforting me and Father Mark presumably went back to his map. I must've cried myself back to sleep in the end, because the next thing I knew, I lay with my head in Bane's lap and the shadows were lengthening.

"Bane?"

"I'm here. How are you?"

"I'm all right." My voice sounded rather small, disappearing into the trees like the mist now creeping back out of the forest. "Have they searched for us yet?"

"Not yet. They shouldn't. Plan was they'd think we'd gone with the Resistance in their trucks—be led a merry dance. And since some of us did go, they're even less likely to realize they've been had." His tone was dark.

"I thought you said no one would—"

"No one was meant to go with the Resistance, Margo," he said with a lack of apology that told me whatever had happened was not his fault. "But most of the boys took off with them. No loss: they were completely uncontrollable. S'pect the Resistance will make an example of one or two and the others will fall in line. Anyway, eleven boys bolted into the woods, came back when the trucks had left and asked to come with us. Fortunately, too, since we're down as a mixed school."

"Huh? School?" My stomach and thighs were burning. I shifted restlessly, but that made it even worse. Under the unzipped sleeping bag laid over me I was dressed in my own clothes on my top half—my bottom half was loosely wrapped in that plastic sheet. The idea of putting my jeans on... I shuddered and pain flared even more.

"Hey, don't move. Take these." He fed me a handful of pills, interspersed with swigs from a water bottle, pill, swig, pill, swig, pill... It went on forever.

"That's a lot of pills, Bane," I objected at last.

"We don't have any painkillers up to the job. These are shop-bought types you can sorta take together. Father Mark counted them out for you. He said take them and don't read the packets."

"Oh..." Wearily, I swallowed the last few and relaxed in the circle of Bane's arms. His chest was so broad now. How long had we been apart? Four months? It felt like forever and yet no time at all. I'd always hoped he wouldn't fill out too *too* much and become all hulking, but this, this was fine. More than fine. Like curling up in the shelter of one's very own protecting wall. Lovely. The pain was easing a bit. Perhaps I should renew my question about his school comment...

...The light was going...it was dusk. I blinked, disorientated. Why was I so tired? I suppose stress and skinning accounted for it. Bane didn't seem to have moved.

"Are you all right there? Aren't your legs going to sleep?"

"I'm fine, Margo. You're not *that* heavy. Anyway, I wasn't going to wake you, you were sleeping like a baby. You look very pretty when you're asleep."

"And not when I'm awake?"

"Definitely when you're awake too. But you don't have that cute look on your face. Though you drool less."

"Awww. Sorry!"

He bent his back into a U shape to kiss me. "I'm hoping to have you drooling on me for the rest of my life, so I think I'd better get used to it."

I had to smile. It pulled muscles on my forehead and made the cuts twinge. The smile slid from my face.

"Oh, Margo, I don't like that shadow in your eyes. What can I do?"

"Hold me. For about a hundred years."

His encircling arms drew me closer. "That is the point of this whole exercise, isn't it?"

I lay nestled to him for a little longer, then finally looked around. My eyes fell on Jon, sitting nearby, munching an unappetizing looking food bar. "Jon! Are you okay?"

His head turned towards me and his gray-blue eyes frankly glared. "*Me?* I'm fine. What possessed *you* to pull that crazy stunt?"

I flinched from his harsh tone. Frowned. "Jane's life," I whispered.

"Well, it was crazy," he snapped. "And you lied to me!"

"I did not!" I quavered. "I said I was going to bring up the rear and I did!"

"It was crazy!"

I hid my face against Bane's coat. My insides trembled like jelly and my eyes burned. What was the matter with me? I seemed raw inside as well as out and I couldn't bear his anger.

"Didn't you realize you'd be caught! Didn't you—"

"Quit yelling at her," growled Bane, "or I'm going to pound you, Jon!"

"Oh, you think it was a good idea, then?"

"It was a stupid thing to do! But you were even more stupid for walking out of there without her! I can't believe you took your eyes...ears...off her for one second, after this Jane girl was taken! Don't you know Margo at all?"

"Not as well as you, it would seem," snarled Jon.

"No, you don't! So don't you *dare* yell at her again!"

I put a calming hand on Bane's arm and managed to speak at last. "It wasn't Jon's fault, Bane. I did trick him."

"I didn't say it was his fault. But if he upsets you again right now we're going to have a falling out and that's a fact!"

I snuggled my face into his coat and breathed in his familiar Bane smell. Heaven. Did I have the energy to try and change the subject? "What were you saying about a school?"

"Oh, well, I'd better explain things in order. We're going to stay here near the caves for forty-eight hours, 'til we're fairly sure they're not going to search the Fellest. Caves would block infrared cameras, y'see. Then we're going to set off on foot and walk to York."

"York?" I drew away from his jacket so I could look up at his face. "It must be over a hundred kilometers to York!"

"Yes, a hundred kilometers of Fellest—passes, ravines, cliffs and all—no one would try to march seventy reAssignees—okay, forty-four—all the way to York, right? Think it through. They should be convinced we're kilometers away with those trucks they'll be trying so hard to find. But they're bound to up security in all the closest towns and cities just the same. But not in York because it's too far away. That's why we have to go there."

"But—"

"Don't worry, we have everything we need. Spare sneakers and foil blankets and rations and everything. We'll do it in a few days. And in York we've got school uniforms waiting and a bus booked and all the necessary arrangements made for a school trip to the continent."

"Where on the continent?"

"Somewhere people like you will be safe."

There was only one place on the continent where people like us would be safe. And it wasn't part of the EuroBloc.

"Was this all your idea?"

"Well...I talked it all through with Father Mark."

"Wonderful, Bane," I yawned.

"Don't go to sleep again yet, you'd better eat something. How about some room service over here?" he called.

I lost track of a few moments then, as I waited, snug in Bane's arms. I didn't feel at all hungry.

"Margo?" I looked around and found Jane crouching beside us, Sarah beside her. Jane sounded unusually hesitant. "Here's some food. Are you...okay?"

"Yeah." I tried to sound light-hearted about it. "Teach me

to run faster, huh?"

Jane didn't smile. "*Seriously*, Margo...*thank you*. Not just for me. For...for everyone..." She gestured, and looking further away for the first time, I saw a mass of girls and a few boys spread out at the far end of the glade, talking and eating from some sort of ration packs. "We're free because of you."

"It was hardly just me, Jane. And we're not safe ye..." I broke off, with a quick glance at Sarah. "That is, we've a long way to go yet, you must see that."

"Yeah, I do. All the same, we have a chance. And you can be as modest as you like, but *you* gave it to us."

I blushed and tried to think of something to say as Bane took the ration pack from Jane and began unpacking it.

"Okay, Margy?" asked Sarah anxiously.

"I'm fine, Sarah." That definitely wasn't the most honest thing I'd ever said, but it satisfied her.

"Margo?" said Bane. "There's baked beans and sausage—that's supposed to be breakfast but who cares—or corned beef hash. What do you fancy?"

"Nothing."

"Let me rephrase that. What are you *going* to eat?"

"Oh...corned beef hash, sounds the most comfortable thing to be force-fed."

"It actually hardly tastes any worse than the stuff back in there." Jane jerked her head vaguely towards the trees. "Loverboy's clearly been spoiled by home cooking."

"Yeah," said Bane, unrepentantly, "your mum's cooking, Margo. My mum congratulated me on passing Sorting by saying I was an adult now so I could blinking well cook for myself. That was about two months ago and your mum took pity on me, so I've been eating well since then."

He added, "Actually, it worked rather well. As far as my mum could see, I *was* cooking for myself and your mum didn't disillusion her. So your cousin Mark's been well fed. In quantity though not in quality, needless to say."

He ripped the top off one of the silvery sachets and produced a fork. "No fires, sorry. Too risky."

Cold food or ending up back on the gurney. "I'm not complaining."

"Didn't think you would be."

I spooned slowly, almost too tired to chew the mush, listening to Sarah chattering to Jon about the fascinating forest.

"Squirrel...you hear, Jon? Squirrel said 'chitter'. You hear it?"

"Yes, I did. Was it a big squirrel?"

"Very big. Very furry tail. And it said 'chitter'. And ran off. Can I have a pet squirrel, Jon?"

"Not right now. Perhaps if you work hard and save up you can get a hamster."

"Sarah will work hard! What work?"

I tuned out again. Sarah had a future now. She would have a job of her own that she could take pride in.

Well, providing we got out of the EuroBloc.

...It was almost entirely dark now. Bane still didn't seem to have moved, bless him. Jon sat nearby, his head slightly on one side as though he was listening hard to the sounds of the Fellest around us. Jane and Sarah must have rejoined the other girls.

"Awake, Margo?" he said.

"Umm."

"Are you feeling better? I'm, uh, sorry I was so cross before."

I peered at him in the dim light. His expression was rather...closed and his voice had an odd reserve in it. And a touch of sadness. Oh. For the best part of four months I'd cried on his shoulder, sought comfort in his arms and told him my every fear and worry. And waking, earlier, I'd screamed for Bane and not even remembered Jon's existence until the third time I woke up—not until I saw him. Suddenly I felt awful.

"I'm...fine. I'm feeling better." I had to say something, but how to find the words? "Um...I think I...leaned on you rather hard in there. More than was fair. I'm...I'm sorry."

He snorted, but his head turned away slightly. "Don't apologize. We leaned on each other. That's...that's what friends are for, huh?"

What more could I say? *I'm afraid you're in love with me and I'm sorry?*

"Well, I'm glad you looked out for each other." There was only a faint edge to Bane's voice, though his arms tightened around me.

"You're welcome." Jon's voice was rather flat. "Well, I think I'm going to turn in."

He took up a shiny silver square and began to unfold it with a lot of rustling. And unfold it. And unfold it. Quite hypnotic watching it become a blanket. Rustle. Rustle. Rustle...

...Full dark, now. Where was Bane! He no longer loomed over me...*where?* Oh...there. Lying beside me. I remained tucked in his arms. I relaxed, my breathing steadying.

"Okay, Margo?" He'd felt my flinch, or he'd been awake.

"Fine. You're here. It's all fine." I lay and thought about the clever plan he'd laid out to me, for getting the best part of fifty reAssignees to the other side of the continent. A school group. Yes, it was probably the only way. But... My thoughts ground on and my heart sunk. I swallowed hard. *Oh Lord, I don't feel like being brave right now, or strong, or doing the right thing. I just want to hide in Bane's arms for about a million years.*

"Bane?"

"Yes, Margo?" Resignation filled his voice.

"You...you do realize we can't possibly go with the others, don't you?"

"Why's that, Margo?"

"Because...I don't think I'm being arrogant when I say that my picture is probably going to be on the front page of every newspaper in the EuroBloc."

"Too late. It already is."

"Well, then. *I* certainly can't go with them. They've got a good chance of getting through, on their own."

Bane sighed. "I know. It's all arranged."

"It is?"

"Yes. We'll be going separately."

"Oh. Why didn't you say before?"

"Because..." His arm tightened around me, protectively. "Because I'm a lot more selfish than you, Margo, and if you hadn't said anything, I wasn't going to either. Because I reckon our chances of making it are a heck of a lot higher with the others. But...I knew you'd probably point out their chances were lower and refuse to go, so...I made other arrangements."

"Which are?"

"Don't freak out, okay? But...we'll be posing as New Adults backpacking before university."

It took a moment for it to sink in. "*Walking?* We're *walking* all the way across the EuroBloc! I've no skin on my thighs, Bane!"

"It's okay. Father Mark says you'll heal quite quickly. I'll carry you to York, then we'll go with them on the bus across the Channel bridge and split off from them on the other side. Pitch camp for a few days or however long and then start ambling in easy stages until you're all better. It'll be fine."

"*Carry* me? All that way? And how will we get *food* on the continent? We won't be able to buy from shops, we can't scan our IDs at the cash registers—"

"Calm down, Margo. It's going to be all right, okay?"

Maybe, maybe not. But I didn't seem to have the energy to argue about it right now.

Someone lying nearby rolled over with a rustle of foil blanket and Jon's voice came from the gloom. "And what are you planning to do with *me*, Bane? I can't go with the others either. I'm far too recognizable. And wherever you leave me, they'll know you've been there and bang goes the idea we're all with those trucks. I told you you should've left me outside the Facility."

"Well, you're coming with us, aren't you?" I said. "Bane?"

Bane's hesitation was only momentary. "Yes, Jon's coming with us."

"You've got what he needs?"

"Yes, I got stuff for three. Since I had a feeling you'd manage to drag him out of there and there's a whole list of reasons why we can't leave him behind."

"You seriously intend to haul a blind person all the way across the EuroBloc?" said Jon. "Doesn't sound like a good plan to me."

"Oh, don't give me that *poor little blind boy* rubbish," retorted Bane. "One of us to guide you, and you'll be fine.

Anyone would think you *wanted* to be back in the Facility waiting to die!"

There was silence for a moment.

"Good night," said Jon stiffly, and rustled over onto his other side again.

I lay quietly, my cheek resting on Bane's arm. "Listen!" I said after a while. Wolf song came floating over the forest's blackness.

"Great. Just. Blinking. Great." From the rustling sound, Jon had pulled his blanket over his head.

"They're not going to bother us," I said sleepily, and lay listening to the wild music...

Then Doctor Richard bent over me, the eye scooping instrument in his hand.

"Such beautiful green eyes. Just what we need."

Major Everington walked into the Lab, head bowed, hair hiding his face.

"You said you forgave me, young lady," he whispered hoarsely. Blood covered his hands. "You said you forgave me! Why did you let them do it?"

"Don't fret, sir," said Doctor Richard. "I'm taking care of it."

"You can't fix things," said the Major, still not looking at me. Blood dripped from his fair hair. "No one can fix things."

Doctor Richard reached out with the scoops and the Major turned his face to me at last. Empty eye sockets stared bloodily from his white face.

"But it's my eyes I want," he said.

"These are close enough." And Doctor Richard plunged the instrument into my eye.

I screamed...

"Margo, Margo, wake up, it's all right. It's all right!"

I opened my eyes—my intact, undamaged eyes—and found myself looking up into Bane's face, glowing golden in the first light of dawn. "Bane!"

"It's all right! Wherever you were, you're not, you're here, you're all right! Did that make any sense?"

I let out a long breath and huddled to him. "Enough." But after a moment spent drawing in his calming scent, I said, "The Resistance helped you and Father Mark get back in to get me, didn't they? Was anyone killed?"

"Resistance? Who cares, they asked for it. Blowing up that stupid helicopter while you were all just underneath! Wouldn't listen to me, wouldn't *wait!*" He was literally snarling and it was his turn to take a calming breath. "*Sorry*. I was just so mad at them after that."

"It wasn't the brightest thing to do but, I meant, guards?"

Bane gave a helpless shrug. "I don't know, Margo. I *honestly* don't. Most of the psychos had to stay outside in command positions, if it makes you feel better. The helicopter pilot bought it, *God help me*, I was so angry. Though..." his voice grew almost inaudible, "s'pose I can't throw stones now."

Oh. *That*. We needed to talk about *That*. I needed to see if he was all right. But...not right now, not yet, I just couldn't.

After another moment's silence, he went on firmly, "Anyway, no one was boasting about killing anyone, after, 'cept one guy who claimed he'd shot the Facility Commandant or something, only everyone else reckoned this Major chap had ducked and wasn't hurt at all, so who knows. But they actually weren't there for killing, Margo, they really were after some good press and everything."

"Hmm." I didn't want to dwell on what he'd told me, couldn't dwell on it. Doctor Richard still lurked over me with his instruments and I shuddered, then flinched in pain from the shudder. The agony was swamping me again.

"It's all right, Margo, it's all right." He kissed my forehead, beside the cuts, stroking my hair. "You can have some more pills now, Father Mark put them ready, before he went on watch."

He fed me pills again, pill, sip, pill, sip, pill, sip... Drew me close. "Just rest, Margo, you're safe now."

I was dozing off again, but... "It's not like you to lie to me, Bane."

"I was speaking comparatively," he murmured into my hair.

"Oh. That's all right, then." Oh yes, I could accept some 'comparatively' just now.

"Rest. You're safe. You're safe."

He'd drawn me so close my head rested on his chest again and his heart drummed me to sleep. Safe-safe. Safe-

safe. Safe-safe. For how long? No, safe. Right now, safe. It was enough.

Deo gratias. *Thank you, Lord.*

DON'T MISS
BOOK 2

THE THREE MOST WANTED

3 New Adults
2000 kilometers
A EuroBloc-wide manhunt

Safe?

Not even comparatively...

OUT NOW!

TURN OVER FOR A
SNEAK PEAK!

Paperback: ISBN 978-1-910806-08-1
ePub: ISBN 978-1-910806-09-8
ASIN: B011SMOPOA

unSeen

Find out more at:
www.UnSeenBooks.com

I AM MARGARET
THE THREE MOST WANTED
CARNEGIE MEDAL NOMINEE
CORINNA TURNER

THE THREE MOST WANTED

SNEAK PEAK from CHAPTER 1

Everything echoed in my ears. The sun was rising above the trees, a brighter patch in the mist, and Jon was carrying me. I'd no memory of night. I squinted against the cruel light, focusing on the flat dirt track along which the crocodile was moving. Oh. Not a dream. Bane and Father Mark both exhausted? Or taking advantage of this flat track to get some extra time off?

Sarah walked beside Jon, raising a hand and touching his arm when he veered slightly to the left.

"Hi, Margy. You feel better?" Proud in her little job as Jon-aimer.

"I'm fine." I tried for a reassuring smile and Sarah stared worriedly at me. But getting words out was like lifting lead to my lips.

"It's too early for more pills, Margo," Jon told me after a while. Had I said something? He looked worried.

"M'fine," I muttered. Another lie. Major Everington was walking alongside with his empty eye sockets turned towards me, blood trickling down his calm face like tears. He held out a hand, palm cupped as though to receive something. *Eyes?* I shuddered.

"I do think it's very decent of you." I could hear his well-bred voice. "But if you're not going to need them anymore."

"Go away! *You're not really here.*"

"Am I not?" He raised an eyebrow, making one empty socket gape horribly. I shut my eyes tight.

"Sarah *is* here, Margy. I *is.*"

"It's okay, Sarah." Jon's voice. "I don't think she's talking to you."

"Then who Margy talking to?"

"Someone who's not there."

"A ghost!"

I whimpered. Not a ghost, please, Lord?

"No, no, not a ghost, Sarah. She's running a temperature, that's all. It makes people...see things."

I dragged an eyelid up and risked a peep. The Major was gone.

For now.

ACKNOWLEDGMENTS

As my book ideas sometimes (but not always) do, this one came to me in a dream. I was on retreat with the Dominican Sisters of St Joseph at the time, and the idea was certainly one of those that had to be written, not typed up and filed away 'just in case.' So I'd like to thank the Holy Spirit for the idea and the Sisters for all their support and wise words over the last six years.

I would also most especially like to thank my parents, for all their care and love, and for generally being such wonderful parents; and all my family and friends for their support and encouragement.

I'd like to thank my proofreaders, No. 1 being my Mum, whose honesty results in such massive improvements—an invaluable quality in a proofreader! No. 2 has to be Lucy O., with her brilliant analytical skills—'Corinna, Margo's book was actually published on a Tuesday, you know...'—and also Anne H., Caroline Green, Cat I., Ellie S., Emma T., Eoin Colfer, Georgina P., Penny C., Rachel Fraser, Stewart Ross and Sr. Mary Catherine B. O.P.—thank you for your time and your feedback: I hope you enjoyed it! Thanks also to Sr. Tamsin G. O.P. for helping with my awful Latin!

I'd also like to thank Amanda Preston, my agent, from whom I have learnt so much about editing my own work—a painful skill every author needs to learn. And especially Regina and Andrew at Chesterton Press, who have given so much help with preparing this edition.

Not to forget those who have helped me by proofreading earlier work—Ehren S., Fiona T., Ann H., Sam M., Diana T., Clifton M. and anyone who has slipped my mind!

And last but not least, my Guardian Angel (because they're so under-appreciated).

Thanks must also go to the generous developers of these beautiful Open Source fonts:

Quattrocentro Roman, Source Sans Pro, Note This, Daniel, Courier Prime, Jenna Sue, WC Rhesus A Bta, BPreplay, Rosario, IMPACT LABEL REVERSED and Almendra.

ABOUT THE AUTHOR

Corinna Turner has been writing since she was fourteen and likes strong protagonists with plenty of integrity. She has an MA in English from Oxford University, but has foolishly gone on to work with both children and animals! Juggling work with the disabled and being a midwife to sheep, she spends as much time as she can in a little hut at the bottom of the garden, writing.

She is a Catholic Christian with roots in the Methodist and Anglican churches. A keen cinema-goer, she lives in the UK. She used to have a Giant Snail called Peter with a 6½" long shell (which is legal in the UK!), but now makes do with a cactus and a campervan!

Did you enjoy I Am Margaret*? Please consider leaving a review on Amazon or your favorite retailer. Thank you!*

Get in touch with Corinna...

Facebook: Corinna Turner - *Twitter*: @CorinnaTAuthor

or sign up for **news** and **free short stories**,
including several I AM MARGARET stories, at:
www.UnSeenBooks.com

DOWNLOAD YOUR EBOOK

If you own a paperback of *I Am Margaret* you can download a free copy of the eBook.

1. Go to *www.UnSeenBooks.com*
          or scan the QR code:

2. Enter this code: MXB7377G

3. Enjoy your download!

Made in the USA
Middletown, DE
27 January 2022

59751337R00182